Tropic of Orange

Also by Karen Tei Yamashita

Anime Wong

Brazil-Maru

Circle K Cycles

I Hotel

Letters to Memory

Through the Arc of the Rain Forest

Tropic of Orange

KAREN TEI YAMASHITA

With an introduction by Sesshu Foster

COFFEE HOUSE PRESS
Minneapolis
2017

Cover design by Carlos Esparza

Book design by Bookmobile

First edition published by Coffee House Press in 1997

Coffee House Press books are available to the trade through our primary distributor, Consortium Book Sales & Distribution, cbsd.com or (800) 283-3572. For personal orders, catalogs, or other information, write to info@coffeehousepress.org.

Coffee House Press is a nonprofit literary publishing house. Support from private foundations, corporate giving programs, government programs, and generous individuals helps make the publication of our books possible. We gratefully acknowledge their support in detail in the back of this book.

LIBRARY OF CONGRESS CATALOGING-IN-PUBLICATION DATA

Names: Yamashita, Karen Tei, 1951– author.
Title: Tropic of orange / Karen Tei Yamashita.
Description: Minneapolis : Coffee House Press, 2017.
Identifiers: LCCN 2016057048 | ISBN 9781566894869
Subjects: LCSH: Interpersonal relations—Fiction. | Los Angeles (Calif.)—Fiction. | Magic realism (Literature) | GSAFD: Science fiction.
Classification: LCC PS3575.A44 T76 2017 | DDC 813/.54—dc23
LC record available at https://lccn.loc.gov/2016057048

PRINTED IN THE UNITED STATES OF AMERICA

26 25 24 23 22 21 20 19 3 4 5 6 7 8 9 10

For my immigrant family.
For Ronaldo, Jane Tei, and Jon.

Contents

SUNDAY: Pacific Rim

HyperContexts

	MONDAY Summer Solstice	TUESDAY Diamond Lane	WEDNESDAY Cultural Diversity
Rafaela Cortes	**Midday** *–Not Too Far from Mazatlán* CHAPTER 1	**Morning** *–En México* CHAPTER 10	**Daylight** *–The Cornfield* CHAPTER 18
Bobby Ngu	**Benefits** *–Koreatown* CHAPTER 2	**Car Payment Due** *–Tijuana via Singapore* CHAPTER 12	**Second Mortgage** *–Chinatown* CHAPTER 15
Emi	**Weather Report** *–Westside* CHAPTER 3	**NewsNow** *–Hollywood South* CHAPTER 9	**Disaster Movie Week** *–Hiro's Sushi* CHAPTER 20
Buzzworm	**Station ID** *–Jefferson & Normandie* CHAPTER 4	**Oldies** *–This Old Hood* CHAPTER 13	**LA X** *–Margarita's Corner* CHAPTER 16
Manzanar Murakami	**Traffic Window** *–Harbor Freeway* CHAPTER 5	**Rideshare** *–Downtown Interchange* CHAPTER 8	**Hour of the Trucks** *–The Freeway Canyon* CHAPTER 19
Gabriel Balboa	**Coffee Break** *–Downtown* CHAPTER 6	**Budgets** *–Skirting Downtown* CHAPTER 14	**The Interview** *–Manzanar* CHAPTER 17
Arcangel	**To Wake** *–The Marketplace* CHAPTER 7	**To Wash** *–On the Tropic* CHAPTER 11	**To Eat** *–La Cantina de Miseria y Hambre* CHAPTER 21

Acknowledgments

In large and small ways, the following people have supported and given sustenance to the writing of this book:

Vicki Abe Betsy Amster
Jane Tomi & Pat Boltz Susan Brenneman
Kerry Burke Bill Burroughs
Chris Fischbach Craig & Ruthie Gilmore
Ted Hopes Ben Huang
Ryuta Imafuku Marialice Jacob
Jimmie Khuu Sally Kim
Seokjin Kim Allan Kornblum
Casey Krache Russell Leong
Audrey Limon Steven Maier
Linda Mathews Karen Mayeda
Michael Murashige Bonnie Nadell
Jeff Nygaard Sue Ostfield
Olivia Regalado & Family
John Retsek Alma Rodriguez
Reyes Rodriguez Hisaji Sakai
Beth Sistanovich Garth Sorensen
Emi Stevens Miyo Stevens
Tim Uyeki Rosa Velasquez & Family
Chip Williams David Welna
Asako Yamashita Onna Young
KCET Channel 28

With gratitude to all and to those who have written and continue to write about L.A., but especially to Ronaldo Lopes de Oliveira, who brought the original orange from São Paulo and that other Tropic.

Introduction

BY SESSHU FOSTER

This is the ultimate book about Los Angeles because there's no ultimate book about Los Angeles. There's no last stop on the L.A. railway whose yellow trolleys went out of service in 1958; there's no end to Oaxacans, Zapotecs, Mixtecs, Central Americans, and Bengalis inventing new lives in Koreatown; no one's heading to the Ambassador Hotel on Wilshire to disrupt the assassination of Robert F. Kennedy; there's no end to white hipsters and "creative types" coming to Los Angeles from NYC and points East to make it big—just like there's no last off-ramp on the 10 freeway heading across the desert to Texas and Florida. Which is to say, as the last city of the American civilization before the Pacific Plate subducts under North America and uplifts the ranges of the West, L.A. never stops, it never stops—L.A. never stops. *Tropic of Orange* dares to go there.

L.A.'s the city at the end of the continent that grinds out industrial daydreams and nightmares for the rest of the planet. "Hollywood will not rot on the windmills of Eternity / Hollywood whose movies stick in the throat of God," Allen Ginsberg wrote. "Money! Money! Money! shrieking mad celestial money of illusion!" This city industrialized the imagination of the species. This city unspooled reels of Buster Keaton and W. C. Fields, killed Sam Cooke and Janis Joplin, buried Marilyn Monroe and the shadows of ten thousand Indians, Japanese, and Vietnamese who dared to attack John Wayne and his cohort of innocents. Driving Route 66 to the edge of the continent, L.A. arrived at the end of the world first. Giant ants, earthquakes, aliens from outer space. The city limits, *The Outer Limits*. Time and again, even as it was wiped out by Martians in 1953 in *The War of the Worlds* or in 1971 while Charlton Heston drove the empty avenues of downtown in *The Omega Man* looking for vampires to machine-gun, the city plowed the civilization's subconscious and planted alien pod plants.

Roman Polanski's 1974 noir classic, *Chinatown*, ostensibly set in 1937, makes no mention, of course, that in 1936 most of Chinatown was razed and buried under the newly built Union Station. Dodger Stadium commemorates in no way the Chicano neighborhood of Chavez Ravine, whose residents were forcibly evicted, whose properties were buried under landfill for baseball parking lots. Entire Japanese American neighborhoods were emptied of residents for concentration camps during World War 2; East San Pedro Japanese American residents were given forty-eight hours to pack and leave—their fishing village then razed, their boats sold or burned. Entire Mexican American neighborhoods were razed and buried under famous freeways. Displacement, dispossession, and dislocation continues these days under the guise of gentrification. These are stories that Hollywood can't seem to imagine, because they're actually happening. Look in vain for them in *Chinatown, Blade Runner, Short Cuts, L.A. Confidential.* The ostensibly intergalactic imagination of the movies doesn't begin to approach hard-bitten realities reflected in the lives of the seven characters central to *Tropic of Orange.*

Tropic of Orange refracts the city's passion like skyscrapers against the setting sun. This book holds in solar heat like a piece of granite. Even as the desert east of the San Gabriel Mountains refracts the city's energy like dream lightning in murky dreams of ex–L.A. hipsters gentrified out to Joshua Tree, in sun-bleached dreams of old rock guitarists and rock climbers, as wind scours trinkets of aluminum and plastic across the sand and gravel. Out there, across the sand and gravel of his artist's compound, Noah Purifoy's human-scale monuments broadcast South Central passion to the cholla, the creosote, and the stars. Out there, young black and Latino families from the Marine base shop at the Yucca Valley Walmart. Out there, errant music recorded in L.A. wafts like lost heat waves. Those lyrics, those phrases and rhythms reemerge inscribed in these sentences, in these chapters. *The revolution will not be televised,* recalls *Tropic of Orange* on page 187, even as a romantically entangled Chicano and Japanese American couple, journalists, tragically try to prove it wrong.

If L.A. is that recombinant hybrid of the culture's imagination and the civilization's final history, of its weird and frequently terrible desires taken to their ultimate logical ends (freeways and car culture, cults and crazies, a police state hidden behind sunglasses and suntans), few novels live to tell actual Los Angeles stories and effectively take anything like its full measure. *Tropic of Orange* takes that apocalyptic tale on with surrealist nerve and futurist verve. Karen Yamashita looks on what the civilization wrought on this place, unafraid—she doesn't turn away; five years after the 1992 riots ("the largest civil disturbance in modern times . . . Sixty dead, one billion dollars damage . . ."), columns of smoke still rise from those conflicts of race and class. Seven voices, each distinguished by a distinct voice and POV, tell stories that sojourn the Pacific, traverse the Sonoran Desert, cross mean streets and ethnic divides to meet, folding into one another in a wild (and wildly imagined) seven days in Los Angeles.

In 2011, as visiting professor of creative writing at UC Santa Cruz, I wandered into the lunch counter at a cafe that Karen liked and found her hosting a party of out-of-town visitors. She invited me to join them, and as I pulled up a chair, one of the visitors, Robert Allen, was talking about the Port Chicago Mutiny, the largest mass mutiny in U.S. naval history, when fifty black sailors were court-martialed in 1944 after seven hundred men were blown apart (320 died) loading munitions aboard ships heading for the war in the Pacific. "Robert!" I said, jumping up. "You're the only person I've ever heard talking about Port Chicago!" I ran over and gave him a hug. "The last time I saw you was in Nicaragua! How long has it been? Twenty years?" He'd written a book about Port Chicago and edited the *Black Scholar* journal for decades. I'd learned about Port Chicago more than twenty years earlier and more than three thousand miles away, in Managua, in 1987, when Robert told me about it as we sat at a table with Alice Walker. I've only heard the story of Port Chicago twice in my life, both times by luck, the kind of luck and the kind of stories you get when Karen Yamashita invites you to sit at her table. *Tropic of Orange* invites you; try your luck—pull up a chair or just open this book—you're in for seven kinds of L.A. stories that fold into an origami flower of razor-sharp titanium.

Tropic of Orange

A city named after sacred but imaginary beings, in a state named after a paradise that was the figment of a woman's dream; a city that came to fame by filming such figments; a city existing now on sufferance from the ever-hotter desert and the ever-rising sea, and that feels every day, to so many of us, like a mirage as it waits for its great quake. Its suffering is real enough, God knows. But its beauty is the beauty of letting things go; letting go of where you came from; letting go of old lessons; letting go of what you want for what you are, or what you are for what you want; letting go of so much—and that is a hard beauty to love.

—Michael Ventura, "Grand Illusion"
Letters at 3 am: Reports on Endarkenment

It's against the law in California to walk on the freeways, but the law is archaic. Everyone who walks walks on the freeways sooner or later. Freeways provide the most direct routes between cities and parts of cities . . . Some prostitutes and peddlers of food, water, and other necessities live along the freeways in sheds or shacks or in the open air. Beggars, thieves, and murderers live here, too.

. . . the freeway crowd is a heterogeneous mass—black and white, Asian and Latin, whole families are on the move with babies on backs or perched atop loads in carts, wagons, or bicycle baskets, sometimes along with an old or handicapped person. . . . Many were armed with sheathed knives, rifles, and, of course, visible holstered handguns. The occasional passing cop paid no attention.

. . . People get killed on freeways all the time.

—Octavia Butler, *Parable of the Sower*

standing on the map of my political desires
I toast to a borderless future
(I raise my glass of wine toward the moon)
with . . .
our Alaskan hair
our Canadian head
our u.s. torso
our Mexican genitalia
our Central American cojones
our Caribbean sperm
our South American legs
our Patagonian feet
our Antarctic nails
jumping borders at ease
jumping borders with pleasure
amen, hey man

—Guillermo Gómez-Peña,
"Freefalling Toward a Borderless Future"
The New World Border

Gentle reader, what follows may not be about the future, but is perhaps about the recent past; a past that, even as you imagine it, happens. Pundits admit it's impossible to predict, to chase such absurdities into the future, but c'est L.A. vie. No single imagination is wild or crass or cheesy enough to compete with the collective mindlessness that propels our fascination forward. We were all there; we all saw it on TV, screen, and monitor, larger than life.

MONDAY

Summer Solstice

CHAPTER 1:

Midday *Not Too Far from Mazatlán*

Rafaela Cortes spent the morning barefoot, sweeping both dead and living things from over and under beds, from behind doors and shutters, through archways, along the veranda—sweeping them all across the deep shadows and luminous sunlight carpeting the cool tile floors. Her slender arms worked the broom industriously through the air—already thickening with tepid heat—and along the floor, her feet following, printing their moisture in dark footprints over baked clay. Every morning, a small pile of assorted insects and tiny animals—moths and spiders, lizards and beetles—collected, their brittle bodies tossed in waves along the floor, a cloudy hush of sandy soil, cobwebs, and human hair. An iguana, a crab, and a mouse. And there was the scorpion, always dead—its fragile back broken in the middle. And the snake that slithered away at the urging of her broom—probably not poisonous, but one never knew. Every morning it was the same. Every morning, she swept this mound of dead and wiggling things to the door and off the side of the veranda and into the dark green undergrowth with the same flourish. Occasionally, there was more of one species or the other, but each somehow always made its way back into the house. The iguana, the crab, and the mouse, for example, were always there. Sometimes they were dead; sometimes they were alive. As for the scorpion, it was always dead, but the snake was always alive. On some days, it seemed to twirl before her broom communicating a kind of dance that seemed to send a visceral message up the broom to her fingertips. There was no explanation for any of it. It made no difference if she closed the doors and shutters at the first sign of dusk or if she left the house unoccupied and tightly shut for several days. Every morning when the house was thrown open to the sunlight, she knew that she and the boy had not slept alone that night. Hummingbirds and parakeets fluttered across the rooms, stirring the languid humidity settled by the night, frantically searching for escape through the open lace curtains, while crawling lives hid beneath furniture or presented itself lifeless at her feet.

When she first came to the house, she couldn't find a broom to accomplish this daily ritual, not to mention for sweeping the clouds of cobwebs from the dark, rough-hewn rafters. Gabriel had left an American vacuum cleaner in a closet—an old steel Electrolux purchased at the Rose Bowl swap meet for thirty dollars. When the electricity wasn't shut off, Rafaela dragged the vacuum—the hard Bakelite wheels bumping over the clay tiles and the woven throw rugs—from one room to the next but soon depleted Gabriel's supply of vacuum bags. Recycling these bags was nearly impossible, and she did not have the heart to dump them without releasing the trapped animals inside. One day, attempting to use the vacuum cleaner without the bags resulted in jamming the gears with pieces of the crab, not to mention everything else, and that was the end of the Electrolux.

When Rafaela told Gabriel that the Electrolux had died, there was an uncomfortable silence on the other end of the line, probably because Gabriel had had some idea that a stainless steel vacuum cleaner was something incredibly wise to have in the salty humidity of Mazatlán and also because he had lugged it one thousand miles on one particularly sacrificial trip made in a borrowed Volkswagen van. The story about the crab seemed unlikely. His land was much too far from the sea. Yes, it sounded impossible, but why would Rafaela make such a thing up?

"I bought a broom," she said, pressing the back of her hand against the sweat of her forehead. "If things get better between us, maybe I can get one of those upright vacuums from Bobby. Actually a dry-wet vac would be best. Bobby swears by them."

"Don't worry about it." Gabriel shrugged. "Did you talk to Rodriguez?"

"Yes. He's coming over tomorrow, maybe with some help. He's going to put the windows in the bathroom and fix the tiles so the door will close. And I got him to come down in price." Rafaela tried to sound professional. She wanted Gabriel to know that despite breaking his vacuum, she could be a very good housekeeper. She was also very good with money matters and managing workers. Well, she came with good experience. Hadn't she been doing this for Bobby all along? She would have his place fixed up in no time. "Don't worry. You're gonna have a really nice place to retire to someday."

"Retire? I can't wait that long," moaned Gabriel. This project had already been going on for eight years. It had begun one summer when Gabriel felt a spontaneous, sudden passion for the acquisition of land, the sensation of a timeless vacation, the erotic tastes of chili pepper and salty breezes, and for Mexico. And there had been one additional attraction: the location. It was marked exactly by a sign on the highway shoulder beyond the house: Tropic of Cancer. In Gabriel's mind the Tropic ran through his place like a good metaphor. If it were good enough for the Tropic, it was good enough for Gabriel. He put his entire savings down and every cent he could spare on top of that. In the beginning, he went every summer, every free weekend, but the cost of travel, the headache of fighting the bureaucracy to get the right paperwork, and the difficulty in finding building materials and good construction workers frayed his original passion. Even though he tried, he was not a hands-on sort of person; he didn't understand plumbing, foundation work, masonry, electrical wiring, or even gardening. After all, he was a journalist; he just wanted a quiet place to write. Maintenance was the problem.

And speaking the language was not enough. Everyone could tell he was green and took advantage of it. The workers, who all eventually abandoned their work, smiled graciously and wondered at this young Chicano who had a college education and whose grandfather had fought with Pancho Villa and ended up in Los Angeles. Nobody remembered the grandmother who supposedly came from right around there—a little girl who got kidnapped by the grandfather and taken away North. Some people pretended to remember or suggested that so-and-so might remember; they felt bad because he seemed so sure and proud about it.

Still the project continued in alternating states of disarray or progress. He seemed to be building a spacious hacienda, maybe a kind of old-style ranchero, circa 1800, with rustic touches, thick adobelike walls and beams, but with modern appliances. But then again, finishing depended on having money and being able to translate his vision to others. He showed the workers scraps of photos torn from slick architectural magazines: tile work, hot tubs, wet bars, arches, decks, and landscaping. Everyone agreed his ideas were all very beautiful. Old-fashioned, but beautiful. The plans expanded, then diminished; swelled with possibility, then shrank with reality. It seemed that if he took one step forward, he would then take two backwards. After eight years, the house—the part that was finally constructed—needed painting again. The metal window insets he had gotten for such a good price were rusting and probably needed to be replaced with aluminum, and the doors were full of termites.

Now Rafaela was there. Gabriel was doing her a favor, letting her hide with her little son until she and her husband Bobby could make up their minds about their marriage. In return, she was going to help finish what his romantic impulse had begun. Rafaela was from Culiacán, thirty miles north of Mazatlán. About the time Gabriel was buying a piece of the Tropic of Cancer, Rafaela was crossing the border North. In eight years, while his Mexican project floundered, she had learned English, married Bobby, helped start their janitorial business, borne a baby, and got a degree at the local community college. She was smart, savvy, and eager to take on the tasks at hand. Gabriel couldn't ask for better. If this didn't work, he was going to have to sell the place, probably to another romantic tourist, and try to at least make back what he put into it.

"I planted more cactus and peppers today, and my herbs and sunflowers are blooming all over," she announced. "And yesterday, I went into town to price some toilet bowls and fixtures. You won't believe what they're asking. Maybe you ought to check out the prices over there. I'm going to make a list, and the next time you come down—"

"You want me to bring toilet bowls down from L.A.?"

"Well, since you got this gigantic cistern dug and the piping is all copper, maybe, well you know what Bobby says. You get what you pay for, except that's not really true here, but I just want to save you some money."

Gabriel thought about toilet bowls and his money. It sounded crazy, but he knew she was probably right. He wanted to ignore the toilet bowls and said instead, "Don't worry about the fixtures. I ordered some from a catalog and mailed them down. You should be getting them any day now."

"Mail? Are you sure that's wise?"

"It's the chance you take."

"My brother Pepe comes down all the time you know. The last time he brought me some things from Culiacán, from my mother, to dress up the house. Knickknacks."

"From your mother?"

"It's nothing at all. She wants you to have them. Just to make things pretty. Why don't you send me some copies of *House Beautiful* or *Sunset*? I can get some good ideas."

"House Beautiful?" Gabriel seemed to choke on the other end.

"Anyway, you could send stuff with Pepe. He really fills up his Chevy, but maybe he has some room. If you pay the gas, maybe he will come down this far."

"Maybe. How is Sol?"

"Kid's okay. I don't know how to thank you."

"Forget it."

Rafaela hung the phone up and nodded to Doña Maria who was playing with Sol.

"He's such a dear," Doña Maria cooed at the little boy. "He's got a little of your curly hair and your coloring, but really he's such a little Chinese," she marveled. "A true mixture."

"Yes," admitted Rafaela, pushing back the dark waves of her bushy hair, then combing her fingers through her son's. "He really looks like his daddy." She looked wistfully at Sol and thought about Bobby. Lately she found herself talking to an invisible Bobby, consulting the air about this or that as if he were there. Bobby was such a handyman; he would have shaped up Gabriel's place in half the time.

"So your mother was born in Culiacán?" Doña Maria was digging for information.

"No. She was born in the Yucatán. And my father's people came from even farther south. Ayacucho in the Andes. They say my great-great-grandfather brought his family across the mountains and through the jungles to get here. But that was a long time ago."

"The old-timers knew how to endure."

"They say my mother's people were weavers, and my father's people built the looms. They couldn't talk to each other at first. They talked through their weaving and fell in love." Rafaela remembered that she and Bobby couldn't talk much at first either, but Bobby learned fast. He had already been fluent in some kind of Chicano street talk, but she herself had never bothered to learn Chinese. Maybe she should have.

"Such pretty stories," the old woman nodded as if they weren't true. "But why did your people leave the Yucatán?"

"One day the weaving stopped. The looms were old. The work was slow."

"Times changed," Doña Maria sighed. "And did you learn to read palms from your mother?" she asked.

"Oh no," Rafaela smiled. "I don't know why I read palms. I've always just done so."

"Lupe says you are very good at it."

"It's just nonsense. Something to pass the time," Rafaela demurred. Perhaps Doña Maria wanted her palm read, but Rafaela had a strange intuition. She did not want to read the woman's palm.

Doña Maria did not press her, but commiserated. "You look a little tired today. It's a big headache. Believe me, I know. My son went crazy building this place for us, and then Benito died, God rest his soul. He only saw the foundation. Now such a big house for one old woman. But at least when my son was building it, he was always here, back and forth, back and forth. Now, I only get phone calls. But I thank God for this telephone."

"Please let me know how much it is when the bill comes, Doña Maria." Rafaela took the boy's hand.

"Oh, I almost forgot. My son sent me new chairs." Doña Maria pointed to two rather ornate blue velvet cushioned pieces with shiny wood knobs and feet. "But it's such a shame. The old chairs are perfectly new, and I wondered if they might be of any use to you. That house could use some chairs of course."

Rafaela thought about the old chairs that were as Doña Maria said practically new. If she remembered correctly, they weren't much different from the new chairs, except they had brass knobs and feet. She wondered about this decorating scheme, but before she could say anything, Doña Maria offered, "I will have Lupe send them over. You will see. They are just what the house needs."

Rafaela didn't want to offend the woman by saying no, and after all, chairs were needed. Gabriel had talked about leather and carved dark wood benches. Not very comfortable but then again, blue velvet was probably not his preference. Well, he could get rid of them later. "Thank you," she said.

"Of course. Please, any time at all. We are neighbors. Well, it's a little far, but you are just across the highway. I have always told Gabriel, any time at all. He used to walk all the way to the hotel. I have nothing against the hotel, but then again, it's not such a nice hotel. Well, we don't get the tourists like Mazatlán, but that's why my son and Gabriel, too, like it here. They say it's quiet, away from the commotion. But I do get lonely."

Rafaela smiled. She knew Doña Maria preferred to stay in Mazatlán with her sister but put off her plans just to be around to check out Rafaela and this story that she was some sort of housekeeper for Gabriel. Offering the use of her telephone was a perfect way to get information. And perhaps Doña Maria thought Rafaela would be lonely in that big unfinished house on that big unfinished property, but Rafaela had been too relieved to be away from her problems with Bobby and kept too busy to feel very lonely. To be able to sweep with a broom across tile was somehow a very satisfactory thing, so much better than pushing the noisy vacuum over dull carpets from office to office. How could she explain this to Bobby? This wasn't just dust; it was alive.

Rafaela and little Sol crossed the two-lane highway, walked along the barbed-wire fence on the west side, passing a group of cows absently chewing their cud, big green plops of fresh dung steaming everywhere. She went to check the fencing where Gabriel's property began. The cows had tramped over a fallen post and into the garden, destroying Gabriel's lattice with the wild roses. Not that it had looked that beautiful, but it was a nice idea. Probably one of Gabriel's magazine cut-outs. Now the roses were twisting along the ground and up a banana tree. The idea of having fruit trees was a nice one too, except that the soil was sandy and required a lot of dung and compost. Every day Rafaela threw kitchen leftovers and fallen fruit into the trough at the bottom of the banana tree. It knew how to make use of fresh refuse, but composting trees like peach and plum was a more delicate business.

Over the years, Gabriel had planted an orchard full of different trees. He had a thing about planting a tree every time he came. He tried not to be discouraged when they died, telling Rafaela, "They gotta take care of themselves. Survival of the fittest." Needless to say, the fittest were the mango and papaya trees. At this time of year their fruit rotted in steaming ditches everywhere. The sweet stench floated above the earth swirling around as Rafaela's body cut a meandering path through the garden, wondering why Gabriel insisted on planting trees that couldn't survive in this climate. Evidence of their dried twigs supporting creeping vines and hidden behind the now robust vegetation was everywhere. She planted cactus and sunflowers, chiles and corn, kitchen and medicinal herbs. Still, she was hoping to make some miracle happen in this orchard, just to surprise Gabriel. Produce from his exotic northern trees. A sweet gooey marmalade from his orange trees, perhaps.

But perhaps not. The variety of citrus trees was commendable: Italian blood oranges, mandarins, valencias, Mexican limes, their green foliage spreading a rich blanket across the land. But Rafaela was only concerned about one tree in particular. It was a rather sorry tree, yellowing perhaps from lack of some nutrient or another, but for some reason, she had been watching it every day. It was the only citrus tree in the garden that had a fruit on it. Gabriel had actually brought this tree from Riverside eight years ago. It was a navel orange tree, maybe the descendent of the original trees first brought to California from Brazil in 1873 and planted by L.C. Tibbetts. This was the sort of historic detail Gabriel liked. Bringing an orange tree (no matter that it was probably a hybrid) from Riverside, California, to his place near Mazatlán was a significant act of some sort. Gabriel had taken some pains to plant the tree as a marker—to mark the Tropic of Cancer. Actually there had been two trees, one on either side of the property—two points on a line, but one had died. Rafaela didn't think much about Gabriel's fascination with an imaginary line, but she knew instinctively the importance of the surviving tree.

The tree was a sorry one, and so was the orange. Rafaela knew it was an orange that should not have been. It was much too early. Everyone said the weather was changing. The rains came sooner this year. "What do they call it?" mused Doña Maria. "Global warming. Yes, that's it." Rafaela had seen it herself. The tree had been fooled, and little pimples of budding flowers began to burst through its branches. And then came a sudden period of dry weather; the flowers withered away, except for this one. Perhaps it had been the industriousness of the African bees, their furry feet dusted heavily in yellow pollen, that had quickly mated the flower to its future, producing this aberrant orange—not to be picked, not expected, and probably not very sweet.

But from the very beginning Rafaela somehow felt this particular orange was special. Perhaps it was her desire to see a thing out of season struggle despite everything and become whole. As time went on, she found herself watching the orange, wandering out to the tree every day even in the rain, feeling great contentment in the transition of its small growing globe, first from green and then to its slow golden burnish.

But there was something else. Just where its tiny bud had broken through the tree's branch, Rafaela noticed a line—finer than the thread of a spiderweb—pulled with delicate tautness. It was most visible in the dewy mornings as the sun rose from the east; at other times, it was barely visible. But she always sensed its presence. If she could not reach out and touch it, she sensed its peculiar, very supple strength. Perhaps it was something like a thin laser beam or light passing through an optic fiber. Rafaela was not sure. She only knew that it ran across Gabriel's property. In fact, she sensed that it continued farther in both directions, east and west, east across the highway and west toward the ocean and beyond.

In the days when the orange was a blossom of soft petals, its fragrance surprised her. She had passed beneath the orange several times, drawn to its sweet scent before she had discovered it. The perfume could only be emanating from that curious flower. She came often then to secure the whiff that tingled her deep memory; it was as if she knew this scent intimately. It was then that she noticed the line; it seemed to shudder with pleasure, if lines could shudder with pleasure. And when the baby orange appeared, it seemed to grasp that line as its parent, if a line could be a parent. As expected, the orange did not grow to be very big or seem very succulent, but it did begin to hang rather heavily. And when the salty wind blew west from the sea rocking it back and forth like a small cradle, the curious line—now running through the growing orange—rocked back and forth with it like a lullaby.

Rafaela and Sol walked hand in hand past the orange tree, careful not to disturb the lizards and beetles waiting breathlessly beneath scattered leaves and brush. For three days now, it had not rained. And yet any cool surface bled the air's moisture. Rafaela felt this wetness; it gathered in tiny molecules over her skin. It was a little before noon, and the sun was particularly bright and oppressive that day. If Rafaela had bothered to look at the calendar, she would have noticed that it was Monday, June 22. She might have also noticed the lunar signs in the corner of the calendar and the small print that said summer solstice.

She glanced briefly at the orange with some satisfaction and hurried toward the house. "Come on Sol. It's much too hot out here today." His little quick steps pattered behind, dancing around the young trees, and then ran forward. She followed Sol who seemed to be following a path of his own, but upon closer inspection, he was tracing the path of a very thin but distinct shadow stretched in a perfectly straight line along the dirt and sand. There were no telephone cables or electric lines above, nothing to cast such a shadow, and yet it was clearly there. Sol danced back and forth, his little legs jumping this way and that, over the soft sand and gravel, crossing the brick paths, hopping the line cut like a sharp blade across the earth. Rafaela glanced back toward the orange tree and the single orange, suddenly aware of the only possible and yet entirely impossible thing that could obstruct the intensity of the sun's light at this hour, slicing the heavy atmosphere with cruel precision. Indeed the sun was a great ball of fire directly above the orange tree. It seemed even to point at the tree, at the strange line, at the orange itself.

Rafaela ran after Sol into the cool shadows of the house. There was a sudden gust of tepid wind, and from the corner of her eye, she thought she saw the line's razor shadow dip away, south. Rafaela felt a dizzy nausea. She did not realize that the orange had fallen irresistibly from a height of two meters, rolling in dusty turbulence down a small slope, under the barbed-wire fence, and just beyond the frontiers of Gabriel's property to a neutral place between ownership and the highway.

CHAPTER 2:

Benefits *Koreatown*

Check it out, ése. You know this story? Yeah, over at Sanitary Supply they always tell it. This dude drives up, drives up to Sanitary. Makes a pickup like always. You know. Paper towels. Rags. Mop handles. Gallon of Windex. Stuff like that. Drives up in a Toyota pickup. Black shiny deal, all new, big pinche wheels. Very nice. Yeah. Asian dude. Kinda skinny. Short, yeah. But so what? Dark glasses. Cigarette in the mouth. He's getting out the truck, see. In the parking lot. Big tall dude comes by with a gun. Yeah, a gun. Puts it to his head and says, GIMME THE KEYS! It's a jacker. Asian dude don't lose no time, man. No time. Not a doubt. Rams the door closed. WHAM! Just like that. Slams the door on the jacker's hand. On the jacker's gun! Smashes the gun! Smashes the hand. Gun ain't worth shit. Hand's worth even less. Jacker loses it bad. He's crying. Screaming. It's not over. Asian dude swings the door open. Attacks the jacker. Pushes him up to the wall of Sanitary and beats the shit out. Dude don't come up to the jacker's nose. But it don't matter. Got every trick in the books. Bruce Lee moves. Kick. VAP! WHOP! Damn. Don't mess with this man. By now Sanitary's called the police. Crowd's seen it all. Jacker's a mess. Blood everywhere. Never seen so much blood. But not a drop on the Asian. Not a drop. Never took off his shades. Never even stopped smoking. Turns over the jacker's remains to the police. Don't say nothing. That's it. Goes into Sanitary. Picks up the mop handles, Windex, rags. Gets in the pickup. He's gone. That's it. That's it.

That's Bobby. If you know your Asians, you look at Bobby. You say, that's Vietnamese. That's what you say. Color's pallid. Kinda blue just beneath the skin. Little underweight. Korean's got rounder face. Chinese's taller. Japanese's dressed better. If you know your Asians. Turns out you'll be wrong. And you gonna be confused. Dude speaks Spanish. Comprende? So you figure it's one of those Japanese from Peru. Or maybe Korean from Brazil. Or Chinamex. Turns out Bobby's from Singapore. You say, okay, Indonesian. Malaysian. Wrong again. You say, look at his name. That's gotta be Vietnam. Ngu. Bobby Ngu. They all got Ngu names. Hey, it's not his real name. Real name's Li Kwan Yu. But don't tell nobody. Go figure. Bobby's Chinese. Chinese from Singapore with a Vietnam name speaking like a Mexican living in Koreatown. That's it.

Bobby's story. It's a long story. Gotta be after hours for Bobby to tell it. And then, he might not. He was twelve. His brother eight. Dad had a bicycle business in Singapore. Mother dies. Business went bad. Can't sell no more bicycles. Dad says, you wanna future? Better go to America. Better start out something new. For the family. You better go. Don't worry about us. You start a future all new.

Bobby's only twelve. How you get from Singapore to America? It's 1975. People getting on boats, rafts, dinghies, anything, swimming south out of Vietnam. Get to Singapore, but Singapore don't want them. They tell the Americans, it's your problem. Put them in camps. Keep them there. Count them. Sort them out. Ask questions. Americans lost the war. Gotta take care of the casualties. Call them boat people. Call them refugees. Call for humanitarian aid. Call for political asylum. Meanwhile, they're in camps. Singapore don't want them. What's America gonna do? Count them again. Sort them out. Ask more questions. Pretty soon refugees get put on planes. Little by little. Distributed to America.

Every day, Bobby gets up early. He and his little brother. Walk over to the camp. Gates open in the morning. Walk in. Stand around with the refugees. Eat with the refugees. Guards don't notice. Who's gonna notice? But he's there every day. Maybe he belongs there. So maybe they notice. Bobby and his brother. Looking like orphans. Sad situation. Orphans everywhere. The war did this. Got to help the children. It's the children who suffer. Bobby and his little brother don't understand nothing. Don't understand Vietnamese. Just get some language here and there. That's all. Looks like they can't talk. Why not? War does that. You can't talk. Gets to be nighttime. Bobby and his brother go home. Slip out. Walk back into Singapore town. Go home and eat. Sleep. Get up early. Go back every morning. Spend the day sitting and eating with refugees. It's like that every day. Every day for months. That's it.

Then, pretty soon Bobby and the brother get counted. They get sorted. Get questions. Bobby's gotta have a name. He says Ngu. Everybody's Ngu. He's Ngu too. He's on the list. He's counted. Brother's counted, too. Get their pictures taken. Get some papers. American passports. Bobby's dad gives him money. U.S. money. Saved from the black market. Hides it in his pants. Sews it there. It's everything his dad can give. Money's there. Ready. Just in case. Every morning, Bobby gets his brother up early. Every morning, they slip into the refugee camp. Every night they slip out. One night they do not come home. One night Bobby's dad and the two sisters eat dinner. They leave two bowls out like always. They stare at the bowls. Silent. Staring at the two bowls.

Bobby'll tell you this story. But only after hours. After some beers and lots of smokes. He don't have time to tell stories. Too busy. Never stops. Got only a little time to sleep even. Always working. Hustling. Moving. That's why he beat that guy up and never stopped. Just kept on going. Never stops smoking either. Gonna die from smoking. He can't stop. Daytime, works the mailroom at a big-time newspaper. Sorts mail nonstop. Tons of it. Never stops. Nighttime got his own business. Him and his wife. Cleaning buildings. Clean those buildings that still got defense contracts. Bobby's got clearance. Got it for his wife too. Go around everywhere. Dump the stuff that's shredded. Wipe up the conference tables. Dust everything. Wipe down the computer monitors. Vacuum staples and hole punches and donuts out of carpets. Scrub the urinals. Mop down the floors. Bobby only stops for a smoke with the nighttime guard.

Bobby's wife likes to study. She's got a Walkman in her ears. Running the vacuum and the Walkman. It's not music. She's studying English. She's Mexican. Bobby don't teach her English. Speaks to her in Spanish. She's got to learn by herself. She's smart. Really smart. Got her degree at LACC. She told Bobby, janitors like them got to make better money. Got to get benefits. Some don't even get the minimum. Can we live on $4.25 an hour? No way. She joined Justice for Janitors. Bobby got mad. This is his business. He's independent. All the money is his. What's she talking about? It's solidarity she said. Some work for the companies. They need to organize. For protection. Bobby don't understand this. He says he works the morning job and gets benefits. Why is she complaining?

Maybe this was the reason. Maybe not. Bobby got in an argument with his wife. So she split. She took the boy with her. Drives him crazy. He can't see straight. Never been so happy as when he got married to that woman. Can't explain. Happier he is, harder he works. Can't stop. Gotta make money. Provide for his family. Gotta buy his wife nice clothes. Gotta buy his kid the best. Bobby's kid's gonna know the good life. That's how Bobby sees it.

It's not just the kid and the wife. Bobby's gotta send money to his dad. Back in Singapore. Keep the old man alive. Wanted the old man to come to L.A., but he wouldn't do it. Says he's too old. Says Bobby's got the future. All new future. And Bobby's baby brother. He's in college. Smart kid. Gets all A's. Bobby put him in college. Pays for everything. Books, dorm, tuition, extras. Got him a car, too. Bobby don't forget his baby bro. His carnalito. Don't forget the kid cried every day when they arrived. Every day for two weeks. Cried for his mom who was already dead. Cried for his dad. For his sisters. Cried. Carnalito don't cry no more. Bobby don't forget.

Used to be, back in Singapore, Bobby had it easy. Dad had a factory. Putting out bicycles. Had a good life. Good money. Only had to go to school. One day, American bicycle company put up a factory. Workers all went over there. New machines. Paid fifty cents more. Pretty soon, American company's selling all over. Exporting. Bicycles go to Hong Kong. Go to Thailand. To India. To Japan. To Taiwan. Bobby's dad losing business. Can't compete. That's it.

But that's the past. Everything had to change. Change like the seasons. Rainy season. Dry season. Rainy season'll come again. Bobby's working on it. Gonna flood with the rainy season. Gonna fly back to Singapore and see his dad. Gonna see his sisters. See his nephews and nieces. Gonna bring the kid bro and the family along, too. But he's gotta get that woman back. Gotta bring the boy home. Can't be happy without his family. Can't work. Can't keep running. Can't keep fighting. After hours, Bobby keeps thinking. What's he gonna do? Rafaela said he's gotta stop smoking. That's it.

After hours, Bobby goes home. House's in Koreatown, edge of Pico-Union. Maybe it's Koreatown, but he owns it. Stucco job with two palm trees in front. Nobody home. Just him. Woman said to stop smoking. That's it. That's the last cigarette. Boil some water. Get out the ginseng. Get a good piece of the root. Grind it up good. Hot water. Ginseng. Steam goes up just like the root. That's the smell. Clean up the system. Clear the head. It's an old root. Takes a long time to grow. Don't waste it.

CHAPTER 3:

Weather Report *Westside*

"That film noir stuff is passé. Don't you get it?" Emi told Gabriel over her Bloody Mary. She squeezed the lime, dumped it in, shook in the Tabasco, more black pepper and stirred the whole mess with the celery stick, licking her fingers, watching him, watching the waiters, watching the cocktail hostess walk away, watching the entire clientele in the restaurant, taking hold of the situation as if she had produced it herself. "Stop being such a film buff. Raymond Chandler. Alfred Hitchcock. Film nostalgia. I don't give a damn if *Chinatown, The Player,* or everybody in Hollywood owes these old farts their asses. I'll give you this: at least they're in color. Except for *Roger Rabbit,* if I have to spend another evening with you viewing another video in black and white, this relationship is over." She laughed, tossing the silky strands of her straight hair over her padded shoulders. She didn't mean it. She never did.

She had started dating Gabriel because he was Latino, part of that hot colorful race, only to find out that, except for maybe his interest in tango (and even that was academic), he wasn't what you call the stereotype. But that was back in college (the things you learn in college); since then, they had been on again/off again. And considering someone like herself—so distant from the Asian female stereotype—it was questionable if she even had an identity.

"Hot colors," she said sipping the Bloody Mary. "Color TV. When I was born, black-and-white TV was already passé. Monochrome monitors are passé for godssake. The other day I saw a thirty-inch Super VGA. Know what it looks like? Like my hand. Here." She pointed with the celery at her other hand, at the big ruby ring and the red nail polish. "Next step is high-def. You know what I say?" She stopped scanning the ongoing surrounding scene long enough to look Gabriel in the eyes. "Colorize 'em all."

Emi watched Gabriel's reaction, watched his dark eyes under powerful brows, the aristocracy of his Incan nose, his trim goatee. Wouldn't you know it; his lips turned in a subtle grin. He was chuckling. Maybe he was even secretly hoping that everyone in the restaurant could hear Emi. They were all an assortment of Hollywood types—screenwriters, producers, wannabees, gophers of varying dispositions, moguls of varying degrees of power or lack of, graduates of the UCLA film school. Here they were at the very center of the Westside power plays, cushioned in pastels and glass bricks and remakes of David Hockney, and she was trying to be obnoxious. And he was smiling. Go figure.

Emi looked at her watch. "Don't worry. I can take a long one today. Only I gotta be back to segue the weather report. Can you believe it? We got a sponsor for a midafternoon cut to weather report. Ninety seconds. Didn't want the heat of anything controversial so probably suggested *wea-tha.* Also ultracheap time slot, not to mention short. In L.A. how can you lose? Monday. Overcast in the morning. Sunny in the afternoon. Tuesday. Overcast in the morning. Sunny in the afternoon. Temperature holding at seventy-eight degrees. That's what's wrong with your precious L.A. detective films. It's always raining. It never rains here! The only reason it rains in those films is so Bogie can wear a trenchcoat. What's the point? It's like those freeway signs that tell you you're in traffic. So what's new? It's either overcast or sunny. And you know who bought the slot don't you? Some tanning lotion company. Summer's over and it gets dumped."

"Summer solstice today," Gabriel mentioned since the subject seemed to have changed to the weather. "I was thinking about my place in Mexico. The Tropic of Cancer runs right through it." He picked up a knife and sliced the air. "That means the sun is right there, directly on top of my place. Now." He looked at his watch.

"Does it affect broadcast reception?"

"I don't know," Gabriel shook his head.

"I thought the sun could do that. Why am I asking you? I should ask one of my technicians. On the other hand, I shouldn't. You ask a technical question and you want a yes or no. But these guys are starved for any little talk. They'll technilese you to death. Really, they get off on it, like sex. All I wanna know is if my program is gonna get up and for godssake don't screw up the commercial."

Gabriel sipped his water.

"At least order Perrier. This is on me you know. I'm expensing this one." Emi crunched into the celery and waved around the stringy end of it. "Order a Sauvignon Blanc. Go ahead. For my sake, you could try to blend in with this crowd." Blend in with this crowd. Blend in with all these white studio types. That comment should get his goat.

"*You* blend in," he quipped and pushed the glass of water toward her. "Try this. Tap water from Northern California. It's got a very subtle bouquet."

Emi smiled. Being obnoxious with Gabriel was a great pastime. She liked trying to push his buttons. For example, she liked trying to be anti-multicultural around him. Right in the middle of some public place, she might burst out, "Oh you're so Chicano!" Oppressing him with images of television was another tactic. He was such a film aesthete, it made her sick. Sometimes she really made him mad, and he'd cuss in Spanish. On occasion, he'd walk out. Oops. Went too far. Oh, well. But today it occurred to her that Gabriel was on to her, on to this purposeful (for whatever purpose) display of obnoxiousness. He seemed to be sitting there waiting for it to pass.

Her mother had said her big mouth was always getting her into trouble and that it was no wonder any boyfriend didn't stick around very long.

"Whatsa matter with you? Your dad and I don't talk like that. Your brother and sister don't talk like that. In fact no J.A. talks like that."

"Maybe I'm not Japanese American. Maybe I got switched in the hospital. There were three sets of switched kids on the daytime Donahues last week: *Montel Williams, Rikki Lake,* and *Sally Jesse Raphael.* (Ratings were all up. Caress sold a lot of Caress.) But get this, they discovered each other by genetic testing. If three talk shows found three different sets, imagine how many more of us there must be! There's probably a support group out there for people like me. I should check the net."

"It's your dad's genes. Not mine. We Sakais keep our mouths shut, that's what. Besides, I like Gabriel."

"Really? I like Gabriel, too."

"If you like someone, how can you treat him like that?"

"He can take it. Think of it this way. I'm not hiding anything from him. What he sees is what he'll get. It's really just a test. Rigorous, but hey, some fail. Like *Human Feats* on cable. Like paddling across the Pacific in a canoe. Crossing the Sahara on bikes. Climbing Mount Whitney."

"It's more like jumping off Mount Whitney." Emi's mother rolled her eyes. It was useless to talk seriously about these things.

"If there's one thing you and dad taught me, it's that you can never appreciate anything that just comes to you. You've got to struggle for something to really appreciate it. Like when you made me make my payments on my Civic. Or when I saved to buy my first Panasonic VCR. I really struggled. That's what Gabriel is doing. Struggling."

The most Gabriel was struggling with at the moment were the foreign words on the menu. *"Pappardelle con funghi al vino marsala,"* he muttered.

"As menu items go, it's probably passé. But it *is* to die for," she suggested. "I know the chef. Go ahead. Die."

"Poison fungi?" he asked, attempting a mild joke.

But she said, "Fugu. Fugu's poisonous. If you wanted Japanese, you shoulda said so."

"Fungi." He looked up. "Mushrooms. Fungi are mushrooms. Some mushrooms are poisonous."

She took a swig of Bloody Mary and licked her lips. The Tabasco burned her lips. She licked them again and puckered, "So. What? It's just a little oral gratification. Afraid to die?"

"No shit. I'll go to hell, and you'll be there, with your big mouth, dumping on me till eternity."

"That's the trouble with you. Live on the edge I say. Live to the max. It's like riding the crest of a wave, staying current with it, right there, on top, top of the news, before it breaks."

"I'd rather be in Mexico."

"You'd rather be in the nineteen thirties back in black and white with that detective Philip whatshisname. It's not like I'm not interested in your habit. I mean this Philip Morris—

"Marlowe."

"—Marlowe guy could have a revival. Then okay. But otherwise, strictly current affairs for moi."

Gabriel had heard this harangue before . . . he didn't even seem to be listening. His thoughts were far away. He didn't try to defend his hero or even the possibility that a Chandler revival might be more than just a current affair. He knew that she knew. It was just one of those absurd conversations with Emi. He changed the subject.

"I talked to Rafaela at my place near Mazatlán. I think I'm finally going to get the house finished."

"That's great."

"I'm thinking of going down in a couple weeks."

"Maybe I'll go with you." She reached down and pulled the electronic scheduler from her purse, entered some items on the screen and said, "You should get one of these. Then you'd have all my numbers and your calendar all together. I'm going to get you one for your birthday."

"I like my calendar book better."

"This is what the future is about. A paperless existence. Gabriel, you're murdering trees." She paused, "Two weeks from this one, I could get a Friday off. Make it a three-day weekend."

"I don't know. Actually, I'm thinking of driving. I may have to take some toilet bowls down."

"Toilet bowls? What's wrong with Mexican toilet bowls?"

"Rafaela says they're too expensive."

"I can't believe that."

"That's what she says."

"Gabe, this back-to-nature thing of yours? It's a nice vacation, but how about golf?"

"I don't know how to explain it. I get a kick out of planting a tree every time I go. It's not like this news business. I plant; I get fruits. I get to make something I can actually touch and eat for a change. Seriously,

I sometimes think to hell with all this." Gabriel's eyes wearily surveyed *all this*.

So did Emi's. "I read somewhere that these days, if you are making a product you can actually touch *and*," she emphasized *and*, "making a comfortable living at it, you are either an Asian or a machine."

Suddenly a beeping. Emi reached in her purse and turned it off. Then she scrambled with the rest of the contents in the purse until she found the folded cellular phone, pulled out the antenna and punched in memory. "I knew this was gonna be a weird week. We're calling it Disaster Movie Week. Every night we've got another disaster movie. Tonight it's *Inferno in the Tower*. Tomorrow *The Northridge Quake*. Then it's *Canyon Fires. Airport III. Bomb Threat at the Pacific Exchange. Burn Baby Burn*. And for the final insult, *The Day After*. Can you believe it? The lives of ordinary people with petty problems who now have *a big problem*." Emi grimaced at Gabriel and directed her voice into the phone. ". . . You paged? This was supposed to be an easy day. Yeah, yeah. No! Shit. Oh shit. Whadyamean you can't find the tape? I put it in your hands personally. Personally. Remember? That's not what you said. Okay, so what's the problem? What mix-up? We're not going to lose this. No way. Or it's your pay. You pay for the slot! Okay. I'm coming. I'll be there in ten minutes." She slapped the phone together. "Gotta go. You eat my linguini." She pulled out a lipstick and a mirror, twirled up the baton, and quickly reformulated her lips. "Wrap it up. Bring it home. Damn. Damn weather report. Three minutes. Prerecorded this morning. I saw it myself. Perfect for tanning lotion. Like I said. Overcast in the morning. Sunny in the afternoon. The second spot comes up in an hour and no tanning sponsor tape for the time. Damn." She flung the purse to her shoulder and headed away from the table rushing past the waiters with their steaming plates of pasta. "I'll call you this afternoon."

Gabriel stared down at the *pappardelle con funghi al vino marsala*, the sweet fragrance of wine and rosemary rising, the delicate slices of wild mushroom limp and appealing coyly to his senses just under and between the firm ribbons of pasta. But this was passé. So what was in? Probably burgers.

Someone was knocking at the glass in the window pane next to his table. He looked out. It was Emi. Her two fists were clenched in front of her face, a kind of demonstration of frustration and boxing technique all at once. He watched her mouth and lips move, trying to decipher her silent scream through the thick panes. "It's raining!" Her lips formed the ridiculous words. In fact, the terrace and street beyond were awash, water pouring as if from a thousand chrome-plated faucets, pouring out of the gray L.A. skies.

CHAPTER 4:

Station ID *Jefferson & Normandie*

Buzzworm figured that some representations of reality were presented for your visual and aural gratification so as to tap what you *thought* you understood. It was a starting place but not an ending. Buzzworm tapped your worst phobias. Seemed like he was who he was to offend you. If he sauntered in with an attitude, it was because no matter how he sauntered in, you couldn't miss him. Might as well make a statement. Besides, how many people got their information from film and TV and the company they keep? Just about everybody thought they knew the truth.

So he could understand the li'l punk who came round here, dissed him bad. Bad. Buzzworm, he didn't say nothing. Just raised his eyebrow a bit like so. Said, "Homey, I got your number. If you're bad now, think about when you're my age, going on forty-five. You be plenty bad. If you alive."

"Why I gots to be alive when I'm forty-five? Lots don't make it. So what?"

"You got a point. Guess time goes on, life gets more precious. If you don't survive, you ain't nothin'. Anybody can lay down and die. Survivin's the hard part. I should know. I survived a war. Every day, I wake up, say I made it, one more day. If I can do it, so can you."

"I's survivin'. Everybody in the hood survivin'. All the mamas survivin'. Get a check and survive. Dealin' and survivin'. On the street and survivin'. Fuck that survivin' shit."

"When I talk about surviving, I don't mean pushing a needle up your veins and waiting for the next time. That's dying. Surviving is what you choose to do. Takes some courage. Takes some sense."

"Sense. Shit. You don't make no sense."

"Little homey like you pack a twenty-two. Think you're cool. And whatcha doing? Out with the crew marking your territory like some dog. Some other dog come piss on your wall, you gonna shoot him. And *I* don't make no sense?" Buzzworm got up. "Catch you later, brother."

Beeper went off. Was a call from someone just outta doing time in county jail. "Gotta go." He fiddled with the volume on the Walkman; readjusted it in his ear. Looked at the time and moved on out. Buzzworm didn't like to waste too much time with those who didn't want to be reformed. He figured he could be around when the time's right. Time for everything. Bible said it. For every season, there is a time.

You saw Buzzworm walking the hood every day, walkin' and talkin', making contact. Had a wad of cards in his pocket. Card said:

Buzzworm
Angel of Mercy
Central & South Central
Pager # 213-321-BUZZ
24 hrs/7 days

Must be everyone on the street got his calling card with something jotted down on the back: rehab number, free clinic, legal services, shelter, soup kitchen, hotline. He was walking social services. Weren't for him, been more dead people on the street. Twenty-four-hour service; he meant it. Some poor nobody in trouble at three a.m. paged him, and he was there long before anyone, especially the police.

Everybody knew him. "Hey, Buzz, whassup?" You saw him coming from a long way. Big black seven-foot dude, Vietnam vet, an Afro shirt with palm trees painted all over it, dreads, pager and Walkman belted to his waist, sound plugged into one ear and two or three watches at least on both his wrists.

How many times he'd been stopped for all those watches on his arms. Cops figured he was fencing the things. But like Buzz said, "These part of my collection. Got over two hundred of them, most of them in working mint condition. Worth nothing to nobody but me." And he was right. This wasn't no Rolex collection. "Rolex?" Made Buzzworm laugh, "I'm no fool." The Buzzworm Watch Collection included so-called priceless pieces like one of the first Seiko just-shake-me-up-no-winding watches, a solar-powered watch, a genuine 1961 Mickey Mouse original, a glow-in-the-dark with fluorescent green numbers, a square LCDer with big half-inch numbers, case you had trouble seeing. Stuff like that. Picked out at flea markets. Buzzworm swore by the swap meets where life and death meet, he liked to say. Life for a set of pink Bakelite dishes left by your dead Aunt Polly. Life for a bunch of has-been watches.

Everybody was saying, "Hey Buzz, what time's it?"

Buzzworm'd say, "Time you dropped in get tested for TB. Epidemic's in town, just to let you know." Hands out a card with a number.

"Is it true what they say?"

"What's that?"

"Old Loco's in jail?"

"Nah. It's rehab for the fourteenth time."

"Do you never give up?"

"Never," Buzzworm smiles. "I never give up. How about you? Using?"

"Me? Ahn ah. Just plain homeless. Doin' time without the crime."

Then someone'd ask, "So what you sportin' today?"

Buzzworm might point to the middle watch on his left arm. He always had what he calls a conversation piece. Could be a silver thing with a gold trim. All the numbers in gold paint. "This one's a got a long history." If you wanted to hear a story, you came round to listen, 'cause Buzzworm always had one. He said, "Belonged to a Creole named Cisco. 'Fore that belonged to his dad. Got the initials on the back. See here, F.D. Francisco Duprey. So I'm told Cisco, the son, pawned this piece off six times. Every time Cisco went back to get the watch, but the sixth time, it wasn't there. And it was the only thing left of his dad's legacy. Dad give it to him before he died when Cisco was just a kid. He near went crazy. Pulled the dealer out by the collar. 'Who'd you sell it to?'

"Dealer says, 'To you. Don't you remember? You came in yesterday. It's yours. Always has been. Always will be.'

"Cisco says, 'I oughta know if I came in here yesterday. What I be doin' here today, if I got my watch yesterday?'

"Dealer can't understand it, 'I swear. It was you. Course you looked kinda strange. Dressed different from usual. Wearin' a hat. Nice suit too. Double-breasted pinstripe. Don't you remember? I asked you where you were going dressed up like that.'

"'I don't own no pinstripe and don't wear hats neither.'

"'Said you was going to a funeral.'

"'Funeral?'

"'Don't you remember?' says the dealer. 'About your tie. It was some crazy tie with a lotta colors. I said you oughta change the tie. Wouldn't do for no funeral.'

"Cisco about turned green. Pulled a photo from his wallet and showed it to the dealer. 'This the man?' Sure enough it was a young dude in a pinstripe with a hat and bright colored tie.

"'That's you!' shouted the dealer.

"'Nope,' says Cisco. 'My old man. Died maybe twenty-five years ago.'

"'Damn. Guess he came back to get his watch.'

"Two days later, Cisco gets killed walking across the street, hit by a car. Despite he's never had any money, he's got this insurance policy for a nice funeral. They lay him out nice and tidy, and just before they close the casket, someone notices the watch. He's wearing his dad's watch. This watch."

So what was Buzzworm doing with Cisco's watch? "That's another story," he said. "Point is: Dead come back."

That was the way it was. Every watch had a story. And with Buzzworm, just about every story had a watch or time or the philosophy which was as aforementioned: Time for everything.

Like it was time to be listening to Papa John on *The Blues Hotel*. Program from noon to two p.m. on 88.9 FM. Twenty-four hours, Buzzworm was listening to the radio. From station ID to station ID. Unless he meant business, he had it plugged in like supermarket music, just in the background to help you shop, give a little light rhythm to the situation. It was even hooked into his ear when he was sleeping, just whispering like a suggestive dream. And he listened to everything. He listened to rap, jazz, R&B, talk shows, classical, NPR, religious channels, Mexican, even the Korean channel. Didn't know a thing they were saying, but he liked the sounds. Fact is, he listened to the sounds so much he could imitate them.

So one day he went to see his Korean friend, the hapkido master, and repeated some sounds he'd been hearing. "So Kwon, what's it mean? What am I saying?" But Kwon was laughing so hard, he couldn't talk. You ever seen a hapkido master fall over on the mat laughing? It was a scene. Turns out it was a commercial for a laxative.

Buzzworm said the radio's a habit. He went through rehab twice before he discovered the radio. Now he didn't do nothing, not even smoking. Cured the smoking, cold turkey. Cured everything. Maybe it was the sound waves bouncing around the brain cells, massaging the nerves. No need for coffee neither. And it didn't need to be loud, just there, soft in the background, like an inner voice. Sometimes he tried tapes or CDs, but they were not the same. Not as effective, he claimed. Radio had a special wave, a pulse. AM or FM, it didn't matter, long as it was coming over the air. When Buzzworm'd unplugged himself from his Walkman, meant he was unplugged from his inner voice, and that had to be a little scary. Not for Buzzworm, but for the one he'd unplugged it for. That's when you maybe had to watch it. Some thought he wasn't paying no attention with that thing in his ear, but he was paying plenty attention enough.

Used to be Buzzworm spent all his money on dope and smoke. Now he spent it on batteries. Buzzworm had batteries on him like some people got matches or a lighter, Tums or chewing gum. Maybe it might be cheaper to smoke. Batteries're expensive. Think about it. Maybe fifty cents apiece on the triple-As for the Walkman, another fifty cents each on the double-A for the pager, special jobber for the cellular, little jobbers for the watches. One day he figured it out. Conceivably he could spend somewhere around $7.38 a day just for energy. Anybody said they've got an expensive habit, Buzzworm reminded them about his. But he said, it's totally legit. Surgeon General didn't get on his case either. Even if he might be changing seven, eight batteries of various voltages per day, he did try to conserve; unless there was an emergency, he used rechargeables on a regular basis, and he always had those little puppies recharging. Lately he had got himself a solar-powered radio. Plugged himself direct into the sun. Used it during the day and saved the Walkman for nighttime.

Buzzworm had a thing for palm trees too. Maybe 'cause they're skinny and tall. Maybe if he put his ear to the trunk of a palm tree, he could hear the radio waves descending from the scraggly fronds at the top. And he really knew his palm trees. Family Palmaceae. Four thousand species. Tall ones called Washingtonia Robusta or Mexican Fan Palm. Similar ones with thicker trunks were called Washingtonia Filifera. Mostly you noticed the tallest Robustas. Buzzworm was always talking about them like he was their personal gardener. You caught him staring at palm trees, seemed like he was talking to them.

Sometimes he made people come out of their houses and appreciate what was on their own front lawn. They came out past their screen doors to take a look up at two spiky trunks topped with what, for all they cared, were giant mops. Green giants in dreads is what. But Buzzworm said, "These here are Phoenix Canariensis."

"Phoenix Canary what? Buzzworm, what's this got to do with social services?"

"You understand the species of trees in the neighborhood, you understand the nature of my work."

They shook their heads, but Buzzworm pointed to the palms, "Could both be more than fifty years old by the looks of them. This one on the right's female. See the orange blossoms? That's a female. They'll turn to fruit soon. You must have noticed them before. Look like dates. One on the left is male. Someone planned it that way. Pair of male and female. This is a very nice pair. Could use some trimming inside here. Also they could use more water. Some people think palms don't need water, but some water helps. They might well last another fifty years."

People in the house didn't know what the hell he was talking about. They probably rented the place and only watered every other week. They didn't know what good two giant palm trees were except to mark the house where they lived. Seemed like they made a mess when the dead fronds fell, the orange fruit got all over the sidewalk, and the birds made a mess nesting and squabbling about. They said to Buzzworm, "You like these damn palm trees, dig 'em out and haul 'em away. Be our guest."

"I just want to let you know the age of these fine specimens. Been standin' here a long time and will continue to long after you and I are gone. These trees're like my watches here, markin' time. Palm tree's smart, knows the time for everything. Knows to put out flowers and fruit when the time's right, even though out here don't seem like there's any seasons to speak of. Suppose we could all learn something from a palm tree that knows the seasons better than us."

Buzzworm was born and raised near about the corner of Jefferson and Normandie. Said when he was growing up, never noticed trees. No trees to mention. Bushes, dried-up lawns, weeds, asphalt, and concrete. Consequently, no shade this side of town. What's trees? he always wondered. Never sure about trees, even though he learned to spell it, learned to copy the pictures other kids painted in tempera, two brown strokes for a trunk and that green amorphous *do* on top, sometimes with red dots they called apples. Never saw one of those in the neighborhood. It was a puzzlement. No trees in this city desert.

One day, however, he was walking his block like always, and he suddenly noticed that row of poles planted every so many yards into the grass or dirt to one side of the sidewalk. His eyes followed the gray-brown poles up to the sky, and for the first time, he recognized what he believed to be a tree. They don't draw it certain, he thought. Not at all. Brown trunks should be much longer, top *do* a bush, and absolutely no apples. After that, he started to draw these trees all the time. Too high to see if birds live in them. Too high to check for fruit. But he was sure he had the tallest trees of anyone in the class. He thought if you could get to the top of them, you could see everything. Those trees could see everything. See beyond the street, the houses, the neighborhood. See over the freeway.

And they didn't seem to need water, just some trimming from time to time, but the wind did that. Blew down the giant fronds making a mess on the street. Sometimes a city crew came by with a man in a basket on a crane and buzzed the old stuff off. Buzzed everything till there was nothing but a little green mop at the top. Looked ridiculous. One time made a mistake and buzzed the whole thing off the top, nothing left but a damn pole. Bald thing for pigeons to sit on from time to time.

Other kids said, "What you drawin' them ugly palm trees for? If anybody had some sense, they'd hack these poles down and plant some real trees with real shade."

"Poor people don't get to have no shade. That's what porches are for."

"These palm trees are a mistake. Somebody thought they would grow short; turned out they giants."

"That's cause they gotta see over the freeway, over the hood to the other side."

"Eventually, they gonna cut the tops off. Turn them into telephone poles."

One day, Buzzworm got taken for a ride on the freeway. Got to pass over the Harbor Freeway, speed over the hood like the freeway was a giant bridge. He realized you could just skip out over his house, his streets, his part of town. You never had to see it ever. Only thing you could see that anybody might take notice of were the palm trees. That was what the palm trees were for. To make out the place where he lived. To make sure that people noticed. And the palm trees were like the eyes of his neighborhood, watching the rest of the city, watching it sleep and eat and play and die. There was a beauty about those palm trees, a beauty neither he nor anybody down there next to them could appreciate, a beauty you could only notice if you were far away. Everything going on down under those palm trees might be poor and crazy, ugly or beautiful, honest or shameful—all sorts of life that could only be imagined from far away. This was probably why the palm trees didn't need any water to speak of. They were fed by something else, something only the streets of his hood could offer. It was a great fertilizer—the dankest but richest of waters. It produced the tallest trees in the city, looking out over everything, symbols of the landscape, a beauty that could only be appreciated from afar.

CHAPTER 5:

Traffic Window *Harbor Freeway*

The third movement was excruciatingly beautiful. But that was his rule about third movements. One should hang breathlessly on every note, a great feeling of anguish nearly spilling from one's heart. It was mostly strings, violins accompanied by violas and cellos, exchanging melodies with the plaintive voice of the oboes. When it was really good, it brought tears. He let them run down his face and onto the pavement, concentrating mightily on the delicate work at hand. One slip of the baton, one false gesture, and he might lose the building intensity, might fail to caress each note with its tender due. In some deep place in his being, he wanted desperately to lose his way through these passages, but he would not give up his control. He must hear every measure, cue every instrument at its proper moment, until the final note. This was the work of a great conductor and the right of the composer.

Manzanar Murakami sensed the time of day through his feet, through the vibration rumbling through the cement and steel, and by the intervals of vehicles passing beneath him. At that moment, cars swooped at steady intervals, trucks trundled but trundled quickly. Traffic was thick but moving. It was manageable traffic. People in this traffic could count themselves lucky. They might reach their destinations ten to fifteen minutes early. Manzanar calculated that it would probably be twenty past the hour or ten 'til. It was prior to or after the amount of time it took for workers to normally leave their offices, pack their belongings, descend in elevators, retrieve cars from parking lots, plod through city streets, wait on ramps for traffic meters, then to finally merge onto the great freeway system. They had not yet all arrived, or a great wave of them had already plowed through in a slow grumpy mass. Those who cruised by at this reasonable speed, considering the hour, were the early birds or riffraff of the great mass. They took advantage unknowingly of what Manzanar knew to be a traffic window—a window of opportunity where a traveler might cruise between the congested clumps of aggravated rush-hour traffic.

Such a traffic window was essential for the third movement. There was just enough tension and yet the possibility of reverie. Not the stoned reverie of night traffic at seventy miles an hour, but a controlled reverie of rhythmic cadence and repeated melody. An incredible yearning went forth, perhaps of love and desire. Even if it were only the simple hunger for dinner, it was a hunger Manzanar sensed in a brutal and yet beautiful way. There was an inexplicable clarity about the third movement, a sweetness tinged with pain. It was as if his very heart tilted forward, his arms offering and yet containing this heart, opening and closing as the wings of a great bird, coaxing the notes tenderly to brief life, conducting sound into symphony.

Those in vehicles who hurried past under Manzanar's concrete podium most likely never noticed him. Perhaps there were those who happened to see the arching movements of a man's arms, the lion's head of white hair flailing this way and that, the silver glint of the baton or a figure of strange command outlined starkly between skyscrapers in the afternoon sunlight. And perhaps they thought themselves disconnected from a sooty homeless man on an overpass. Perhaps and perhaps not. And yet, standing there, he bore and raised each note, joined them, united families, created a community, a great society, an entire civilization of sound. The great flow of humanity ran below and beyond his feet in every direction, pumping and pulsating, that blood connection, the great heartbeat of a great city.

From the beginning of daylight saving in April, the city watched its days lengthen until the solstice, when daylight lingered across the skies as long as possible. It was the end of the school year, and children had or had not graduated from one class to the next, eager to wake to listless days at the beach, on cool porches, under sprinklers, or before the interminable TV. Never mind that they had been signed up for summer camps, Y camp, work camp, athletic camp, leadership camp, swim school, remedial reading, remedial math, college for kids, year-round school, summer school, summer jobs, a job at McDonald's, a job a Disneyland, jobs for youth, the family business, keep kids off the street, the family vacation, vacation with grandma, vacation with dad who lives in Florida or mom who lives in Dallas, a trip to Epcot, a tagging crew, gangs, or detention. Never mind. Today none of that had started. It was Monday. It was hot and listless and expectant. All the TVs in L.A. were turned on. Maybe no one was watching, but they were turned on, turned on to cartoons—Warner Brothers, Disney, Hanna-Barbera. It was summer, the first day of freedom.

All this Manzanar knew. Gone were the yellow school buses, the sporty Nissans and Mazdas favored by the college-bound, the Tercels, Corollas, Accords, and Tauruses favored by educators, the mothers and their early-morning Chrysler and Previa vanpools. When education left the freeways, a certain unclogging was achieved. Manzanar likened it to lowered cholesterol in the blood stream. It was the same when bureaucrats were given holidays. And it was the reason for the unusually good window in traffic. The first day of freedom might mean many things. For Manzanar, it was this extra elbow room on the usually densely occupied freeway. It called for more expansive gestures, a greater elasticity in the musical measure.

Manzanar Murakami had become a fixture on the freeway overpass much like a mural or a traffic information sign or a tagger's mark. He was there every day, sometimes even when it rained, but it rarely rained. After all, this was L.A. There was a schedule of sorts, a program, an appropriate series of concerts and symphonies in accordance with the seasons and the climate of the city. As noted by many others, climatic change in L.A. was different from other places. It had less perhaps to do with weather and more to do with disaster. For example, when the city rioted or when the city was on fire or when the city shook, the program was particularly apt, controversial, hair-raising, horrific, intense—apocalyptic, if you will. There was an incredibly vast repertory, heralding every sort of L.A. scenario. Particularly eloquent was the Overture to the Santa Anas. Few contemporary composers rivaled the breadth and quantity of his compositions, and no one had yet dedicated their entire repertoire to one city, not to mention L.A. Few composers of his category were so unknown, so unheard, so without recompense for their art, so maligned, and so invisible.

To say that Manzanar Murakami was homeless was as absurd as the work he chose to do. No one was more at home in L.A. than this man. The Japanese American community had apologized profusely for this blight on their image as the Model Minority. They had attempted time after time to remove him from his overpass, from his eccentric activities, to no avail. They had even tried to placate him with a small lacquer bridge in the Japanese gardens in Little Tokyo. But Manzanar was destined for greater vistas. He could not confine his musical talents to the silky flow of koi in a pond, the constant tap of bamboo on rock, or manicured bonsai. It was true that he had introduced the shakuhachi and koto to a number of his pieces, but he was the sort who imagined a hundred shakuhachis and a hundred kotos. Indeed, he had written a piece for a hundred shamisen—the sound of their triangular bones beating on strings echoing through the stretched skins of a hundred cats was deafening and thrilling. No. Only the freeway overpass, the towering downtown horizon rising around it, would do.

It was suggested that he could be taken by helicopter and left on a mountain top—certainly a grand enough vista for a hundred shamisen or a thousand cellos. But those who knew Manzanar knew that he would find his way back, track the sounds back to the city, to the din of traffic and the commerce of dense humanity and the freeway. The freeway was a great root system, an organic living entity. It was nothing more than a great writhing concrete dinosaur and nothing less than the greatest orchestra on Earth.

CHAPTER 6:

Coffee Break *Downtown*

It was about four o'clock in the afternoon, an hour before the five o'clock deadline, mid-June, summer solstice, and it had rained. Out there, steam rose from the hot streets, the pungent odor of wet concrete wafting over the downtown landscape. At eighty degrees, in an hour it would be dry again, but for the moment, everything out there had a wet reflective murky glow, the clouds parting into what I typically call pewter skies.

As usual, Emi called. "Hey, Gabe! Break time!" she announced over the phone. "Get away from that monitor before you catch cancer!"

I put her on hold. "Listen," I said to Terry on the other line, "You're right about the pewter skies. I got carried away. Strike it." Actually I never get carried away. Well, rarely. It's just a joke around the office. It's how I test out new editors. See how they handle an edit. When a new editor like Terry comes on board, I always find a way to plant a *pewter skies* line into the body of my story. About a week later, someone will say to the newcomer, "Pass the pewter test yet?" The smart editor may simply strike it without a word. The shy editor may wander through previous articles nervously trying to find a precedent or whether I'll bite. One editor changed it to *putrid skies.* Another suggested *buffed tin* or *tarnished silver,* or was it *stainless steel*? Someone left the pewter in and added something about how it *darkened the Southern California landscape like heavy metal.* Most editors are polite or politely sarcastic, but one editor said haughtily, "I've only been here one week, and it's already obvious you guys can't write to save your behinds. Major L.A. newspaper my ass." Clearly, this editor was God's gift to the business.

I didn't feel like giving Terry a hard time. I had met him in the elevator. He complimented me on my mothers of gangbangers story. He seemed wise and bookish, a true editor type. He didn't seem like the sort who would become a problem; he wasn't a wannabe reporter. Wannabes could be trouble. Years of turning sloppy, albeit perhaps creative, writing into terse cogent prose could make an unsung talent pretty damn frustrated. But Terry was probably one of those editors whose finely tuned sense of grammar was a source of modest pride. Knowing how one word should follow another, one sentence follow the last, and one paragraph unfold upon the next, and applying those rules to sometimes unruly text seemed to be, for Terry, the whole of his fulfillment. Oh yes, and he was a precision speller. I could write a book about the pewter test, but that's beside the point. All this to distinguish myself as a reporter who understands the worth of a good editor. In this oftentimes cutthroat business, I might even be considered sensitive in this regard.

Perhaps you've seen my *by*: Gabriel Balboa. I do the local news and sometimes the East L.A. metro beat. I'm one of a handful of Chicano reporters on editorial staff. I did a rare thing: worked my way up from messenger. Did this all through college. To be honest, I did it for completely idealistic reasons at the time, not necessarily because I could write or even liked to. It was because of Ruben Salazar, the Mexican American reporter who was killed at the Silver Dollar during the so-called "East L.A. uprising" in the early seventies. Of course I never knew him personally but had read about and been inspired by the man. By the time I got my first story, he was long dead, but I was there to continue a tradition he had started. That's the way I felt. This was going to be my contribution to La Raza, to follow in his footsteps. Now I'm not so pretentious as to think I'm some kind of modern-day Salazar, but remembering my roots can keep me on track, steer me away from the petty jealousies that seem to pervade this office. So I might be considered idealistic in that regard. On the other hand, I must say I keep a handle on the nitty-gritty. It's the detective side of this business that gives me a real charge, getting into the grimy crevices of the street and pulling out the real stories.

"Gabe! So what are you working on now?" Emi nearly yelled into the phone. She knows this is the most loaded question she can ask a reporter in a crowd of other reporters. You only need to lose one scoop on a story to learn evasiveness on the phone.

"Rained you out today, eh Angel?" I answered.

"Can you believe it? I wasn't gonna lose the commercial. No way. We played the tape. Bob whatshisname-the-weatherman is talking like a fool about sunshine in the afternoon, and it's pouring out there."

"The paper predicted rain. And that was yesterday as of five."

"Who reads the paper for godssake?"

"We know you don't read, but who tunes in for the weather at two-thirty in the afternoon?"

"Surfers? Who knows. Hey," she interrupted herself, "Hot tip. Invest in rubbish. At one point four billion, it's our tenth biggest export item."

"I believe it."

"Did you wrap up the linguini?"

"It's in the back of the car."

"It's going to rot in this heat."

"It's part of the plan, although I doubt salmonella can kill you. Besides, you owe me. You left me with the bill."

"Did we have great sex last night or what?" This was another one of Emi's tricks. "Come on, Gabriel. Say it out loud. Repeat after me: We . . . had . . . great . . . sex. God," she whined, "it's so stuffy over there. Okay, then. Say it in Spanish."

"I only speak Spanish with my family, with my mother and her priest. I can't talk dirty with you," I joked.

"And I thought you were bilingual." She said *bye-lingualll,* like she was licking her lips.

"Gotta go. Gotta interview."

"What time tonight?"

"That's what I meant to tell you. It's gonna be a long haul tonight. I haven't even started."

"Then I'm going to the gym."

"Do me a favor? That video store next door to the gym. See if they've got *Angel Beach.*"

"No way. This is disaster movie week, remember? I'm taping the series. We're gonna watch real TV, color TV, commercials and everything."

"*Angel Beach* is a disaster. An artful disaster."

"See you lay-ter." She hung up.

Knowing Emi, she would find *Angel Beach* for me. That's the way she was. The complaining and the bitching were the surface of a very big heart, the most generous I had ever known. The character of our relationship only seemed stormy. It had started out that way, with the smart talk and mouthing off, the snide repartee of two people who hate each other's guts and then fall into bed together. I admit Emi had it all over me; she never lost her cool, but I could really get mad. And she knew it. "I thought you had some hot blood," she crooned. She could be wicked, but I admit I loved that side of her. I loved her fast tongue, her spontaneity. She had said so herself. "Gabe, you're *then.* I'm *now.* For a reporter, you oughta be more *now.* Let's do it now." She kept dragging me into now. Most of the time, I felt grateful. But I had one thing over her. She *acted* like she didn't care. I knew better.

I snuck into Beth's office, one of those glass enclosures earned by seniority. Beth was always good about letting me have a private conversation when necessary. She wasn't around at that hour, but she wouldn't mind me using her phone. I paged my contact and waited. Usually it was a five minute wait, but never more than ten. I looked at my watch. Three minutes. Buzzworm was in form that day.

"Balboa? You? You paged me on my coffee break."

"It's the other way around, Buzz. I paged you on my coffee break."

Buzzworm laughed.

"So what's up, buddy?"

"Strange day, dude. Strange day. Rain over your way?"

"Yeah, sure did. Hey, turn that thing down. Sounds like a bad connection." I could hear Buzzworm fiddling with his Walkman. He was never without his radio. Asking him to turn it off might make him hang up the phone, but I had learned he wasn't entirely unreasonable.

"Okay." He was back. "Write this down. L.A. River. I'm checking out the transvestite camp along there. We get a wall of rain. And I mean a wall of rain. Flood conditions. Dumps a whole foot in five minutes. I timed it, so you know I know. Shit floating down the river. Car parts, hypodermics, dead dogs, Neanderthal bones, props from the last movie shot down there, you name it. Folks in the bridge rafters tossing avocados and screaming. Got a cross-dresser who was doing his regular laying around, near drowned with his wig on. Had to pull him out and pump the lungs. Brother saw God. It was like a baptism. Then it was all gone. Concrete bed's dry. My pants're dry. Like it never happened. And you look up. The sun's up. I mean up. Like it's never gonna go away. And by my synchronization, it's near going on seventeen hundred. Daylight saving my ass. This is like Alaska."

A flash-flood-L.A.-river-transvestite-drowning story with a happy ending. I thought about it. "What else you got?"

"What else I got? Balboa, you always saying, *what else you got?* I know you're producing pulp. I even read it from time to time. Not that it isn't good pulp. Who else but Balboa's gonna write about us? But around here, brother, we recycling your pulp as beds. Maybe you can turn the stuff back into trees and build us some real beds."

"I'm trying, Buzz. I really am trying."

"Hey, I know what I was gonna tell you. Yeah." Buzzworm's pause was pregnant. "This one is good. Real human interest. But he's shy. Been around a while now, but moves around a lot. The easy thing is he only moves around the freeway system."

"Freeway system's big, Buzz."

"Yeah, but you can't miss him. Picks an overpass, see. Looks out over the traffic, the freeway, and—" I could sense Buzzworm making gestures through the phone, "conducts."

"Conducts?"

"Music. With a baton and all. You know. Like Leonard Bernstein. Like Esa-Pekka Solanen. Conducts."

"Conducts what?"

"I could get philosophical with you man, but so what if he's crazy. We all crazy!"

"He was a conductor?" I scratched my head.

"Is Seiji Ozawa still around?"

"I think so."

"Then it's not him," Buzzworm confirmed.

"He's Japanese?"

"Probably an American breed. Hey, you downtown. You never see him? Thought by now somebody'd see him. You too busy on the car phone, man. Don't bother to look up and see the sights."

"I don't have a car phone."

"Ever notice the Washingtonia Robustas?"

"Buzz. The story. Give me the story."

"Hey, I read this story where a writer and a palm tree face it off. Wouldn't you know it, the palm tree wins."

"I don't have all day, Buzz."

"Okay. So, I offered him mental health services. He just laughed. Maybe he's schizo, but maybe not. They can fool you good. Totally lucid. And somebody takes care of him. He's out on the streets, but he's got a stash somewhere keeps coming to him. Come winter, he's got a jacket. Come summer, he's got a hat."

"So what's the angle?"

"I gotta write the story for you, Balboa? Look him up. See for yourself. You wanna humanize the homeless? Then humanize the homeless."

"Don't be sarcastic."

"It's a wake-up call, Balboa. All these people living in their cars. The cars living in garages. The garages living inside guarded walls. You dump the people outta the cars, and you left with things living inside things. Meantime people going through the garbage at McDonald's looking for a crust of bread and leftover fries."

"Can I quote you?"

"Weren't for the deal, you could go to hell."

"Don't count on any deal, Buzz. I made a promise to you. That's all."

I felt myself squirming. Buzzworm had a stake in my stories, deeper and hungrier than that of the most competitive reporter. He wanted desperately to see in print the stories of the life surrounding him, to see the wretched truth, the dignity despite the indignity. When I first met him, I had no idea that I was making a pact with a taskmaster more demanding than any editor. He was ruthless in his criticism, his disdain for my soft educated style. "East L.A. boy makes good and gets out of the barrio. Get real, Balboa." So I said if I ever got a Pulitzer, he could take the prize money. "Fifty percent is fine. Otherwise you got no incentive," he smirked, but he never forgot this. He was always waving this thing in front of me like he was the one giving out the Pulitzers himself.

"You Pulitzer material or not, Balboa?" he now injected into the conversation.

"Maybe I should quit this business and do something really altruistic. Like go into teaching."

"You won't. Teaching is a recognition of talent, Balboa. First kid you flunk gonna go out and get himself a million-dollar record deal. At least out here on the streets, you have me. If you'd been connected before, you wouldn't have gotten your ass kicked by that Webb reporter in San Jose."

"Right." What was there to argue? "So where do I find him, and what's his name?"

"Last sighted: Harbor overpass, near Fifth. Name's Manzanar."

"Sounds vague, Buzz. Maybe we better go back to the drowning."

"Trust me on this one. It's gonna be big." Buzzworm liked to taunt me with banter he believed to be newspaper talk. "I got a hunch," he said, as if this should seal the story's fate. Trouble with dismissing him was that lately he knew better than me.

"So what's the latest conspiracy theory on the street?"

"Word is the players change, but the game's the same. And on that note, Balboa: that other hot tip you been waiting for? Tomorrow a.m. LAX. Mexicana. Ten twenty. C. Juárez. No luggage. Carry-on only."

"That's it?"

"Just be grateful." He hung up.

I went back to my desk, opened my afternoon mail, flipped through some personal stuff like the copy of a bank transfer of money to my account in Mazatlán. I thought about Rafaela down at my place in México. It had taken so many years to build the place, I didn't really care anymore. I just wanted to see it finished even though I knew it would never be finished. I imagined Rafaela there, padding across the tile floors in her bare feet, her dark hair crinkling in the summer humidity, her soft Afro-Mayan features bronzed by the Mexican sun slipping in and out of the green shadows. I imagined the industry of her hands and mind, running my accounts, paying the workers, planting, placing, arranging, completing my foolish love affair.

How many friends, how many women had I taken there, forcing them to share my excitement, enduring their veiled compliments, knowing it was just another vacation for them? If I were ever to live there, my friends would not follow me, least of all Emi. There were only variations of nothing to do. Or as Emi commented, "There's only so much sex and tequila you can stand." It was the sort of place writers love. But as time went on, I had to admit to myself that I was really not a writer: I was a reporter. The current event, the late-breaking story, the three o'clock budgets, deadlines, secret sources I had painstakingly built up over the years, and the cutting edge of the interview: I realized I could never abandon this life for the endless lull of a private paradise.

And yet lately I found myself thinking constantly about Rafaela. I remembered her fingers lightly tickling the lines in my palm. "It seems you will encounter some big adventures," she suggested. "And a long life." She followed my life line. I couldn't imagine her returning to her husband, returning to her janitorial jobs, ever again running the vacuum under my feet in the evenings and gently complaining, "Gabriel, drinking coffee again at this hour. It's bad for you. Time to go home. Come on now. You're in my way. How can my crew do its job when you reporters never leave?" This was a world I was sure she had left for good, and I could now only imagine Rafaela in my place, in my home, there.

I took the stairs down, my heels squeaking on the last flight of marble steps and out the foyer. The rush of heat and humidity outside the glass doors was sudden and oppressive. I walked quickly through scattered crowds and traffic, all moving as if in unison in one great stoic groan, languishing under the hot sunlight. And then I realized how strange this was: in the middle of towering thirty- and forty-floor buildings there was not a single shadow, not a sliver of a cooler gray to slice the concrete walks. The sun had aimed its rays straight down into the downtown canyon. At this hour it seemed impossible. Everything had the eerie tones of searing white and grimy black.

I walked west with some urgency, determined to find my subject. I marched toward the bridge over the Harbor Freeway, but no one stood out. About midway over the bridge, I paused, looked over into the river of traffic below. A sooty heat and din emanated from there, pressed against what I imagined to be all the elastic parts of my body: my lungs, my diaphragm, my tympanum.

And as I looked across, I saw him. Buzzworm was right. There he was larger than life, under the raging sun and a disheveled shock of white hair, a face both of anguish and incredible peace, his arms reaching and caressing the air for the sound and rhythms of . . . of what?

CHAPTER 7:

To Wake *The Marketplace*

No one knew where he came from,
or how long he had lived,
how many years,
decades,
and yet he seemed a child,
yet not such a child to be without season
nor such an old man to be without reason.

When he removed his clothing, he revealed weathered skin stretched like fragile paper over brittle bones, revealed the holes in the sides of his torso and the purple stain across his neck, the solid scars of tissue that padded both his feet. He possessed the beauty of an ancient body, a gnarled and twisted tree, tortured and serene, wise and innocent all at once. Here, in this body-tree—more like bamboo than birch, more like birch than oak, more like oak than pine, more like pine than sequoia, more like sequoia than cactus, more like cactus—was the secret of his youth and the secret of his age.

He said that he had come from a long way away, from the very tip of the Tierra del Fuego, from Isla Negra, from the very top of Macchu Picchu, from the very bottom of the Foz do Iguaçu, but perhaps it was only a long way in his quixotic mind. And yet his voice was often a jumble of unknown dialects, guttural and whining, Latin mixed with every aboriginal, colonial, slave, or immigrant tongue, a great confusion discernible to all and to none at all. *Yo soy el Frito Bandito,* he said. *Bebes Coca-Cola?* Stuff like that.

Of course this was part of an accomplished performance, but no one was ever certain whether it was just a performance. No one was certain where or how he had perfected his art. He was actor and prankster, mimic and comic, freak, a one-man circus act. He did it all himself—the animals, the scenery, the contraptions, the music, the sound effects, all the characters, the narration, advertising, and tickets. He did big epics and short poetry—as short as a single haiku—romantic musicals, political scandal, and, as they say, comical tragedy and tragical comedy. And he was not beyond doing provocative, exploitive, or sensational work; timing was everything. Across the border, they had a name for such multiple types: they would call him a performance artist. This designation would entitle him to local, state, federal, and private funding. Well, he didn't know it yet, but that's where he was going: North.

He had performed with the greatest, with La Argentina in Buenos Aires, with Carmen Miranda in Rio de Janeiro and Ornitorrinco in São Paulo, with El Teatro Nacional in Santiago, with Cantiflas in la Ciudad de México. At one time he was called the Latino Ronald Reagan—a facetious comparison of his own making, but of course he said he had always turned down Hollywood. He had performed for the people, for the masses, on street corners, in cabarets, in dirty saloons, in churches and plazas, in bordellos and cemeteries. He performed for the rich, the famous, and the infamous; for household names: for Che in Bolivia, for Eva Perón, for Pelé, for Pinochet, and Allende before that, for El General Stroessner, for Pablo Escobar and the DEA, for Noriega, for Vargas Llosa and Fujimori, for Somoza and Sandino, Borges and Neruda, for Archbishop Romero, Porfirio Díaz, and Fidel. When they put him in jail, he performed for his torturers. And when they tortured him, he performed for his fellow inmates. He died a thousand deaths, but they could never shut him up. They could never stop his body, his face, his physicality, the innuendo of a mere muscle, the silence of his presence, the fear of his glare, the emotion of his beating heart, the scream of his absence.

In one installation he wore wings and sat in a cage. Gabriel García Márquez himself came to the opening, drank martinis and tasted ceviche on little toasts in the society of society. Occasionally someone went to the cage and threw in bits of caviar and the olives from their drinks. Then someone noticed that the wings didn't seem fake, weren't strapped on or glued to his back, but were growing there. Arcangel. That was his name. His professional name. He turned to the black tie crowd and spread his wings, his thin decrepit body an angular mass beneath those magnificent appendages. Someone turned to García Márquez to ask the meaning of this, but he had disappeared.

And then there was that time in Montevideo on the steps of the opera house when Arcangel played the prophet. Chilam Quetzal, he called himself. (He didn't sport wings this time. Prophets usually don't.) He predicted doomsday based on the ancient belief that doom comes in fifty-two-year cycles. The only problem was to decipher when the first doom had occurred and other dooms hence. Perhaps there were a series of small dooms in consecutive fifty-two-year cycles. It was difficult to know. And yet, he stood there at the top of the steps with his calculator, gesticulating and prophesying, his thin body a writhing mass of anguish and foreboding.

The end of the world as we know it is coming!
It will come in 2012,
exactly ten cycles of fifty-two years
from the time Christopher Columbus
discovered San Salvador, Cuba, Haiti,
and the Dominican Republic in 1492!
Think of it!
The last greatest doom that marked
the end of the world as we knew it.
The great discovery!
The great curse!
And this because of a lousy bunch of spices
to hide the putrefaction of meat!

However, he said, it was possible to judge the first doom in the Western Hemisphere as having occurred in 1494 when Columbus discovered Jamaica or in 1498 when he discovered Trinidad and Venezuela. Others might place the first doom in 1502 when Columbus discovered Martinique. By these calculations, doomsday could be predicted to be 2014, 2018, or 2022.

Repent, sinners!
Prepare for the worst!
The fifty-second year is approaching!
Now, if we calculate the first doom
from the time John Cabot discovered
Newfoundland and the North American continent,

he cried, waving his arms, punching numbers into the calculator and reading from the flickering LCD in the sunlight,

then I predict doom will come,
as sure as I am standing here,
in the year of 2017!

Perhaps people thought that doom could be pushed forward and away, that the fifty-second year could be recalculated from a later date, but doom, Arcangel assured everyone, would come anyway. The tremor in his voice was enough to convince everyone.

Ah woe is the great land of Brazil,
discovered in 1500
by Pedro Alvares Cabral.
Doom! Doom! Doom!
Doom in the year 2020!

Or,

Woe is Patagonia
discovered by Ferdinand Magellan in 1519.
In this year also,
Hernán Cortés discovered México.
Ah, all is lost!
Doomed.
Doomed to destruction in 2039!
And what of Argentina
discovered by Magellan in 1520?
Think of it!
The year 2040 is not so far away.

He pointed to a young man.

In your lifetime, you will see it!
If you believe that you will be spared,

think again.
Only death will spare you.
Every year
there has been a historic discovery of our lands
to make the dates of doom a certainty.

It was as he said. In 1524, Giovanni da Verazano discovered North Carolina and the New York harbor, and later, in 1528, he discovered the site of the Panama Canal. In 1534, Jacques Cartier discovered Canada, the Saint Lawrence River, and Quebec. In 1513, Vasco Núñez de Balboa discovered the Pacific Ocean. In 1542, Juan Rodriguez Cabrillo discovered the islands of California, Santa Catalina, and San Clemente and the bays of San Diego and Santa Monica and the Bay of Smoke of San Pedro. In 1602, Sebastian Vizcaíno discovered the Bay of Monterey. In 1610, Henry Hudson discovered the Hudson Bay. In 1621, the Pilgrims discovered Plymouth Rock. There was no escape! If doom did not come as he first predicted, in 2012, then it could also be expected in 2044, 2048, 2054, 2062, 2070, 2078, or 2087.

Doom! Doom!
Look to the past and know the doom that awaits you!
The doom of discovery!
The doom of conquest!
And worse yet,
who among the discoverers
did not plant their seed in this land of discovery?
Now all is lost! We will pay dearly!
I, Chilam Quetzal, the soothsayer, have spoken!

But that was in Montevideo, many years ago.

Lately he had been seen on street corners in México City, juggling balls representing the planets of the solar system while spinning a replica of the sun on his nose. He, like E.T., was very good at this, keeping Pluto on the outer ring, juggling everything—Saturn, Uranus, Venus, Jupiter, etc., even the moon around the Earth—in great ellipses. Children and passersby agreed to hold candles around him to represent the stars. The spectacle produced sudden wonder and, eyes glistening through tears, people emptied their purses and pockets into his waiting hat.

Occasionally he could be persuaded to demonstrate the usefulness of the holes in the sides of his torso. It was shocking, but profitable. Occasionally.

Now, it was Monday, and he awoke. He awoke to all the metaphors that come from the land. He had followed a path across the continent that was crooked, but always heading north. Now he was in Mazatlán. He could hear the waves lapping at the edges of the sand, feel the already-heating breezes flowing from the Sea of Cortez.

He had had a dream. And when he awoke he could still see the dream like a miniature Aleph reflected from his mind to an indefinable point on his visual horizon.

TUESDAY

Diamond Lane

CHAPTER 8:

Rideshare *Downtown Interchange*

Manzanar lifted and dipped his baton, feeling his way carefully through the early morning traffic. It was a red convertible Porsche. The two young men wended their way north toward Hollywood, peeling oranges, bouncing flippant ideas for a storyboard back and forth. It was overcast but so what; the forecast was always sun. Not that Manzanar knew; he was just a conductor. The terrible pain of this moment flashed: the screech of tires, the groaning wail of the monstrous semi pulling forty thousand pounds of liquid propane under pressure in its shiny stainless steel interior—its great twisting second-half tumbling and thundering over itself, and the horror in the face of the driver who knew the consequences of this payload. All this played against the metallic crash and crunch of the unfortunate who shared the same lanes, the snap of delicate necks, the squish of flesh and blood. In both directions of the freeway, spread across ten lanes, hundreds of cars piled one onto the other in an almost endless jam of shrieking notes. Perhaps, perhaps someone had caught it all on video. There was always someone out there catching unsightly things on video. Perhaps not. In any case, Manzanar had fearlessly recorded everything—every horrible, terrifying thing—in music. The sad refrain, not meant to be insipid, was the gentle notes of ridesharing. He had seen the friendship of the two young, and indeed beautiful, men, their brief encounter with happiness, and the possibility of success.

Ridesharing, when it was practiced in greater proportions, alleviated flow, increased rhythm while enhancing and deepening tone. Manzanar, for one, was grateful. The complexity of human adventure over lines of transit fascinated him. The mass of people flowing to work and play, the activity of minds muddling over current affairs, love affairs, the absence of affairs, in automatic, toward destinations beyond streets, parking lots, or driveways: Manzanar followed it all conscientiously.

Long ago, Manzanar had been a skilled surgeon. His work had entailed careful incisions through layers of living tissue, excising tumors, inserting implants, facilitating transplants. At what point the baton replaced the knife, he could no longer remember. Perhaps the skill had never left his fingers, but the will had. He could as easily have translated his talents to that of a sculptor in clay, wood, or even marble—any sort of inanimate substance, but strangely, it was the abstraction of music that engulfed his being. One day, he left a resident to sew up a patient, removed his mask, gloves, and gown, strode through the maze of corridors, down the elevator, through patient waiting, to become a statistic under missing persons.

Manzanar imagined himself a kind of recycler. After all he, like other homeless in the city, was a recycler of the last rung. The homeless were the insects and scavengers of society, feeding on leftovers, living in residue, collecting refuse, carting it this way and that for pennies. In the same manner, who would use the residue of sounds in the city if Manzanar did not? This was perhaps a simplistic interpretation of his work, as simplistic as, for example, the description of his utilizing the sounds of cars whooshing down freeways to imitate the sound of the ocean. Poetic, but false. Everything had its own sound. Genius disguised, as always, with innocent simplicity.

There are maps and there are maps and there are maps. The uncanny thing was that he could see all of them at once, filter some, pick them out like transparent windows and place them even delicately and consecutively in a complex grid of pattern, spatial discernment, body politic. Although one might have thought this capacity to see was different from a musical one, it was really one and the same. For each of the maps was a layer of music, a clef, an instrument, a musical instruction, a change of measure, a coda.

But what were these mapping layers? For Manzanar they began within the very geology of the land, the artesian rivers running beneath the surface, connected and divergent, shifting and swelling. There was the complex and normally silent web of faults—cracking like mud flats baking under a desert sun, like the crevices in aging hands and faces. Yet, below the surface, there was the man-made grid of civil utilities: Southern California pipelines of natural gas; the unnatural waterways of the Los Angeles Department of Water and Power, and the great dank tunnels of sewage; the cascades of poisonous effluents surging from rain-washed streets into the Santa Monica Bay; electric currents racing voltage into the open watts of millions of hungry energy-efficient appliances; telephone cables, cable TV, fiber optics, computer networks.

On the surface, the complexity of layers should drown an ordinary person, but ordinary persons never bother to notice, never bother to notice the prehistoric grid of plant and fauna and human behavior, nor the historic grid of land usage and property, the great overlays of transport—sidewalks, bicycle paths, roads, freeways, systems of transit both ground and air, a thousand natural and man-made divisions, variations both dynamic and stagnant, patterns and connections by every conceivable definition from the distribution of wealth to race, from patterns of climate to the curious blueprint of the skies.

As far as Manzanar was concerned, it was all there. A great theory of maps, musical maps, spread in visible and audible layers—each selected sometimes purposefully, sometimes at whim, to create the great mind of music. To the outside observer, it was a lonely business; it would seem that he was at once orchestra and audience. Or was he indeed? Unknown to anyone, a man walking across the overpass at that very hour innocently hummed the recurrent melody of the adagio.

CHAPTER 9:

NewsNow *Hollywood South*

"Where are you?"

"Doing the Joan Didion freeway thang. You know, slouching around L.A. Sorry, babe, but it's hard to feel exhilarated going five miles an hour."

"Be serious."

"All right." Emi sucked her nostrils together and intoned, "Do you read me Mothergoose? Come in Mothergoose. I'm on the Hollywood South, following the *NewsNow* van to a site."

"Where on the Hollywood?"

"Just passing Silverlake."

"Shit!"

"What?"

"My car! Didn't you see it? Stalled on the right shoulder!"

"Gabe, we're looking for a major SigAlert, not your stalled car. Besides, they're saying it's a red convertible Porsche Carrera Four or what's left of it, not a decrepit faded orange BMW with no bumpers and no muffler. I told you to buy a new car."

"The transmission blew up. Shit. It took forever to get this far anyway. It's like the freeway is longer or something."

"Well, it is pretty stacked up." Emi looked out all her mirrors. "Red convertible Porsche. Imagine, no L.A. native would buy such a thing. What are the chances? Breathe freeway air and get cancer. Lose your hair. Get jacked easy. Or just get shot straight on. Must be an ex-pat from the East. Came to L.A. to die."

Gabriel groaned. "Listen, get off at the next exit and pick me up."

"At this point, it would easier for the *NewsNow* copter to pick you up."

"Emi, this is important. I've got to meet a plane in the next half-hour. I've got a lead to follow. In fact, it's stuff you like. Might involve some genuine espionage."

"Ouuu. Where are you?"

"At a gas station phone booth. Two blocks north on Silver Lake off the Hollywood."

"If you'd get a decent car, you could keep a car phone. Cell-u-lar. Get it? We could do cell-u-lar to cell-u-lar." She said it like it was sex.

"Emi, I don't have time for this. Beam me out of here, okay?"

"Ay ay, Cap—" The line went silent. Emi followed the *NewsNow* van under the overpass and then to a standstill. The major SigAlert couldn't be too far away now, or then again, it might be really far away, and this was the residual result of stopped-up traffic. In any case, it was impossible to talk to Gabriel from a tunnel of concrete. But it also looked like it would be impossible to save him from his predicament. It was wall-to-wall cars. Emi pulled on the hand brake and got out of her car. She walked up to the *NewsNow* van and tapped on the window. "Guys, I gotta go save a friend. Did you see that old stalled orange BMW back there?"

The guys shook their heads.

"Well, that was him."

"You gonna walk?"

"I know what you mean." Emi surveyed the line-up of cars.

"Air shots from the *NewsNow* copter look good, but we can't even get up on the shoulder to drive through. It's the next overpass over. See?" the *NewsNow* driver pointed. "Porsche ran into a semi. Semi jackknifed. Thing's sprawled out across five lanes. Porsche looks like a Classic Coke can. Squashed for recycling.

"Anybody hurt?"

"I guess we'll find out."

Emi thought about this. Every now and then, she and usually some other sensation seeker at the station would get the word and go chasing after the *NewsNow* van, just to be there on the scene. It was one of those days when she just felt like a little adrenaline high for real-life horror. Maybe because it was disaster movie week. So far she had been to a fire, to the scene of a robbery, and had chased the *NewsNow* van chasing cops involved in a two-hour car chase that started in Burbank and ended up in Whittier. But the thought of seeing mangled bodies in a car wreck suddenly churned about in her stomach. She could always see it on TV. "Hey, if I can maneuver my car out of here, I'll see you back at the station."

Emi spotted Gabriel on the corner near the gas pumps. He was looking in the other direction, his dark features a striking profile, black hair slicked back into a ponytail, Ray-Bans focused across the street at nothing in particular. He was wearing a black shirt, black suspenders, and the purple tie she had given him, looking rumpled as usual and probably sweating like a horse in this heat. "Hey you," she yelled through her tinted power window as it slid down, "Prince of the Aztecs! Are we too late?"

Gabriel nodded a cool recognition at the sight of Emi's sleek black twin-turbo Supra. As Emi liked to say, everything about her vehicular possession purred, *Detail me. Detail me.* She gunned the motor to let anyone watching know she was picking him up.

"Plane could be late. Then there's customs. It's worth a try."

"Bradley International?"

"Yeah."

"What's with this mobster look? Aren't you hot?"

"Don't remind me. It was—"

"Overcast in the morning," she finished the sentence. The light turned. "Hold on," she warned. "We gotta cut through the red tape." No one maneuvered a car like Emi. She wasn't afraid to merge. She slipped in a CD. Piazzolla for Gabriel. Merging music, she called it. As she had explained to Gabriel long ago, "I was brought up next to the Ascot in Gardena. My brother and my cousin used to race. I learned to drive from them. No wimpy driving here, baby." Emi gunned the Supra around the corner, jammed into first, second, third, fourth, fifth, sixth, dancing up and down each gear to the vehicle's purring acceleration. "I love to shift gears," she gripped the stick and confessed over the wailing tango.

Gabriel feigned nonchalance. He usually let her drive. Like the house in Mazatlán, his old BMW 2002 was another aspiration of his—to take a classic with character and make it run like a panther. He never had time. Usually it ran.

"Something's wrong today," Gabriel observed. "Yesterday too. Haven't you noticed it?"

"If you mean that the garage door opener broke, there's no paper in the fax machine, and my car alarm went off for no good reason, you're right."

"I mean the length of the day. The weather. The light for godssake. Time. It's got something to do with time. Place. Damn!" Gabriel squinted. "Every which way you turn, the sun is in your windshield.

"I've got an earthquake kit in the back with bottled water and aspirin. Maybe we should break it out. You don't sound so good."

"Buzz mentioned the same thing yesterday. He was talking about the rain, how it flooded, how the sun was out right after like it never happened. Something about it being like Alaska. The sun never going away."

Emi shifted gears and changed the subject. "I talked to your mom today."

"So what's new?"

"She wanted to know why we missed your grandma's birthday party. From the sound of it, all two hundred and thirty-three members of your family were there except you. Even your cousin Joe got out of jail for it."

"Do you know how old my grandmother is? One hundred and eight. Ever since she turned a hundred, we gotta have a party like it's the last one. So I've been to seven out of eight."

"She's the one who knew Pancho Villa?"

"Yeah. She's full of stories. She started the East L.A. Ladies Garment Workers Union. Hey, I've got it all down on tape and notes. And that's what counts. Nobody understands." Gabriel fumed.

Emi gunned the Supra down surface streets and two freeways, then swerved the Supra to the curb. "Twenty-eight minutes flat with two to go. Get out and be a reporter." She pointed at Bradley International. "I'll circle once. That enough time?"

"You may have to stall."

"No problema."

Gabriel burst from the car. Emi had put the punch back into his always grim resolve. No matter what was wrong with today, Emi could ignore it or use it to her purposes. She was right. There was work to do. There was a story to follow. "You saved my ass," he admitted, and ran from the car but not far enough before she called him back, Piazzolla chasing notes in minor.

"I got it!" she yelled from her driver's seat. *"Angel Beach!"* She waved the videotape in its Blockbuster container. "They say it's a goddamn classic!"

Piazzolla's bandoneón moaned. The black Supra moaned. Emi moaned. "For godssake," she bit her lip, "You make me feel so horny."

Gabriel turned on his heels, impassioned anguish embodied in his dark figure, disappearing into Bradley International.

CHAPTER 10:
Morning *En México*

In the mornings, Rodriguez worked on the fencing and the brick work in the garden. By afternoon, when the rains inevitably fell, however, he was safely inside the house, placing tile, stuccoing the chimney, or painting the bedroom. On Tuesday, he seemed particularly unsettled for some reason. He was usually a very industrious man who, despite the heat, always insisted on finishing a particular task before going on to something else or before taking a snack or even a drink of water. Rafaela noticed him several times in the afternoon, standing on the veranda, looking past the garden through the drizzling rain—his old eyes cloudy but concentrated, shaking his head.

"What is the matter, Señor Rodriguez?" she asked. "Are you worried about something?"

"I do not know how to tell you this," he paused. "But you will notice it sooner or later, and I fear you will be very angry with me. I cannot afford to lose this job, but I know you to be a very fair person. I am a very skilled worker. I cannot understand what has happened. Perhaps— " His voice broke off. He looked as if he were about to cry.

"Señor?"

"I am not such an old man. I have done this work all my life. I have made some mistakes, but you see my work all over these parts. I come recommended."

"Of course. Of course."

"I cannot receive my pension so soon. Do you understand?"

"No, I really don't." Rafaela tried not to sound exasperated.

"Do you know the ways of the curandero?" He asked suddenly, almost darkly, accusingly. "Maybe it is not me. Maybe it is this place." Rodriguez had worked himself around his own conversation and now stared accusingly at Rafaela as if the source of his confusion were no longer a vision he had been observing through the drizzling rain.

Rafaela stepped away from the man's stare. Perhaps he was referring to her palm reading, but it was nothing really; something she had always done for fun. Yet, she wondered if the man sensed her own fear, a fear of intuitions too keenly felt. Lately she read fearful things in the palms of others, things she dared not speak. And for example this morning, sweeping the house as usual of its entourage of insects and animals, she remembered feeling her body twist as the snake curled first to the right, then to the left. She spoke quickly, "Perhaps you are tired. This has been enough work today."

"Yes. Yes, maybe that is it." He shook his head and began to gather his tools. "Nothing has been right today. First it was the crabs. Then the eggs."

"Crabs? Eggs?"

"Two crabs. Can you imagine? Two crabs in the house this morning. And then the eggs. Two yolks. All the eggs this morning had two yolks."

"Crabs are not normal?"

"Of course not. Who ever heard of such at thing? It would take a man many hours to walk to the beach. But a crab!"

Rafaela watched Rodriguez hurry off, a small sack of his belongings on his back. She saw him pause near the brick foundation of the fence he had been working on in the morning and then run off in agitation. She smiled to herself. Rodriguez reminded her of Bobby in that he was so conscientious, so proud about his work. She remembered that Bobby loved his work no matter what it was. To want a better kind of work didn't make sense to Bobby. No work was better than another. She had been thinking about Bobby and his good points lately. She was beginning to miss him.

By now the rain had subsided, and Rafaela could see Doña Maria closing her umbrella and nodding to Rodriguez as she hurried along the brick path toward the house. "Oregano and tarragon," she pressed a plastic bag filled with dirt and plants on Rafaela. "Lupe sends them," she added. "I would have been here sooner," she said out of breath as if she had anything else better to do. Of course, she could have sent Lupe, but she came herself. "But you can't imagine the amount of traffic on the highway. Cars and trucks, one after another. I was afraid to cross." She looked back toward the highway. "Where is that Rodriguez going so early? You are much too easy on the man. And with all this work to do," she said looking around at the unfinished projects around the house.

Rafaela wanted to defend the old man, wanted to say that after so many years of work, perhaps he deserved some rest, deserved to leave work early. But this was México. This was the way of her country. Her relationship to

Doña Maria depended on her ability to pay Rodriguez and to get what she paid for. She remembered her arguments with Bobby. They had a business together. They had to agree to pay the people who worked for them and to follow the rules, American rules about paying them, and there were so many others. She couldn't remember anymore. Were they arguing about the rules? And what were the rules? If she asked Doña Maria, the woman might say that she was a God-fearing person and that the poor would always be with them. But Bobby would never say that. Sure Bobby thought he was one of the poor, and he wasn't going away, but he wasn't going to lie down and die either. He was going to take care of himself, so he wanted to know why she wanted to take care of everyone else in the world. "Take care of Sol first," he said.

She asked Doña Maria instead, "Are you thirsty? Would you like a drink? A cold glass of passion fruit?"

"Perhaps a little. Passion fruit makes me sleepy. Where is Sol?"

"Taking a nap."

"Dear thing." Doña Maria followed Rafaela into the kitchen, but not before adjusting the lace doilies over an antique chest and fingering the wooden candlesticks placed as an altar to Frida Kahlo. She stared at the monkeys and Frida who stared back, but she never understood what tourists saw in that woman. Frida was an old fixture, but the doilies, candlesticks, the array of glass and porcelain vases, hanging clocks, and framed reproductions of Van Gogh and Picasso were Rafaela's doing. So were the sunflowers placed in vases all over the house. Maybe Gabriel had been trying to achieve a rustic old México look what with that heavy dining table, the big leather chairs, and that giant mirror framed by a colorful Quetzalcoatl, not Doña Maria's personal preference; she liked what she called a French Mediterranean look—marble staircases, Louis the 14th cherrywood side tables, silver candlesticks and porcelain figurines behind beveled glass. She saw her two blue velvet brass-knobbed chairs near the fireplace and nodded approvingly, "The house has a woman's touch now. I can tell you have done a nice job, Rafaela. Gabriel, what was he thinking? Such a sweet young man, but here all by himself. Sometimes there were others, but he never introduced me. There was that gringo couple, and then I remember an African woman. No really, African. She had her hair like long twisted black noodles in a beautiful blue scarf. Do you know what I mean? The last I remember was the Chinese woman. Gabriel, Gabriel," she sighed as if he were her own son. "He really should be married by now."

Rafaela didn't know who these friends of Gabriel might be, but the *Chinese woman* must be Gabriel's current girlfriend, Emi, who wasn't Chinese but probably Japanese and Japanese American at that. Rafaela didn't care to gossip about Gabriel with Doña Maria and only nodded and smiled. The Gabriel she knew in L.A. was self-assured and assertive. She was grateful, but even his helpfulness was assertive. "Do it this way," he seemed to tell her. Now, in México, in the disorder of his dreams, it occurred to her that maybe Gabriel was rather lost. She understood how Doña Maria might think of him as her son, that he seemed to be the sort that required mothering.

"Doña Maria," Rafaela wanted to change the subject, "Rodriguez told me that crabs are not usual here."

"Crabs? How funny for you to say so. The first time in all the years I have lived here, there is a crab in my house. Where did it come from? How did it cross the road?"

"Are they good to eat?"

"Eat? I don't know. But how could this crab be a crab in the ordinary sense?"

"Perhaps the crabs fall out of the trucks coming from Mazatlán," suggested Rafaela, wanting an explanation.

"Crabs? This was just one crab in my house this morning. It is very strange."

Rafaela remembered Rodriguez's stare. She did not want to say how she swept a crab out—not to mention everything else— from the house every morning.

But Doña Maria was more interested in gossip of the human rather than the animal kind. "The Chinese woman was always in a bikini. But that was the dry season. Hardly any mosquitos. Think of her now."

"Mami!" Sol's voice could be heard across the corridor.

"Sol's up," Rafaela announced.

"I will say hello to Sol and be on my way." Doña Maria bustled down the corridor, adjusting Gabriel's hanging assortment of black-and-white photos, oblivious to their scenes of a distant childhood in East L.A., and greeted the boy tugging at the neck of his T-shirt. "Sol," she said patting him on the head, "such a sleepyhead. When are you coming to my house? I may have a surprise for you." She nodded at Rafaela. "My son sent for men to put up a satellite dish. They are doing it right now! Imagine, two hundred channels! How many with cartoons, yes, Sol?" Sol followed Doña Maria to the veranda. "I just hope it doesn't take me so long to cross the highway again. When you walk out there, be careful with Sol. Well, you will see," she waved to Rafaela, scrutinizing a giant potted cactus, the health of trailing ferns, and toeing the corner of a throw rug into place. Retrieving her umbrella, she turned suddenly, "How silly of me. I almost forgot to tell you. The very reason I came here. The hotel called to say that you have a package waiting there. The bus left it this morning."

"It must be from Gabriel."

"Bring a strong sack with you. It is not such a big package, but they say it is heavy."

Rafaela smiled. Sometimes the woman's probing ways could be helpful.

Rafaela pulled the small straps through the buckle on Sol's sandals. The other foot dangled back and forth, Sol watching it from one side of the milk bottle planted securely in his mouth. She found a strong canvas bag, the umbrella, and the folded stroller. Sol might make it to the hotel walking, but walking back was another thing. She had had to carry him all the way back the other day. She was taking the stroller today. Then again, Sol might refuse to get in the stroller, and she would have to carry him and the stroller and the bag with the package all back home again. And if it rained, she would have to do so and hold the umbrella above their heads. That was a chance she would have to take.

Indeed it was as Doña Maria had said, the highway was unusually busy that day. The noise of trucks and cars rumbling and whining down the searing asphalt road never seemed to stop. The pungent smell of tar stung Rafaela's nose.

Rafaela watched the undulation of their shadows across the steaming green undergrowth at the side of the road. It occurred to her that the sun was still somewhat low for that time of the day, actually still west. But the afternoon rains had come and gone, and Rodriguez had come and gone as well. And Sol had awoken from his afternoon nap. Rafaela paused and looked back. No, the hotel was south down the highway, of course. The long shadows were disconcerting, but she continued on, Sol prancing forward with the simple pleasure of moving his legs.

She signed for the package. It was small but heavy as Doña Maria had warned. The hotel manager seemed to be waiting for Rafaela to open the package. "What could that be anyway?" She decided to open the package, a small concession to the manager who might find the pleasure of knowing its contents payment enough for his trouble. She pulled the newspaper from around the thing and uncovered a pair of faucets. The shiny chrome reflected the manager's gaze. They were modern-looking things with a sort of industrial look, the sort that Gabriel seemed to like. Rafaela was indifferent to this style. It still had a surface like any other that had to be cleaned.

The manager took the liberty of turning the fixtures in his hands and then stopped and chuckled. "Hecho en México," he read with amusement.

Rafaela sighed and shook her head. "I'd better be going. It will get late."

"Yes," agreed the manager, "before the afternoon rains."

Rafaela looked up with a start. The big clock above the hotel desk read 11:45.

"Oh, it's a little fast. How far do you have to go?"

"Not far, but that is the correct time?"

"Ten minutes fast, I'd say. But what difference does it make?"

Rafaela felt Rodriguez's mixed expression of confusion and fear in her own features as she wrapped the faucets back into their newspaper packaging.

About halfway down the road, Sol began to drag his feet and then to cry. "Sit here, Sol." She offered the boy the open stroller. This was not satisfactory at all. Sol grabbed her blouse and pulled and jumped. Rafaela slung the bag with the package into the stroller, pushing it with one hand and cradling Sol next to her hip. Now the sun was pulling itself to the ceiling of the sky, and the shadows were almost nil. Across the horizon however, Rafaela could see the great billowing wall of an approaching thundershower. The sun's intensity would not last for long. Thin streaks of lightning darted across the approaching wall. "Sol, how about the stroller? Please?" She pleaded, trying to get the boy to sit down.

Sol kicked and struggled, grabbing her neck with tenacity. She wanted to leave him in the road, but shifted him to the other hip and pushed the stroller and the heavy faucets with the other hand. Small drops of rain flew around the sunlight. A great rainbow pulled itself across the sky. "Look, Sol, a rainbow." But Sol wasn't interested, and he was getting heavier every step, and the stroller with the faucets wandered clumsily along the dirt road, jammed in the gravel and the frequent ruts.

The great rainbow slipped into oblivion, and the black sky approached with a vengeance. Rafaela put Sol down, to his great displeasure, and frantically worked at the rusty catch of the umbrella. The umbrella flew open and out like bat wings—good for hanging bats, bad for pouring rain. Sol was stooping near her feet and screaming as if he were hungry and very tired, as if he had never had his nap. Finally she picked him up and got him momentarily concerned about having the responsibility of carrying the umbrella. This turned out to be a bad idea because Sol wanted to hold the umbrella by himself, but the wind and downpour tossed it violently in every direction. Rafaela clung to the boy and blindly managed her forward momentum, alternately drenched and pressed against the embankment, fighting to avoid being flung onto the highway. The path was soon awash, and Rafaela could barely see anything. Vehicles careened through the rain and sprayed the greasy water from the asphalt in sheer walls. Rafaela struggled to higher ground and then crouched there in frustration, rivulets of mud flowing around the stroller and through her sandals, Sol sobbing unhappily.

Suddenly she noticed them. Just like the crabs she swept from the house daily, but hundreds of them, large and small, crawling frantically sideways in every direction, washing down with the river of rain. Rafaela forgot the necessity of the umbrella's protection or the value of the heavy fixtures in the stroller. She hugged Sol, securing her hand over the back of his head and ran, crabs grappling the earth and crunching beneath her feet.

Approaching the house, Rafaela looked for the usual landmarks: the orange tree, Rodriguez's brick work, and the new fence. Perhaps it was the rain—a thick wet lens through which she perceived this wet world. She was not sure, but the fence was somehow curved, or maybe even longer, or stretched. That was it. The fence stretched south in a funny way, like those concave mirrors in drug stores and 7-11s in the States. Rafaela was not sure.

Stripping off Sol's clothing and encasing his body in a dry towel, Rafaela looked through the starched lace curtains at a hazy visage of the world and remembered. The orange. That orange. It was not there.

Out across the garden, the sun's light began to dapple through the parting clouds and rising mist. Somewhere a snake slid into a shadow. And it was still morning.

CHAPTER 11:

To Wash *On the Tropic*

Arcangel stood in the rain that flowed like a waterfall from heaven, splashing over his head and naked body in an exuberant torrent. From a distance and through the gauze of the rain, it would seem that he was clothed. The stark white of his torso and legs contrasted sharply with the deep brown of his head and neck, arms, ankles, and feet. He ran the bar of coconut soap over his body, through his hair, under his arms, and between his legs, frothing and rinsing, white foam slipping down his legs, swirling with mud and the rainbow of grease toward the highway. He bent over, his back toward the flow, to enjoy the pounding massage. He tilted his head back and spread his arms, swallowed and sputtered the rain from his mouth. He massaged his penis and ejaculated into the foam. Then, he peed into that.

The rain seemed to subside, allowing him to pull one of those disposable plastic razors this way and that across his face, carefully feeling his way against the hollow of his cheekbones. He felt his face, the rugged places and the soft places, and he thought to himself that he had had the same dream again.

In the dream,
a woman was pushing a cart
filled with cactus leaves.
Fresh nopales.
The woman was pushing her cart along a highway
toward the city,
only to come upon an orange,
out of season,
there along that horizontal line
where the sun sliced the tropics.

Yes, thought Arcangel, that is the Tropic of Cancer. That is a border made plain by the sun itself, a border one can easily recognize. And there was the orange, rolling away to a space between ownership and the highway.

The woman paused with her cart
to avoid the orange.
She stooped, scooped the thing up,
threw it in the cart with the cactus and shrugged.

As suddenly as they had appeared, the clouds with their torrents lumbered away, and the rain slipped across the horizon perhaps to the sea. Arcangel shook himself from his head to his feet much like a shaggy dog except that he was somewhat hairless. The water sprayed forth from the loose attachments of his old skin, especially the sagging lobes on either side of his torso, in a way that seemed to please him. The sun appeared to do the rest.

He carefully unfolded a wrinkled but clean set of clothing—a simple shirt and loose-fitting pants. Of course he could wear any number of costumes, but artists like himself always traveled incognito. He repacked his traveling menagerie in his worn leather suitcase, pushed his shirttail into his pants, and walked toward the marketplace.

A truck with a load of oranges was stalled in the street just at its narrowest place. Behind it was a line of cars and trucks and carts filled with produce, meats—dead and alive—grains, and kitchen utensils, all temporarily stalled in their progress toward the marketplace. The commotion behind the stalled truck was becoming fiercer by the moment as lettuce wilted and the rising stench of ripening fruit began to dash any hopes of a morning trade. Occupants in the houses on either side of the road stuck their heads out of the windows and yelled at the line of stopped vehicles. Some took advantage of the situation and bought produce through their windows. The man with the stalled truck was nervously tinkering with a wrench under his hood as impatient merchants with merchandise piled on their heads and shoulders struggled by on foot, yelling epithets. "Stupid! Have you checked the gas tank?"

Arcangel assessed the situation and made his offer. "I will move your truck for you," he announced, flexing his skinny biceps.

"Old man, I don't need your jokes, too," the truck driver snapped.

"I have moved such trucks before. I will do it for you." He climbed to the top of the truck and faced the long crowded corridor of angry people and fuming vehicles. His voice was powerful, the voice of a true performer. It drowned the commotion like an approaching tidal wave, thundering with fearful authority. His arms lifted, and his body seemed to glow against the morning sunlight. In each hand flashed a large metal hook.

I will demonstrate the incredible strength
of the human body.
With the aid of a steel cable
around the axle of this truck,
these two solid hooks
and the skin of my body,
I will myself move this vehicle.
What is it worth to you to see such a feat?

"Old man, you are crazy!"

"We are stuck here anyway. Let him do his trick. At least we will have a good laugh!"

"I give you my profits today!"

"What profits? You are never getting to the market to make any profits!"

"So what is there to lose? I give him my profits!"

"I give him a chicken!"
"A sack of beans!"
"A kilo of tomatoes!"
"Two kilos of tomatoes!"

Arcangel nodded and climbed down the truck. The crowd scurried forward to observe his movements, watching him secure a coil of steel cable from his suitcase. A young boy scampered up and offered to crawl under the truck to draw the cable around its axle. Meanwhile, Arcangel removed his wrinkled but clean shirt with a quiet flourish, exposing his thin white torso. When the cable was in place, Arcangel secured both ends to the two hooks and drew the hooks through the very skin of his body, through the strangely scarred lobes at the sides of his torso. He moved slowly forward until the entire contraption was taut, until he was harnessed securely as an ox to its plough. "Put the thing in neutral!" someone yelled.

Arcangel clenched his fists and moved forward.

The skin against his abdomen
spread itself
as tanned leather over a drum, the hooks
drawing the large lobes of skin
backwards. In fact,
the entire surface of Arcangel's person—
from the skin on his face and his flowing white hair
to the legs of his pants—
seemed to be drawn back toward the truck,
as if he were facing
a great tunnel of wind.
Slowly, his torso leaned into his footsteps
one at a time,
gripping the surface of the asphalt and
pulling inch by inch
the truck and its entire load
of oranges.
Those who witnessed this performance
felt themselves the excruciating weight
of the machine and its fruit
tearing at their bodies.
People choked with amazement and fear

that they might see a man
stripped of his fleshy covering.
Why should they allow him to do such a thing?
What were they thinking?
They should push the truck themselves!
Fools!
But they all strained themselves
with watching and yearning in hushed awe
that the feat should be achieved.

And so Arcangel, attached to his great burden, inched his way down the street toward the marketplace, every muscle in his body intent upon its task. By the time he had traversed fifty meters, women and children had run forward to spread flowers in his path, to cup their hands to catch the blood and sweat from his torn stigmata; people tossed coins; fruit and vegetables were collected on his behalf. Another fifty meters and the street was clear. Arcangel unhooked himself, recoiled the steel cable, repacked his baggage, while gathering, exchanging, and distributing his gifts and tokens of appreciation. He wiped the glistening layer of sweat from his body and slipped his arms into his shirt. The traffic flowed past him, and the street was once again engulfed in the business of the day.

As he had meant to, he continued on to the marketplace. It was perhaps more than a coincidence, but

the woman in his dreams,
with the cactus leaves,
was sitting there on a crate,
carefully slicing the thorns from the leaves.

She looked up at Arcangel. "The very freshest. Cut today."

He nodded. He could see

the orange tossed to one side
with the refuse of thorns and
green shavings of cactus skin.

"I will take a bag of cut nopales." He had just pulled an entire truckload of oranges with his bare skin, but still he said, "And that orange, too. How much do you want for it?"

"This orange? Worthless. I'll be honest with you. It is not imported. A local fruit out of season."

"I have a need for the taste of an orange."

He opened his suitcase and put the orange and the bag of cactus leaves in one corner.

"Where are you going with that?" the woman pointed at the suitcase.

"North," Arcangel smiled. "I am going north."

CHAPTER 12:

Car Payment Due *Tijuana via Singapore*

Letter came today. Go figure. Never heard of this cousin, but he's got it all right: name of Bobby's dad, name of his mom, name of his uncles. Bobby reads it again. Reads it three times. Cousin from Hong Tian in Fujian, same village as his mother's father. Gotta be a distant cousin. Could be a trick, but could be legit. Besides, how'd he find him? How'd he know Bobby was Chinese from Singapore? Knows everything. Knows Bobby's Chinese name. Knows about the family bicycle business. Cousin's in trouble. Musta got smuggled in. One of those boat people. Most never make it. This one might not either. All he's got is Bobby's name and address. Now the smugglers want their money. But where's the cousin? Tijuana. Just turn over the money. Five thou to get the cousin across. If he makes it, five thou to get him free. China to Chinatown. That's the deal.

Nothing from Rafaela. What about the boy? What about Sol? Goddamn woman. What's he done to deserve this? How many years it's been? Ten? At least. First he knew her brother Pepe. Pepe got himself over the border. Pepe got a story like any other. Still, it's a story. Not as bad as some, like the Guatemalans, the ones from El Salvador. Not as bad. But still they don't want you in the Unaite Estays. Pepe didn't pay no coyote. Just crossed the Rio Tijuana with a bunch of others. Got caught twice by la migra and sent back. Third time he made it. Crossed I-5 dead of night. You don't understand traffic till you dodge cars going seventy miles an hour across ten lanes. Pepe didn't want the same for his sister, but she was crazy to come. He was making her wait in Tijuana. Meanwhile he was having to hustle it on Pico and LaBrea. Folks back in Culiacán were worried. Pepe was telling Bobby he's gotta find a way for his sister. Maybe Bobby'd wanna help him out. Marry her maybe. To help out. You loco! That's what Bobby said.

Then next best thing was to do Pepe a favor. Take some money and a letter to his sister. Wire the money and mail the letter Bobby said. Couldn't do that. Sister was not in a place you could trust the mail. As for money, it was out of the question. Hadn't heard from his sister in a while. The money'd probably run out. She was too proud to go home to Culiacán. Anything happened to her, he was in big trouble. Folks'd say he was responsible. What was there to do?

Bobby got his instructions. Wasn't an address. More like a map. Go to the center of town. Calle Malinche. Two streets this way. Five streets this way. Go straight. Two kilometers. Go left. Go right. He'd never been to Tijuana. Spoke Mexican, but was gonna be a miracle if he found Pepe's sister. Was a house between a luncheonette and a tire place. La lonchería y la vulcanizadora. Did you have any idea how many luncheonettes and tire places there are in Tijuana? Rafaela Cortés. That's Pepe's sister's name. She had wavy brown hair and brown eyes and a pretty smile. Hey! Bobby said, this gotta be a description of every chica in México! Don't worry, said Pepe. She was gonna be the pretty one.

Bobby made it to the house between the luncheonette and the tire place. Rafaela Cortés? Bobby just missed her. She'd moved out two days ago. Where? Somewhere where the rent was cheaper. But how cheap could it be unless she wanted it free? This place wasn't much, but at least it was safe. If her brother only knew. She just couldn't be convinced. It was friendly advice. Call her brother up North they suggested; he'd be making money by now. Send her enough for the rent. It was friendly advice; after all this was a business. She owed us the past month. Never said a word and left. That's the thanks. We all have bills to pay. Bobby pulled out the past month's rent. But Bobby wasn't dumb. He held it out. Found out first where he could find Rafaela. Heard maybe she's working at a shop on the Avenida Revolución selling American T-shirts. That's it.

Bobby found the T-shirt shop on the Avenida. It was like Pepe said. She was the pretty one. Pretty soon, Bobby was in Tijuana every weekend. He doesn't know how this happened. He never felt this way. No one ever looked so good next to a bunch of American T-shirts. UCLA. Nike. Princeton. Bulls. Lakers. Dodgers. Reebok.

That was ten years ago.

And what about this Chinese cousin? Bobby hasn't been to Tijuana since. There's an address in Chinatown. Better check it out. Ten thousand dollars.

Are they crazy? Ten years ago, cost him four thou. Paid the lawyer to get Rafaela a green card. Goddamn lawyer. Goddamn smugglers. Goddamn border.

What's today? June 23rd. Car payment due. It's Rafaela's car. The one he bought her. Red '96 Camaro Z28. Sitting out there on the street all new with The Club on the wheel. Pretty soon someone's gonna notice it's abandoned. Then it's gone. Might as well. How come he's gotta pay for it now she's gone? How come she didn't take it? Didn't take the car seat neither. Can't go nowhere without the car seat for Sol. Where did she go where she don't need a car seat? Where?

Maybe Pepe knows, but he's not telling. Bobby thought Pepe was his friend. Now he's just a brother-in-law. Shit. Pepe says he can't help out. It's between the two of you, he says.

Celia Oh from next door comes by. She's Korean-born Brazil side. Talks to him Portuñol. Wants to know about Rafaela and the kid. Didn't know Rafaela split. At least it wasn't a raid; every time there's a raid somewhere, folks get split up. Get deported to the border while the babies get left behind. Her mother's been taking care of a baby like that. Cries for its momma who can't get back to this side.

Meantime, Celia's been down in the garment district twenty-four hours ever since her dad's photo place burned down. Rebuilding L.A. with a sewing machine. Brother got shot in the head. April 1992. Some kinda quincentennial pre-blowout. Bobby found him on the street. Dragged the body home. Maybe Bobby's hurt is not so big anyway.

Celia Oh goes home, but first she says she's gonna put some water on Rafaela's herbs. How come he's letting everything die? He can hear the water going outside, just like Rafaela's home. Celia brings in a sunflower. Sticks it in a vase. He stares at it like it's gonna attack him. Goddamn sunflower.

Bobby needs a smoke. He needs one bad, but he made a promise. He's drinking pure ginseng like crazy. Day number two without a smoke. He's gotta get help. Gotta go to Chinatown anyway. Better get some herbs. Get a custom concoction from a Chinese pharmacy. That's it.

The phone rings. Hello, he says.

Yuespequespanish?

Every night he gets these calls. Of course he speaks Spanish. But it's the wrong number. They call. They leave messages. They want work. *Trabajo de limpieza. Yes, he's got a company. But, no he never put in no ad. It's the wrong number. El número equivocado. But isn't this 953-5351? Yes, but he doesn't have work. Sí. No. Sí. No.* Ever since she left, it's been like this. Phone calls like this every day. Everybody looking for work. Work.

Ever since he's been here, never stopped working. Always working. Washing dishes. Chopping vegetables. Cleaning floors. Cooking hamburgers. Painting walls. Laying brick. Cutting hedges. Mowing lawn. Digging ditches. Sweeping trash. Fixing pipes. Pumping toilets. Scrubbing urinals. Washing clothes. Pressing clothes. Sewing clothes. Planting trees. Changing tires. Changing oil and filters. Stocking shelves. Lifting sacks. Loading trucks. Smashing trash. Recycling plastic. Recycling aluminum. Recycling cans and glass. Drilling asphalt. Pouring cement. Building up. Tearing down. Fixing up. Cleaning up. Keeping up.

Rafaela told Bobby, people like him doing all the work. Couldn't he see that? Of course he could. Hey, he coulda been gangbanging weren't for his little bro. Maybe he wasn't bonafide Vietnamese, but wasn't too long ago some V Boys come 'round recruiting, suggesting he could take in the scene at the Asian Garden Mall. They could use his expertise, hype some chips, pocket a Mercedes. Easy money, but so what? First here, he was stupid; used to hang with a mixed gang, but it was having its toll on his carnal. Saw his homies die at gunpoint, go to juvey. He didn't want that life for the brother.

But she kept talking, saying we're not wanted here. Nobody respects our work. Say we cost money. Live on welfare. It's a lie. We pay taxes. Bobby knows he pays taxes. She said since Bobby smokes like a chimney, he probably pays more sales taxes than anyone else. That's it. He said he pays enough taxes. He'll quit smoking. So what's the point?

Bobby thinks about this now. Rafaela was serious. He didn't want to listen. She was serious. She respected his work. But she wanted more. She left the cherry-red Camaro Z28 with the car seat and The Club. She left the house and the 32" Sony KV32V25 stereo TV with picture-in-picture and the Panasonic PUS4670 Super-VHS VCR, the Sony Super-ESP CD player, the AT&T 9100 cordless phone, the furniture, the clothing, the two-door Frigidaire with the icemaker, the Maytag super-capacity washer and gas dryer, the Sharp Carousel R1471 microwave, everything. She just took some books, Sol's clothing, and some toys. She just left. Didn't even lock the security door. Left. She didn't want any of this. She wanted more. It's like his kid brother in college. He keeps sending him money. Paying for tuition. Paying for books. He's so proud of the bro. But when they get together, there's nothing to say. Bobby's too busy working. The kid brother wants something more. Rafaela wanted something more. Maybe she was right.

CHAPTER 13:

Oldies *This Old Hood*

Buzzworm studied the map. Balboa'd torn it out of a book for him to study. *Quartz City* or some such title. He followed the thick lines on the map showing the territorial standing of Crips versus Bloods. Old map. 1972. He shook his head. Even if it were true. Even if it were true, whose territory was it anyway? Might as well show which police departments covered which beats; which local, state and federal politicians claimed which constituents; which kind of colored people (brown, black, yellow) lived where; which churches/temples served which people; which schools got which kids; which taxpayers were registered to vote; which houses were owned or rented; which businesses were self-employed; which corner liquor stores served which people; which houses were crack; which houses banging; which houses on welfare; which houses making more than twenty thou a year; which houses had young couples with children; which elderly; which people been in the neighborhood more than thirty years. And where in Compton did George Bush used to live anyway? If someone could put down all the layers of the real map, maybe he could get the real picture.

So far he was thinking how he owned his house. Owned it outright. Paid for it a long time ago. Like those plates say, *Don't laugh; it's paid for.* Took up where his grandmother left off, paying like clockwork every month. Old lady was proud of it. Never missed her payment day. Could go without food or clothing, but not her house. Eat out of the garden out back. Patch up the clothing, starch it, dye it another color. But pay for the house. Day it was paid for good and clear, Buzzworm paid a visit to her grave site. Took the paperwork to prove it. Taken thirty years, double that and then some, counting the time to save the down payment—her lifetime and some of his. The house itself couldn't be worth nothing. Only so much repair he could afford to do. Been meaning to paint it now some five, six years. Kept the lawn mowed and the flower bed weeded. Was it the land? The garden? Some real estate person come round and offer hundred thou, maybe be a blessing. Was this his territory? According to the map, it was in Crips or Bloods territory.

Buzzworm remembered conversations he had with people saying they used to live here or there. Now here or there is a shopping mall, locate the old house somewhere between Mrs. Field's and the Footlocker. Or here or there is now the Dorothy Chandler Pavilion, or Union Station, or the Bank of America, Arco Towers, New Otani, or the freeway. People saying if they coulda owned the property, if the property had been worth anything at the time, if they'd a known then every square foot of that land was worth millions. If they'd a known the view'd be so expensive. If they'd a known. And then Buzzworm thinking about before that. About the Mexican rancheros and before that, about the Chumash and the Yangna. If they'd a known.

Somebody else must have the big map. Or maybe just the next map. The one with the new layers you can't even imagine. Where was his house on this map? Between Mrs. Field's and the Footlocker? Somebody's parking lot? Somebody's tennis court? Or just the driveway to some gated community? Roll over grandma. He could never go to heaven to tell her such things. He'd have to go to hell.

He remembered years ago. Neighborhood meeting at the old recreation center. City bureaucrats come over to explain how they were gonna widen the freeway. Move some houses over, appropriate streets, buy out the people in the way. Some woman just like grandma stood up and wanted to know what the master plan was. How'd she know it wasn't gonna be more than just widen the freeway? How'd she know wasn't gonna be more than one ramp? Wasn't gonna be some other surprises? An airport maybe? Condominium and hotels and convention halls? Who was gonna guarantee she was gonna have a place to live under the master plan? Bureaucrats unveiled their poster boards and scale models. Everything in pastels, modern-like. Made the hood look cleaned up. Quaint. Made the palm trees look decorative. This was the plan. Just a little freeway widening. Wasn't gonna affect her house. Her house was her house. Wasn't gonna affect her.

Bureaucrats acted like she was crazy paranoid. But they knew better. Anything can happen. Time and paper on their side. By the time the freeway could be widened, people forget what they got promised. Politicians who promised could be gone. Situations change, bureaucrats don't. So they said it wasn't gonna affect her. They'd be around to make sure. Make sure it took five years to clear out the houses. Make sure the houses left to be broken into and tagged. Let the houses be there for everyone to see. Use for illegal purposes. Pass drugs. House homeless. Make sure the ramp took another five years. Slow down the foot traffic and the flow. Break down the overpass crossing the freeway. Make it impossible for people to pass. Stop people from using the shops that used to be convenient. Stop people from coming to her dress shop. Used to be a respectable shop. Anybody who's anybody, she did it custom. Haute couture. Entire wedding line-ups. Now homeless, dope dealers, prostitutes only ones passing her shop. No master plan. No ma'am. Wasn't gonna affect her no way.

Was no wonder you could make a map. Call it all gang territory. Was no wonder homies tagging their territory. They wanted it all back. Claim it for the hood. Futile gestures without a master plan. Leave it crumbling and abandoned enough; nothing left but for bulldozers. Just plow it away. Take it all away for free.

Buzzworm had a plan. Called it gentrification. Not the sort brings in poor artists. Sort where people living there become their own gentry. Self-gentrification by a self-made set of standards and respectability. Do-it-yourself gentrification. Latinos had this word, *gente.* Something translated like *us.* Like *folks.* That sort of gente-fication. Restore the neighborhood. Clean up the streets. Take care of the people. Trim and water the palm trees. Some laughed at Buzzworm's plan. Called his plan *This Old Hood.* They could laugh, but he was still trying to go to heaven.

He thought about his palm trees like jeweled fingers. They towered in the sky. Formed the true diamond lanes of the city. Somebody wrote something about his palm trees. He read it somewhere. About them being "long rows of phallic palm trees with sun-bleached pubic hair." He was appreciative of the image. Sexy and tropical. A naked beach-like representation. Still, if he saw the beach once a year, it was an excessive count. Beach was an imagined thing skirtin' the far Westside. He had heard the downtown high-rises referred to as phallic, too. Maybe his palm trees were standing up giving everybody the finger.

Today, he was doing the rounds with the street peddlers. They had their unspoken territories, too. He never saw them get in fights about it. They were very civilized about territory. Plenty of corners to go around. Plenty of freeway ramps. El Norte was big. L.A. was big. Grande. Sí. He had these conversations all the time. Get your business license, see. Fill this out. Put it in the paper. *La Opinión* will do. A few were old-timers, but most moved on. It was too risky if you didn't have documents.

"Margarita, what's on sale today?"

"Everything on sale. Otherwise gonna rot. Business's not so good today." Margarita smiled. She always smiled, even when business was not so good. Even though she got her boys out of El Salvador to escape the mano blanca death squad and now they were gangbanging in L.A. with the Mara Salvatrucha.

"I'll take a bag of peanuts."

"Señor Buzzworm, you always take peanuts."

"I'm an elephant for peanuts."

"Take bananas. They gonna rot." She forced him a bunch. "What's the music today?" She pointed at the Walkman in his ears.

"For you, Margarita, oldies."

"Aretha Franklin."

"How'd you know?"

"I know. I know you listen to mariachi también."

"Los Camperos. The very best."

"Sorry," she shook her head. "Is not my culture. I, Salvador."

"You," he pointed at her. "Aretha Franklin. Don't be such a purist."

She laughed. "Look. I got nice oranges. This not the season see. So is imported from Florida."

"Naranjas," he nodded, but he thought he'd better set Margarita straight. "If it's Florida, it's not imported. Same country, see. If it's México, it's imported."

"Por qué? Florida's more far away than México."

"You got a point, Margarita."

"You bet. You buy bananas? I throw in one naranja free."

"I'm a sucker, Margarita."

"No, Señor Buzzworm. You're a good customer."

Buzzworm walked away with his bag of peanuts and bananas. Orange in his pocket. Crossing the street, he heard shots and the screech of tires hauling off. He ran around the corner, found a kid glued to a chain-link fence turning several shades of green. Kid recognized Buzzworm and blubbered something about curving bullets.

Buzzworm looked the kid over—not dead, a survivor— remembered he was the same kid mouthing off yesterday. Same little homey looking foolish, looking the other way, pawing the concrete with his Air Jordans sticking out his baggy pants. "Sounds like you had yourself a religious experience." Buzzworm was almost sympathetic. "Course, you could be dead and having yourself a religious experience in a few days, depending on when they scheduled the funeral."

"I ain't lyin'."

"Why should you lie? Few days ago, getting shot at was just things as usual. Surviving was no big deal."

"So it ain't. I just saw the bullets is all."

"Like Superman, you saw the bullets."

"Like slow motion."

"Bullets coming at you at twelve hundred feet per second."

"Movin' from the barrel stickin' outta the car."

Buzzworm pulled the orange from his pocket. "Better eat something. Take the edge off the experience. Food is best." Handed little homey the orange like it was a hamburger. "So you dodged the bullets."

"No. They curved by me sudden-like."

"Some say when your time comes, you see everything timelessly. I suppose you oughta see the bullets coming your way."

"Weren't my time. Wasn't like that. Was more like space curved. Shit. Ain't nobody gonna believe me."

"I believe you." Buzzworm nodded. "You got some vision." He took off one of his watches. It was a waterproof one with a calculator. "Individual who owned this watch did calculations in the shower. Went on to teach math and invest in the stock market. Say he was wearing this very watch when he shook hands with the great Muhammad Ali. Now it's yours."

"Ah man." The kid could probably find himself a better one, but something about Buzzworm. Something about something so simple. Just believing. Made this watch priceless.

Like Buzzworm said, every watch has got a story. Everybody's got a timepiece and a piece of time. Watch was an outward reflection of your personal time. Had nothing to do with being on time. Had to do with a sense of time. Sense of urgency. Sense of rhythm. Cadence. Sense of history. Like listening to oldies with Margarita. Time could heal, but it wouldn't make wrongs go away. Time came back like a reminder. Time folded with memory. In a moment, everything could fold itself up, and time stand still.

CHAPTER 14:

Budgets *Skirting Downtown*

I checked the giant arrival/departure board over the international gangway at Bradley International. KAL from Seoul ARRIVED. VARIG from Rio ARRIVED. QANTAS from Sidney DELAYED. JAL from Tokyo LANDING. MEXICANA from Mexico City LANDED. I could see the wave of Koreans pushing their carts with luggage up the ramp. Then there were scattered

American tourists with the peeled look of happy lobsters baked to near melanoma on the beaches at Ipanema. The Mexican contingent would be in the third wave. I had made it in time. Buzz's description had been vague. No luggage. Maybe a simple wide briefcase or carry on. That could be anyone. The name was also vague. C. Juárez. I walked to a courtesy phone and requested the page.

"C. Juárez on Mexicana flight 900. Please contact your party at the nearest courtesy phone."

I watched a man in a suit with a large briefcase wander out past the guard. A woman with a child in her arms struggled with a big baby bag slung over her shoulder. She was searching the large hall for something, probably a familiar face, and trying to adjust the bag. I watched her from my phone as she bumped into the man and apologized. I waited, but the man with the single briefcase disappeared through the glass doors to the street. "Please repeat the page," I made my request again and searched for another possibility.

Suddenly, a voice came over the phone. "Hello?" It was the voice of a woman. "Hello?"

I could see the woman with the baby at the courtesy phone on the other end of the hall.

"Excuse me," I said. "I'm waiting for my page. Are you trying to page someone too?"

"No. I was just paged," she said.

"Obviously you're not Charles Juárez."

"No," she said, and hung up.

I could see her rush away from the phone with the kid and her baby bag. She had no other luggage. This would be strange for a mother traveling with a child. I ran out the door.

Emi was circling her Supra like a tigress of some sort. She had the back trunk open with the almost defiant expectation of an imminent passenger. And Piazzolla was still jamming. *La Muerte del Angel.* "Damn it Gabe. You can only keep these guys at bay so long."

I slammed the trunk down. "Come on. See. The woman with the baby and the yellow bag. The taxi's pulling out right now. Let's go for it."

Emi slammed the Supra through five out of six gears, wandered over four lanes and back three, and planted us neatly behind the taxi. "He's heading for the Century." The Century Freeway was empty, and we flew east over Inglewood in a matter of minutes. "Okay, looks like north on the Harbor.

It's probably gonna be the same mess going toward the downtown interchange. Semi's still turned over."

"Taxi knows it. He's taking streets."

Emi maneuvered the Supra east following deftly behind the taxi. "Damn light," she muttered and stepped on the gas. The timing might just let the taxi pull away. I could hear the siren from behind and groaned. "Ambulance." Emi watched the taxi with one eye and the mirror with the other. "If the taxi pulls over, I pull over. Is this a plan?"

"That's the plan," I agreed. We pulled over behind the taxi, and the ambulance sped around us, lights flashing urgent and hysterical. We pulled out with the taxi and found ourselves following the path of the ambulance to the emergency entrance of a hospital. Emi drove past the entrance and circled round. I watched the woman struggle out with her child and the bag and hurry into the hospital.

"Gabe. What is this? Why are we following an innocent woman with a kid to a hospital?"

"You don't get off an international flight without any bags and rush to a hospital."

"Maybe you do. Maybe she's got a sick relative. Maybe the kid's sick."

"Maybe not."

"Well, if she's hauling drugs, maybe it's legal shit. Anesthesia. Antibiotics. Colombian aspirin."

"Come on."

"Right."

"I'm sick."

"Right. Poison fungi."

"Good. Thanks, Angel."

I hobbled into the emergency lobby on Emi's arm, but we didn't have to keep up this pretense too long. A hospital aide walked from the elevator and greeted the woman. She held the baby while C. Juárez opened her big baby bag and produced a small Igloo cooler. It could have been baby bottles or baby food. The aide tickled the baby's chin for a moment before handing her back, took the blue cooler, and headed for the elevator. I nodded to Emi and hobbled forward in distress. "Going up!" and the aide was obliged to wait for me. I nodded at her choice for the floor and followed her out far enough to see her disappear behind doors marked, SURGERY—AUTHORIZED PERSONNEL ONLY. Maybe Emi was right. Anesthesia or Colombian aspirin. I walked to the nurse's station and feigned stupidity. "I'm sorry. I'm lost. Where am I? I'm supposed to meet Doctor . . . Doctor . . ." I pulled my GP's name out of the air, "Steven Maier." I looked at the forbidden doors and lied, "He's a surgeon."

"The name's not familiar. There are all sorts of surgeons. Does he do transplants?"

"Transplants?" Maier did obstetrics too. "Do babies count?" I offered.

"Well, we specialize in infant heart and kidney."

When I got back to the lobby, I could see Emi on the other side of the glass doors outside making time with a CHP whose uniform fit him a few donuts too tight. He had his boot in the car door and his flip-tops flipped up. Better to see Emi. She was leaning into his car like it was just any old Crown Victoria painted black and white, like she could hold him up and not the other way around. She flicked her silky hair about—a gesture which could indicate a lot of things including *flip you off*. "There's my boyfriend now." she smiled.

"Hope you're feeling better," he nodded at me with dumb compassion. She must have told him I had my stomach pumped or some damn thing like that.

"I'll be all right." I walked quickly to the car. Like hell I was going to feign limping for anybody's amusement.

"See you at traffic school," Emi waved much too sweetly behind her and caught up with me. "Hey, I told him you had to have an enema. You know, poison mushrooms. Bad scene."

"Thanks."

"Don't be mad. It was for a reason. Listen. The ambulance. It was the guy in the Porsche, his passenger and the truck driver. You know the big accident on the Harbor downtown with the semi? The Porsche (by the way, did I tell you it was an '89 911 Carrera 4?). Anyway, the Porsche was at fault. Guy went off. Traveled across two lanes, careened around and right into the semi. The *NewsNow* van never got close. In fact, they started evacuating everybody. Are you listening? Because, the semi was hauling propane. Police started yanking open car doors and telling people to get the hell out. But too late. *Kaboom!*" Emi gestured luridly for effect. "If you were a gawker, you got it in the face. Cop saw it blow in his rearview just as he followed the ambulance up the ramp. The blast took an entire overpass with it. Says the Sig's currently *a firestorm in a crater.* Not to mention the concrete and steel rubble, buried cars, and the pile-up for miles. Can you imagine? And get this: Driver in the Porsche Carrera was DOA. Passenger survived miraculously. Just walked away. The truck driver is in critical condition. And, they suspect drugs. An overdose. But the passenger denies it. Says, he was peeling oranges and handing the sections to his driver friend to eat. Says his friend chewed up a piece of orange and passed out. He swears it was the oranges. Can you believe it? Wait 'til I tell the guys in the *NewsNow* van. They missed everything!"

It wasn't my story. I couldn't care less. I should have been amazed at Emi's uncanny ability to scrounge information, but I was sore at her for making up stories about me to satisfy her need for the sensational.

"What about the woman and the baby?" I asked, wounded by her defection from my story line.

Emi taunted but did not disappoint me. "Woman? Oh yeah. I talked to her. She speaks perfect English. No accent. She said she pumps her breast milk and brings it here every day."

"From México City?"

"Her kid is a little big to be breast feeding, and frankly, she looks a bit flat," Emi quipped. "My sister didn't do it past six months, but then they say you can do it for years. La Leche says, just keep pumping."

"Where'd she go?"

"Taxi stood by, meter running, and off she went. International breast milk. Who'd a thought!"

"The benefits of NAFTA. Mexican wet nurses. I wonder if Nestlé knows about this."

"Is this serious? I mean, really Gabe. A breast milk conspiracy? Is it spiked?"

"Spiked oranges. Spiked breast milk. Give me a break, Emi."

"I know. I watch too much TV."

Emi hit the diamond lane on the on ramp. "Always take advantage of passengers I say. You know, there's something about being in the diamond lane. Like you're doing something good for humanity. This is my positive contribution today. I'm the reason there's hope for the future of L.A."

I pointed to southbound traffic, still inching along. "My car's on the other side. Sorry, Angel, I guess you'll have to abandon your altruistic duties and get off at the next ramp."

"No problem." The woman instantly slid over three lanes while I strained to see my stalled car through the traffic.

"Did you see my car?"

"Nope."

"Damn." It wasn't there. "Someone stole my car!"

"Towed. Get real. Who'd want to steal it?" Emi made some calls from her cellular. I'd have to get the car out of hock, pay some fines, and did I know my car was blocking the fire lane, and considering the Sig on the Harbor today, I was lucky I wasn't causing a life-or-death scenario. Life-or-death scenario. That's what the bureaucrats in parking violations said. Scenario.

"Gee, Gabe," Emi commiserated. "Missed a chance to use your AAA membership." She dropped me off downtown, and I ran up to my desk with about an hour to pitch my budgets. I paged Buzzworm and waited.

"Buzzworm. Angel of Mercy. At your service."

"Buzz. LAX thing went to a hospital just skirting downtown. What's the deal?"

"Got me."

"Go back to the brother who untapped it and get me some specifics. I don't think it's drugs."

"What about the article on my symphony man Manzanar? If I see it in print, maybe we might risk it."

"Buzz. This isn't about tit for tat. One's a feature. The other's hardcore."

"Both're hardcore. Drugs's hardcore. Homelessness's hardcore. Forty-two thousand citywide. Hundred-fifty countryside. That enough homeless for you? Only thing, it's not a crime to be homeless. Some jive radio show host saying should put 'em all to sleep. Could bring the Nazis back to do it too! Go back and interview Ted Hayes again, but don't be giving me that feature bullshit. You see homeless bobbing like pigeons in the streets. What you think? Dropped their contact lenses? They looking for diamonds? Il legal tender? Oh yes. Turn a trick for a piece of the rock. Pathetic. It's all part of the same system."

"Do I have to argue ideology? It's too late in the day."

"Did you know I knew Salazar personally?"

"Lot of Salazars, Buzz."

"The reporter. One who got killed. If he wanted to know something, he'd go to jail to find out. If he could, he'd be reporting now, direct from hell."

"Salazar's in heaven. Aztlán, Buzz."

"No wonder he's not saying nothing. Nothing to report."

Between Buzzworm and Emi, I needed a serious vacation. But I said, "Your man Manzanar wouldn't speak with me. Reticent. Maybe if you came along."

"Maybe. Gimme a buzz."

I punched in my budgets: continuation of series on homelessness—overpass conductor (as in symphony orchestral); interview with Richard Iizuka, Supervising Agricultural Inspector for L.A. County Dept. of Ag, for update on medfly situation; Father's Day postmortem—single fathers coping in South Central and East L.A.; gangs, contracts, and the attorneys who work for them. And, what the hell: possible spiked orange cause of major freeway SigAlert.

Suddenly I felt really tired, reached for the cold coffee next to the keyboard. Maybe Rafaela would give me a call. Just a short call would do—my fix from down South. If I associated Emi with caffeine, maybe Rafaela was like Prozac. It was a balancing act. Who was I kidding? Mine was a mind game. L.A. was out there.

WEDNESDAY:
Cultural Diversity

CHAPTER 15:

Second Mortgage *Chinatown*

Bobby got time to kill. Time before he meets the Chinatown snakehead gonna set his cousin free. Still don't know this cousin. Got a call in to Singapore. Better talk to the folks. Find out the truth. Meantime, Bobby got time to kill. Hang out round the Chinese pharmacy. Check out the goods. Ginseng. $98.98/lb. On sale. Tangui. $8.89/lb. On sale. Woman's root. Been some time, Bobby took Rafaela to Chinatown. Made her take tangui tea. After that, Sol got born. Got born fast. This time, check out a recipe to stop smoking. Maybe they got something like that. Sure enough. Shen qi jie yan ling. Miraculous Stop Smoking. Developed by the Institute of Clinical Immunology of Contemporary Traditional Chinese Medicine, No. 1 Shang Yuan Cun Hadian District, Beijing, China. Telephone: 8327721. Fax: 8328275. Awarded a gold medal by the thirty-seventh Brussels Eureka World's Fair for Invention in 1988. Got medicative herbs: *Fols Carthami, Radix Ginseng, Borneolum, Radix Sophorae Flavescents, Fadix Astragali, Pericarpium Zanthoxyli, Bulbus Fritillarae Cirrhosae, Fructus Corni, Rhizoma Atractylodis Alba,* etc. Put the liquid near the nose and inhale once a day for ten to twenty-five minutes. Take deep, even breaths. After seven days, you lose it. In ten thousand cases, 98 percent lost it. Give it up. *Miraculous Stop Smoking* Powerful stuff. That's it.

Bobby looking at the photo plan. They got a Plan A for thirty-five bucks and a Plan B for thirty-five bucks. Difference is in the photo sizes. A, you get two 8 x 10s, ten wallets, and eight 4 x 5s. B, you get one BIG ONE, ten wallets, and eight 4 x 5s. First married, he took Rafaela over and got the B plan with the big photo, 12 x 15. He wanted one big for himself. Then, when Sol's born, they went back. Got another Plan B with a 12 x 15 of Sol. Put them in frames. On the wall in the hallway. Both of them still there in the hallway, staring back, looking beautiful. Big as life. 12 x 15. His whole life, staring back. Plan B.

Next door, there's the clothing. Fancy stuff. Not just made in Taiwan. Styled in Taiwan. Silk shirt. Looks silk but maybe polyester. Black and white. Pleated job. Down the pleats, it's open like vents. Show some skin. Got these black ribbon strips to hold the openings together. Skinny tough guy like Bobby look bad in digs like these. Bad for a Singapore Chinese. Bad if you live in Phnom Penh, Bangkok, or Ho Chi Minh City. Something scarce however for a cholo like Bobby. Life coulda been different. Coulda been hanging with the boys in Singapore with a black-and-white silk shirt with slits. Just like this one. Showing some skin. Looking like the Asian dude in the poster. Two Asian beauties in tight dresses puckering up to either side. Suave sophisticated. Fingering a cigarette. Some brand named 555. Says it in English: *Where smoothness is everything.* Coulda been smooth. Don't matter now. Bobby given up smoking. That's it. Plan B.

Next stop, it's a video store. Chinese videos. Some's Hong Kong. Some's Vietnam. Some's Thai. Some's Cambodia. Action/Adventure. Kung Fu. Gangster. Romance. Bobby thinks Action/Adventure maybe. This way you get the Kung Fu *and* some story. Chow Yun-fat. He's the man. That's it. Then there's Erotic. Cover posters with naked women. Got their heads pulled back, cat eyes narrowed to slits, tongues just slipping through their teeth. Men got their backs to the poster or maybe their sides, pawing the women, making it happen. Everybody's looking hot and steamy. Coulda taken these near the giant pots of boiling noodles, over giant woks with bok choy and peanut and sesame oil, back of a Chinese kitchen. It's hot. A real workout. Still it makes Bobby itch. He could use some action. Man, he could really use some action. No sex. No smoking. He's dying. Any video will do. Maybe make it worse. But how could it get worse? One Action/Adventure. One Erotic. That's it.

Bobby's time to kill is up. He's gotta meet the snakehead. Get a stall in a restaurant. Second stall on the right. No one there yet. Bobby orders tea. He could order a beer, but he doesn't. Against his rules. Beer for after hours only. Lately, though, he could screw the rules.

Man slips in the stall. Slips in from nowhere like maybe he works in the kitchen. Like he's a snakehead. Nods. Speaks Mandarin smooth. Speaks friendly like he knows Bobby and always has. Like he knows the family. Maybe he does. He's got a picture of the cousin. Puts the photo down in front of Bobby like a trump card.

Bobby wants to cry, but he remembers to look cold. It's not a he. It's a she. Photo looks like his sister. That's right. It's a girl cousin. But how come it looks like his sister? Can't be. Sister used to look like this. Sister's older than him by ten years. So who's this? Bobby says, "Don't know her."

"Funny. She looks like you."

"How old is she?"

"Only twelve."

"How come she's alone? Where's her family?"

"There was a brother. Nineteen. The Lucky Golden Dragon couldn't dock. Looked like it was going back to China. He was desperate. Left all his belongings with this sister and jumped ship just off the coast of Baja. Maybe he could swim. Maybe not. Never found him. Body never turned up. Maybe the sharks got him."

"Then who wrote this letter?" Bobby takes out the letter.

"What does it matter? The information is reliable, isn't it?"

Bobby's thinking. Older sister had some kids, but these can't be them. Sister's in Singapore. Maybe it's a trick. Fake picture.

Snakehead says, "She could be your sister or even your daughter. The resemblance is amazing. Are you from Fuzhou?"

"When was this picture taken?"

"Just before departure. Passport picture."

"Passport? If it were a passport picture, she'd be here already."

"If her brother hadn't jumped ship, she'd be here. Now who's going to guarantee for her? Who's going to pay her way?"

"She's a girl. She didn't cost anything. Everyone knows you bring in the girls free."

"This one was guaranteed by the brother. She wasn't going to be a prostitute. Such a shame. All alone. So young. Unspoiled. A very nice girl. I'm sure you wouldn't want to abandon her."

Bobby don't fall for this talk. "You said he left all his belongings with her. Probably left enough to buy her freedom."

"Some clothing. Books. Mementos. Poor people. Besides, if you bring anything of value on a trip like this, it will be stolen."

Bobby don't believe it. "How did you find my name?"

"It was written in a book in his things. There's a letter as well." Snakehead spreads a folded piece of paper out. Chinese characters Bobby can still read pretty well. It's his dad's handwriting. The same as always. The letter says to look up his son in America. Here's the address. Good to have friends. One shouldn't be alone.

Still Bobby remembers to look cold. The price is too high. Anyone knows the price at the border. Five hundred dollars max to cross by car. Fake documents. Door-to-door service. But that's the Mexican price.

"Ten thousand is too much," Bobby says.

"Ten thousand is cheap. She cost us a boat trip. Every day she's eating. We could stick you for the brother, too. He owes us thirty. To be frank, either we unload her on you, or we just unload her."

"Where is she?"

"She's safe. Tijuana. Waiting. Waiting for your answer."

"Let me see her first."

"It will cost you. Better to pay now. We'll have her here next week. From today, every day you make us wait, it will cost you. Room and board."

"How do I know she's real? Anyone can come up with a picture and a letter."

"Maybe I'm wasting my time. Maybe she'll just have to take her chances."

"How much to see her?"

"Five hundred."

"Too much. I'll give you two."

"Four hundred."

"Three." Bobby pulls out three big ones.

Snakehead nods. "Walk through the gates to the Mexican side from the end of the line at San Ysidro. Stand at the corner to one side of the taxi stop. Tomorrow. Noontime."

"Give me her picture."

Snakehead shrugs. Hands Bobby the letter too. What's it to him. Easy ten thou. Slips out.

Snakehead said tomorrow. What day's today? Wednesday; 24th. Second mortgage due 24th of every month. Take it out of his checking. Where's he gonna get ten thou? Gotta be another way. Rafaela might know. She could help. Rafaela knows Tijuana.

Bobby stares at the photo looking like his sister when she was a kid. Even if she's not blood connection, she sure looks it. Bobby tries to feel cold, and he can look cold, but he's not like that. Rafaela knows this. He knows she knows this. So why'd she disappear? But he's not gonna cry. Walks out to the street. Got to get something to eat. Down the corner, there's a sign: Chinese burritos. Fish tacos. Ensopada. Camarón chow mein. Hoy Especial: $2.99. Comida to go. Por qué no?

Bobby's got the takeout, the medicinal herbs, the *Miraculous Stop Smoking,* the photo, the letter, and the two videos. He gets it all in the house, past the security door and the dead bolt. Gets the water boiling, the tea steeping, the takeout nuked. Studies the letter. Stares at the photo. Twelve years old. So? He was twelve when he came. Tea don't go with the takeout. Chinese burritos. Chinamex. Who they trying to kid? But it's not bad. Probably need to change the diet too. Tea don't work with this food. But it's not bad. Unwraps another. Gets it nuked, too. Gets a video in the machine. Check out the Erotic. Check out the messages. Eleven messages. All asking about *trabajo de limpieza.* Still working that wrong number. Nothing from Rafaela. Nothing. *Trabajo de limpieza? Trabajo de limpieza?* Everybody's asking. If there's work, they want to do it. Got families to feed. Got rent to pay. Got dreams. Got hope.

He's sipping his tea and sniffing the *Miraculous Stop Smoking.* Medicinal. Smells like every herb in the pharmacy. Taking long deep breaths. Adjusting the yin. Adjusting the yang. Gonna lose that smoking urge. Meanwhile, the erotic video gets to brass tacks fast. Licking and humping. Working the hips. Working the thighs. Pressing the breasts. Sucking the nipples. Pumping the buttocks. *Trabajo de limpieza? Se busca trabajo de limpieza?* Pumping. Breathing deep. Working. Hard. Adjusting the yin. Adjusting the yang.

CHAPTER 16:

LA X *Margarita's Corner*

Time was x was Malcolm. *Newsweek* said now it was Shaq; he being the x Generation. What did they know? Hood'd changed. Now it was *La x. La equis la equis noventa y siete punto nueve!* Everybody was listening to the Mexican station. Doing banda and stepping to the quebradita. Buzzworm was not about to be behind this eight ball. He was listenin' up too. Keeping up on the news. Keeping up for Margarita and all the others doin' time in El Norte. Keeping up so's to be ready with the dialogue. Some wanted to pit black against brown, but looked like one side got the crack, other got the weapons. And everybody got one helluva war, but who was the enemy? To keep it in perspective, somebody had to be there to get the sides to see eye to eye. Order to see eye to eye, had to get with the program. Far as Buzzworm was concerned, program was the Mexican station. It might not have been the *source* source, but it was tapping it. Course, Buzzworm listened to everything the air had to offer, but he'd been trying to let the brothers know they had to expand their horizons. Couldn't be tuned into the Beat or the Power only. Not just Hammer, Boyz 2 Men, Snoop Doggie Dog, Kid Frost. Not just the hop over some smooth woman's vocals. Yeah. Oooo. Oooo. Had to get behind another man's perspectives. Hear life in another sound zone. Walk to some other rhythms.

Course, Buzzworm knew it just might be a question of maturity. Hard to get a young homey to change channels when it was like the clothes you wear, what defined you, kept you part of the thing. Couldn't get caught listening, for example, to The Wave; someone bound to think you'd gone cerebral or New Age, lost your ability to hop. Not many big enough to listen to his or her own mind. Still Buzzworm'd convinced some to try jazz. "Try it nighttime," he suggested, like it was evening dress or dinner food or a nightcap. "Jazz," said Buzzworm, "is the music of the night." Hip hop in the day, but reserve jazz for the evening hours. Trust Buzzworm; he should know.

Once he had you listening to the jazz station, then he'd be talking to you about personalities, syncopation, improvisation, blues, fusion. Pretty soon, he was piling on the details, insider stories, anecdotes, hearsay. It got complicated. You had to listen to the station more, call in for requests even, get you some tapes and CDs, find out what you like, participate in the give and take. Pretty soon, you'd find you getting yourself an education. History of jazz followed the history of a people, black oppression, race, movement of the race across the Earth, across this country. Ended up here in South Central. Count Basie and the Duke playing on Central Avenue. 5-4 Ballroom on 54th and Broadway. Charlie Parker, Fats Domino, and Ray Charles at Club Alabam Saturday nights in the fifties. Found out you came from somewhere. History. Buzzworm, he'd catch you if he could.

Had to figure this was the plan when he took some time with the homey who saw bullets curve in space. Kid who saw bullets curve in space either got some kind of imagination or genius. Then too, maybe drugs'd spliced the mind. That was a possibility Buzzworm had to consider when he got the word the boy came up DOA at County Gen. Personally, he didn't think so; kid had an attitude, not an addiction—that is, of the chemical sort. Buzzworm had a sense about him; thought the boy'd make a fine revolutionary. Still that's what the report said. Direct cause of death: high doses of a very pure form of cocaine and unidentified chemicals found in the stomach and digestive tract, probably ingested orally.

Buzzworm accompanied the boy's mother to the morgue to identify the body. "What have they done to him? What have they done to him?" she kept crying. He was beat up bad; hardly recognized the kid. Eyes were two big swollen purple bruises. Mouth and nose same thing. Head blows. Body blows. The whole anatomy all punched out. Kid had one of those thin builds with a fast metabolism on a sudden growth spurt. Now everything was swollen flesh. "What are they talking about? Drugs. Coroner's saying he OD'd. Boy was beat to death. It's obvious. What are they trying to hide?"

Buzzworm changed the station and shut his eyes. He had to think about this one. Meanwhile, the mother collected the boy's things. The watch was there with a few coins, pocketknife, X cap. Watch was still good. Calculator working just fine. How come the watch could go on, but the boy could not? This would be all a mother could bring home of her son—a few worthless tokens in a brown envelope. Maybe this homey had been right. Why did he have to be alive when he was Buzzworm's age? Well, he wasn't gonna be.

"You got another son, too? Younger?" he wanted to confirm.

The woman nodded.

He scribbled a number on the back of one of his calling cards. "You ever heard of the ROCers? Group of mamas ROC-ing. Means Reclaim Our Children, see? Can't do it all by yourself."

She put the card in her purse.

Homey's crew was particularly quiet. No one was talking. Nobody pointing fingers. Nobody saying it was them that did it. "What about the drive-by yesterday?" Buzzworm wanted to know. "What was that all about?"

"Just general shooting. Nothing personal. Happens all the time."

"Boy was beat up. Nothing personal?"

"Beat up happens too."

"Who did it?"

"Dunno. Coulda been kickin' it. LAPD come round jacked him good."

"Maybe kid was jumped out. That what happened?"

"Dunno."

"Why'd he want out of the crew?"

"Who says he wanted out?"

"Could be took his life to get jumped out." Buzzworm figured maybe the homey took a beating to end his commitment to the crew. Got beat up to get in; got beat up to get out.

"Can't prove none of that. Dude's too tough to die that way. If he got beat up, he walked away. Can't nobody take his respect away. Gotta give him that."

"Walked away?"

"So they say."

"Walked away where? Over a cliff?"

Crew laughed. Cliffs in Watts would be good. Too bad it was all urban flatlands. Only cliffs around: maybe freeway rubble. So they suggested, "Into traffic. Hit and run. Could be."

"What about the cocaine? Since when you messing with such pure stuff?"

"What?"

Buzzworm couldn't figure this one. They were just a tagging crew, running around marking up the walls. Bunch of kids running. It was mostly an overdose of hormones and poverty made them run. Running fast, but not fast enough. Things were aiming to catch up with them: drugs, petty theft, assault, robbery. But it wasn't time for homicide, Buzzworm thought. Wasn't time. Maybe they were telling the truth. The dead boy had walked away.

One kid in the crew was listening to a Walkman. "What you listening to?"

"What's it to you?"

Buzzworm smiled, unperturbed. "Gimme a hit off those headphones of yours."

Kid shrugged and handed him the phones, but Buzzworm was genuinely surprised. "Son," he said, "this is classical."

"So?"

"So when'd you go cultural?"

"Trying to listen for this thing."

"Thing?"

"Shit."

"I'm listening."

"Thing in my head. Sounds like this stuff here, see."

"Beethoven?"

"Bay who?"

Buzzworm gave him back his phones. He felt confused, first about the dead boy who saw bullets curve and now about another homey who listened classical.

Then he remembered Margarita who listened to oldies. Buzzworm looked at one of his watches. It was lunchtime. Maybe he'd wander over and see Margarita at her corner. Sometimes she had her homemade pupusas. He liked the ones filled with potatoes and carrots, but any kind would do today. He got onto the Mexican station; he wanted to razz Margarita with a little mariachi, try to sweet talk her with some Spanish cooing, sing her the Cucaracha, tell her how everything south of the border was México, tell her her kids were all gonna end up marrying Mexicans, make her mad enough to cuss him out in her Pipile language. Maybe even get a few Chupacabra stories in. But Margarita wasn't there.

Margarita was dead. He got the page. Met the family in a one-room duplex, Pico-Union projects. Margarita had been in the kitchen at the sink, peeling oranges, eating, washing dishes, chopping vegetables, stirring up dinner, doing everything at once. Just like Margarita, doing everything at once. Then all of a sudden: boom. Slips to the ground. Looks like she's sleeping. Mami! Mami! Wake up! Wake up! What's happened? They dragged her to emergency. It took hours to get in. The older kid knew when she was dead. He couldn't hear her heart, couldn't hear her breathe anymore. Sat there in the waiting room, holding her head, keeping the news to himself, scared to tell the younger ones, wanting to know what he was supposed to do, wanting to be young and stupid again. What he couldn't understand was what the folks at emergency were trying to tell him, trying to tell him it looked like his momma died of an overdose. Looked like she finally took too much. Too much of what? he wanted to know. Too much of work?

There it was again. Someone trying to tell Buzzworm that an overdose was responsible for death. People who conceivably ought to drug the daylights out of their poor miserable lives but never did, who withstood beating both physical and spiritual, who anyway, they said, had succumbed. Buzzworm couldn't buy it.

He went back to Margarita's corner and stared at the grease spots on the pavement where her cooking once dripped, the scatter of peanut shells and orange peel in the gutter. He searched the waves for Aretha but couldn't find her. Someone was on a talk show talking about some music in her head, humming it on the radio. Could they play it please? Could anyone identify it? It was driving her crazy. This wasn't a music program lady but maybe someone would hear her humming and call in and identify the tune. Sure enough, a caller came through humming the same stuff, but no identification as yet. Only thing they knew was it sounded classical. What the hell. Buzzworm zipped into Mexican territory. Maybe he would luck out with some cumbia at least. It was the best he could do for poor Margarita. *La equis la equis noventa y siete punto nueve!*

CHAPTER 17:

The Interview *Manzanar*

Like Buzzworm promised, I got my interview with the homeless conductor. We met around Pershing Square and tried to get comfortable on one of those curved bus benches that won't support a sleeping homeless person. I passed out the McMuffins and the coffee and tried to be inconspicuous while Buzzworm did the interview. This was my understated pretense until the end when this homeless character looked me in the eyes and said, "Since you haven't taken any notes, I'm assuming you're taping this."

"Why no. I'm not."

Buzzworm smiled. "Don't worry. He's good," he assured the man. "Has an almost audiographic memory." And before I could protest, Buzzworm made further assurances: "Besides, guaranteed you see the copy before it goes to press. Right Balboa?"

Audiographic memory. I could have strangled Buzzworm on the spot. Pretty soon, he'd want every homeless person in L.A. to verify my quotes and critique the copy.

"It's about trust, Balboa," Buzzworm tried to justify. "And respect."

"The president of the United States doesn't get this privilege, goddammit!"

"You weren't interviewing the president. You were interviewing Manzanar Murakami, the first sansei born in captivity. Did you hear that?"

"He's crazy."

"That's what you gonna write?"

"No." Buzzworm was right. There was something important about this man, so wise, so completely honest. He deserved my respect. He probably did deserve to see my copy as well. It wasn't going to be easy. For the moment I couldn't see any way to do justice to the story. He might just look like one more crackpot homeless figure who got stepped on by the system. But this was a case where the man had side-stepped the system. And there I was without a pen or an audio recorder, without words.

I hurried back to my desk, tried to reconstruct the interview, reorganize Buzzworm's circuitous style. It drove me nuts. I was always the hunter, calculating my moves, getting ready for the kill. Of course, finesse was involved; I was subtly brutal. I'd be out of there before anyone remembered what happened.

But Buzzworm played the interview like a social soccer game, moving in, dancing with the ball, a foil there, sparring, dribbling the thing around to no obvious purpose. Or he was editorializing for my benefit with upstart questions like: "When you're conducting and look up at these downtown skyscrapers, maybe one-third of them empty, as somebody homeless, what do you think?" or "You ever come to make the connection between the fall of the Berlin Wall and the rise in homelessness in L.A.? Some think if we gotta blame someone, it still oughta be the Russians." or "Most everyone on the street's got a conspiracy theory. What's yours?"

Still I had to admit that when Buzzworm finally nailed the goal, it caught me by surprise.

"So you been out on the streets how many years?"

"You composing your own stuff or what?"

"How come you never use my services?"

"What did you do before you moved to the streets?"

"How about jazz? Coltrane? Miles Davis?"

"Where were you born?"

"You come from a musical family?"

"You ever been seen for psychiatric care?"

"What about Bach? Mozart? Dvorak?"

"What did you eat today?"

"How old are you?"

"When did you graduate UCLA?"

"How's your eyesight? Sure you don't require some eyeglasses?"

"Where do you camp out?"

"What hospital did you work in?"

"How about your folks?"

"If you could get a job, then what?"

"Maybe you should get yourself a partner."

"What about medication or drugs?"

"You play an instrument?"

"What kind of surgery did you do? Anybody ever die?"

"How's your general health? How about the bowels?"

"Now, I know you're conducting, but how's it work? I mean, what's going on when *you're* out there?"

"How you making out? You picking up welfare?"

"Is that your real name?"

"You're an educated man; you don't consider that you might be crazy?"

Manzanar Murakami did not consider himself to be crazy. I had read about cases of schizophrenia where people could be completely convincing in various roles. It was not his real name, so perhaps he had never been a surgeon, never graduated UCLA. Perhaps it had been one of his former roles. I couldn't be sure. He had created his name out of his birthplace, Manzanar Concentration Camp in the Owens Valley. He claimed he was born there during the war. That would have been over fifty years ago, and he looked to be well over fifty.

He had smiled wryly under a bush of white unkempt hair that he must shear off himself from time to time by simply grabbing it on top and hacking. His clothing was worn but not tattered. Even in the heat of June, he wore a black trenchcoat—good quality with a lot of pockets and zippers just like Buzzworm said; like other homeless, he carried all his belongings on his person. Said he had a "modest place" in an encampment hidden in freeway overgrowth; Buzzworm knew the place. The man had a blackened appearance like a chimney sweep. Like the underbelly of the overpass itself, it seemed rather permanent. Beneath this sooty exterior, however, I noticed a powerful body, broad chest and strong arms, as if the man worked out. What a lousy baton could do for the body! There was something of the stevedore about him. The elements of the urban outdoors had not worn him down, yet. I imagined he could simply take a shower, don a white jacket, and be transformed very suddenly into Dr. Murakami.

What struck me was that Manzanar was probably not crazy. There was a subtle quality about him and an honest reticence that seemed to reflect a true kind of modesty. He had a clarity of mind and speech; no glitches that I could notice. But then, who am I to say? After all, he lived on the street; he conducted an orchestra no one could see and music no one could hear. But his attitude was monkish, like a character in a Kurosawa film who shaves his head and forsakes all worldliness—a kind of head start toward nirvana. And yet he was funny. His words and manner were laced with irony and intelligent humor. I figured if he were crazy, a lack of humor would be a dead giveaway.

Buzzworm had no opinion about this. It didn't matter if he were out of his mind. Look at Buzzworm. He was crazy. So what? Still, it wasn't your typical homeless story, if there were such a thing. It could be said that Manzanar had chosen homelessness as a way of life. This probably wasn't the message Buzzworm was trying to convey. Buzzworm was trying to get jobs, housing, health care, rehab, and mental services for the folks. Manzanar wasn't exactly a case for any of these things, but Buzzworm said, "Balboa, forget the social agenda. Just tell the story. Point is there's people out here. Life out here."

One final thing struck me; it was that there was something I had to learn from this man, something I needed him to impart to me, not as the subject of an interview or an investigation, but something he could teach me, as if he were some sort of conducting shaman, as if he held a great secret, as if he knew *the way*. Of course I couldn't admit this to Buzzworm; it was purely absurd. I was the journalist of current events, hellbent on getting the story out. Still, not knowing this secret would only mean that Manzanar would continue to be just another crazy old man.

I didn't make the Asian connection until I got Emi's habitual afternoon call; but then why should I connect Emi to Asianness? Maybe Emi never let me forget I was Chicano, but it was easy to lose track of Emi. She defied definition. "Ever heard of a Manzanar Murakami?" I asked. "He's sansei," I added as if it would help.

"Oh-kay," she said, like she was dealing with a hypothesis of some sort.

"He's homeless."

"Do I know anybody homeless?"

"Do you know anything about your community at all?"

"Gosh, what do you figure, Gabe? Twenty thousand of us? Fifty? A hundred? I'm supposed to know one homeless Asian?"

"Your people take care of each other. This guy is very noticeable. I bet someone's noticed him. I bet your mom's heard of him."

"True. My mom reads the *Rafu* cover to cover. Too bad you don't write for the *Rafu*. That would really impress her."

"She likes me anyway."

"But she doesn't read your stuff much. *Rafu*'s got the L.A. obits. She never misses a funeral. Do you know what koden is?"

"No."

"Well, she's spent a fortune in it."

"Ask her about Manzanar Murakami, will you?"

"What kind of name is that?"

"Sansei hybrid."

Emi changed the subject. "Now I know all of you over there only get your news from printed matter, but did you at least hear the second semi blow? They can't contain the fire. Don't you get out? It's got to be smoking your way. Even imprisoned behind four inches of glass, you must have heard the blast."

"I thought they cleared it up. That was yesterday."

"How did you get to work?"

"I had an interview six a.m. I took side streets to pick up coffee. Wait. You said second semi. There's more than one?"

"Where have you been? Turns out a second semi—no apparent relation to the first—knifed a few minutes later about a mile back of the first. This time, it was just ten thousand gallons of sloshing gasoline. One more giant Molotov cocktail on wheels. Besides which, a truck crashed into the second semi spilling thirty-three thousand pounds of meat. That's when the whole thing blew up. It's dead cows all over the freeway. Can you imagine the barbecue? An entire mile of cars trapped between two dead semis, not to mention two craters, fires, and the debris from the blasts. Find a TV for godssake! There's a very weird view from the *NewsNow* copter. Cars on fire, all the ivy, palm trees, brush, signs. Worse yet, the Santa Anas are blowing through like the one-ten was a canyon in Malibu."

"There's a homeless encampment in the overgrowth around there."

"It's not Malibu. It's gonna burn."

"I gotta go." I hung up and paged Buzzworm.

"Cardboard ramshackles've gone up in smoke," he reported. "You believe there's maybe two-three-hundred of 'em live up in here?"

"Where're they now?"

"They're headed down onto the freeway."

"What?"

"Traffic's at a standstill. Folks abandoned their cars. Explosions, fires. You'd run for it too. Some didn't make it. Homeless're in the cars now."

"Buzz, whadya hear on your radio?"

"Sports."

"What happened to the news?"

"Balboa, ain't we got enough news yet?"

"Give me fifteen. I'll be there." I paused and decided to ask while I remembered, "Buzz, at the interview this morning, what were you tuned to?"

"You mean what was I on?"

"Yeah."

"Just talk."

"Howard Stern?"

"What I be listening to New York for?"

I thought about this. "Rush Limbaugh?"

"Listen, Balboa. I take it all in. KFI, KLSX. Might as well be KLAN as in *Ku Klux*. People out there starved to talk, try their excuses for brains out on the airwaves."

"Yeah," I agreed, but I was gonna miss the homeless taking over the one-ten. I hurried on like the reporter I am. "We'll talk more. See you in fifteen."

"Balboa," he stopped me. "The C. Juárez thing? I got some addresses for you, but they all lead South, meaning maybe México. And I think you're right. It's not just about illegal medication. Cartel's into diversification."

"Damn," I said.

"There's always a price attached to these addresses. Can you pay up?"

"Depends."

"Looks like it's not a monetary price. More like a political one. They figure a journalist like you has connections, see."

"I'm listening."

"They insist on a meeting. Mexico City. Need to size you up to make an offer, I guess."

"You guess! I can't be everywhere," I complained.

"It's your call. I myself don't go nowhere. Hell, L.A. don't go nowhere, and look at this. Shit just comes to us."

I didn't say anything. I was being lectured to again.

"About Manzanar. You wanted to know?"

"Right."

"SigAlerts and weather. Commuter Classics. Was I wrong?"

"I guess not." I hung up and grabbed a Power Bar from the top desk drawer, washed the chewy consistency down with a gulp from my mug of always-cold coffee. I paused over the mug's significance. Emi had given it to me. An eyeball floated by means of a ceramic post in the middle of the black liquid—a mercurial gray under these artificial lights. With the smoke rising from the freeway fires out there, the eyeball was looking like the sun in my L.A. pewter skies. The mug read sardonically, "Here's looking at you . . ."

CHAPTER 18:

Daylight *The Cornfield*

Rafaela rubbed the salt between her fingers, pelting the corn lightly, and gave it to Sol whose small hands encircled the thick ear eagerly. He sunk his baby teeth into the soft sweet kernels at one end and wandered after his mother. She slung a canvas bag with Sol's bottle in it over her shoulder and called after the boy, "This way, Sol. We're going to see Doña Maria."

Together they skirted Rodriguez's unfinished wall following its pregnant bulge. Strangely the curve in its features seemed even more accentuated than this morning when she and Rodriguez had stood solemnly before it, speechless. Both watched a long thin snake wend its way along the wall, its fine head curiously rising and dipping, searching for a passage. Rodriguez did not move to kill the snake as he might have because, she thought, the snake's path skirting the wall seemed oddly straight. If only the snake could define the nature of a straight line... She did not have the heart to ask Rodriguez to tear the wall down, and she hoped that Gabriel would not expect such perfection either. But she would call and ask. Sol tugged at her fingers, and they continued down the path toward Doña Maria's.

She had been thinking about calling Bobby, practicing her conversation. She had needed to go home to find out what that felt like; it had been too many years... that would be her excuse. He should see Sol, so tan and healthy these days. Maybe they could find a way to go to Singapore. At least he could go home to see his family. It might help. She was going to suggest it.

A highly polished black Jaguar was parked conspicuously in the shade in front of Doña Maria's porch. Rafaela eyed the car warily and paused, absently reading the gold numbers across its back, XJS 12, wondering whether it might be best to leave, but Sol was already running up the steps, and Doña Maria seemed to be waiting for them at the door. Rafaela sighed. She had better look in on the woman. Perhaps the Jaguar belonged to a stranger.

"You have come at a good time." Doña Maria clapped her chubby hands together. "You can meet my son Hernando. I suppose you thought he didn't exist. I'm always talking about him, but he never visits. But what's a mother to do? He's so busy."

Rafaela could hear a man's voice yelling.

Doña Maria waved in that direction. "On the phone. He's been on the phone since he arrived last night. Always business. Such a headache. He hasn't touched his coffee. Come on. Sit down. Sweet bread for Sol?"

Sol was still clinging to his corn. Pieces of the yellow kernels stuck to his cheeks and nose. Rafaela wiped them away and tried to take the corn from Sol's hands. Sol pulled away. The corn was precious to him.

"Is it that good?" Doña Maria laughed. "We have an entire field of it. You can have as much corn as you want. Shall we take a look?"

Rafaela nodded but glanced back in the direction of the phone. Doña Maria's son was still yelling. Something about a shipment of oranges. "I want to know every detail, every stop, every person who had anything to do with it from the time it got to Honduras!" He paused. "Those Brazilians are sons of bitches, but they're not so stupid!"

"I'm sorry," apologized Doña Maria. "Of course you want to use the phone."

"I can come back another time," Rafaela protested.

"Did you see the satellite dish? He came to check it out." She pointed in the direction of the television. "For me, such a blessing, a little television now and then. Don't you miss it?"

Rafaela hadn't seen television for weeks now. She thought about Bobby and his Sony television, how he had chosen it so carefully, how much he wanted to impress her with this gift. Everything was a gift to her and Sol: all those amazing things he loved to buy. She had scorned his materialism, but it was his way of showing his love, of trying to delight her with the nice things that other Americans had. That is what he wanted to tell her. No, she didn't miss television, but she missed Bobby.

"Sons of bitches!" Hernando yelled.

Doña Maria rolled her eyes. "Come." She pushed Sol out the door. "Let's get some corn. Maybe when we get back, he'll be off the phone."

"What is your son's business?" Rafaela wanted to know.

"Oh, he dabbles in this and that. I don't really know. Export. Import. I never know his business. This time it's oranges from Brazil. Some problem with them. Poor Hernando. It's such a headache." She shook her head. They walked on. Doña Maria's property extended over several acres. "See?" she pointed for Sol. "Corn. Rows and rows." The stalks towered above their heads, thick with ears of corn, silk drying in brown curls.

"What will you do with so much corn?"

"Eat it, of course. As much as you want. The rest, Lupe will take to market for cash." Rafaela knew Lupe did everything on Doña Maria's place. Lupe cleaned, cooked, gardened, planted, and harvested. She fed the chickens, collected eggs, fattened the pigs, and slaughtered them when the time came. Rafaela thought about her argument with Bobby, about how she and Bobby did all the work without benefits, about exploitation. Now she had crossed the border and forgotten her anger. Lupe did all the work. Someone was always at the bottom. As long as she was not, did it matter?

"How stupid of me," Doña Maria pouted, "I've forgotten the basket. And it was right there at the kitchen door."

"I'll go back," offered Rafaela. "Besides," she pointed at the canvas bag, "if you don't mind, I'd like to put Sol's bottle in the refrigerator." Rafaela hurried toward the house which seemed quite near, but looking back, Sol and Doña Maria seemed suddenly quite far. It was perplexing to see the way in which the corn seemed to tower around them and swallow them up. As she stepped into the kitchen, she expected to hear Hernando's loud voice still over the phone, but now there were two voices, speaking in even tones, pulsing heavily through the thick air.

"How many months?"

"This one's not a baby. Two. Two and a half years."

"What do they need?"

"Kidney."

"One?"

"Yes."

"Blood type?"

"It's all there as usual."

"How desperate are they?"

"Very."

"Was the price suggested?"

"Yes. They agreed."

"We'll see what we can do."

"Tell them to be careful. Not just any starving two-year-old."

"They're not getting the stomach. They're getting a kidney."

"The child shouldn't be yellow, jaundiced."

"Kidneys are cheaper. The child can live on just one. No?"

"It's the same work."

"I'll call in a few days."

"The doctor wants to go on vacation. We expect delivery Friday."

"And today, what did you bring me?"

"A heart. It's hard to believe they're so small. The size of a golf ball." The voice was approaching the kitchen.

Instinctively, Rafaela slipped outside the door and listened to the footsteps, the sound of the refrigerator door, and the soft clunk of plastic on the cold shelf. When the kitchen seemed empty again, she slipped in and opened the refrigerator door, foolishly gripping Sol's bottle as an excuse. Cold air bathing her hot skin, she seized the handle of what she recognized to be a small hard plastic cooler. It was the sort she used to carry around back home to keep Sol's bottles of milk chilled. It wasn't very big at all. With the ice packed in, she could, at most, get a small bottle and a fruit in it. Perhaps because it seemed so familiar reminded her of her attachment to Sol—she was able to snatch that blue and white container nestled between leftover cake and a piece of cheese as if it were her own and stuff it into the canvas bag.

Export. Import. It was not just any conversation spoken in a bubble of intrigue. It did not make any sense, but it made Rafaela's heart race. Suddenly she realized her recklessness. From the corner of her eye, she caught sight of Dona Maria's son Hernando, a fearful meeting of faces in reflective glass. Who was this man whose yell and whose whisper both worked a terrible knot at a tender place in her womb? *Not just any starving two-year-old.* What could it mean? Sol. Sol was not starving. He was not just any two-year-old.

Rafaela stumbled from the kitchen, racing toward the field of corn with her new possession feeling suddenly very heavy, but the more she ran, the farther it seemed to be. She could see the distant figures of Doña Maria and Sol with his salted cob wandering in and out of the corn, wandering as if in some timeless space, at every moment farther and farther. Her heaving breath pummeled in her ears. How long would it take to run such a distance? Breathless, she stretched her arms reaching toward Sol. To everything there seemed to be an eerie liquid elasticity. How far must she race? How far must she reach to touch her Sol?

CHAPTER 19:

Hour of the Trucks *The Freeway Canyon*

Manzanar concentrated on a noise that sounded like a mix of an elephant and the wail of a whale, concentrating until it moaned through the downtown canyons, shuddered past the on-ramps and echoed up and down the one-ten. There was an instinctual recognition of this noise by those who could hear it. The salutary marching orchestral backdrop à la Yojimbo/Atom Boy hinted at the original Godzilla theme. It was slightly cartoonish, and the timing was purposely out of sync as if the entire thing—even Godzilla's wail—were dubbed. This was *The Hour of the Trucks* which Manzanar conceived of in his strangely organic vision, appropriate if one were to compare the beastly size of semis, garbage trucks, moving vans, and concrete mixers to the largest monsters of the animal kingdom—living and extinct, all rumbling ponderously along the freeway.

Manzanar knew the frustration of the ordinary motorist wedged between trucks—the nauseous flush of diesel exhaust and interrupted visibility—but he also understood the nature of the truck beast, whose purpose was to transport the great products of civilization: home and office appliances, steel beams and turbines, fruits, vegetables, meats, and grain, Coca-Cola and Sparkletts, Hollywood sets, this fall's fashions, military hardware, gasoline, concrete, and garbage. Nothing was more or less important. And it was all moving here and there, back and forth, from the harbor to the train station to the highway to the warehouse to the airport to the docking station to the factory to the dump site.

The slain semis with their great stainless steel tanks had sprawled across five lanes, bleeding precious fuel over the asphalt. The smaller vehicles of the automotive kingdom gawked with a certain reverence or huddled near, impatiently awaiting a resolution. Police cars and motorcycles, followed by ambulances and fire trucks, sirened and blinked meandering and treacherous paths between lanes and over shoulders to the sites. Helicopters hovered, swooping-in occasionally for a closer shot, a giant vortex of scavengers. The great land-roving semis lay immobile, dwarfing everything—even the formidable red fire trucks, poising themselves defensively around the victims.

When the tanks blew and the great walls of flames flew up the brush and ivy along the freeway canyon, Manzanar knew instinctively the consequences, knew that his humble encampment wedged against a retaining wall and hidden in oleander would soon be a pile of ash. To leave his perch and abandon his music to save his home would be a useless and dangerous enterprise. Anything of personal value he carried in one of his numerous pockets. He would lose some books, magazines, a lantern, cooking utensils, bedding, a change of clothing, soap. For those who had nothing, this was everything.

Manzanar continued to conduct, watching the fire engulf the slope. Even he, who knew the dense hidden community living on the no-man's-land of public property, was surprised by the numbers of people who descended the slopes. Men, women, and children, their dogs and even cats, bedding, and caches of cans and bottles in great green garbage sacks and shopping carts moved into public view, sidling along the lines of abandoned cars, gawking into windows and kicking tires, remarking on the models, ages, and colors, as if at a great used car dealership. From Manzanar's perspective, and given its length of one mile, it was the greatest used car dealership.

The vans and camper trailers went first; then the gas guzzlers—oversized Cadillacs with their spacious pink and red vinyl interiors, and blue Buicks. A sleek white limousine with black interior was in particular favor. A spacious interior with storage space was favored, while the exterior condition of a car was deemed of secondary importance. Never mind the bondo sanding projects in the works, a falling muffler, or the crushed brake light patched with red plastic. Boxy Volvos and Mercedes, and Taurus station wagons, had the advantages of space and sturdy structure. Some wondered if good tires weren't a necessity. Compacts were more popular than two-seater sports cars. Porches, Corvettes, Jaguars, and Miatas were suddenly relegated to the status of sitting or powder rooms or even telephone booths (those having cellular phones). Convertibles remained as before: toys. Children clambered over them; adults sat in them and laughed.

In a matter of minutes, life filled a vacuum, reorganizing itself in predictable and unpredictable ways. Occasional disputes over claims to territory arose, but for the moment, there were more than sufficient vehicles to accommodate this game of musical chairs. Indeed it was a game, a fortunate lottery, and for the transient, understandably impermanent and immediate. Besides, great walls of fire raged at both ends. What to do now? What to do next? Kids lined up next to a black Beemer with smoked windows to call a 1-800 *How Am I Driving?* number. A commissary truck opened for business, as did a recycling truck. A moving van was emptied of its contents: washing machines, refrigerators, ovens, chairs, tables, sofas, beds, carpets, barbecue pits, lawn mowers, etc. Watermelons, bananas, and cantaloupes were hauled off one truck, as were Wonder Bread, Cacique tortillas, and Trader Joe's fresh pasta. Someone passed out bottles of Tejava and Snapple. Cases of cold Perrier were taken to the fiery front.

A scattered chorus of car alarms honked and beeped. Why in God's name anyone should evacuate a car on a freeway and trigger the alarm one could only speculate; the decision had been made by at least a dozen motorists. The variety and frequency of these car alarms fascinated Manzanar who accommodated them in his score with appropriate irony. These sounds joined the thudder of helicopters, the sirens of fire trucks, the commentary of newscasters, the opening and slamming of car doors, hoods, trunks, and glove compartments, and the general chatter of festive shopping and looting. It was one of those happy riots. Manzanar wondered if the storming of the Bastille could not be compared to the storming of this mile-long abandoned car lot. Perhaps not.

The Hour of the Trucks was an hour outside of the general rush, but it created its own intensity. In this case, it was quite a mess. As the semis went up in flames, there were the usual questions of traffic safety, whether trucks should be confined to operation during the hours between midnight and dawn or to truck-only corridors. As the homeless flocked onto the freeway, there were also the usual questions of shelter and jobs, drug rehabilitation, and the closing of mental health facilities. And as car owners watched on TV sets or from the edges of the freeway canyon, there were the usual questions of police protection, insurance coverage, and acts of God. The average citizen viewed these events and felt overwhelmed with the problems, felt sympathy, or anger and impotence. There was also an imminent collective sense of immediate live real-time action, better than live sports whose results—one or another team's demise—were predictable, and better than CNN whose wars were in foreign countries with names nobody could truly pronounce. Of course everyone remembered the last time they had gathered on freeways to watch a spectacle; white Broncos had since become the vehicle of choice. Not surprisingly, the CHP and AAA together reported at least a dozen instances of white Broncos driven to some finality: E on the gas tank, over a Malibu cliff, to Terminal Island, etc.

Manzanar pressed on through the spectacle that the present circumstances would soon become, the chatter of silly and profound commentary, the cruel jokes, and the utterly violent assumption underlying everything: that the homeless were expendable, that citizens had a right to protect their property with firearms, and that fire, regardless of whether it was in your fireplace or TV set or whether you clutched a can of beer or fingered a glass of Chardonnay, was mesmerizing. All of these elements shifted bizarrely through the movement barely controllable by Manzanar's deft style. Sweat poured from his brow, spattered from the tips of his white mane. Fear rose to his throat, clutching terribly. For the first time, he considered abandoning his effort as he had once abandoned his surgical practice, and yet an uncanny sense of the elasticity of the moment, of time and space, forced his hands and arms to continue. He was facing south on his overpass podium, and he knew the entire event was being moved, stretched. And he was quite sure that the direction was south. Yes, south, for the time being.

CHAPTER 20:

Disaster Movie Week *Hiro's Sushi*

"Have you ever seen an *I heart* L.A. sticker? People here *heart* everything else—Ensenada, Hussong's, Taos, Alaskan Huskies, Guatemala, even New York. That *L.A. is a desert paradise, sunshine, blond people, insipid, romantic* is B.S. Nobody hearts L.A." Emi straddled the stool with crossed legs, toes balancing a black heel, her skirt slipping up and down her thighs. She leaned away from the bar momentarily and carefully masticated and moaned. Albacore, wasabi, shoyu, vinegared rice. To die for. Her eyes narrowed and glanced over at Gabriel's conservative offering of kappa and tekkamaki. She watched him pincer a cucumber roll and swab it in shoyu.

"Hmmm," Gabriel stuffed the thing in his mouth and nodded. "But I thought you liked the Rose Parade. All those Pasadena señoras," he swallowed and continued, "playing Castilian Ramonas in black lace shawls on rows of prancing Palominos and bending bosoms to get an interview with Bill Welch."

Emi grimaced. "Try that," she pointed through the glass. "Just try it. It's gooey duck, but I swear it's not gooey. He wants that," she announced to the sushimaker, then continued, "Did I tell you? A green-type from Colorado asked me whether we recycle the flowers after the parade. I told her we donate it all to a sachet business that retails in expensive Beverly Hills boutiques which in turn supports a home for battered wives and kids."

"Maybe we do."

"Speaking of sachet. I couldn't get past the first chapter of that book."

"Chandler? What's the problem?"

"Orchids don't smell. They don't overwhelm you with a languid trop-i-cal perfuuume. Have you ever heard of orchid sachet? Fragrance de Catalaya? Ask any J.A. gardener. Ask any J.A. Ask my dad. Does his greenhouse make your head woozy?"

"Maybe black-and-white orchids smell. The famous Noir Orchid, Angel. I'm surprised a J.A. like you never heard of it." The sushimaker plopped the gooey duck couple in front of Gabriel. "You may have to eat it yourself," grimaced Gabriel.

"Just try it. We've got to find something else you'll eat besides those kappas. You might as well eat in any supermarket deli. My *mom* makes those."

"I like your mom's better. She puts sesame seeds and jalapeños in mine. I even like the politically incorrect Spam ones and those tofu bags, too."

"Footballs."

"Yeah."

"Picnic sushi," Emi sneered. "I can't take you anywhere."

"Take me to a Japanese American picnic," he quipped.

Emi poured another round of tepid sake and stared over the head of the sushimaker at the TV. "I'm glad you have a TV," she complimented him. "Some sushi bars are too Zen to have one."

"I like sports," said the sushimaker.

"Sports sushi," nodded Gabriel. "Why don't you make footballs?"

Emi rolled her eyes. The sushimaker continued, "Usually I got on ESPN, but people want a update on the freeway fire."

Emi nodded. "And it's hump day. Movie of the week tonight: *Canyon Fires*. Do you think it can compete?" Emi waited for Gabriel to be appalled.

"Compete?" He shook his head. After all, the movie was on full screen, but the station had conveniently carved out a corner box with continuous coverage of the freeway fire from the *NewsNow* copter. From time to time, captioning strutted by announcing a dead fireman and how many charred vehicles. The station couldn't lose. Commercial time rolled along, and so did live action news.

"No difference," observed the sushimaker. "Fire here. Fire here." He pointed to the screen and subscreen.

At home, Emi had a set with its own screening boxes. "Look at this," she had announced to Gabriel when she bought the thing. "I can watch four stations at once if necessary." This feature had almost finished the relationship. It was taking things to the edge when Emi tried it in conjunction with one of Gabriel's classic black and whites. He came back from the kitchen with Dos Equis, salsa, and chips only to find *Murder, My Sweet* in the lower left quarter of the screen, competing with *Hard Copy,* CNN, and *The Three Tenors.* If Emi had her way, she would watch TV at Circuit City. She was used to being in a control room watching her network and the competition simultaneously. At any moment, she could judge which channel had the more exciting screen.

"Looks like McDonald's, Coca-Cola, KFC, and even Nike took a dive this prime time," she cooed. "With a live offering like this, a remote control could go into automatic. Tsk. Tsk," she clucked.

"The way you pay attention to this, you'd think you were the station chief," Gabriel derided.

"I have a five-year plan."

"How about a reality check?"

"Hey, I don't wanna hear about your glass ceiling, okay? We're not going to weep into our sake today, are we?" Emi leaned over, snatched one of the gooey ducks and wiggled the long meaty end of it at Gabriel. "I worked hard to make it this far, but I don't have any illusions about what I do. I take a show, speed it up electronically, and if that's not enough, we slash and burn. Mostly it's very delicate. You hardly notice. Cut. Cut. Snip. Snip. Snip. The point is to keep the integrity of the show (well, sort of), and still get everything to wrap around the commercials. I get it to the second, mind you. There are people below me who would kill for my job, and there are producers who would kill me if they knew who I was. Mostly it's second-rate stuff. So do I care?" Emi chomped on the gooey duck.

"What's the point?"

"The point is that anybody can do it. You just have to want to. It's just about money. It's not about good honest people like you or about whether us Chicanos or Asians get a bum rap or whether third world countries deserve dictators or whether we should make the world safe for democracy. It's about selling things: Reebok, Pepsi, Chevrolet, AllState, Pampers, Pollo Loco, Levis, Fritos, Larry Parker Esq., Tide, Raid, the Pillsbury Doughboy, and Famous Amos. Them that's smart took away the pretense and do the home shopping thing, twenty-four hours. Hey, we're all on board to buy. So who needs a reality check?"

"It's depressing talking to you."

"Let's change the subject," Emi agreed.

This time Gabriel did the rounds of tepid sake.

"How's that gooey duck?"

"Crunchy."

Emi looked down and around, following the curve of the counter, scrutinizing the customers in varying stages of filling their faces with sushi, tea, and ginger. "Ouu. Let's people watch."

Gabriel moaned. This was one of those high school pastimes that Emi had turned into a kind of sophisticated voyeurism. Usually she did it while driving, peering into cars and speculating about the owners and passengers. Emi had a gift for fabricating the most intimate details about other people's lives. She could easily have written for the *National Enquirer.* She also had a gift for spotting famous people in bizarre places. Emi called these *sightings.* Gabriel never recognized half of them, as famous as Emi insisted they might be. Exchanging stalls with Uma Thurman in the women's room of the Formosa Café or reaching for sausages with Quentin Tarantino in the meat section at Hughes seemed long shots, but there was always a good story.

"Gee, Gabe," she perked up. "Here we all are, your multicultural mosaic. There's you and me and the gays at the end of the bar and the guy with the turban. And how about those Caucasian Japanophiles who talk real Japanese with the sushi man? Can we count them too?"

"Sure. Why not." Gabriel felt generous.

"There's even white people here."

The woman sitting next to Emi turned and glared momentarily. Emi absorbed the glare like it was a tanning lamp. Gabriel looked the other way.

Emi continued, "Over there, that woman must be Persian and her friend's gotta be Cherokee."

"Cherokee?"

"Okay. Navajo."

"Sorry to bust your bubble. The one you think is Persian is Chicana."

"Hey I know a Persian when I see a Persian."

"Chicana. I know my people, see."

"What about her date?"

"White."

"Oouuu, he likes wasabi. Yeah, definitely white meat. Humph." Emi tossed her hair and swiveled around. "That couple over there is South African wouldn't you say? And her, what do you think? I figure one-quarter Micronesian, one-quarter Armenian, and one-half Mesoamerican."

"Her parents met in New Delhi."

"Yeah her father was a nuclear physicist working for the Soviets, and her mother was a stewardess for Air Peru."

"He lost his job when the Berlin wall came down."

"She died in a crash in the Andes."

"Very tragic."

Emi paused, mulling over the tragedy of it all—the end of communism and the plane crash over Cuzco, and crossed her legs in the other direction. "Gabe, it's all bullshit."

"I know."

"Cultural diversity is bullshit."

Gabriel sighed. Of course it would come to this. As usual, Emi would pronounce a new sacrilege.

"Do you know what cultural diversity really is?"

"I'm thinking."

"It's a white guy wearing a Nirvana T-shirt and dreads. That's cultural diversity." Emi looked up at the sushi chef. "Don't you hate being multicultural?" she asked.

"Excuse me?"

The woman next to Emi bristled under her silk blouse and handcrafted silver. She looked apologetically at the sushimaker and said, "Hiro-san, having a hard day?"

"Hiro," Emi butted back in. "I hate being multicultural."

"Can't you calm down?" The woman never looked at Emi, but offered up a patronizing smile for Hiro-san. "We're trying to enjoy our tea. By the way, Hiro-san, it's just delicious today."

"See what I mean, Hiro? You're invisible. I'm invisible. We're all invisible. It's just tea, ginger, raw fish, and a credit card."

"Whatever is your problem?"

Gabriel knew better than to introduce more ammunition. He said plainly, "I'd like a California roll."

The woman went on. "I happen to adore the Japanese culture. What can I say? I adore different cultures. I've traveled all over the world. I love living in L.A. because I can find anything in the world to eat, right here. It's such a meeting place for all sorts of people. A true celebration of an international world. It just makes me sick to hear people speak so cynically about something so positive and to make assumptions about people based on their color. Really, I'm sorry. I can't understand your attitude at all."

Emi stared into a compact mirror and reapplied a glossy layer of red lipstick before she turned around in her seat to meet her sushi bar neighbor in her full frontal glory.

"Emi—" Gabriel felt a sudden panic.

Emi sighed. She noticed the woman's hair was held together miraculously by two ornately-lacquered chopsticks. Maybe there was some precedent for this hairdo. Gabriel later remembered something about Oedipus blinding himself with his mother's hairpins. Not an Asian myth however.

Emi said, "Hiro, could we have two forks, please?"

Hiro quickly motioned and signaled for the occidental eating utensils.

Emi examined the forks carefully and held them up for her neighbor. "Would you consider using these in your hair? Or would you consider that," Emi paused, "unsanitary?"

The woman blanched. Gabriel missed chomping into his California roll. For some reason, the entire sushi bar seemed to tilt and sag with an indescribable elasticity. Gabriel's elbow lost its surface, and that seaweed, rice, crab, and avocado delicacy tumbled and tumbled.

CHAPTER 21:
To Eat *La Cantina de Miseria y Hambre*

Arcangel sat alone at a table outside the Cantina de Miseria y Hambre. It was a cantina like any other, but he had chosen it for its name, Misery & Hunger—perhaps not an auspicious one for such a business, but perhaps not inappropriate. All day and night long the tables and chairs of the Cantina of Misery & Hunger were filled with people. Of course, some were miserable, some hungry, some miserable *and* hungry. They saw the sign from a distance as they crossed the street, wending their way through life's travails to a place of commonalities. As such, it could be construed as a miserable and hungry place, filled with miserable and hungry people, but it was in fact bustling with life. It was as life is: spilling its guts and filling its belly, endlessly.

The waiter came with his plate of nopales. "Don't I know you from somewhere?" the waiter asked.

"Where were you born?"

"Near San Cristobal de las Casas, in Chiapas. My people have worked an ejido there for three generations."

"You were born in the cornfields?"

"How did you know?"

"How old are you now?"

"Almost twenty."

Arcangel nodded, "Has it been that long?"

The waiter was baffled and took the liberty of sitting down while Arcangel began to fill his mouth with forkfuls of the steaming and slightly slimy nopales. "So it's true that I know you then?"

"I think so." Arcangel scrutinized the puzzled young man. "Yes, but you've changed a bit since I last saw you."

"You have not changed at all," the waiter said, "but I do not know how to explain how I know that."

Arcangel shrugged and pointed at his plate. "My compliments to the cook."

"Perhaps you would like a beer?" the waiter suggested.

"Perhaps."

"It's on me. For old time's sake." The waiter returned with a can of Bud Light.

"Beer in cans? What's this?"

"Bud Light."

"What other sort of beer do you have?"

"We have Budweiser, too. Schlitz. Hamms. Michelob. Coors. Miller. Miller Lite. Samuel Adams."

"You don't think it strange?"

"Strange? That I remember you from my birth?"

"No. About the beers. All American beers. But we are in México, are we not? Where are the Mexican beers?"

"Perhaps you would prefer Coca-Cola or Pepsi?"

"Perhaps I would like a hamburger, Fritos, and catsup."

"It is our special today."

It was true. Arcangel looked around at all the hungry and miserable people in the cantina—all eating hamburgers, Fritos, catsup, and drinking American beers. Only he, who had asked the cook the favor of cooking his raw cactus leaves, ate nopales. He scratched the rugged stubble in the hollow of his cheek and ran his fingers across his chin. "The cantina is very full today. Is it always so?"

"We do a good business. But today, even better. Most of these people are on their way to the cockfight."

Arcangel left with the crowd, their prizefighters hidden in sacks, resting in the dark before their perhaps final events. He followed them to a small arena, watched the owners groom their proud birds, sun glancing off the satin sheen of their black and emerald feathers and the terrible glare of the knives at their heels. He watched the money exchange hands, the excitement of the deal, the glint in the eyes of both men and birds. He wondered when his time would come, when he would be forced to spar with knives at his heels, to meet the final destiny of those with wings. The slain bodies of the most elegant, well-fed, and trained roosters were carried sadly away. The victors who remained strutted the ring, seemingly boastful, but only the owners were foolish enough to be truly boastful.

Now it was Arcangel's turn to strut to the center. Unseen by anyone, he had transformed himself into a motley personage: part superhero, part professional wrestler, part Subcomandante Marcos. Ski mask in camouflage nylon, blue cape with the magic image of Guadalupe in an aura of gold feathers and blood roses, leopard bicycle tights, and blue boots. Someone shouted, "It's El Gran Mojado!" Instant recognition. An awe-struck murmur ran through the crowd. Could it be? Indeed *the man going north* had appeared. "El Gran Mojado, what are you doing here?" someone in the crowd wanted to know.

"Fool. He is going north, of course." Everyone knew his story. His manifest destiny.

"Ah," said El Gran Mojado, lifting a can of Budweiser, "But for the moment the North has come South."

"Haven't you heard? It's because of SUPERNAFTA!" someone shouted. "While you are busy going north, he's here kicking ass. And he's saying we are North, too!"

Another said, "It's all hot air what he says. What's the good of being North when it feels, looks, tastes, smells, shits South?"

"That's right! If Martians landed here, they would know. They would swim nude in Acapulco, buy sombreros, ride burros, take pictures of the pyramids, build a maquiladora, hire us, and leave."

"El Gran Mojado! Stay here and save us! Why do you want to go North and save those bastards up there?"

"He's afraid of SUPERNAFTA! He hasn't got the balls!"

"GRRRRR!" El Gran Mojado roared. He strutted to the edges of the crowds, gesticulating. Everyone backed away. "You can spread rumors of what you have heard, but it is what you see and hear for yourself that matters. You can see me! I have come to you! But who has seen this SUPERNAFTA anyway? Anyone?"

A murmur ran through the crowd. No one had actually seen the wrestling giant. "We have seen his picture. His posters are everywhere. They say his silver clothing is made of titanium. His hair is on fire, and he has the power to duplicate, even triplicate, himself. And he is twice your size. You are a skinny old man compared to him!"

"A picture can be made to look like anything. That's why you never see pictures of me, yet everyone knows El Gran Mojado. I," he beat his chest, "am a vision in your very minds!"

"What good is a vision up against something like SUPERNAFTA? When he appears, where will you be? In our heads?"

"I have made a challenge to this super-fake no one has ever seen. If he is indeed the fighter his posters declare, then he will find me. Me, El Gran Mojado! He will come to where I am, like a true warrior, and fight to the death!" El Gran Mojado gestured widely. His voice reverberated everywhere even long after he was silent. The cocks shifted in their canvas bags or crowed like crazy from their cages. No one could mistake the intention of his words. He continued,

Have you forgotten 1848 and the
Treaty of Guadalupe Hidalgo?
With a stroke of the pen,
México gave California to the gringos.
The following year,
1849,
everyone rushed to get the gold in California,
and all of you Californianos who were already there
and all of you indígenas who crossed
and still cross the new border
for a piece of the gold have become
wetbacks.
My struggle is for all of you.
El Gran Mojado derives his great strength
from the noble hearts of his people!
Let's see if this SUPERSCUMNAFTA is not a

coward!
He is only concerned with the
commerce of money and things.
What is this compared to the great
commerce of humankind?
His challenge is doomed to failure!
So be it!
He will know where to find me.
All of you,
his finger threatened the crowd,
will point the way.

The crowd and its menagerie of birds parted a path northward, and El Gran Mojado disappeared.

"It will be the greatest battle ever witnessed!" The declarations were immediate and exaggerated.

"Imagine! Two great champions to the death!"

"I will wager everything on El Gran Mojado!"

"But I have heard this NAFTA has a secret hidden weapon. It will not be a clean fight."

"This NAFTA will draw blood."

"A fight not to be missed!"

"A historic event."

"If I see nothing in this life, I will see this fight!"

In a moment a great turbulence had been created. Already, it was being billed as the Greatest Fight of the Century: El Contrato Con América. And the others would also be there, superheroes and supervillains alike: Super-Barrio, La Chingada y El Gran Chingón, Super-Migra, Super-Ilegal, Super-Chicano, Super-Gringo, and La Raza Cósmica.

And the crowd, lusting for battle and blood, moved North with its Latin birds and American beers.

How does this novel portray the problems and concerns of a cultural community?

- Theme of interconnectivity
- Categorizing cultures when celebrating cultural diversity

THURSDAY:

The Eternal Buzz

1. What imagery is most powerful? How does it relate to the idea of cultural oppression and dominance?

2. what did you learn about the use of setting to depict social standing?

Assignment
1-2 paragraph summary of novel
Brief discussion of primary themes

CHAPTER 22:

You Give Us 22 Minutes *The World*

The world teeter-tottered. That was as near as Buzzworm could define it. Whoa. Maybe this twenty-four-hour attachment to the waves was doing it. Doing it to his brain. But, on a scale of reality to substance abuse, it was definitely the vision thing. Time stood still momentarily. Time stood still eternally. Whatever it was doing, it was standing. Just standing. Buzzworm was sure of that. Second hands on the watches never moved. Seconds on LCD displays neither. Twelve noon just standing there. It could be one watch might not be in sync, but not all the watches. Actually, watches weren't the real tip-off: radio stations on every dial were holding their notes, their words, their voices, their dead air. Just holding. Howard Stern saying sex like seeeeeeeeeeeeeeeeeeeeeeeex forever but never getting to the x. Reminded Buzzworm of the sportscasters on Mexican radio doing the goooooooooooooooooooooal thing. Then there was some call-in cop talking about an assault with a deadly weapon and *this individual, this individual, this individual, this individual, this individual* like a broken record; coulda been an entire population of individuals. Jazz station had Miles blasting his piston at an eternal and breathless high C wanting to break your drums, your amps, your resolve. It kept on keeping on. Maybe Miles coulda done it anyway without time standing on it. Buzzworm didn't know, but it filled his head and his chest with a long hurt. And then there were those stations with the dead air like a dead hum, a buzz: the eternal buzz.

Then it was back to normal-like. Baca Boyz calling their sisters, "Baby-girl! Nicole of Paramount got her a birthday today! Happy Birthday, baby-girl! And have we got some faxes today. You all faxin' in your hellos. Got one here arriving now from La Puente! Another from West Covina! You all gonna get free passes to the Power event. Yeah, tell me about it!"

Buzzworm thought about Nicole of Paramount. Chicana with maroon-brown twenty-four-hour lipstick don't come off even at Raging Waters. Even if she's kissin' a storm outside the Power event. Did she run with a girl crew? How old was she today? Did she know she got some extra eternal buzz minutes on her life for free today?

Buzzworm caught the news. *You give us twenty-two minutes*... First twenty-two minutes it was: *spiked* orange alert. Several oranges found to be laced with unidentified chemical. Possibly extra vitamins. Possibly alcohol. Possibly marijuana. Possibly Prozac. Public alerted to report and turn in any suspicious fruit. No reports of polluted orange juice, concentrates, or orange derivative products. Several Van Nuys supermarkets reportedly removing all fresh oranges from consumer stock. Sunkist and Dole orange reps to make public statement at 5:00 p.m. Pacific Daylight Time. FDA investigators, local Health Department inspectors, and FBI agents working around-the-clock.

But the talk shows were saying things like, "Fresh-squeezed orange juice. Some people have probably forgotten the taste of it. One orange every day, freshly squeezed, will clear up the complexion in one week. By the end of two weeks, your insecurities will be gone; you'll be getting dates and going to parties."

Next twenty-two minutes, the new update came in: spiked orange *scare!* Deaths of two Van Nuys residents traced to spiked oranges. Three hospitalized. Oranges now believed to be injected with a very lethal form of some unidentified chemical. Buzzworm shook his head. Maybe it wasn't just Van Nuys. Maybe Margarita and the little homey had made it home the same way. But they weren't the names on the news. 'Course they'd probably never be. They got under some other statistics. When the class action suit came 'round, they'd be left behind. Buzzworm stopped in his tracks and did what he rarely did— dropped the earphone from his ear. Class action his ass. Margarita's words came back. *One free naranja imported from Florida.* He'd given it to that righteous little homey. Where did Margarita get her oranges? Where did any of the street vendors get their oranges? They had them piled in bags on shopping carts or in the backs of trucks. They were on every street corner, every freeway off-ramp, every intersection. A bunch of oranges got smuggled in and took a detour. Some detour. A dead end was what. And it wasn't just Van Nuys.

But the talk shows were saying, "Joining Weight Watchers changed my life. I lost thirty pounds in one month. Now I'm a new person. I have lots of energy and renewed self-confidence. I just like myself better and feel happy now. And one of my own secrets is to have a tall glass of fresh orange juice every morning . . ." Do O.J. and be healthy, wealthy, and wise.

But, next twenty-two minutes it was: *illegal* orange scare. Chemical breakdown of spiked substance in oranges traced to cocaine. Highly concentrated liquid form. A single orange could be worth maybe one kilo.

Buzzworm started running. He was going to have to make the rounds quickly. Going to have to find all the Margaritas and the Margaritos on all the street corners and ramps in the city. Check out the distribution patterns on oranges.

Talk shows were still talking, "Fresh O.J. will end your problems with arthritis, give you a mental boost, increase your muscular surface naturally."

But Buzzworm could already sense the consequences. The entire LAPD was lined up on either side of the Harbor Freeway readyin' up to catch any homeless wantin' to flee the canyon. They were all preoccupied with looking down on that situation like a bunch of buzzards. Meanwhile, every peddler in the orange business was seeing his merchandise confiscated at gunpoint. Some were slugging it out. Some knew the value of the merchandise and were finding ways to hide it. Oranges were being shoved under floors, into holes dug in the ground, under the hoods of cars and into ice cream carts, into every available crevice out of sight. Before Vons or Lucky could blink, their oranges disappeared. They went out the front by the bags and out the back by the crates. You mighta thought it was only gangs or druggies or the mafia going after them, but it was everybody, like it was a lottery. Housewives and yuppies, environmentalists and meat-eaters, hapkido masters and white guys in dreds with Nirvana T-shirts—all going for the spiked oranges. How badly did a person need a screwdriver? How badly a psychedelic orange? What were they thinking? Buzzworm wanted to know. Didn't they hear about the two people dead? Others in critical condition? Didn't they understand the addictive effects of drug use? Couldn't they just say no? Couldn't they dare to say no?

Maybe not. Talk shows were talking about, "You take orange peel and grind it up, add one tablespoon olive oil, one tablespoon Vaseline Intensive Care. Spread it over your shoulders, your body, everywhere. Then you bake yourself in the sun fifteen minutes. It's an instant tan you women can wear with strapless dresses or you brawny men in tank tops." Avoid ingesting; just use topically.

But it was already too late. You give us twenty-two minutes was coming in loud and clear: *illegal alien* orange scare. Like Margarita said, imported. But not from Florida. Rainforest Russian roulette oranges. Unidentified natural hallucinogen plus traces of rare tropical snake venom. You got high, saw God, and got killed.

Talk shows never stopped. "Scientists are reviewing evidence that regular doses of vitamin C during a human lifetime may directly affect genetic formation in areas of intelligence and physical strength."

"But now that O.J. is out of the question, Tiffany, what do you suggest?"

"Well, fresh is best. You could go to tomatoes and pineapple, but here's an insider tip: passion fruit. It's always had more concentrated amounts of vitamin C, plus it has the benefit of soothing your nerves naturally."

Next twenty-two minutes: *Death oranges.* Minute doses produce exquisite high. Exquisite death. DEA was now involved. Mexican government, too. Everybody down South being looked into.

Oranges went underground. The word was emphatic: All oranges were suspect. And deemed highly toxic. Waste companies hauled the rotting stuff by the tons to landfills. Environmental experts declared them toxic waste. Sniff the chalky fungus and you could be dead fast. The poison could leach into the water system. Fruit flies could spread it too. County Ag Inspector Richard Iizuka said it loud and clear: See an orange? Call 911.

Talk show Tiffany didn't miss a beat: "That's right. Passion fruit is all the rage. Minute Maid is selling it under the trade name, *Passion*™. Make the change now. *Passion*™."

Buzzworm scratched his head. Looked like you could take out an entire industry in just twenty-two minutes flat. Nothing to it. Why should he be surprised? Put the crack industry in in 'bout the same amount of time. Problem was, was taking longer than twenty-two minutes to take it out.

He looked up, up at his palm trees catching the light, fluttering like tinsel, unlike any other trees. Called his city tinsel town. Wasn't because of the palms, though. Palm trees looked like they were all bending, all stretching their necks in the same direction. Pointing. Trying to say something.

Buzzworm thought he'd seen everything. But lately things were going off in their own direction. And some people were looking down the barrel of a deadly party in the center of an orange. Looking for the eternal buzz.

CHAPTER 23:

To Labor *East & West Forever*

Arcangel shoveled more sand and cement into the wheelbarrow, tossed in another bucket of water, and mixed the heavy gray slop with a hoe. Rodriguez came to check the consistency of the mixture and nodded, "You have some experience in this business I can see." He pointed at the unfinished brick work. "How are you at walls?" He smiled and shook his head. "The other day,

I must have been ill. I could swear that this wall that I planned very carefully to be straight was suddenly curved. I ran my hands across it like this, and it seemed to have this great dip in it, all along here." Rodriguez pointed it out to Arcangel. "Can you believe it? Impossible! It's perfectly straight. Maybe it's my eyes."

"Is that so?" Arcangel pulled the wheelbarrow heavy with wet mortar up to the wall and wiped his brow with the sleeve of his shirt.

Rodriguez scooped the stuff up with a trowel, carefully placed a brick and tapped it lightly. He continued, "Everyone knows my work around here. 'If you want a straight wall, call Rodriguez,' they all say. Imagine. I must be going crazy. Too much praise is a bad thing. You begin to doubt yourself."

Arcangel nodded.

"A young journalist, a Chicano," Rodriguez waved his trowel about for special emphasis, "from the north, owns this place. Every now and then he shows up. The girl is only housekeeping for him, but she at least has brains. He must have wasted hundreds of dollars on plants and materials he brought from the north. Most of it has died, rotted, or rusted. Our climate requires hardier stuff. Finally, she has made the garden grow. And this wall, it should have been built years ago."

The two men worked side by side laying mortar and bricks with a kind of rhythm that would suggest they had labored together all their lives.

"I'm glad you came along," confessed Rodriguez. "I'm getting too old to do this work alone."

"I can only work for you today."

"Too bad. This place has work for a lifetime."

Work for a lifetime. Arcangel pondered this.

"Where will you go? A factory further north? The government has a long-range plan, but don't be fooled by that. A lot of big words about programs and production, but who does the work? They always forget the people who sweat for their bread. Unless it's an election year, there's nothing in it for people like us. No," he shook his head, "stay here with me. This," he pointed at his wall, "is work you can see." He stood back for a moment and stared proudly at the wall.

Arcangel smiled. "Yes, it is a good wall."

"Some people work with their brains. Like the journalist who owns this place. You and I, we work with our hands. But it is work just the same. Good work."

"Noble work."

"A good word. Noble." He paused to think. "You and I. We are old men. No one thinks like this anymore." Rodriguez looked sad. "My son said I am working all these years only to die."

"He was drunk," Arcangel said as if he had been there listening.

"He said poor people are doomed to work to their deaths. That we eat and drink all our earnings because anyway we will die."

"It's true. Anyway we will die."

"But I am not working to die," Rodriguez protested. "I work to live!" He looked as if he would cry. "All these years with the little I earn, I worked for my children to live. Even soldiers who labor with death, labor to live! Even my youngest son who ran away—" Rodriguez could not continue.

Arcangel sympathized. "You are right. Death is a strange excuse for poverty." Rodriguez's youngest son had run away to be a soldier and died in an ambush. Arcangel had held the dying heads of so many soldiers in his arms. Most of them were boys; they had not even seen the end of a second decade. They foolishly believed.

Believed in everything:
revolution,
illegitimate uprisings,
coup d'etats,
communist takeovers,
nationalization of the private sector,
populism,
military dictatorships,
leftist dictatorships,
destabilization tactics,
covert operations,
inflationary policies,
corruption,
unionism,
cultural assimilation,
development, and
progress.

Whatever it was, they believed.

"He was only a boy." Rodriguez shook himself out of an old grief. "You must be hungry. We will stop here for now." Arcangel watched the man's stooped walk to the shade of the orange tree. He sat at the base of the tree and rummaged through the contents of a small bag, beckoning Arcangel. "It's nothing much. Tortillas. Some fruit."

Arcangel walked over with his great suitcase that never left his side. He opened it and produced the gifts he had received the previous day at the market: tomatoes, onions, potatoes, corn, limes, cookies, fresh tortillas, small sacks of grain, cans of condensed milk, and the orange. The orange seemed to sleep swaddled in a soft bed of shirts in one corner of the suitcase. Arcangel gently patted it.

Rodriguez looked on with surprise. "You are a walking market."

"No. I am a walking kitchen," he smiled, producing a pan and a knife and a portable gas stove. He pointed at the stove. "This is American. I got it in Nicaragua. Left behind with the garbage in a mountain camp." In a matter of minutes, he produced a hot meal for the astonished bricklayer. "I have been traveling a long time."

"How long?"

"Five hundred years."

"Impossible," Rodriguez laughed at the joke.

"Perhaps. I have seen more than a man may ever wish to see." He closed his eyes for a long moment. He could see again

the woman who sold him the nopales in the plaza
and this Juan Valdez picking Colombian coffee
and Chico Mendes tapping Brazilian rubber.

He could see

Haitian farmers burning and slashing cane,
workers stirring molasses into white gold.
Guatemalans loading trucks with
crates of bananas and corn.
Indians, who mined tin in the Cerro Rico
and saltpeter from the Atacama desert,
chewing coca and drinking aguardiente to
dull the pain of their labor.
Venezuelan and Mexican drivers
filling their trucks with gasoline,
their cargos of crates
shipped by train,
by ship, and
by air and
sent away,

far away.

He saw

the mother in Idaho peeling a banana for her child.

And he saw

lines of laborers gripping
soiled paychecks at the local bank.

All of them crowded into his memory in a single moment. Now there was this bricklayer Rodriguez and his family as well. Everyone was so busy, full of industry. But Eduardo Galeano had himself explained to Arcangel that

this industry was like an airplane.
It landed and left with everything—
raw materials,
exotic culture, and
human brains—
everything.
Everybody's labor got occupied in the
industry of draining their
homeland of its natural wealth.
In exchange
they got progress,
technology,
loans, and
loaded guns.

Arcangel saw his thoughts as a poem scratched across the unfinished wall, but Rodriguez interrupted. "This is very good," he complimented the chef. "You will come to my home tonight, and I will also fill your belly with good food."

"You remind me of a man I once knew in Colombia," Arcangel reminisced.

"Did he lay bricks?"

"No. He was a gravedigger."

"Well," Rodriguez shrugged. "He too worked with the earth."

Arcangel thought about this. "José Palacios. I worked for him for six years. In six years, we buried six hundred bodies. Side by side, they formed a line of dead longer than this wall. We dragged them out of the Cauca River. Bloated bodies. The stench was terrible, but no one came to claim them. We marked the graves N.N. No nombre."

"A war?"

"Yes, the war over an innocent indigenous plant."

"The traffic," Rodriguez nodded. "It all goes north to the gringos. If they want it so much, why don't they plant it in their own backyards? Make it in their own factories?" He stood up suddenly with anger. "How many people run along this road. Every hand is greased. My first son. Such a fool. Such a big shot. He used to carry a gun and fly a plane. He used to bring things: hard liquor, cigarettes, perfumes. I made him take it all away. It was only a matter of time. They shot him in the head through the window of his car. He used to brag to me, 'Drugs,' he said, 'have come to kill our poverty and marry our politics. It's a very powerful marriage. Join the honeymoon while it lasts.' My first son was not a bad boy; he was only foolish— another stupid hero of a narcocorrido. He didn't want to be poor anymore."

Rodriguez returned to his work. Only work could make him forget that he only had one son left, and that son drank every night and scoffed at his work, at his straight walls, his careful laying of one brick after the other, because after all he would die, and the bricks that depleted the earth did so to make room for his body. Two bricks for his head, two bricks for his hands, two for his feet. Knowing this, Arcangel set the bricks with special care, blessing and naming each brick, reconstructing Rodriguez's dying body again and again into that very straight wall. But it was a strange mumbling mantra, and Rodriguez, peering over the wall at his laboring partner, thought Arcangel might be chanting in Latin:

Trade balances and stock market figures.
Negatives and positives.
Black and red numbers.
Percentages and points.
Net, gross, and dividends.
IMF debts.
Loans and defaults.
A twenty-eight billion dollar trade deficit?
Devaluate the peso.
A miracle!
No more debt for the country. Instead
personal debt for all its people.
Free trade.

Arcangel remembered seeing the slain body of Emiliano Zapata, killed in an ambush by a vain young colonel named Jesús Guajardo and thrown across a mule as it passed through Zapata's homeland, through the Villa de Ayala from the Hacienda Chinameca on April 10, 1919. By the end of the day, when the body was flung to the ground and peeled from the dirt to reveal the familiar and handsome features—the dark brows and thick mustache, Arcangel recalled—it was just another body, its blood thickened to clay. Now, from the mountains of Chiapas at the border of Guatemala, that very name had been reinvoked by the people who called themselves Ch'ol, Lacandón, Tzeltal, Tzotzil, Tojolabal, and Zoque.

Tierra y Libertad.
Revolution reinvented,
but consistently the same:
the hard labor of people at the bottom
with nothing,
nothing,
to lose.

It was only political poetry, but he couldn't help it. It was always there carousing around in his brain. Such a nuisance. Arcangel made several trips with the wheelbarrow hauling bricks. Then he stopped to mix another slop of mortar. Rodriguez worked with a trowel quietly and carefully at one end of the long perfect wall. Arcangel wondered if it wasn't a wall that could conceivably continue east and west forever. Labor for a lifetime.

CHAPTER 24: **Dusk** *To the Border*

Rafaela felt Sol in her arms. She encircled him with every part of her body that could possibly touch his and rocked him there between the rows of corn. Sol squirmed; after all, it was hot, and he was slippery with sweat.

"Whatever is the matter?" Doña Maria looked on with her bundle of corn.

"I just missed him."

"It's been less than five minutes."

"No. It's been an eternity. I can't explain it. I really can't." Rafaela looked back on the house and clutched the bag with the baby cooler. Terror rose in her throat again. "We really need to get back." She needed an excuse and blurted out, "Rodriguez will be around soon."

"Isn't it rather late for him? Time for supper soon. Don't forget your corn."

"There's only the two of us." She grabbed three husks almost impolitely, clutching them and Sol to her breast, shouldering her bag and hurrying away.

Doña Maria trotted after them, panting, "What about your telephone call?"

"It can wait," she waved the old woman back and then stopped anxiously. "Will you be all right?"

"Yes, of course." Doña Maria was confused, but she said, "Bring Sol back for a little television."

Rafaela did not know what to say. She had come home to México to be by herself, to be somewhere familiar. Everything was as she had always known it to be and yet nothing was. Had she never noticed? This elasticity of the land and of time. This sensation of timelessness, of yawning distances, of haunting fear, of danger. Perhaps it was just here, just as Rodriguez had noted, just at Gabriel's place. And ever since the orange—that orange—had disappeared. Perhaps if she could get back to her parents in Culiacán. Perhaps if she had been able to call Bobby. And why had she taken this thing from Doña Maria's refrigerator? There was no turning back now. Finally, she understood what Bobby always felt: this fear of losing what you love, of not feeling trust, this fear of being someplace unsafe but pretending for the sake of others that everything was okay.

Rafaela ran with Sol across the highway and into the house. With panic but firm resolve, she dumped Gabriel's water faucets from their box and stuffed the cooler into the newspaper and foam popcorn, repackaging the whole thing. She could feel the weight of the ice and chilled liquid within, but she didn't dare look. Adjusting Sol in the strong cradle of her right arm and the canvas bag with its boxed contents in her left, Rafaela wiped her brow on the sleeve of her cotton blouse and crossed the highway heading south toward the hotel.

At the corner of Gabriel's property where Rodriguez had abandoned his masonry, an old man squatted against an old fig tree and slept at the side of the road. He was leaning into a large old suitcase and snoring. The dappled shade wandered over his features, moist with humidity. A snake coiled itself like a cat at his side. It was a peaceful sleep. Rafaela stared at him for a moment and noticed that he seemed strangely tangled in the wisp of a thread. It was indeed the same thread, the same line that she had noticed before running tautly across Gabriel's property and through the only ripening orange in the grove. Perhaps the line was so thin, so transparent, he did not notice it. He did not seem encumbered by the fact. The strands wound about him gracefully, tenderly, like strands of silk hair. Rafaela peered into the man's open palms and gasped slightly at the length of his life line. He stirred in his dreaming.

It was getting late. Rafaela hurried on to the hotel to dispatch the box. The bus would be there soon to pick up the afternoon mail.

Sol was still clinging to his corn. He ran back and forth across the tiles in the lobby. Rafaela watched him from the telephone and listened to her own voice on the message machine in L.A. What would she say to Bobby on the machine? What could she say in two minutes or less? Should she tell him where she was? How could she explain her situation? What would he understand? He must be furious with her. And Sol. Sol belonged to Bobby too. Eventually she would have to bring him back. Eventually they would have to talk this out. And there was so much to explain, so many things she needed to tell him. Suddenly she really missed Bobby; he would know what to do. But Rafaela listened to her own voice on the machine in L.A. She hung up and dialed again.

"Gabriel?"

"Rafaela. I've been waiting for your call today."

"I'm sorry. Doña Maria's phone was occupied. Her son, Hernando—"

"I see."

"Rodriguez has been working on the wall on the south side of your property. He's very upset."

"Why?"

"The wall does not seem straight. At least the last time I saw it."

Silence.

"But I don't think you want him to do it over, do you?"

"What will it cost me?"

"Gabriel, maybe your property is not straight. I don't think it's Rodriguez's fault."

Rafaela heard Gabriel change the subject to hide his exasperation. "Did the faucets arrive?" he queried.

"Yes. How much did you pay for them?" Rafaela wanted to know.

"Enough."

"They're made in México, you know."

"Can't be."

"Gabriel, what is the Tropic of Cancer? I mean I know what it is, but what *is* it?"

"A line. An imaginary line."

"Gabriel, I'm afraid."

"Why?"

"Doña Maria's son Hernando. Do you know him?" Rafaela asked.

"No."

"He's an importer/exporter I think. Oranges and something else."

"Is this important?" Gabriel seemed to ask in his reporter's tone of voice, then more anxiously, "Is he bothering you?"

"I overheard a conversation. About—"

"What?" Gabriel coaxed.

"Body parts. Kidneys for a two-year-old. Do you think . . . ?" Rafaela clutched her throat. Her thoughts were unspeakable.

"What?"

Rafaela heard the screech of the car tires outside before she saw the shadow of the black Jaguar. She spoke quickly, "I'm sending you a package. I was afraid to look. Maybe it's nothing, but maybe—" She had only seen the man's eyes. He had only seen hers. But she could not be sure what eyes could betray. "I've got to go. Maybe we'd better tell Bobby. Would you?"

"Raf—"

Rafaela ran across the lobby, swooping upon Sol and scuttling with him toward the back exit. She ran through the crumbling brick patio and between the refuse of junk cars hidden behind. Where to go? Her heart raced in panic. Why had she taken the thing? Gabriel's place would not be safe, but it was the only place she had. Perhaps she should gather their belongings and close up Gabriel's house. She and Sol could flag down the next bus to Culiacán or even Tijuana. Perhaps.

Her eyes searched the most lush part of the terrain for a hidden route toward Gabriel's place. Scanning the horizon, she saw Rodriguez's unfinished wall, the fruit trees, and the orange tree at the edge of Gabriel's land, even the broken trellis of wild roses and a portion of the house. But it could not all be this close to the hotel. Even without the burden of Sol in her arms, it was at least a twenty-minute walk, and yet Gabriel's place seemed to be creeping up, step by step toward the hotel.

And then Rafaela saw him: the old man with the large old suitcase and the transparent strands of silken thread wound about him. The thread glistened in the now waning light as if wet, but the old man seemed oblivious as he stepped with his slow but sure gait. Rafaela ran towards him. "Señor, where are you going?"

"To take the bus. I hear it stops at that hotel."

"Where will you go?"

"North."

"Culiacán?"

"Farther."

"To the border?"

"Yes."

Rafaela looked back. Indeed the bus with its Tres Estrellas de Oro was trundling up the highway. The black Jaguar remained parked before the hotel. "The bus is here. Such a coincidence. We are going that way too."

Rafaela followed the old man, up into the bus on the skirts of the tangled threads. The bus was already full except for two seats at the very back next to the toilet. She could see the hotel manager bringing the mail bag. Her box must certainly be in there. As the bus pulled away, she turned to look out the window. A man was running toward the black Jaguar. His eyes were obscured by expensive dark wire glasses which he now removed. Rafaela saw his eyes and hugged Sol close to her in the seat and leaned against the old man.

The old man turned to her and smiled. "The boy likes corn I see."

"Yes." The three ears of corn fell into her lap. She still had them despite everything. "Would you like one?" Rafaela handed him an ear as if it were very natural to travel north with raw corn.

The man opened his luggage. "Thank you. It will keep my orange company."

Rafaela peered into the strange mess of his suitcase, an assortment of colorful costumes, steel cable, hooks, books, and papers. The words on a flyer caught her eye: *The Ultimate Wrestling Championship: El Contrato Con América. No holds barred. El Gran Mojado meets the challenger* SUPERNAFTA. The suitcase should have been extremely heavy; yet he carried it as if it were filled with air. As he said, the orange was neatly confined in a bed of clothing to one corner. He placed the corn next to it. Rafaela knew the orange as she knew the face of her child. The strands of the line extended from two ends of the orange, reaching out of the suitcase, tangling about Arcangel, and slipping across the bus, through the windows, and across the land. On either side of the bus, the landscape was continually familiar to Rafaela, as if they were moving but not moving. To the left, Gabriel's land and the unfinished wall stretched and slid along, never leaving the bus to its northern destination, like a child clinging to its mother's skirt. *The Tropic of Cancer,* she whispered to herself, tentatively touching the delicate strand protruding innocently from the suitcase. She looked at the old man for an answer, but his eyes turned under their heavy lids toward a sleeping dream.

Eventually, the dusk settled in its graying tones across everything, and behind, the black Jaguar followed but never caught up.

CHAPTER 25: **Time & a Half** *Limousine Way*

The line was dead. I tried to reconstruct the conversation onto my notepad just as I had heard it. What I said. What Rafaela said. It was a dumb conversation; hardly worth it. Something in her voice made me take it down. Like the reporter I am. There was something there to decipher. It wasn't because throughout the hassle of the day, hers was the only call I really hoped to get, craving her voice—that touch from the south. I knew the thing in her voice wasn't her affection for me. But in the end she said maybe we should tell Bobby. *We* tell Bobby *what?* Well, I could fantasize, but as Emi would say, it was all crap. No. Something in my guts told me Rafaela was in trouble.

At the same time I wanted this excuse to rush down south, I had to admit my resentment at the timing. Big stories were breaking all around town. My homeless series was practically spread all over the front page, not to mention the freeway canyon. And my homeless conductor was conducting. The news never stopped; it just kept coming twenty-four hours a day. It seemed that for every hour I worked on it, there was another half-hour hidden away that I had to catch up to. Time and a half. If I could punch a clock, I could make some real money. In this case, I was under time compression. The news stretched; time compressed. Meanwhile, I followed Buzzworm like a beagle, sniffing into every campfire, car, hovel or the remains of, every stewing pot in every soup line, every ring of shopping carts, every newspaper bedding.

"*Les Miz* à la L.A.," Emi called it. "Like they spilled out the Shubert. If only they could pack 'em back in."

"These are real people," I reminded her pompously.

"Real people paid sixty a pop to see unreal people." She pointed at the TV. "If you don't mind the commercials, you get to see real people here for free."

"It's obscene."

"Which? Paying or not paying?"

"Both."

"You're such a purist. You think people should only get the news by reading it."

"You think news is entertainment."

"It isn't?" Emi smiled her smile. "Gabe, you want it to be like B-complex stress vitamins or eating veggies."

"The stuff of informed responsible decision making. Citizenship." It was disgusting. I sounded like *MacNeil/Lehrer.*

"That's not news, Gabe."

She was right. News was the spice of life. The thing that broke up the day. News was change. Gossip. I loved news. I worked for news. I lived news. News was my life. Who was I kidding?

"Hey." Emi remembered something. "When I said *Les Miz,* I wasn't being facetious you know. Seriously."

"I know."

"About the singing?"

"Yeah, I was down there. They're all singing, humming. I mean it's sporadic, but yeah. Homeless singing, harmonizing. Something."

But later in the day, Buzzworm was more emphatic: "There's a goddamn choir down here!" he reported.

"What would you say?" I asked. "Gospel? Revival?"

"If you wanna call Beethoven's Ninth revival. More like the Mormon Tabernacle I'd say. Weird. I heard even the goddamn Triforium is playing it."

"What do you make of it?"

"What do I make of it? People living in abandoned luxury cars, creating a community out of a traffic jam. There's already names to the lanes, like streets! South Fast Lane and North Fast Lane. Limousine Way—that's the off-ramp at Fifth. There's dealing down here! There's a truck could be a Seven Eleven. Got everything—beers, Cokes, even nuke you a burrito. Only thing missing's the lottery tickets. FIRST A.M.E. feeding people on the right shoulder southbound at Olympic. Hey, get this. Somebody found an espresso maker; I got a latté for fifty cents! Get us a Versateller down here, and we're cookin'! And this singing. People busting out singing. Just busting out. Some guy over here on top of a Maserati singing like he was Pavarotti. Meanwhile, the fire on the two ends of the freeway is creeping in. Saying that the blast tapped a natural pocket of gas below the freeway. Can you confirm this?"

"I'll look into it."

"Goddamn Eternal Flame. Ain't never gonna blow out. You talk about hot! Smoke covering everything like a big black tent. Is this hell?"

"Are you asking that rhetorically?"

"Balboa you fool! Hell yes!"

"Hey, what about this orange crush?" I interjected. "What's the scoop on the ground?"

"Word is oranges were supposed to be just a form of transport. Squeeze those babies and reconstitute. Sells with a slight orange zest."

"How much you figure came through?" I queried.

"Truckload at most. But who'd a thought it could be that toxic? Principle's imaginative, but acidity enhanced the poison. Sorta like fugu, that poison blowfish sashimi." I was always amazed by Buzzworm's savvy. He continued, "Bit of poison gives you a rush, see. Time goes by, and it gets stronger. Packs a bigger punch exponentially, shall we say."

"Guess they didn't figure."

"Not at all."

"Looks like transportation got crossed," I added.

"Looks like. Maybe even some DOUBLE-crossing."

"Who's involved? Who's the originator?"

"That's just it. Looks like it's C. Juárez and company."

"Damn. One hundred and one ways to move shit."

"They're moving on that meeting. It's México City or nowhere. Tomorrow soon enough for you?"

"Timing couldn't be worse," I groaned.

"Like I said, it's your call. But what about my man Manzanar?"

"He approved my copy, not that he liked it much."

"Is that so?"

"Said I wrote it with my head, not my ears." I was feeling hurt, but Buzzworm wasn't going to commiserate.

"I know what he means."

"Whaddya mean you know what he means?"

"You can't hear his music, can you?"

"What's that got to do with it?"

"Way I see it is this. Manzanar used to be a doctor. Now, he's a kind of witch doctor. He sees and hears things nobody else can. What he's doing up there is a kind of interpretation. You can't write about what you can't see nor hear." Buzzworm waxed philosophical.

"I gotta go up there and conduct?"

"Maybe."

"Bullshit."

"Look at it this way. Homeless are like the dead. You the medium. We gonna talk through you, Day of the Dead like."

I thought about this. "I don't do magic, Buzz." Like Emi said, I was strictly noir.

"Don't feel bad. Neither do I. Besides, don't need magic for no Pulitzer."

"Where're you calling from?"

"Car phone in a gold Mercedes. You just line up and take your turn." Buzzworm paused. "Now I wanna know if you got your info. So where is the LAPD? Where's the National Guard? What's the fix on this? This ain't a riot yet, but in this town we all know people value their cars above their spouses. Can't last forever."

"Seems like they're concentrating on the fire first. When the fires go out, you'll all look like Custer's Last Stand."

"Don't think there's not some thinking down here 'bout this. At the very least, they're gonna jumpstart these vehicles and make a move."

"Phone's cellular, Buzz. Better keep it to yourself. Could be a reason for letting you use it."

"You coming down?"

"Gimme an hour."

"Limousine Way?"

"Limousine Way."

I grabbed my stuff, stashed my notes in a folder. While I was talking to Buzzworm, I had been circling a word in Rafaela's conversation. It popped out of the notes on the page: *Package*. She was sending me a package. What package? One hundred and one ways to move shit. I made my decision; I would make that meeting in México City, get a reading on C. Juárez and the orange connection and take a detour to my place to check up on Rafaela. Even though Buzzworm had counseled me on the nature of hardcore news, I knew what he knew: the homeless weren't going away. On the other hand, the very tail of a conspiracy was whipping about just out of my reach; either I grabbed it now or never.

CHAPTER 26:

Life Insurance *L.A./T.J.*

The beeper goes off. Who's it gonna be? Maybe it's that postediting place in Hollywood. Go into editing some movie night and day. Trash cans get stuffed with pizza boxes and takeout. Toilet paper disappears. Toilets get clogged good with paper towels and shit. Bobby seen 'em clogged with condoms and syringes. Bobby don't ask no questions. He just comes in twice if they give him the call.

Or maybe it's the place in El Segundo makes bombs. Gotta haul out the shredded paper. Anybody ask any questions, he's got a clearance. After everything, they never figured out he's not Vietnam. Not no orphan with no connections to nothing. Orphan refugee can't be communist. Gotta be happy he's alive in America. Saved by the Americans. New country. New life. Working hard to make it. American through and through. Clearance proves it. He can haul out all the shredded documents he can carry. Doing America a favor. Doing his duty. That's it.

Anybody ask, he's legal. Casualty of the war. Responsibility of the victor, the aggressor, the big loser. Nowadays, they're saying you can go back. See the homeland. It's not a problem. Vietcong'll let you in. Everything's cheap in Vietnam. You can live there like a king. Don't he know? All the Vietnam folks owning donut shops are taking the trip. He don't say nothing. Pretends he was too little to remember. Too little to remember Saigon. Now it's a musical. Miss Saigon. Miz Saigon. Don't you miss Saigon?

Bobby misses Singapore. Only thing people know about Singapore is you can't do graffiti. Even white kids get flogged. People saying taggers here oughta get flogged too. Flog 'em big-time. Been so long, can't remember the Singapore they're talking about. Skyscrapers, rich people, business like it's never gonna stop. Maybe he shoulda never left; cleaning buildings here, cleaning 'em there. What's the diff? Well, might be being Chinese in Singapore's different than being Vietnamese in the U.S.

Somebody says, "What'd we do without you, Bobby? You saving our lives. Without you nothing gets done around here." It's an exaggeration. Bobby don't hold nothing by it. Way of saying, who's gonna clean up if it isn't you? Gonna be some other refugee needs the work. Still it's likely the job doesn't get done as good. Bobby's proud of his business, proud of his rep. He disappears, they gotta get along with something less than clean.

What day's today? The 25th. Insurance on the life due. Bobby bought himself term. Half's for the wife and son; half's for his brother. They're depending on him. It's a chunk. Not a lot, but a chunk. When he can, he'll put in for more. Pretty soon he'll be worth more dead than alive. Dead, he'll be some kind of lottery. Then again, if he never finds Rafaela and the boy, what's it gonna matter?

For now, he's gotta run. Gotta answer the beep. Turns out it's not Hollywood. Not the war machine in El Segundo neither. It's Gabriel, the Chicano reporter. Gabriel's like the li'l bro. Got an education. Like the kid brother, got consciousness about what's it to be a minority. Required course: cultural politics. Gabriel was reading Rafaela's papers for the community college. Correcting the spelling. Telling her to keep up the good work. Getting articles out of the system to put in the papers. Putting ideas into Rafaela's head. Now he's on the phone, telling Bobby he's got news about Rafaela. They better talk. Figures. Bobby like to smack him, but he better get Rafaela and the kid back first. Then he'll smack him.

Gabriel's saying how about this afternoon? Got a minute to talk? He's between assignments. Has Bobby seen the mess on the freeway? He's really busy, but—

Bobby can't do it. He doesn't say that he's got three hundred dollars to the snakehead to check out the girl cousin cross the border. Today. He's gotta run. Give it to him straight on the phone.

It's more complicated than that. Gabriel's gotta draw a map. Why's he telling Bobby this now?

Because Rafaela wants Bobby to know. At least that's what he thinks. Because he's lost contact with her. Because he's got a lot of things in the works. Someone else's got to get involved. Because there's some kind of trouble.

What trouble?

Don't know.

What's she mixed up in? Gone down to join the Zapatistas? What about the boy?

Gabriel didn't think of that.

Didn't think of that?

No.

What did he think?

Not that.

Didn't he read her papers? Bobby been reading them at night. Taking the Miraculous Stop Smoking and reading. Pile of them left on a shelf. Titles like *Maquiladoras & Migrants. Undocumented, Illegal & Alien: Immigrants vs. Immigration.* Talks about *globalization of capital. Capitalization of poverty. Internationalization of the labor force. Exploitation and political expediency. Devaluation of currency and foreign economic policy. Economic intervention.* Big words like that. Enough to get back smoking again. Maybe he's been too busy. Maybe. But it's not like he don't understand. Prop 187. Keep illegals out of schools and hospitals. They could pass all the propositions they want. People like him and Rafaela weren't gonna just disappear.

But she did.

Bobby wants to know: How's she living? She's gonna need some money.

Don't worry about that for now.

She's my family. That's my son. We don't live off no one. No one.

Listen. Reporter's gotta make a business trip to México anyway. He'll check up on Rafaela, call Bobby soon as he knows something.

Bobby unlocks The Club on the Camaro. Gonna make the ride down to T.J. Been awhile since he done it. Boy's car seat still in the back. Take him two hours if he's lucky. 5 to the 805. Pull up to San Ysidro and make the crossover on foot. Same clanging gates. Like you can't pass quietly. Can't tiptoe in or out. Indian mommas, Mixtecs, and Mayans and their kids lined up on blankets selling Subcommandante Marcos dolls, Our Lady of Guadalupe, bubble gum, and plastic cactuses. Traffic stopped up like usual. Lines of cars and trucks waiting to jump the border, moving up one at a time. Who knows what's crossing to the other side? Gifts from NAFTA. Oranges, bananas, corn, lettuce, guaraches, women's apparel, tennis shoes, radios, electrodomestics, live-in domestics, living domestics, gardeners, dishwashers, waiters, masons, ditch diggers, migrants, pickers, packers, braceros, refugees, centroamericanos, wetbacks, wops, undocumenteds, illegals, aliens.

It's time. T.J. taxi slows down at his corner. Girl's Chinese. Just like her picture, but thinner. Scared. She's staring out the window. Something in her eyes. Maybe if Rafaela could read her palms.... It's not like it's his sister. It's like it's maybe twenty years ago. Like it's him and his kid brother fresh off the boat. It's just a glimpse. But it lasts forever. Twenty years goes by in a glimpse.

CHAPTER 27:

Live on Air *El A*

"Where are you?"

"Creative Cuts."

"You're editing? What poor schlock's B celluloid are you chopping up for prime time now?"

"Gabe, Creative Cuts is my hairdresser's in Torrance. I just got a shampoo and trim. Now I'm getting a cellophane and a weave."

"Trim, cellophane, weave. It still sounds like editing."

"So how's my soft-boiled detective?"

"You'd think I'd be hard-boiled by now judging by the heat down here."

"Ouuuu. Sounds satanic. Where are you?"

"L.A.'s latest gala disaster, Angel. One more day of the locust. You said it yourself. Les Miz on the pedestrian freeway."

"There you go again trying to be part of a book. What do they all say? *El A* is *A*-pocalypse. It's bee ess I tell you. Earthquakes. Riots. Fires. Floods. It's just natural phenomena: earth, wind, fire, water."

"Sounds like a sixties band."

"Gabe, you *can't* be at a phone booth."

"No. I'm running up the tab on a cellular in a gold Mercedes."

"Can you see the *NewsNow* van from there? It's smack dab in the middle. Gabe, look around. Microwave's up at least ten feet. It's a goddamn phallus!"

"*NewsNow* van? What's it doing here? You lower it in by helicopter for the occasion?"

"A fortunate accident really. We're pumping up to CNN. Hey, I can see you now on the baby Sony. Gold Mercedes. 300SEL, isn't it? Gold package. Gold rims. Oouu. There you are, down in the middle of a true current event. Live on the air! You are the reality on TV. God I'm jealous. On the Richter scale from natural to human, what would you give this one?"

"On the Nielson, what would you give this one?"

"Listen. You're pre-empting *The Simpsons, Married with Children,* and *Margaret Cho!*"

"Oh yeah?"

"Gabe, about the orange thing. They've cleaned out the city. I was down at Farmer's Market getting cheese knishes and an espresso. Every last orange's been carted out. It's like the Chilean grape thing but bigger. Bigger than

Tylenol capsules laced with cyanide or syringes in Coke cans. Have you even heard? You're so isolated by your assignments."

"That's what I like about you. The buzz of L.A."

"And don't forget my insider scoop on the boys in the Porsche. Remember, they were eating sex-tions of oranges." Gabriel could almost see her lips move through the cellular. She continued, "Some're saying it's orange trees growing in poppy fields in Bolivia. Others say it's a dangerous tropical virus, like flesh-eating bacteria. Can you believe it? Oranges with cancer. Carves a hole in your brain in twenty-four hours. Who's gonna drink O.J. for breakfast ever again? And you thought coffee stunted your growth."

"Emi, I need a favor."

"Sure. Dump the orange marmalade? It's done. The bath salts à l'orange? Orange pekoe tea bags? Chocolate covered citrus sticks? All history. What about the Trader Joe's chewable vitamin C?"

"We're liable to get scurvy."

"Scurvy. Didn't Columbus bring that disease to the New World?"

"I'm serious about a favor. I need you to take over my beat for a few days."

"You want *me* to go down *there*?"

"We'll be in touch by phone and fax. I promise you won't have to write anything. Just take notes. Keep the details."

"Where are you going?"

"South."

"You mean Orange County? So what? They're broke. Gonna follow that Citrus man to his derivative stock brokers?"

"It's Citron."

"Citrus. Citron. O.J. What's the diff?"

"You drive me crazy. Emi, I'm going to México."

"I know you're stressed, sweetheart, but is this any time for a vacation?"

"It's not a vacation."

"Returning to your roots? Pilgrimage to the source?"

"Are you jealous?"

"Of course. Do you know what a ticket to Japan costs? Dollar to yen dropped again. Do you know what a cup of coffee at Narita goes for? If I had the urge, do I have the financial backing to even get close to my roots?"

"Emi, your roots are in Gardena. It's just a toll call."

"Whaddya want me to do?"

"Talk to my contact here. Get more on Manzanar Murakami. And just stand by."

"And you?"

"It's a hunch. Something's brewing down there, connected to stuff here. I need you to be here. I need you to help me put it together."

"I can't believe you'd leave at a time like this. That freeway story's gotta be big."

"And it's not going away. Besides, you can handle it, Angel."

Emi fumed, "I suppose I should be honored."

"One more favor. Keep a lookout for a package. Let me know if it arrives."

Emi plopped the cellular down and stared deep into the mirror before her. "Evelyn," she apologized to her hairdresser who was carefully wrapping bits of her hair into aluminum foil, "Can you do a stepped-up version? I gotta run."

By the afternoon, Emi had shed the female executive attire for dress-down jeans, Nikes, and a baseball cap, slipped her credit cards, lipstick, gum, and electronic necessities into a backpack, briefcase, and two duffel bags and traded places with Gabriel at the appointed spot on Limousine Way.

"What's with the baseball cap?" Gabriel asked.

"Bad hair day," Emi growled, dropping her belongings at his feet.

"What is all this?" Gabriel moaned at Emi's luggage.

"If I'm going to do this, I've got to be comfortable."

Buzzworm moved his stature into full prominence and took a look at Emi. "Balboa, *this* is your replacement?"

"I am not a replacement," Emi sneered. "Where did they find you? In the extra line for *In Living Color?*"

"Balboa, what we got Judge Ito's smart-assed baby sister for? And how many times a day does she change?"

Two contradictions sized each other up. There was no way in hell they could see eye to eye, but Gabriel said, "Emi, this is Buzzworm, my primo contact in the city scene. Buzz, meet Emi, friend and confidante. I know you're both going to really hit it off. This is going to be a working relationship—"

"Made in hell," acknowledged Emi.

Gabriel nervously noticed Buzzworm swiveling through the channels on his Walkman, searching for a hook. Not a good sign.

"What are you doing?" Emi sassed the Buzz-man.

"Baby sister, I'm looking for some relief. There are no vibes in here to match yours and none to counter them."

"Is he for real?"

Gabriel scratched the stubble on his goatee.

"Listen, let's get on with this." Emi cut a path for herself, crisscrossing through the messy encampment of stalled traffic and temporary housing toward the *NewsNow* van. "If you need anything, I'll be in my office." She handed Gabriel her backpack. "Would you mind?"

Gabriel slumped suddenly under the weight of the backpack and two duffel bags but motioned to Buzzworm to follow. Buzzworm sauntered behind reluctantly. "We look like a goddamn safari," he muttered. "Balboa, you would be attached to some Asian Princess."

"Buzz, trust me. The woman's incorrigible."

"You got that."

Reporters at the *NewsNow* van snapped to happy attention. Obviously Emi was a sight for sore eyes. "Well, how are we today?" she exclaimed like a nurse on duty and proceeded to empty the treasure in her bags. "Luey, have I got something for you," she motioned to the cameraman. "See? Batteries! Half dozen fresh bricks. Fire it up. We got another twenty-four hours!" For Kay Torres, on-the-scene reporter, there was lipstick and mascara and a camouflage jump suit. For Kerry, the technician, there were more batteries and cables, mikes, and a second IFB.

"I'm sorry I didn't help you with that load," Buzzworm said to Gabriel with some residual sincerity as Emi produced everything from Cokes and Big Macs to toilet paper, flak jackets, sunscreen, Bufferin, $350 in small bills, and a gallon Gatorade jug filled with gasoline.

Gabriel rubbed his shoulder. "Why didn't you tell me I could have blown up? What's this for? You planning a revolution? Besides, there's plenty of gas down here."

"It's for the van's generator. Can't take any chances. I've got to plug my stuff in, too." Emi pulled out a laptop complete with modem, connecting printer, and fax. "Luey, draw me a cable and hook us up." A second laptop, twin to the first, she pushed on Gabriel. "It's just like a typewriter, see. Except, you can talk to me." She handed him the credit card modem. "Initiation into the net by fire, Gabe. You take this to México. We're gonna boogie!"

Gabriel looked helpless.

Buzzworm shook his head. "Nope, Balboa. I guess she isn't your replacement."

Emi set her operation up on the dash, settled a thermal cup of latté in its holder and scribbled directives on yellow stickies. "Gabe, this is the pager number. This is the cellular. This is the fax. And this is the address on the net. For godssake, memorize this."

Gabriel stuffed the numbers in his pocket, propped the computer under his arm, and joined Buzzworm in the van door, staring at the action in the small monitors of this mobile tech station. Kerry, the technician, explained, "This is what's on air now. This is the view from the helicopter, and this is what we've just finished taping down here."

"Can you talk to the helicopter and pull in the view of that man on the overpass?" Gabriel pointed.

Kerry channeled up to the copter for a close-up of Manzanar.

Emi leaned back. "Gabe, you'd better go. Got a plane to catch." She pecked Gabriel on the cheek. "Don't leave me here too long."

"That's him," Gabriel pointed at the monitor and Manzanar's full face of anguished concentration.

Emi stared at that face in disbelief. She knew this face. She knew it intimately from some time in the past. She knew this very man.

Gabriel had returned the kiss, spoken his last words of good-bye, said he'd be in touch in a few hours, not to worry, thanks, thanks, take care of her, Buzz, to which Buzzworm had answered, "Who *me*? Take care of *her*?" Yeah, yeah, you know what I mean. Later. Later. By the time Emi could tear her eyes from the reality on the screen, from a real-time moment of recognition, Gabriel was on his way.

CHAPTER 28:

Lane Change *Avoiding the Harbor*

A curious moment of stasis was achieved. Not simply a rest or even a coda, but stasis. Manzanar could liken it to a crossover—the pianist's hand flowing to its destination on the opposite end of the keyboard in one breathless extending and endless motion like changing lanes, straddling the dividing line for a sweet, wistful pause before some rude awakening. Driving in darkness heightened the quality of the effect: the searching distance of headlights spilling across the highway, dimmed to hazy starpoints by adjustable rearview mirrors, following the glowing cinder of taillights, phosphorescent dashboards, and the tiny immutable interior beacon within one's mind focused on a distant point, a question mark, a destination.

Upon these matters Manzanar pondered through the warm night, gazing over the strange encampment below his perch—a trailer park akin only to a giant Arizona swap meet. TV and LAPD choppers hovered—dark angels sweeping their giant flashlights across the unpredictable terrain. Lights flickered within the cars like campfires, flickering out as batteries died. Some had managed to jumpstart the cars, revving engines, now puffing warm exhaust into the night air.

The ability to move forward or backwards was minimal. During the day, attempts were made to achieve a different parking angle; an off-roadie had pulled itself up into the ice plants. A closer proximity allowed for jump-starting with the singular advantage of operating the electrical system, of tuning radios and running interior lights and, for that matter, headlights, taillights, and turn signals for whatever good reason. There was, too, the possibility of playing CDs and tapes ransacked from glove compartments. For the second night in a row, Manzanar could see the terror reflected in the faces of people huddled in a dark van attentively listening to all twenty-four ninety-minute cassettes of a Stephen King novel narrated for Books-on-Tape.

Speculations arose as to how much fuel was required to keep an idling engine idling. How much rev to keep a battery alive. For the most part, however, energy was a minor concern, especially to those who were usually without such a luxury. Only the *NewsNow* van caught in the middle of this Sig disaster anxiously pondered, at the end of the day, the demise of its minicam batteries and the gas indicator closing on E. Maybe someone would syphon the gas in their station wagon in return for fifteen seconds live on the air. To lose even a minute of this event would be tantamount to a transmission failure during crucial testimony in the O.J. or Menendez trials. The *NewsNow* reporters hunkered down like correspondents in a dugout in Bosnia-Herzegovina, occasionally wandering out to interview someone trading a shopping cart for a Volvo, carefully exchanging the contents of one for the other, eating the earthquake supplies, tossing out curious items like 3½" diskettes, mug warmers, and copies of *Buzz*.

"Why are you throwing that out?"

"You want it?"

"What do you think it is?" the reporter asks.

"Beats me."

This long moment of stasis allowed Manzanar to drop his arms, to peel himself away from his performance, his music. It was like an out-of-body experience, better understood perhaps on an overpass in Santa Monica rather than against this rational downtown backdrop of business, bureaucracy, banking, insurance, and security exchange. However, he stood beside himself under a summer moon and saw the man he had become over the years: a strange disheveled grizzled white-haired beast of a man wielding a silver baton. The past flooded around him in great murky swirls. For a moment, he saw his childhood in the desert between Lone Pine and Independence, the stubble of manzanita and the snow-covered Sierras against azure skies. He remembered his youth, the woman he loved, the family he once had, a nine-year-old grandchild he was particularly fond of. He remembered his practice, his patients, his friends. Curiously. He remembered. The past spread out like a great starry fan and then folded in upon itself.

Encroaching on this vision was a larger one: the great Pacific stretching along its great rim, brimming over long coastal shores from one hemisphere to the other. And there were the names of places he had never seen, from the southernmost tip of Chile to the Galapagos, skirting the tiny waist of land at Panama, up Baja to Big Sur to Vancouver, around the Aleutians to the Bering Strait. From the North, that peaceful ocean swept from Vladivostok around the Japan Isles and the Korean Peninsula, to Shanghai, Taipei, Ho Chi Minh City, through a thousand islands of the Philippines, Malaysia, Indonesia, and Micronesia, sweeping about that giant named Australia and her sister, New Zealand. Manzanar looked out on this strange end and beginning: the very last point West, and after that it was all East. The inky waves with their moonlit spume stuttering against the shore seemed to speak this very truth—garbage jettisoned back prohibiting further progress.

And there was the great land mass to the south, the southern continent and the central Americas. Everything was for a brief moment fixed. Fixed as they had supposedly always been. Of course, with continental drift, the changing crust of Earth's surface had over billions of years come to this, cracked into continents, spread apart by large bodies of water. Now human civilization covered everything in layers, generations of building upon building upon building the residue, burial sites, and garbage that defined people after people for centuries. Manzanar saw it, but darkly, before it would shift irrevocably, crush itself into every pocket and crevice, filling a northern vacuum with its cultural conflicts, political disruption, romantic language, with its one hundred years of solitude and its tropical sadness.

But for the moment, a strange peace settled over the city. During the day, the AQMD gave updated reports on air quality; citizens wondered how they were supposed to get through the day without breathing. Caltrans trucks with their giant blinking indicator arrows trundled along the shoulders, oblivious as always to any confusion they might cause. Little men in fluorescent orange suits poked along the ivy and oleander for trash. Convicted taggers did social service, sluggishly painting over graffiti. Mild excitement was created over the discovery of an old *Chaka* tag hidden all these years by climbing ivy. Some kids ran over to palpate the peeling Krylon as if it were an Egyptian hieroglyph. The MTD rerouted itself across the landscape, avoiding the Harbor, tooling down parallel corridors, down Fig or Vermont. Some folks even used the Blue Line. SigAlerts continued: the usual big-rig wrecks on right shoulders, over center dividers, two-car collisions, stalled vehicles, spilled contents, slowing traffic southbound, northbound, eastbound, westbound.

At sundown, Manzanar had recognized the motorcyclist in a pink suit and pink helmet—a regular on this freeway—wending her way between lanes, waving and throwing kisses to the new occupants of hundreds of stalled vehicles. She was followed by Hell's Angels and Heaven's Devils and a rubbie or two in leather on Harleys, scouting the scene first hand, come to share a beer at the Bud truck. Two lovers had wandered down on foot; they cuddled together in a convertible Mustang tucked behind a Greyhound bus. Oblivious to the world, only their passion engulfed them

Manzanar's hand had lifted the great billows of smoke in sharps and flats, luminous clouds tinged with the fading sunset, casting beautiful shadows against the tall glass structures. Darkness followed with artless dissonance. Propellers chopped the night, their thunder following searchlights striking without discrimination. And now the great fires burned clean blue flames at either end of this dark stretch of freeway.

FRIDAY:
Artificial Intelligence

CHAPTER 29:

Promos *World Wide Web*

"It's a fascination with water, pools, and pastels. You wouldn't understand," Emi shrugged. "It's a Westside thang."

"Baby sister, don't patronize me," Buzzworm pointed. "I've seen the David Hockney retrospective. He don't come to my part of town."

"What? No light and space? No stucco and tile roofs? No shrubs, brick paths, bougainvillea? No poison oleander?"

"No," Buzzworm growled. "And no jacaranda, climbing roses, topiary, sidewalk bistros, tanning parlors, pillowed weenie-dogs, golf courses, or decaf espressos either!"

"Tsk. Tsk."

"Not to mention major supermarkets, department stores, pharmacies, medical and dental clinics, hospitals, banks, factories, and industry. In this city, you have to risk your life; go farther, and pay more to be poor."

Emi typed everything into her laptop and nodded. "I think I've got some good stuff here. What else makes you mad?"

"Don't you think it's about time to go up there and meet that man?" Buzzworm pointed to the man flailing a baton on a distant overpass.

"I'm thinking about it."

Buzzworm looked at his watches. "I wouldn't think you're the type to lose your nerve, but I could be wrong. Whenever you get good and ready, but I can't wait all day. Meantime, I got some business to take care of." He sauntered away, making necessary adjustments to his Walkman.

Emi looked toward the overpass and her assignment rhythmically swiping at the smoky sky. He looked like a priest blessing a multitude, interminably. She bit her lip. "Damn!" Of course, Emi thought, he was crazy, but she understood how denial might be a favorable attitude. Wasn't everything from Alzheimer's to schizophrenia genetic? Damn. Damn Gabe. Damn this character Buzzworm. Damn that old deadbeat on the overpass. Damn.

The funky shrill tones on the fax interrupted Emi's thoughtful ruminations. Usually fax tones were random tweets, but these had a certain melody, a melody she could not place but knew. Electronic tones representing numerical information, i.e., music. In the distance, an insane and homeless conductor thrashed in silence to the same rhythm. What in the hell was that? Fax paper spit itself out in slippery coils. *Your job (since you're down there anyway) is on-site producer. Put on the show, so to speak. Good luck. As soon as you get this fax, get on-line for chat to chat.*

Emi signed on and typed in a question, *What about program coordination?*

The message typed back, *Any prerecorded material gets edited on sight. Slash and burn to max five-minute segments. You're good at that. Live material—keep it short: three minutes with cut-tos. Keep it moving!*

But why? This is continuous live on-air public service. Who cares how long the features are? Or are we going to special updates only?

No way. This is day four. The public has been served. Sponsors are banging at the door. You see CNN *stopping their commercials? Watch your monitor! Here it comes right now!*

Emi stared at the on-air monitor. Sure enough, Tide was selling cleaner whiter brighter, and Minute Maid had wasted no time in moving on to *Passion*. She looked down from the van's window at the tattered and soiled man curled in the back seat of a Buick. It seemed to make sense. But a second commercial cut to a Buick sailing down coastal roads. The poor man next to her rolled over on his other side. Emi shrugged. Whatever. She typed in for the hell of it, *Who's watching this?*

Everyone!

Cut to station identification and . . . Buzzworm? Emi looked on. He cut an imposing figure. He had a certain charm. "Kerry?" she turned to the tech, "What do you make of this?"

"Well, Kay Torres *was* doing the interview. Guy's smooth. Conversation got going and somehow, suddenly, *he's* doing the interview. Now he's got the mike."

They watched as Buzzworm commanded the cameraman, "Luey, let's move on over here. That's it." Luis panned an apparent audience of homeless people, sitting on car tops and hoods, a few lounge chairs, and some furniture removed from moving vans. Smack dab in the middle was Kay Torres in her camouflage jump suit settled in like it was all fine with her. They were all facing the back of a pickup with three more homeless characters sitting on a beat-up sofa. Buzzworm stepped back into view and announced, "Our three guests today all have something in common . . ."

Oh my god. I'M PRODUCING THIS? Emi typed in caps.

YOU'RE ASKING US? Real-time yelled back. *HAVE YOU LOST YOUR C-DRIVE?*

Buzzworm continued, "Let's welcome: Smokey, Pick-n-Save, and Pollyanna!" Luis panned the applause.

"Kerry, talk to Luey," Emi ordered.

Kerry adjusted his headphone. "Luey, what's the deal?"

Luis answered, "So what am I supposed to do? Turn the camera off?"

Emi moaned. "Production value sucks."

Kerry quipped, "It's free."

They both watched someone with a wooden crate on his shoulders. It got plopped in front of the three guests with tin mugs of coffee and a paper cup with California poppies. Emi groaned, "With my luck, the stage crew will unionize."

"Hey, look at that," Kerry pointed. "They've got cue cards!" Sure enough, someone raised the APPLAUSE! card to an obliging audience.

Real-time screamed, *CUTTING TO COMMERCIAL NOW!*

Emi scrambled out of the van, weaved through the cars, following the path of the umbilical cable to Luey's camera. She jammed her body between Buzzworm and his motley audience. "What the hell are you doing?"

"Would you mind?" Buzzworm purred. "This is where we get comments from the audience."

"Hey," someone yelled. "Wait your turn!"

"Yeah, sit down!"

"Yeah, let B.J. finish!"

Emi eyed the oppressive crowd but feigned her always imperturbable presence. "We just cut to commercial," she spoke through her teeth to Buzzworm. "You're off the air."

"How much you wanna bet we'll be back?" Buzzworm smiled. "Listen, baby sister. I've got some other ideas. How about a cookin' show? Mama on the northbound's doing a show with her mobile hot dog stand."

"Are you serious?"

"And there's Sammy over here." Buzz pointed. "Recognize him? Used to be an actor. Maybe you're too young to remember. And Mona—" Mona sidled in and forcibly shook Emi's hand. "Yeah, Mona was a writer. Hell, we got a lot of has-beens."

Mona handed Emi two pages from a notebook. "Sorry for the poor presentation, but here's a proposal."

Emi read the heading. It was for a sitcom. "Ah, I'm being paged." She extricated herself and talked into the intercom, "Kerry? What now?"

"You better get back. Net's talkin'."

She pulled the phones off her head and jammed them on Buzzworm. "Try this instead of that Walkman. When I get back to the truck, *talk to me.* Do you hear?"

Emi scampered breathlessly back into the van and read the messages: *You got the go-ahead! Momentum is building. Phones won't stop. Who is this Buzzworm? Man's synonymous with telegenic. We might be 75 percent and climbing! Sally Jesse Raphael, bye-bye!*

Emi rolled her eyes, donned a new pair of phones, and tugged at the baseball cap. "All right, Buzzworm? Can you hear me?"

"Loud and clear, baby sister."

"Can we work together?"

"Depends."

"Kerry's gonna prompt you to the breaks."

"What's that mean?"

"Station breaks. FCC requires them."

"You mean commercials."

"That too."

"So we got a budget?"

"Can we talk about this later?"

"Poor people can't perform for nothing."

"You gotta prove this thing to me first."

"Try me for an hour, but then we're talkin' nitty-gritty."

"Oh-kay."

Cellphone rang. "Gabe? Where are you? México City? I hope you're in something four star, at least a Hilton. Something that gets CNN. Are you watching this?"

"Is that Buzz?" Gabriel queried over the cellular. "It looks like Buzz."

"Of course it's him."

"But what's he talking about? Artificial intelligence? Is that a homeless topic?"

"Oh god, Gabe, you've lost a chip."

"What?"

Emi put one ear to the audio. It was true. One of the guests stood up and announced, "For all you know, I could be a goddamn bladerunning replicant," to which the audience cheered, and he bowed several times.

The guest to the left leaned over and said, "Now if I said we ought to think seriously about wiring this entire place into the World Wide Web, that a so-called Local Area Network is traditionally designed to provide maximum capabilities, flexibility, and growth in the future, and the priority should be to achieve total saturation, i.e., e-mail functions, software delivery, database access, if I said that, you would think to yourselves, he's *intelligent*? Or his intelligence is artificial?"

The guest to the right piped, "Easy. Artificial. Artificial. Definitely robotic."

The guest in the middle asked, "Are you schizophrenic?"

"Hey," the guest to the left protested and waved some papers, "I'm just reading this shit I found in a Saturn."

Buzzworm cut in through the laughter. "We'll continue right after this commercial break. But remember, Second Baptist is collecting your donations: blankets, canned goods, and powdered milk for the kids. And look for our next special: *Homeless Vets: From the Jungles to the Streets.*"

Emi sighed. "Gabe, can you believe this? I think the world as we know it is coming to the end. Nostradamus predicted this." She was silent for a moment, "Gabe, I got a confession to make."

"What's that?"

"I had sex last night."

Pause. Breath, then, "I guess it wasn't with me."

Beat. "It was over the net."

"Net?"

"Yeah. Does that count?"

Silence.

"And there's something else. You know that homeless conductor on the overpass?"

"Manzanar?"

"He's my grandfather."

Gabriel stared at the TV screen in México City. Emi stared at it in the van. They saw the same simultaneous image, give or take for satellite lag and time code correction. Did their eyes therefore touch? Did this count?

Buzzworm's face had already been captured digitally, cut and pasted onto a cartoon body complete with Walkman and watches and palm trees batiked onto his dashiki. His new configuration sauntered over the freeway landscape, Chyroned lettering promoed his new show: *What's The Buzz?*

CHAPTER 30:

Dawn *The Other Side*

Sun-kissed:
radioactive whispers through
licking tongues blue on fire,
grinning white ash and glowing gums,
molten lips pressed, consumed.
Orange of its desire:
C pearls succulent,
health encased in sheer tissues and
lacey webs, leathery skin and fragrant oils.

The myth of Columbus:
eyeing the interrupted flight
of a moth, crossing that orange globe,
its wings—miniature sails unfurled—
skirting the edge of its curved horizon,
making his case
for a round world.

The myth of discovery:
when we—a sun-kissed people—
were watching,
from the halls of Moctezuma,
from the seat of Atahualpa,
from the fires of Patagonia,
from the song of Guaraní,
awaiting the moth's return,
searching for the great golden eyes painted
across its wings, singed irreparably, but
holding in those pupils the memory,
the sin of paradise lost,
transferred, absorbed, become
the language,
the Church,
the round world.
Mi casa es su casa.

Mi tierra es su tierra.
Mi mundo es su mundo.

Sun-kissed.
Orange of its desire.

Arcangel penned his poem on the back of an Ultimate Wrestling Championship flyer and gave it to Rafaela.

"But it's written in English," she queried, "except for—"

"Some things can't be translated," he answered.

"Is there a title?"

"Perhaps," he answered. "It is for the boy who sleeps in your lap. His name?"

"Sol."

For Sol, he wrote.

Perhaps hearing his name in his sleep, the child shifted uncomfortably, turned from his stomach but still reached to cling to a piece of Rafaela's hair. Sweat glistened from his cheeks, red and mottled with the folds and buttons of his mother's blouse. Rafaela fingered his small palm. He would have a long life. He would survive. But could she be sure?

Hot air billowed through the bus—a pumping furnace on wheels, with no respite from the sun that seemed to follow the vehicle interminably. Occasionally the pungent reek of urine flung itself from the bus toilet as did the stale odor of someone's yawn. And the aisle was crammed with standing and crouching bodies, standing and crouching all the way to the border.

"Thank you." Rafaela shifted the boy to one side, folded the paper, and tucked it into her pocket. "What is this championship?" she asked.

"A symbolic travesty at best," the old man said seriously.

"Will you see it?"

"Yes. I am traveling for that very reason." He had an elegant manner of speaking, contrary to his dress, his guaraches, the deepening tones of his skin.

"Then you are a poet?" she asked, fingering the flyer in her pocket.

"No not at all," he waved his hand. "I am merely a character in a poem."

Rafaela wondered about that, but said, "How long do you suppose we have been on this road?"

"It is hard to say."

Rafaela wanted to know if the old man knew. She asked, "Have you noticed that the scenery has not changed after all these hours of travel? That wall for example," she pointed at Rodriguez's unfinished work, "is the same wall, the very wall that encloses the house where we live. But we should have passed it hours ago."

"It would seem so, looking out these windows to either side of the road as you do. But you must look forward as does the driver. Otherwise, it is indeed tedious to see the same terrain hour after hour."

"Perhaps you are right." She looked back. The same eyes behind the same dark glasses behind the same smoked windows in a black Jaguar followed at the same distance. But beyond that, the road seemed to have accumulated more than simple traffic. A growing crowd of people walked along the shoulder. Some bore signs. Rafaela strained to read them: *El Gran Mojado! Hero of the People!* And behind them, an even stranger sight: A great church on wheels. Was it not the Basilica of the Virgin of Guadalupe? And there, the pyramids! Indeed it was the great Zócalo of México City, Tenochtitlán swelling with its multitudes, slipping like a single beast across the landscape. And behind that, what more?

Rafaela turned around in excitement wanting to confirm this vision, but the old man had fallen asleep, oblivious.

Without warning of course, the bus came to a sudden stop. Only the bus driver, who as Arcangel suggested looked forward toward their destination, had recognized the restaurant/Pemex station marked by an enormous satellite dish at the top of the plateau. Rafaela looked back anxiously. The black Jaguar stopped too. Wilted passengers tumbled out the bus wearily wandering to the toilets or to the smell of barbecued chicken. Rafaela clutched Sol to her waist and followed Arcangel closely out of the bus. She had decided deliberately to follow Arcangel when she noticed that the old man would be descending the bus with his suitcase that enclosed the orange and its tangled line. Whether proximity to the orange would provide a measure of safety or the answer to some mystery, she did not know.

Looking back at the bus, Rafaela noticed the driver executing the transfer of mail bags from the luggage compartment. The bags were thrown unceremoniously through the doors of a postal truck. Beyond the truck, she could see in the distance the driver of the Jaguar stepping from his vehicle and walking toward the toilets. Indeed, he faced some difficulty getting to the door at all. For some reason his steps veered away, and he found himself ridiculously walking in circles. Rafaela, despite her fear, watched with amusement as the villain finally rushed off in frustration to a gnarled growth of cactus and unceremoniously unzipped himself.

With some relief, Rafaela followed Arcangel to a line for asada. She said hesitantly, "I know this is an odd request, but I wonder if you would take care of my son, I mean, in case anything should happen to me on this trip."

"What are you worried about?" Arcangel queried the mother as he piled his plate of asada with radishes and green onions.

"I am not sure, but will you promise?"

"Yes, of course. Of course. If it will make you feel better. To be honest with you, I am very good with children," he reassured her as if mothers made such requests every day.

They walked together with their plates of chicken and asada, salsa and tortillas. Arcangel put his large suitcase on the ground, and the three of them shared a seat on it. "You see, it's very useful as furniture."

Rafaela folded a soft tortilla around a tender piece of chicken for Sol and nodded. She saw the frustration in the face of the hungry villain who could not push his body past an invisible barrier. His confusion turned to anger. He ripped away his dark goggles as if they were the failed magic through which he had lost control of his world.

When they had finished their meal, Arcangel opened his suitcase and removed a small bundle slightly larger than his palm and wrapped in cloth. "Perhaps you will have use for this?" He handed it to Rafaela.

Rafaela pulled the cloth away, the long cotton wrapping uncovering a small pocketknife. Its silver handle was inlaid with turquoise and mother-of-pearl. "It's very beautiful. I really couldn't accept."

But Arcangel wasn't listening. He had also removed a stack of Ultimate Wrestling flyers from his suitcase which he passed out to the passengers and clients at the rest stop. Rafaela watched the tired nods of those who received the flyer change to excitement. Pretty soon people were toasting their Cokes and Tecate over the possibility of seeing the greatest fight the world would ever witness. Rafaela wondered about this; she had been away too long. How strange that a mere border could close the doors on the current events of one's home. Everyone seemed to know this El Gran Mojado.

Rafaela, watching the villain imprisoned for whatever reason several hundred yards away, wrapped the pocketknife in its cloth, and stuffed it in her pocket. She looked wistfully south only to see Sol skipping aimlessly in that direction. "Sol!" she screamed in horror as the boy danced farther and farther away. She ran after him, but Sol thought it was a chasing game and zigzagged happily around and around the trunk of a sweeping palo verde. "Stop! Sol! Come back. No. No!" The boy scurried away.

Now the villain of the Jaguar watched for his chance. He crouched in the dust ready to snatch the boy, but Sol was suddenly stopped in his tracks by music and clapping. Arcangel was juggling the ears of corn, the orange, and various sizes of colored balls. Sol watched with fascination the menagerie of items flying from the old man's hands and ran back north. But Rafaela had missed catching the boy in her frantic chase, skidding perilously south. The strong hand of the villain reached out and clutched her arm, covered her screams, pulled her away.

Arcangel employed Sol to put the juggled objects away in his suitcase one by one, gently nodding in Rafaela's direction. The last object was the orange which Sol felt unable to relinquish for a long moment. Rafaela's eyes pleaded from afar. Arcangel took the boy by the hand and stepped lightly into the bus.

Rafaela, forced into the body of the Jaguar, saw the delicate strand of line straggle with the old man and Sol into the bus and reassert itself through the bus and across the road. The bus's motor gunned to a start, spitting behind it a gust of black smoke, and moved slowly away. And Rafaela saw the sun above following the bus in its interminable noontime, and with it went the sweltering afternoon, the listless evening, the warm dark night, the starry midnight, leaving behind a cruel dawn.

CHAPTER 31:

AM/FM *FreeZone*

Buzzworm had headquarters set up semipermanently in the gold Mercedes. It was the central location, not the digs. Cellphone didn't stop. Messages were piling up. Pager was going every five minutes. Mona was the secretary 'cause she could write. She told Buzzworm there was a reason she sat in the driver's seat. He said, knowing her habits, it was a blessing this thing wasn't going nowhere. He didn't razz her too much; she was pretty good on the job. But he was needing some duplication service, meaning he was needing some self-duplication. Situation was needing a dozen Angels of Mercy.

"Where'd you find this bozo?" Buzzworm propped the phone to the shoulder and leaned back into the leather.

Homey on the other end said, "1-800 number advertisin' your show, brother."

"Don't you know no 1-800 lawyer can be up to any good?"

"Got a brother point five and a motorbike."

"That a workman's comp or a car accident?"

"One or the other."

"I know the brother. Half went to pay the lawyer. Other half's child support, and he's still owing. Motorbike's only thing left."

"So what do I need? A lawyer to beat off another lawyer?"

"'Bout says it. What sort of fix is this?"

"Crips and Bloods. Making a truce. We made a contract. Make it legal binding."

"What you need a contract for?"

"Gets it on paper. Gets respect. Like we corporate-like."

"Crips, Inc.? What's this? Some kinda merger?"

"First up, we were gonna do a joint CD. Talk mean, 'bout blowin' off some slob's head. Make us some money. And then after gettin' it all out (watchu call it, like therapy?), it was just we gonna stop the shootin'. Gonna respect the territory."

"Yeah?"

"Then, question is what's the territory? See we gotta define the territory. Like who gets Van Nuys or what side of the Westside."

"You consult a Thomas Guide?"

"How'd you know? Attorney got it all marked up, annotated in writing."

"So when the LAPD taps an incident, they can go direct to your map, figure who's jurisdiction and peg the correct gang?"

"Hey, it's not even about bangin'."

"It's about trust?"

"It's about how come the map's wrong? It's about shrinkin' and expandin' jurisdictions. How come Adams is this wide and Martin Luther King's got more miles on it than you can walk comfortably anymore. How come a little crew with a bit-time two-block piece of the action now's got a three-mile fiefdom? Contract like this gonna mean some heads get bashed."

Buzzworm sat up straight. "What are you talking about?"

"We might be droppin' out, but the hood's what we know, like the tattoos on our arms. You don't understand the demographics, you don't understand nothing. And someone's movin' it around."

"Maybe this lawyer's pulled the so-called rug from under you."

"What you jokin' about this for? Anybody on the ground'd know what I'm talkin' about."

Buzzworm remembered the little homey with the vision of curving bullets. Homies talking nonsense had to have some sense behind it. He looked out the tinted windows. Folks were all settled in for the time-being. Washed baby socks and panties hanging out the window of a Chrysler van. More wash sunning out on the ivy. Kids were playing tic-tac-toe on all the dirty windows. What didn't make sense? What made sense? Buzzworm scooted forward and popped out the sunroof. Manzanar was still up there vigilant-like. Like he couldn't stop doing it. Somebody oughta take some food up to the man. Buzzworm made a note of it. Suddenly, he got the notion. Brother said, *anybody on the ground'd know.* Could it be? Manzanar's overpass was stretched out, curved and maybe longer even. Could concrete do that? Buzzworm got back on the line, "So now what? You gonna start a war because the ground under you's moving?"

"First off, we ain't paying no lawyer."

"'S not about no lawyer. It's about things beyond our control."

"Most things's beyond our control."

"This is way beyond. Before you go picking fights, better air this out. Do it on my show tonight. Whole world watching. Hear what you got to say."

"Don't guarantee nothing."

"You about to sign a contract. Better to give your word to me."

Buzzworm hopped out of the Mercedes to take a look at the general scene. Made a beeline for the *NewsNow* van. *NewsNow* Asian baby sister (aka Balboa's substitute) was there looking somewhat stressed, but she never lost her ability to try to be wise. She said, "What? You run out of batteries already?"

Buzzworm tapped the Walkman. "If someone'd told me you'd be my supplier, I'd 'a lost this habit long ago."

Baby sister pulled four Triple-As from the glove compartment. "I've been saving these for you."

"We need to talk about sponsors. I don't want no *1-800 lawyers* doing commercials about how they can get a brother off DUI or put him on easy street with a disability check."

"Maybe you don't understand. You don't choose the commercials. They choose you. I wouldn't screw this one up. It looks good for syndication, you know."

"Now let's get a reality check here, baby sister. How long do you think this situation can last? Look around. LAPD's not exactly surrounding us to protect and serve. They're not going to let us live in the middle of a major thoroughfare forever, would you think?"

"This situation can be duplicated."

"I want to ask you a serious question."

"If that's possible."

"See that HOLLYWOOD sign out there yonder?"

"Hmmm."

"I been watching it."

"Right."

"Either it's coming closer this way, or we're going closer that way. Know what I mean?"

"Haven't you learned to talk to me straight yet? I failed English Metaphors and Symbolism 101."

"I *am* talking to you straight." Buzzworm moved into the van. "Kerry, pull down what the copter sees up there."

Everyone peered into the screen—copter's shadow running itself across the greater L.A. street scene. "There," Buzzworm pointed, "that's what I mean."

"What?"

"Can't you see it? Where we are. Harbor Freeway. It's growing. Stretched this way and that. In fact, this whole business from Pico-Union on one side to East L.A. this side and South Central over here, it's pushing out. Damn if it's not growing into everything! If it don't stop, it could be the whole enchilada."

"Kerry, what's he talking about? Do you see something?"

Kerry shook his head.

"Look, there might be some video distortion, but reality is reality. Are you all right?"

Buzzworm wondered about this reality. If they didn't see it, they didn't see it. Like the homeboy said, anyone on the ground'd know. These folks weren't on the ground. They were online or somewhere on the waves. He shook his head. "Forget it. Gonna traipse over to check out the mama cookin' at the hot dog stand. She puts out a red beans 'n rice affair that shouldn't be missed."

Baby sister smirked, "She may be cooking at a hot dog stand, but she put together a contract for her show that calls for Direct TV and cable rights, all foreign rights, even publication and movie rights."

"Mona must've written it. Mona knows the lingo," Buzzworm nodded.

"But movie rights?"

"Why not? Mama's had an interesting life."

"And what about this group called LAPD?"

"Los Angeles Poverty Department."

"So."

"Homeless performance group. They want a piece of the action. We were missing arts and culture. So I said why not?"

"They're doing the news." Baby sister pointed at the monitor. Two homeless anchors were sitting in beat-up bucket seats behind some kind of makeshift desk with decorative hubcaps, the real L.A. skyline draped behind them. Report was something like, "On the local front, memorial services for Newton Ford will be held this evening near the construction heap on the southbound at Expo which has been requisitioned for a cemetery. Ol' Newt died of complications from starvation and the elements.

"On a happier note, Saratoga Sara gave birth to a baby girl last night in the back of a VW bus. Far as we know, both mother and baby doing just fine. Contributions of diapers, baby clothing, and food for the mother gratefully accepted.

"Now here's Mara Sadat with a special report on Life in the Fast Lane."

Cut to Mara Sadat standing in front of the open hood of a rusting Cadillac who said, "I'm standing in the Fast Lane North with Slim City who's got one interesting project going on: an urban garden. Slim, tell us about your project."

Cad occupant said, "Well, since this babe wasn't goin' nowhere, we pulled her guts out and filled her yey high with some good old-fashioned dirt." Camera panned the dirt under the Cad's hood. "And, now we got a garden goin'. Something we always wanted. Got lettuce in this corner, some baby carrots over here, tomatoes here. A patch like this'll do some good feedin'. Folks in the Fast Lane a little distant from the right shoulders where the plantin's easy."

"What's that climbing the antenna there?"

"Passion fruit. Down here we get our Cs too."

"So here's a solution in self-sufficiency. I'm Mara Sadat for urban gardens here on the Fast Lane."

Baby sister turned to Buzzworm. "Are they for real?"

"They're for real. Why don't you catch a workshop? John Malpede and Luis Alfaro. Consummate artists in the field of performance. Next one's up at four."

"Meanwhile the real LAPD is up there."

"That's right. And the man who owns that dirt-filled Cad is probably putting together an arsenal of AK-47s to take it back."

Baby sister looked serious at Buzzworm for maybe the first time. "What's gonna happen?" Then she waxed nonchalant, L.A.-like, "Maybe we'll be surprised for a change."

"What's gonna surprise you, baby sister? An outright war? That news enough for you? Looks funny for the moment, homeless comedy, doing the local news. But it's too sweet. Homeless sweet homeless. Like we are the eye of a storm coming this way. Everything's colliding into everything. No place for these people to go. What they gonna do? Put us all in jail? At forty thou per head, doesn't seem too cost effective."

Baby sister checked the time. "You got an hour. *FreeZone*'s up next. Who are your guests?"

"Street peddlers come to tell their side of the poison orange mess. Then, an on-site powwow 'tween the gangs." Buzzworm started walking. "Yep. Until the invasion or whatever, I guess we'll conduct business like a FreeZone."

Day ran like that. One show running after the other. TV in the FreeZone. TV from the bottom. Aspirations of the lowest bum on skid row. Lifestyles of the poor and forgotten. Who'd a thought? Buzzworm was producing the hottest property on the net. Baby sister said it was a Hollywood wet dream. Either people'd watch anything, or as long as it was a show, it was cool. People figured: 's long as the tube has to deal with it, it must be outta our hands.

And for the finale: homeless choir numbering near five hundred featuring three homeless tenors, Manzanar Murakami conducting.

CHAPTER 32:

Overtime *El Zócalo*

It was postsiesta on the Zócalo. I had made a quick call to one of my México City contacts, a radio journalist known to the NPR crowd back home, David Welna. His wife, Kathleen, answered and supposed I could find him in front of the Basilica of the Virgin of Guadalupe. Of course, she was being facetious. Two hundred and fifty thousand, maybe more, people were wall-to-wall in México's version of Tienanmen Square or, say, the Washington Monument.

Considering that the city's got twenty-five million inhabitants, that was one percent of the city. It was one of those *Todos Somos Marcos* events. Maybe a quarter of the crowd were sporting ski masks and wooden rifles. As far as I could figure, hundreds of unions and political concerns were all converging. Of course not all of them were Marcos; there was Welna and me and about five thousand federales. For some reason, the whole thing seemed to be swelling and mobile. It felt like being in a school of fish, a salmon run. I had to keep moving, presumably forward, but for all I knew in circles, to keep my relationship to the crowd and to the plaza. I readjusted my backpack, heavy with the notebook computer and modem thrust upon me by Emi. It wasn't a large exertion on my part, at least for the moment.

This moving perceptibly and imperceptibly with the great flow seemed to characterize my existence in México from the moment I'd deplaned. On the major roads to and from the capitol, noticeable were the convoys of federales, Red Cross trucks, human rights observers, United Nations reps, liberation theologians, and press buses crisscrossing each other on the roads to peace and civil war in endless commotion. Soldiers at one checkpoint uncovered a cache of arms and ammunition in a pickup presumably moving south into the mountains, but I was told this was just one checkpoint. The DEA made its moves on a Guatemalan biplane flying a load of cocaine in its fuselage, but I was told this was nothing compared to the seventy tons that regularly made it across the border every year. Two high-level government officials were arrested for fraud, but I was told that the real culprits were too prominent, too powerful to touch. And besides, no one would believe the amount of money that had long seeped out of the country into international bank accounts.

Meantime, I pursued my hunches into Central America. C. Juárez plus a shipment of spiked oranges. My México City meeting was hardly a meeting in the formal sense. I had been told that it would be at their time and convenience. All I had to do was arrive; they would find me. Figures appeared out of shadows and suggested directions to pursue. They seemed to find me anywhere, but their directions got me through a series of loops only to land me at a family planning clinic. I did the loops several times over and found myself at an adoption agency, an orphanage, and a miserable shantytown of abandoned children on the edges of a vast dump. If I took one lead down one road, it brought me around to the same road again. Impoverished kids, orphaned kids, street kids, dead kids, disappeared kids. The whole system was a damn cloverleaf, and I began to have this nauseating sense of moving constantly to no good purpose. I was doing overtime and getting nowhere. I made this confession to Emi over the net.

Typically, she replied, *Knock it off, Gabe. It's México. For godssake, focus. By the way,* she added. *Your package arrived. What should I do with it?*

What's in it?

I haven't opened it. It is addressed to you. The box says faucets. Maybe it's a bomb. Can I find "bomb squad" in the Yellow Pages under B*?*

I can't think about that just now.

I went through my notes again. Emi was right. I hadn't focused. Everything was in this notebook. Interviews with Zapatistas. Notes on collusive military operations out of San Ysidro. A list of recent assassinations. Current value of the peso. Even my last telephone conversation with Rafaela. I proceeded to rip the pages out. I read my cryptic scribble: "Body parts. Kidneys for a two-year-old. Do you think?" The revelation made me gag.

I got Emi back on the net. *What did you do with the package?*

You mean the bomb? We're dismantling it as we speak.

Don't joke. This is serious.

Okay. Okay.

Don't open it. Give it to Buzzworm. Tell him it's connected to "C. Juárez." Let him deal with it.

You mean—

I don't mean anything. Stay out of this. Do you read me? STAY OUT OF THIS!

Alright. You don't have to yell.

The fearful voice of Rafaela rose up from my notes, rattled the old memory banks. Meanwhile, her two-year-old, Sol, chased his imagination in my imagination. The story was in my own backyard. Now I had to find Rafaela; if she had taken what I thought, she was in big trouble.

I made a series of calls to my neighbor Doña Maria. "Lupe went to see," she explained. "The house is wide open, so they can't have gone far. Just a little walk. She's that way you know. What you call a free spirit."

"I will call you back in an hour or two, but perhaps if they can't be found, you should call the police."

"Whatever for?"

I squirmed, remembering Rafaela's cryptic question about Doña Maria's son. How much could the old woman know? "I will be there as soon as possible," I said and hung up.

But for the moment, I was caught in the current at the Zócalo, one more flushed salmon pregnant with expectation. The entire crowd was waving paper money in the air: floating the peso they called it. *Primer Mundo. Ja Ja Ja!*

I got a tap on the shoulder from a ski-masked Marcos. "Gabriel Balboa?" I didn't know how he'd found me, but of course he did. Now it was pay-up time. We made the necessary passwords and signals for proper ID. He didn't waste time, "Have you brought it?"

"In my backpack."

"Follow me." We made our way out of the current, through side and back streets, into a restaurant and out the back, through doors and alleys. The final destination was a small office with a couple of telephones. Marcos pointed at the telephone plug. I took out the computer, plugged in the modem, called up Emi. Marcos handed me a set of disks.

"What's in this?" I asked.

"The first is a database: names, dates, descriptions, work, family, relations, everyone who lived in that village. Everyone who died or was killed or disappeared, and who did the killing if that is known. The second and third have the stories, the past, memories. The entire history of the village since anyone can remember."

I nodded. All these years, computer-stupid, I was supposed to save this man's village. If he only knew the incompetence he trusted. At least, I thought, Emi was on the other side prompting me through. "Copy everything to your hard drive first," she commanded.

I hung my ear over the phone, stared at the monitor, and tried to seem professional. Meanwhile Emi said, "Take it easy. Let's not be premature. Ouu," she purred.

I rolled my eyes, relieved Marcos couldn't hear her. Only Emi could find a database sexy. She moved me through those windows, coaxing this computer virgin into its innermost temples. "Easy on the AccuPoint. Digital manipulation can make all the difference," she purred.

I clicked through the menus, trying to ignore the insinuations.

"Okay, now you've got your very own newsgroup. Voila! Nothing there yet, but wait 'til you post. It's gonna be swimming in news. A reporter's wet dream. Okay, message your posting." She said it like massage. "And, baby, don't forget to CC me." She took me deftly through the last steps. "That's it. You're getting better all the time. A real natural. Attach files. Ready for take-off? Okay, let her rip."

CHAPTER 33:

To Dream *America*

The bus broke down. The engine blew up. The pistons imploded. The diesel ran out through a rusty hole in the tank. And only minutes from the border. They all got out of the bus and looked. Arcangel opened his dusty suitcase and pulled out the steel cables and hooks. He was never without them; one never knew when they might be useful. And this was the second incident this week to prove this theory. Sol was jumping on the seats, pressing his nose into the windows and making faces. He peered into the suitcase and selected the orange from Arcangel's assortment of toys. Arcangel closed the suitcase and sat the boy on top. "Stay right here," he commanded gently.

Sol pressed the orange to his nose, then shook it up and down.

"Good. Good."

Once again, Arcangel offered his services to pull the bus, slipping the steel cable through the axle and hooking his old skin through the metal talons. And once again, the people scoffed at his efforts and gawked amazed as the bus inched slowly along the highway, harnessed to an old man's leathery person, skin pulled taut across his bony chest and empty stomach, minute droplets of blood kissing the earth, dragging everything forward. It was as the burden of gigantic wings, too heavy to fly.

Such a commotion was aroused that no one noticed, either on one side or the other of the Great Border—that Arcangel and a broken bus and a boy and an orange and, for that matter, everything else South were about to cross it: the very hemline of the Tropic of Cancer and the great skirts of its relentless geography.

Televisa, Univision, Galaxy Latin America and local border stations congregated to eyeball the event. If there were a dozen local and national stations, there were a dozen eyes, translating to a dozen times a dozen times a dozen like the repetitious vision of a common housefly. Arcangel strained for this vision even though live television had no way of accommodating actual feats of superhuman strength. The virtually real could not accommodate the magical. Digital memory failed to translate imaginary memory. Meanwhile, the watching population surfed the channels for the real, the live, the familiar. But it could not be recognized on a tube, no matter how big or how highly defined. There were not enough dots in the universe. In other words, to see it, you had to have been there yourself.

Arcangel, despite his pains, looked out across the northern horizon. He could see

all 2,000 miles of the frontier
stretched across from Tijuana on the Pacific,
its straight edge cutting through the Río Colorado,
against the sharp edge of Arizona
and the unnatural angle of Nuevo México,
sliding along the Río Grande,
tenderly caressing the supple bottom of Texas
to the end of its tail
on the Gulf of México.
It waited with seismic sensors and thermal imaging,
with la pinche migra,
colonias of destitute skirmishing at its hard line,
with coyotes, pateros, cholos,
steel structures, barbed wire, infrared binoculars,
INS detention centers, border patrols, rape,
robbery, and death.

It waited with its great history of migrations back and forth—in recent history,

the deportation of 400,000 Mexican
citizens in 1932,
coaxing back of 2.2 million
braceros in 1942
only to exile the same 2.2 million
wetbacks in 1953.

The thing called the New World Border waited for him with the anticipation of five centuries. Admittedly a strange one, but Conquistador of the North he was. Ah, he thought, the North of my dreams.

South of his dreams, it had been a long journey. He could remember everything. Here was a mere moment of passage. As he approached, he could hear the chant of the border over and over again: *Catch 'em and throw 'em back. Catch 'em and throw 'em back. Catch 'em and throw 'em back.* It was the beginning of the North of his dream, but they questioned him anyway. They held the border to his throat like a great knife. "What is your name?"

"Cristobal Colón."

"How old are you?"

"Quinientos y algunos años."

"When were you born?"

"El doce de octubre de mil cuatrocientos noventa y dos."

"Where were you born?"

"En el nuevo mundo."

"That would make you—"

"Post-Columbian."

"You don't look post-Columbian. What is your business here?"

"I suppose you would call me a messenger."

"And what is your message?"

"No news is good news?"

"Is that a question? Say, do you speak English?"

"Yes."

"Where did you learn to speak English?"

"At Harvard University."

"So you've studied in the U.S.? Where?"

"At Harvard at the School of Business. I was there at the same time as Carlos Salinas de Gortari. Then at Stanford University in Economics with Henrique Cardoso. Also at Columbia University with Fidel Castro; I did my thesis in political theory there, you see. And finally at Annapolis; what I studied there is a secret."

"Where is your visa? Your passport?"

"Were you not expecting me? You had better consult your State Department, not to mention the side agreements with labor and the environment. I am expected. Me están esperando." He moved forward, slipping across as if from one dimension to another.

And the words came immediately, "SPEAK ENGLISH NOW!"

The first wave came like a great flood behind him, showing their hands at the border. Ten working fingers, each times thousands. Having to show their fingers meant that they must enter with nothing in their hands,

nothing but their hats to shade their foreheads,

the sweat on their backs,

the seeds in their pockets,

the children in their wombs,

the songs in their throats.

The cockroach. The cockroach. The cockroach.

Customs officials chased after Arcangel. "By the way, are you carrying any fresh fruit or vegetables?"

Arcangel yelled behind him, "Only three ears of corn and one lousy orange!"

"California currently has a ban on all oranges. We are authorized to enforce a no-orange policy," they shouted back.

"But this is a native orange!" he yelled, but his voice was swallowed up by the waves of floating paper money: pesos and dollars and reals, all floating across effortlessly—a graceful movement of free capital, at least forty-five billion dollars of it, carried across by hidden and cheap labor. Hundreds of thousands of the unemployed surged forward—the blessings of monetary devaluation that thankfully wiped out those nasty international trade deficits.

Then came the kids selling Kleenex and Chiclets,
the women pressing rubber soles into tennis shoes,
the men welding fenders to station wagons and
all the people who do the work of machines:
human washing machines,
human vacuums,
human garbage disposals.
Then came the corn and the bananas,
the coffee and the sugarcane.
And then the music and its rhythms,
pre-Columbian treasure,
the halls of Moctezuma and all 40,000 Aztecs slain—
their bodies floating in the canals.
In slipped the burned and strangled body of the
Incan king Atahualpa in a chamber filled with gold.
And then came smallpox, TB, meningitis, E coli,
influenza, and 25 million dead Indians.
After that everything clamored forth:
the spirit of ideologies thought to be dead
and of the dead themselves—
of Bolívar, of Che, Francisco de Morazán,
Benito Juárez, Pablo Neruda, Sandino, Romero,
Pancho Villa, and Salvador Allende,
of conquistadors, generals, and murderers,
African slaves, freedom fighters, anthropologists,
latifundistas, ecomartyrs, terrorists, and saints.
And every rusting representation of an

American gas guzzler from 1952 to the present
and all their shining hubcaps.
Then came the rain forests,
El Niño, African bees, panthers, sloths, llamas,
monkeys, and pythons.
Everything and everybody got in lines—
citizens and aliens—
the great undocumented foment,
the Third World War,
the gliding wings of a dream.

CHAPTER 34:
Visa Card *Final Destination*

Bobby eyeballs the Visa card drag itself through the slit. Jus' like any Americano. Shopping Tijuana. Chinese connection's smooth operation. It's a one-time dumping fee. Free the cuz for half-price. An easy five thou. Put it on the plastic. No muss. No fuss. It's a complete laundry.

Bobby got 'em down fifty percent. It's the limit on his Visa. Forget the paperwork. Forget the China to Chinatown deal. Bobby gonna smuggle the cousin across himself. He figures it won't be even near another five thou. Ten percent of that should do it. She could be his daughter. Who's gonna know?

Been a while since Bobby brought the wife over. But that was different. He was legal, gonna get married. Just a matter of paperwork. Got him a lawyer to do the business. Her brother Pepe always saying Rafaela got lucky. Places 'long the border everybody knows, every woman don't get raped, she don't pass. The price she pays. Next up from the women, it's the poor Indian types. They don't know the language, don't know the ropes. It's gonna be the border rats robbing them. Cross the river. Make a run for it down Zapata Canyon. Lose their money. Their shoes. The clothing off their bodies. Maybe nobody gonna see these folks again. Bunch come floating up the river. It's a fourteen mile *zone.* All lit up. It's a fiesta. Maybe you needing gloves for the trip. Work the barbed wire. Maybe a little barbecue pollo for your last supper. Chiclets? Somebody given up crossing's selling it to you for a price. On the other side, the migra arrests 1,000 per night.

Puts the chivos under thermal imaging. It's high technology with a revolving door. If you lucky, Border Patrol chases you down. Puts you in a wagon and dumps you back. But maybe you gonna be one of them gets shot.

Bobby checks out the market. It's $100 to cross the river. $350 to cross I-5. $500 gets you all the way to L.A. Bobby figures the cuz gets across like his daughter. But just in case, he gets some documentation. Birth certificate. That should do it.

"What's your name?"

"You don't know my name?" The cousin looks worried. Maybe her problems aren't over. Maybe this skinny man's a bad man.

"They say your name's Xiayue, but that could be a phony name."

"That is my name."

"Are you related to me?" Bobby takes a close look. He looks at her sad eyes.

"I don't know. Are you my uncle?"

"I don't know. But now I am your father. You must call me father now. That is how we are going to get across."

"I am already across. They got me off the boat."

"It's not the final destination. Where did you think you were going?"

"America."

"So you still have to cross the border. Actually, it's right over there." Bobby points north. "Not far at all."

"My brother said he would meet me there. That's where there's work for him. He said he'd find me."

"Well, maybe he made it. You never know." Bobby's looking at Xiayue's long pigtails. "Maybe we've got to cut these off. It's not the style. We need to get you some other clothing too."

"My brother knew how to swim. I know how to swim too. I should have jumped with him." Kid looks fierce.

Bobby don't know about the brother, but maybe she'd've made it. Bobby's thinking she's tough, but he's still asking the questions. "Why did you come along? Why didn't you stay home?"

"There's only my brother and me. My parents are both dead. I would have to come sooner or later. That's what they said. I came sooner."

Bobby thinks for some, there's a plan. For others, there's none. Like the cuz here. The brother's gonna work. Work like all the celestials before him. Put down rail ties. Pick oranges. Wash shirts. Sew garments. Stir-fry chop suey. This li'l celestial here, there's no plan. She just came sooner. Bobby's thinking what kinda plan he had when he was her age. When he stepped off the plane. It wasn't any plan either. Just gonna survive was all. Now he's thinking what's the plan now? Still no plan. Rafaela said pretty soon he was gonna work himself to death. Was that the plan? Rafaela didn't want to watch him die. So she left.

In the U.S., can't work much if you're twelve. So right away, he's sixteen. Li'l brother gets put in school. Teacher finds out there's no mom or pop. *Who's signing your report card?* Teacher finds out it's a twelve-year-old parent. Like parachute kids except the folks's poor. Makes Bobby quit work and go to school, too. Puts the boys up and sends them to school. They go to school with the Mexicans and the centroamericanos. Even get some religion at La Placita. That's why Bobby gets a latinoamericano education. Gets in good with the vatos locos. A taste of la vida loca. Who'd a thought? But that was the plan, wasn't it? Surviving. Maybe he and the little cuz on the same plan. Getting by. It's no plan at all.

Bobby takes the little cuz to a T.J. beauty shop. Get rid of the pigtails. Get rid of the Chinagirl look. Get a cut looking like Rafaela. That's it. Now get her a T-shirt and some jeans and some tennis shoes. Jeans say Levi's. Shoes say Nike. T-shirt says Malibu. That's it.

Border's nothing but desks and lines of people on linoleum floors. Bobby's in line like one more tourist. He's got the cuz holding a new Barbie doll in a box, like she bought it cheap in T.J. Official eyeballs Bobby's passport and waves them through. That's it. Two celestials without a plan. Drag themselves through the slit jus' like any Americanos. Just like Visa cards.

CHAPTER 35:

Jam *Greater L.A.*

Despite everything, every sports event, concert, and whatnot was happening at the same time. L.A. marathoners slouched by the droves across the finish line at the Coliseum. At the Rose Bowl: UCLA versus USC; the Bruin mascot had been carried off the field with heat stroke, and the Trojan horse was tied up after throwing its sweaty rider. The Clippers were attempting a comeback in overtime at the Sports Arena. It was the end of the seventh-inning stretch, and Nomo fans at Chavez Ravine hunkered down with their cold beers and Dodger dogs. Scottie Pippen fouled Shaq who sank a free throw for the Lakers at the Forum in the last seconds. The Trekkie convention warped into five at the L.A. Convention Center. Bud Girls paraded between boxing matches at the Olympic Auditorium. Plácido Domingo belted Rossini at the Dorothy Chandler under the improbable abstract/minimal/baroque direction of Peter Sellers. At the Shrine, executive producer Richard Sakai accepted an Oscar for the movie version of *The Simpsons*. The helicopter landed for the 944th time on the set of *Miss Saigon* at the Ahmanson, and Beauty smacked the Beast at the Shubert. Chinese housewives went for the big stakes in pai gow in the Asian room at the Bicycle Club. Live-laughter sitcom audiences and boisterous crowds for the daytime and nighttime talks filled every available studio in Hollywood and Burbank. Thousands of fans melted away with Julio Iglesias at the Universal Amphitheater. Robert McNeil and The Jubilee Choir were jumping gospel at the Greek, and movie music nostalgia brimmed from the Hollywood Bowl with John Mauceri conducting. King Tut had returned to LACMA; Andy Warhol to MOCA. The AIDS walk 5/10K run was moving through West Hollywood. Andrei Codrescu read from "Zombification" at the Central Library. Surfers kicked butt with punks in leather and chains at The Lollapalooza in Orange County. Chicanos marched from the Plaza de la Raza down Whittier to César Chávez in solidarity. Volleyball teams vied for titles all along the beaches from Malibu to the Hollywood Riviera. Street fairs and food fairs and farmers' markets bustled with gawkers in every park and parking lot. Endless lines extending down major freeways waited to get into Disneyland, Knott's Berry Farm, Magic Mountain, Universal Studios, and Raging Waters for their half-price specials. Drag races were underway, deafening the Pomona Raceway, and across the way, a 4-H demonstration of cow milking gathered a crowd at the Los Angeles County Fair. Japanese Americans reenacted the historic 1942 relocation of thousands of legal aliens at the Santa Anita Racetrack. Sin Ying Chang and his wife waited in a line five blocks long for the long-awaited premiere of a new Spielberg film. Political rallies and benefit dinners at one thousand dollars a plate for several Republican presidential candidates clapped themselves toward dessert at the Sheraton, the Hilton, and the Bonaventure. The middle class clamored in malls for summer sales; the poor clamored at swap meets. Chris & Qris inquired at will-call about orchestra seats for Pizzicato 5 at the Japan America Theater. Across town, the Cirque du Soleil was back for the umpteenth time at the Big Tent at the Santa Monica pier. Meanwhile, Stomp stomped trash cans at the Wadsworth. And the horses were running neck and neck at Hollywood Park. . . . Everybody was doing their thing in the greatest leisure world ever devised.

Manzanar saw this thing like a gigantic balloon swelling larger and larger. The most horrific aspect of it was that it would all end at the same time—a Caltrans nightmare. One more L.A. disaster. Of course, this was not planned, although everything else had been, months in advance—subscription tickets, guest invitations, the yearly semifinals, the predictable events of every summer in L.A. Was it possible that anyone could be bored? Individual random and chaotic acts of planning. Coincidental same-day events. Yet how was it possible that everyone could be physically there with the live action and not watching it on TV? How was it possible to leave commercial time—Madison Avenue's wagging tongue—to the infirm and invalid? What did they care about Ford pickups and Nikes? Yes, it was a big screw-up. But only Manzanar could see the undulating patterns and the changing geography corrupting the sun's shadows, confusing time, so that all events should happen and end at the same time.

Perhaps it should have been a comforting idea to Manzanar. A kind of solidarity: all seven million residents of Greater L.A. out on the town, away from their homes, just like him, outside. In the next moment, they would all cram their bodies through exits, down escalators, through arcades, lobbies, and turnstiles, all partake of the outside. And in the next moment after that, they would all head toward their cars, their buses, their motorcycles and limousines, wend their way through giant parking lots several miles square or stories high or deep, all jam their bodies into vehicles of every size, all slam their doors, all buckle their belts, all gun their motors, all simultaneously—a percussive orchestration that even Manzanar found incredible. And CLICK, one two, SLIDE, three four, FLOMP, one two, BLAM, three four, SNAP, one two VROOOM, three four. Just amazing. And then the syncopated REAR VIEW CHECK IT OUT and a one and a two, and AC UP TO THE MAX and a three and a four, and CREEP ON OUT and a five and a six, and MERGE, MERGE, MERGE. They all converged everywhere all at once. Man's most consistent quest for continuing technology in all its treaded ramifications jammed every inch of street, driveway, highway, and freeway. And Manzanar, loathe to lose any moment, writhed with exhilaration and christened it all: the greatest jam session the world had ever known.

To envision the automobile as an orchestral device with musical potential was an idea lost upon the motorist within. In moments such as these, the mechanical and the human elements of Manzanar's orchestra became blurred. The car became a thing with intelligence. He envisioned the person within as the pulpy brain of each vehicle, and when the defenseless body emerged, for whatever reason, he often felt surprise and disgust. A memory was triggered, and he was once again a masked surgeon, cutting through soft tissue. He remembered intimately the geography of the human body, and that delicate, complex thing within each car frightened him.

So when the inevitable impossibility of moving in the greatest traffic jam the world had ever seen made people GROAN one two, UNLATCH DOORS three four, EMERGE five six, Manzanar gripped his baton like a knife. He saw them all with their moving mouths speaking out of sync, as in a Toho Film production of Godzilla, with a strange dubbed language not their own. And yet, it was a babel he understood.

SATURDAY:
Queen of Angels

CHAPTER 36:

To Perform *Angel's Flight*

By the time Arcangel reached San Ysidro, he no longer really had to pull the bus. The great multitude behind pushed it for him. Pushed it and its passengers and the little boy sitting on his suitcase with the orange. Pushed the Tropic ever northward. Still attached by hooks and cables to the bus, however, Arcangel—naked to the waist—continued to press forward toward his destination: The Village of Our Lady Queen of Angels on the River Porciúncula, the second largest city of México, also known as Los Angeles.

"Which way to the Cajón Pass?" he inquired along the way. "I am told Earth has become soft again, and there is a way through the pass to the great basin beyond."

"Go back, old man," people warned. "It's not what you think. What do you think you will do there anyway?"

"I will sell my art. They say there is free trade now, so here I am. I will perform. I will read my poetry. I am making this pilgrimage to perform my greatest work yet."

In the name of the Virgin of Guadalupe, go back old man. Do you have a green card? Do you have a social security card? Do you have any money? When you get there, you will be unprotected. If you get sick, no one can give you care. If you have children, no one will teach them. In the name of Tonantzin and the memory of Juan Diego, go back! You are illegal."

"Is it a crime to be poor? Can it be illegal to be a human being?"

The crowd behind him agreed. They chanted, "Is it a crime to be poor? Is it a crime to be poor?"

But the people already north warned, "Listen to what we say. We have lived here all our lives, even before the others. Our ancestors hunted the woolly mammoth and the saber-toothed tiger. And still we do not belong here."

But the old man was unperturbed. "Tell me. Where is East L.A.?"

And the crowd behind, "East L.A.! East L.A.!"

"Oh, Tío Taco. You're nothin' but a lazy old freeloading mes'kin around here."

Arcangel looked offended. "I may seem old to you, but I am still a *virile* old man. Let me show you." He held out his strong penis for everyone to see. The crowd behind him cheered.

"Put that away, old man. Old Latin lovers are not wanted here."

"I have heard there are so many sights to see along the way. Sea World and Bubbles, for example. General Dynamics and Camp Pendleton. The nuclear reactor at San Onofre is described as two giant white tits embedded in the seascape in a cloud of milky steam. Perhaps you could point them out."

"What do you think you are? A tourist?"

"Can't you see? I am a pilgrim."

"We are pilgrims! We are pilgrims!" shouted everyone.

"Old man, the only pilgrims here came on the Mayflower. And that was a long time ago."

"Ah yes, I remember those pilgrims. I was there at Plymouth Rock when they arrived."

"Old man, you say
you were with Sitting Bull at Custer's Last Stand,
at the Bay of Pigs in 1961 and
on San Juan Hill with Teddy Roosevelt in 1898.
You say
you sailed down the Magdalena River with the
dying Simón Bolívar.
You were with Che in Bolivia in 1967
when he was killed, and likewise
with Leon Trotsky just as he was stabbed in 1940.
You saw Tachito Somoza assassinated in Asunción.
You knew Eva Perón, and
you marched with the Mothers of the Disappeared.
You say you flew in 1906 with Santos Dumont and
sailed with Darwin to Galapagos.
You even kissed the Spider Woman.
You were everywhere every time. How is that?"

"Strange how things happen the way they do." And Arcangel continued on, taking the elevator to the top of Angel's Flight. It was one of those odd moments in liberation theology in which a messenger named Arcangel stood at the top of Angel's Flight, looking out over the City of Angels with his arms raised to the heavens and his body fastened to an entire continent.

Sol scrambled out of the bus and accompanied the old man as if he were his tiny assistant or the monkey dancing to the tune of a hand organ. He sat obediently on the suitcase while Arcangel performed tricks of magic, prophecy, comedy, and political satire. He turned a poor man on the street into a dapper gentleman. He produced a bouquet of roses for a young mother. A young man was brought to tears upon hearing the unknown story of his past and his future. Thousands pondered the meaning of modernity, and an old man died laughing.

And then he introduced the famous professional wrestler, El Gran Mojado, who miraculously appeared from nowhere and announced his scheduled bout in the Ultimate Wrestling Championship known to everyone as *El Contrato Con América*. Like chile con carne, Arcangel said. Flyers were passed out, information verbally reproduced and distributed almost simultaneously with the frenzy of a kind of information saturation. It was probably the last time millions of people were instantly informed of a piece of news without the mechanical aid of television or radio or telephone or newspaper. The entirety of the message was disseminated in a thousand languages, including Spanglish, ebonics, and pidgin, to everyone.

Finally Arcangel juggled the only orange in the city that had not been hidden or confiscated. The crowd surged forward at the sight of the orange, maybe the last good orange in the world. At that moment, its value was incalculable. Its very presence resonated with several thousand oranges rotting in toxic landfills, hidden under floorboards, sweltering in drawers filled with lingerie, or frozen behind the Ben & Jerry's, hidden in dozens of obvious and ridiculous places because they were now illegal. Customs officials who now chased after their stretching border scrambled forward to confiscate a single orange. Public health officials judiciously counted the orange and posted warnings. The FBI got out its stinking badges. But Sol, who loved the orange, grabbed it and ran in circles. And everything in that geographic nexus churned around and around and around.

CHAPTER 37:

The Car Show *Front Line*

Buzzworm made his way up to the overpass, nonchalant-like. He was totin' a thing lookin' like a baby replica of a beer cooler. Igloo Playmate. Coulda been a cold six-pack. Meantime, he was tuned in to some radio talk.

"This is KPFK *The Car Show*. You're on."

Caller said, "Yeah. I got me here a '64 Impala. I did the paint job myself. It's like a Diego Rivera. You know the man?"

"Mexican muralist," said host Frank.

"Married to Frida Kahlo? Yeah we know him," said other host Retsek. It was one of those astute radio car shows. Buzzworm sauntered on. *Car Show* was like a cookin' show. You got filled up just listenin', without havin' to buy or eat nothin'.

"So it's something else, man. I gutted the insides, put in a new 502 with a six speed, lowered it, disk brakes, black leather upholstery—the works."

"Did you blueprint the 502?" asked Frank.

"Yeah, how'd ya know?"

"Sounds like a masterpiece," said Retsek.

"The thing hauls. Hey, didn't you have a guest on sells cars like mine big-time to Japan?"

"Yeah, the Japanese are collecting American muscle cars, but production models."

"It's like, they're into tattooing, aren't they? It's like my car's tattooed."

"That's an interesting observation."

"Wish we could see it."

"That's just it. You wanna see it? It's down there."

"Down there?"

"Yeah. Got a homeless mother and her child living in it. I mean I actually went down to talk to her. At first I thought, shit, if they screw up the upholstery . . . I was gonna go down there, blow 'em away. I put my life into that car. But then, I thought, she might actually take care of it for me. You know, in return for finding her a place."

"That's very good of you."

"Hey, whaddya guys think about this situation? I hear people bitching that they can't get to work. But I been down there. Sat in the car and held the baby for her. It's not so bad. And I think that baby likes me." What did this have to do with cars? What happened to the dirty talk about pistons, lug nuts, camshafts, and drive lines? What about the engine specs and the zero-to-sixty times? But Buzzworm had to give it the nod. He knew the tattooed car and the mother. She was storing baby food and diapers under the trunk hood painted with the calla lilies.

By now, he'd got up to the overpass and made eye contact with Manzanar. Manzanar opened the cooler, pulled a drawstring bag from the melted ice and opened it. Inside there was a Tupperware filled with solution, another bag, and a Ziploc filled with more liquid. "Saline, potassium," he muttered. "Twenty cc dextrose," he added and squinted at something floating in the liquid. It was a tiny purple slimy thing padded tenderly by what was now tepid refrigeration. "Newborn," he said without battin' an eye. "Human heart's consistently the size of your fist. In this case, a newborn's fist."

"Human? Damn. What happened to the rest of the newborn goes with it?" Course, Manzanar didn't have to answer that. Can't nobody live without a heart.

"How did you get this?" Manzanar asked. "I imagine it was harvested for transplant." Buzzworm noticed him grippin' the baton.

Pager went off.

Buzzworm zipped the Ziploc, pushed in the lid on the Tupperware, and pulled the drawstrings. Stuffed it all back in the Igloo. "Thanks for your opinion, doc. I gotta go."

He started to saunter away, but not before looking over that podium and getting a sighting on a constellation of palm trees in the distance. Used to be he could fix his sights by those palms, but weren't the same no more. Manzanar looked at him and confirmed his confusion. "Things are shifting," he said simply.

Buzzworm walked down from the overpass casually gripping the Igloo like it was a lunch box—baby heart sloshing around inside its own baby sea.

Pager was either Mona or baby sister telling him to beat a track to his next assignment. Like the promos said, *the Buzz waz*: "The Reverend Jesse Jackson, actor Edward Olmos, the Police Chief, and the Mayor have agreed to an open forum to be conducted on Limousine Way . . . "

Buzzworm made connections to the same ol' big guns come 'round every time there's trouble. He didn't call them; they called him. Big guns were gonna do the political hip hop. Gonna tell us there's more black men in jail than in college. Gonna let us know the man is glad to see us out here killing our brothers. Gonna be preaching the gospel of hope not dope. Gonna let us know change is in the air. Gonna let us know the real word for riots is uprisin'. Get down and preach the gospel of uprisin'. Gonna let us know the situation is under control. So don't get no ideas.

Then all the rappers gonna be there doing the chorus and the raparounds. Gonna be bad-mouth baby rappers cussin' low-ridin', crack, automatic weapons, and drive-by, smoochin' for the record deal. Then there's the original stuff: Ice-T, NWA, STRAIGHT OUTTA COMPTON. Dispatchin' the action from the urban front line. Ghetto blastin'.

Buzzworm'd been taking a hard look at the urban front line, trying to figure where exactly that line might be drawn. It was all war talk. Even the years he'd been in Vietnam, never was clear. You had to have eyes in the back of your head; you never knew where the enemy might be. Line wasn't something drawn on the ground. When he came home, he realized he was considered the enemy. If he stepped over the invisible front line, he could get implicated, arrested, jailed, killed. If he stepped back, he'd just be invisible. Either way he was dead. Gone to heaven. Become an angel.

Politicos came to the edges to take a look. Take a look into something looking like a big border town. They projected their words in the general direction. Mostly they looked good for the cameras. Whole world watching 'cept the ones concerned. Only bodies in the valley could see their TV images were the folks in the TV van and a bunch packed into the limousine on Limousine Way. Rest had to get a glimpse of the real thing. Buzzworm held the mike and commenced the tour.

Along the way, folks came up to put in their two cents. Brother in a '78 Pontiac said, "Mayor, sir, I consider my occupation of this vehicle a short-term one. I'm just borrowing it. But I want the man or woman who owns it to know I've made considerable home improvements. Washed it good. Waxed it. Spiffed up the insides. There's not a speck of dirt. Made it downright homey inside." Sure enough: photos sat on the dash on either side of an arrangement of California poppies and the Bible; stuffed bear in the back window, decorative hanky over the steering wheel.

Next-door neighbor showed them how he got a tomato plant growing in the dirt coming up through the concrete. "You see here, these blossoms? And here's baby tomatoes. Call it urban gardening. We gonna be feeding ourselves, don't you worry."

Mother with a two-year-old said, "Chief, sir, other day, had a poor woman keel over. Looked to be a heart attack. Did CPR on her and it was a miracle we got her out of the valley. It's a shame. Nine-one-one don't service us down here."

One of the entourage said, "Actually, I'm surprised to see how clean it is down here."

So another brother popped in, "We got regular trash pickup once a day. Bottles, cans, and plastic already get separated."

And another, "We carted the outhouses from the construction work and distributed them at regular intervals, but we could use more. We're gonna be needing running water and a sewage system."

And another, "Every morning at 3:00 a.m., the landscaping sprinkler system goes on like clockwork. Mamas all run out with their kids at the break of dawn to take advantage of the shower. Could the system be timed for the afternoon when the weather's warmer? How about it?"

Políticos didn't say much. That is, they said a lot, but not much. It was a quantitative sort of thing. Not qualitative. It was promises and pledges—sort that could be broken, misinterpreted, or never paid up. Maybe the entourage was prestigious, but they weren't stupid. Wasn't the time to let the axe fall. Not while they were down there in the middle of it. Not in front of the cameras. They knew what Gil Scott-Heron knew: The revolution will not be televised.

Buzzworm was still packin' the baby heart under his left arm. No time to lose it before. Maybe he could just hand it over to one of these politicos like it was a gift. But which one? Who was gonna do right by it? Who knew the value of a human heart?

Baby heart. Might as well be chicken livers. What was he supposed to do with this? Balboa was gonna pay big-time. Who was gonna believe a thing like this could just come in the mail? Easier to account for a bomb. And all the time he'd been touring the bigshots through the valley of the homeless with a baby heart cradled in a cooler like it was a box lunch. Maybe he could lose it under the hood of a car. Maybe he could bury it under a palm tree. He followed the politicos up Limousine Way and, out of some kind of frustration, just kept going. At least no homeless were gonna be implicated in this mess.

Amazing thing was everybody in L.A. was walking. They just had no choice. There wasn't a transportation artery that a vehicle could pass through. It was a big-time thrombosis. Massive stroke. Heart attack. You name it. The whole system was coagulating right then and there. Some of the broadest boulevards had turned into one-way alleys. Cars so squeezed together, people had to climb out the sun roofs to escape. Streets'd become unrecognizable from an automotive standpoint. Only way to navigate was to feel the streets with your own two feet.

So people were finally getting out, close to the ground, seeing the city like he did. He even noticed a couple examining the base of a palm tree, then looking upward with some kind of appreciation. Well, how about that?

Seemed like a crowd was being drawn to the old Bunker Hill, the all-new Angel's Flight. Nothing but an old fellah doing some juggling with some corn and an orange. And damn if it wasn't the last orange to appear in the entire city. People went crazy, grown adults chasing a two-year-old who grabbed the fruit and ran around in circles. They were gonna trample the poor kid. Buzzworm pushed his way in and scooped up the child. Now they ran with Buzzworm's advantage of longer legs, but he began to notice that no matter how fast or slow his pace, something kept the crowd at the same distance. Still, there had to be a way to lose them. He tucked the orange under the boy's shirt, handed him back to the old juggler, and nodded. No one could see the orange, but the old juggler threw his trick voice into the air. "There it is! Under that man's arm!" And everyone chased Buzzworm with his baby heart tucked like a football against his ribs.

Buzzworm ran like a fool. Crowd ran like fools behind. Buzzworm's live heart went ticky-tocky like a charmed watch. Who'd a known he was in such prime condition? Loping along. Blockin'. Twistin' and turnin'. Slippin' by the defense. Some dude was out there like a tight end headin' for some imaginary touchdown. What the hell. Buzzworm took a look back to gauge his elbow room, cupped the cooler with the heart, and let it fly. Tight end twirled up like a damn ballerina, bagged the thing with precision timing, and was off. Buzzworm watched the tight end disappear with the crowd behind. Could be it was miles to the next down, miles yet to a touchdown. Baby heart just kept on going.

CHAPTER 38:

Nightfall *Aztlán*

The villain pressed Rafaela's elbow into the small of her back and jerked her head back by the hair. The sound of her screams traveled south but not north. He jammed her into the leather cavern of the black Jaguar—suddenly a great yawning universe in the night. Springing upon her writhing body, he clawed her throat and pawed her breasts, tearing her soft skin. Her writhing twisted her body into a muscular serpent—sinuous and suddenly powerful. She thrashed at him with vicious fangs— ripping his ears, gouging his neck, drawing blood. He screamed but returned snarling, pounced, eyes bloody with terror, claws and teeth, flashing knives, ripped into the armored scales of her tensile body. Her mouth gaped a torch of fire, scorching his black fur. Two tremendous beasts wailed and groaned, momentarily stunned by their transformations, yet poised for war. Battles passed as memories: massacred men and women, their bloated and twisted bodies black with blood, stacked in ruined buildings and floating in canals; one million more decaying with smallpox; kings and revolutionaries betrayed, hacked to pieces in a Plaza of Tears, ambushed and shot on lonesome roads, executed in stadiums, in presidential palaces, discarded in ditches, tossed into the sea. And there was the passage of five thousand women of Cochabamba resisting with tin guns an entire army of Spaniards, the passage of a virgin consecrated to the sun god buried alive with her lover, of La Malinche abandoning her children and La Llorona howling after, of cangaceira Maria Bonita riddled with lead by machine guns at the side of her Lampião, of one hundred mothers pacing day after day the Plaza de Mayo with the photos of their disappeared children, and Coatlalopeuh blessing it all. But that was only the human massacre; what of the ravaged thousands of birds once cultivated to garnish the tress of a plumed potentate, the bleeding silver treasure of Cerro Rico de Potosí, the exhausted gold of Ouro Preto, the scorched land that followed the sweet stuff called white gold and the crude stuff called black gold, and the coffee, cacao and bananas, and the human slavery that dug and slashed and pushed and jammed it all out and away, forever.

As night fell, they began their horrific dance with death, gutting and searing the tissue of their existence, copulating in rage, destroying and creating at once—the apocalyptic fulfillment of a prophecy—blood and semen commingling among shredded serpent and feline remains.

When Rafaela awoke, the sky above was a shroud of black-feathered creatures, a million pairs of eyes staring down. She focused dimly, through the narrow slit that remained of one eye, on the pebbles embedded in the dirt near her face and the flashing tail of a snake disappearing into the undergrowth. She pushed out a chunk of something fibrous between her teeth with her tongue and was horrified to see a wad of black fur emerge and shift along the dirt like scattering feathers. Retching and gagging, the remaining hair and pieces of skin spilled into a small pool of blood. More blood dripped from her forehead along with handfuls of her own hair, falling into her vomit. The pain of her convulsing body reached from her head to her feet—every part seemed bruised or torn. Despite the heat, she hugged her nakedness, tugging at the few shreds of clothing left covering her battered body.

The villain and his Jaguar had disappeared. Rafaela crawled around in the dirt exploring. A shattered piece of what seemed to be the steering wheel, still encased in its leather cover, and the gold figurine snapped from the hood, were all that remained.

A sharp sting of new pain ran along her arms to her hands, and suddenly she was aware of her fingers clutched in two hard fists. Carefully bending her fingers backward, she stared in horror at the pocketknife in one hand—its inlaid handle thick with blood—and the crumpled leaf of a human ear in the palm of the other.

Suddenly the sky was a chorus of heavenly chanting, a terrible blessing, and a great fluttering of millions of wings withdrawing nightfall, away. Rafaela crouched on her hands and knees in the dirt and bore her nakedness under the malign scrutiny of the now blue sunlight.

CHAPTER 39:

Working Weekend *Dirt Shoulder*

I was making good time on my way from the Mazatlán airport to my place in a rented Nissan called a Tsuru.

I was thinking about Emi and Manzanar; it just didn't figure. No two people could be further apart, much less related. For some reason, Emi was refusing to finish the interview with Manzanar. *I'm like you,* she had typed. *Strictly noir.*

But he's your grandfather.

So I'm in denial, okay?

He's probably not going to recognize you. What did your folks say?

Said they didn't want him institutionalized. That he's not crazy-crazy, see? Just stubborn.

What else?

They don't want to talk about it. They want their privacy. Hey, all these years, they kept it from me. Me! If you know what's good for you, you'll leave my family out of this.

I stared down the two-lane road and thought about Emi's warning.

It would have to wait. This time of year outside Mazatlán, the landscape was lush, the humidity oppressive. No air conditioning in the Nissan. Just a continuous flow of heated air raking through my hair and open shirt.

I don't know why I even recognized her body on the side of the road. I skidded suddenly onto the dirt shoulder; I was sure it was her. She could have been a corpse in the postmortem proceedings of a grisly police investigation. Perhaps I was ready for this considering what I thought I already knew. Perhaps it was the slight curl of her dark hair matted against her cheek, the curve of her neck and bruised shoulder. Maybe it was her scent. Maybe I had always been crazy for her. Her dim pulse pressed against my fingers. "Rafaela?" I carefully opened the palm of her hand, wondering what she herself had read in the now grimy crevices there, wondering if she knew her own danger.

It took a while for her to focus. "Bobby?"

I guess I wasn't what she had in mind. "It's Gabriel," I said, "Fancy meeting you here, Angel," trying to make light of her grim condition, pretending to myself that she wasn't almost dead.

"Angel," she whispered.

Quickly I removed my shirt and draped it over her, suddenly embarrassed I was staring. I cradled her head and shoulders.

"Are we there yet?" she gasped, clutching my shirt.

"Where?"

"Home."

"Let's get you to the car. You're a long way from anywhere."

She shook her head and pointed at an unfinished brick wall. I scrutinized the wall and the house beyond. Why hadn't I noticed it? Maybe it was all those sunflowers and cactus. But it was my house. It was my unfinished wall, and my garden. Those were my trees and my roses. And yes, she was my housekeeper. I felt slightly nauseated, trying to calculate the mileage to my place. It made no sense. I should have had another hour to travel.

Rafaela ignored my confusion and made a great effort to rise. Despite her shattered appearance, she mustered a subtle power from somewhere, refusing my help almost defiantly, and limped ghostlike toward the house. "Sol," she said. "Find Sol."

I helped her into my house, which had been so transformed by her attentions I felt like a stranger. "Is Sol inside?" I asked, making my way through the rearranged furniture, scanning the proliferation of ornaments and pictures on the walls.

She shook her head and pulled scraps of paper from what remained of a shredded pocket. I spread and joined the crumpled pieces of a poem. "Mi casa es su casa?"

"No. It's the other side," she advised me.

I turned the poem over and read the notice about some wrestling championship. If Emi had been there, the thing would have called for a snide remark of some sort, but I simply asked, "What does this mean?"

"This," she paused after every word, "is where he will be." It took great exertion for her to say anything. "Please."

"All right," I agreed, urging her to lie down, pretending to understand. "Rest. Don't worry about Sol. We'll find him."

I tipped a glass of water to her swollen lips and pressed a damp cloth to her forehead. One eye was completely shut by a blackened bulge. Blood and mud formed great scabs across her skull. Incredibly she seemed to have no broken limbs, though there was no part of her that was not bleeding, bruised, or torn.

The tenderness I felt for her saddened me. I had for so long yearned for my place in México, for the tropical privacy of my hideout. If I held a historic connection to this place, it suddenly felt vague. I hadn't recognized my own place; maybe it was those strange brass-knobbed chairs she'd placed next to the fireplace. Where did she get those ugly things? But it wasn't just decorative. No one in my entire family had ever bothered to come here. They called it Gabe's Folly. "Hey, ése, what about investing in the homeland—East L.A.?" they snickered.

And the romantic thing I felt for this woman was maybe only that—a romantic thing. The house felt strange, and so did my feelings. I stared at Van Gogh's sunflowers and wondered how my stupid idea had brought her here, had brought her this terrible punishment, had caused her to lose her child. I didn't understand how this had happened, but I felt accused. I thought I was doing her a favor, but she worked for me in order to have a place to live. I thought I was helping her education, but I was only patronizing her. I thought she might fall in love with me, but she was only fixing up my house, and I was part of a net of favors and subtle harassments that unconsciously set her up. And she had taken this beating for me. It was my story, wasn't it?

"Who did this to you?" I wanted to know anyway.

"I—" Her single open eye seemed to search somewhere inside of herself. "I ate him." She grabbed me. "Is that possible?"

Nothing made sense.

She fell back. "He can't hurt us anymore." There was a brutal satisfaction in her words.

"No. Of course not," I said stupidly.

"The package," she said. "Did you get it?"

"Yes."

"What was inside?"

"You don't know?"

"Was it . . . ? A child's heart," she whispered. "How could they do such a thing?" Her face burned with rage and then sudden fear. "I have to find Bobby. To get Sol back." She jumped up but crumpled to the floor.

"Hey, hey. Take it easy."

"Help me find Bobby. To give him this." She pressed the printed notice on me. "Sol is safe here. Tell Bobby."

I looked over the notice and read the date. Sunday, June 28th. "Tomorrow," I said. "Noon, tomorrow."

"There isn't much time. Will you go?"

"I can't leave you like this."

"I can take care of myself," she glared at me fiercely. She groped at the shredded remains of her clothing and clutched at something tied to her waist. To my surprise, it was a silver pocketknife. "Sol cannot. Besides, no matter what, I won't be far."

There was a voice calling up the path to the house. I looked out the window to see Doña Maria. "Didn't you say it was her son?" I asked quickly.

"She doesn't know anything."

I knew her as a prying old lady, but obviously she hadn't pried enough to sniff out the crimes of her own household.

"Who are the others?" I asked.

"I only heard the other voice. I never saw the face. Be careful," she warned, as Doña Maria's footfalls marched over the tiled patio.

"Rafaela! Have you returned?"

I noticed Rafaela recoil at the sight of the woman, but Doña Maria paid no attention, bustling about the house with nurselike authority, washing and dressing Rafaela's wounds. I justified to myself, even *she* should be helpful in a situation like this.

"I wondered where you had gone. You should have told me. It's not wise to just disappear. Well, you know my Hernando disappeared, but he's always disappearing. Leaves me alone for months. So what else is new? But you. Something terrible could happen. Well, and look at you. It's a wonder you are alive. Let's see. No broken bones. But what are these tears down your back? Like the claws of an animal! Did you lose a tooth? What brute could have done such a thing to you? No. No. Don't talk now. You need to rest. You're bleeding down here. Is it that time of the month? Oh, no . . . no, no, stop crying, dear. Let me wash it away. Close your eyes. It will heal. Close your eyes. Try to forget."

"Doña Maria," I announced. "I'll need to use your phone as usual."

"Of course. Of course. Go on. Lupe's there. Go on." She followed me out the door. "Blessed Mother of Jesus, what a horrible thing. And the boy? What about the boy? Oh my God. The poor child. It's God's wishes. Yes, God's wishes. What are we to do? But what is the world coming to?"

At Doña Maria's, I tried to reach Emi's cellphone. No answer. I hooked up the modem from my notepad and typed furiously. I imagined my words bunched up in some digital holding cell. *The package! What did you do with it? What did Buzz find out?*

Meanwhile Emi's old messages popped up. *It was so goooood last night. Doing it with someone literate is soooo much bettah. Literate SEX. I never knew that conjugating the verb "to come" in four out of four Romance languages could be so thrilling. Now how do the Italians say it? Vengo. Vieni. Veniamo. Baby, how about it? Let's conjugate some verrrbbbbsss.*

Doña Maria's television flickered with some Mexican version of Oprah. I picked up the remote and surfed through the channels on the chance I might pick up some news, some CNN. But the thing that caught my attention was a channel that looked like the L.A. Thomas Guide. Next channel zoomed in for a close-up. I scrutinized the screen and recognized a distorted version of downtown L.A. At least that's what the street names indicated, but distances were skewed and the streets weren't parallel. But it was close enough. A flashing indicator marked x moved around the map. The indicator seemed to be located at the downtown freeway interchange. I calculated it would be right there in that homeless parking lot mess. I watched it move up what was now Limousine Way, blink toward the Music Center, and up Bunker Hill to Angel's Flight. What was it tracking? And how did this system get on Doña Maria's TV? Who else was watching this? I watched the indicator run up and down several streets.

Suddenly I noticed Lupe in the room staring at the television. "Lupe," I asked, "What is this?"

She shook her head. "The men came to put in the satellite dish. Now they tell me this is what you get."

I made her program the remote to remember the channel and pointed to the blinking indicator. "Tomorrow, I'll call you from Los Angeles. Then, you tell me where the X is, understand?"

She shrugged.

I returned to my telephone hook-up while scanning the desk area for notes, numbers, anything. I grabbed what looked like a customs freight receipt and a notepad with numbers. Beneath the notepad was a travel itinerary. The name at the top: C. Juárez. Was it a coincidence? Or did it confirm Buzzworm's strategy: You don't have to go anywhere; things just come to L.A. In any case, it was time to get back there.

I glanced at the TV; the indicator was still proceeding north. Seemed to be in Chinatown now. I had heard they could implant microchips in pets. Transmitters in dope, or maybe in human organs. Insidious and sophisticated. But who were *they?*

I slipped out of the house, refolding the pieces of Rafaela's flyer, customs slips, and C. Juárez's travel itinerary, stufing it all into my pocket. I had some business to take care of and not a lot of time.

When I got back to the house, Rafaela was sleeping. Her breathing was heavy, and I saw her face and body twitch in agitation. Despite my imagined horror of her dreams, I felt relief because at least she was alive.

"Don't disturb her now," Doña Maria pushed me away from the room. "And don't worry. I will take good care of her until you return," she smiled like a nurse. "She will be as good as new."

I took a last hard look. I knew I would never see her again as good as new. I saw the starched lace curtains billow in the window. I had the impression that the house was filled with sunflowers—living and painted—and lace—tablecloths, doilies, bedspreads, pillows, sheets, and curtains—all woven in a sunny tapestry about the house. Had she had me in mind as she dressed the house? I guessed not.

I had little time to ponder any of this. I ran from the house to my car and backed away. I saw my property—my property that I no longer recognized or perhaps had never recognized—become a speck in my rearview mirror. And then it was gone.

CHAPTER 40:

Social Security *I-5*

"I heard you need a special card. A social security card. How do I get this card? What is social security?"

"Do you want to work and pay taxes?"

"I can work." Cuz looks serious.

"Don't worry about it," says Bobby.

"Is it true that people here all have guns, and they can shoot you if you make them mad?"

"Who told you that?"

"I heard it on the boat."

"It's an exaggeration."

"Is it true there are medicines here you can take to make you crazy or make you float, and people here take them all the time?"

"More exaggerations. What else did you hear on the boat?"

"They said there is music. Rock 'n' roll. Music with perverted words you can sing over and over to make you crazy. It's right on the radio."

"Here." Bobby punches the radio on. "Listen for yourself."

"I can't understand it. Is it really perverted? Can they really sing anything they want? Do I have to understand it to go crazy?"

"Don't worry. This is not what's going to make you crazy."

"Is this your car? How did you get such a car?" Little cuz looks out the windows. Everything along the I-5 swooshing by. She's in a cherry-red Camaro, and everything's swooshing by.

"That's Camp Pendleton. That's where *I* landed when *I* came here." Bobby don't tell her how many times he's passed the place. Never been back. Camp's quiet now. Used to be a busy place. Brother and he got bused up the coast. Probably to be sent to some home. They didn't know. Got scared. Escaped from the bus. Scared they'd get somewhere and be found out. Found out they weren't refugees. Found out and sent back. 50,000 refugees, all looking alike. Who was gonna notice two boys? They just ran away. Bobby says, "When I arrived, I was twelve, just like you."

Cuz is hugging her Barbie Doll still in the box. Not gonna be the same troubles Bobby had. Not gonna let her cry like his brother.

"Take it out of the box," Bobby says.

"No. I like it in the box."

"Why did your brother jump ship?"

"He said if he didn't, he'd be sent back. He could die in the ocean or die in prison. My brother was studying. He's very smart. But my mother always said he talked too much. I don't know, but I think he was talking too much."

"Politics."

"They say you can talk as much as you want here. This is good for my brother."

"You talk a lot yourself."

"Why did you come here? Do you know my village?" Cuz takes out a piece of paper folded in a square and folded again.

"What's that?" Bobby suddenly swerves the Camaro. He's thinking this twelve-year-old's maybe a smuggler. Wah Ching got her smuggling. And he's a dope.

"Dirt," she says, opens it carefully, then folds it all back again. "It's my village. The dirt from there."

Bobby rolls his eyes and breathes again.

She just keeps on talking, "You speak a little strange. Why is that?"

"I don't have to speak the language so much anymore. That's the way it is. Do you always ask so many questions?"

"My brother says to ask questions. Then listen carefully and keep my eyes open. I promised to do this until I see him again."

Bobby's not saying nothing about the brother. If he's lucky, he's dead. Or maybe he's hanging out at El Corralón in a fluorescent orange suit costing forty bucks a day. Waiting for immigration. Probably going for asylum. But probably gonna be busted. Nobody to say he's got a big mouth. Nobody to say he's dead meat back in the homeland.

Cuz is staring at her new Nikes. Made in China. Nikes get in. But not the bro.

Seems like the drive's a cinch. Never got to L.A. so fast. But then inside, it's a mess. Wall-to-wall all up and down the 5. Stopped up like a bad drain. Gotta get off the freeway. Take the side streets. Get by through the alleys. Takes hours. Streets stretched and shrunk this way and that. Someone put this city in the washer/dryer. Shrunk 50 percent in places. Then ironed it out 200 percent in others.

Bobby parks the Camaro. Locks in The Club. Automatic locks the doors. Introduces the cuz to her new home. Unlocks the security door. Unlocks the double bolts. House is stuffy. Locks the security door, but keeps the front door open. Opens some windows. Cuz looks out the bars at Koreatown.

Phone rings. It's the Chicano reporter again. "I've been trying to reach you since yesterday," he says.

Seems Bobby's been trying to get home since yesterday.

"Yeah," says the reporter. "Something's gotta give. Like the pressure's building."

Bobby don't know nothing about pressure, but he sure could use a smoke. "I called that number," Bobby says. "Lady answered. Took a message. Said Rafaela and the boy weren't there."

"I don't know how to tell you this. Rafaela's hurt. She's okay, but she got beat up. Some thug. No. She's fine. She's back at my place like I told you. She's gonna be fine. I feel like it's my fault. I mean it's *not* my fault. I feel responsible. Listen. Will you listen? Sol got separated from her. Right. The boy's disappeared. I don't know. I have a flyer she gave me. It's something called The Ultimate Wrestling Championship. Yeah. One of those Lucha Libre events. I know it sounds crazy. She insists the boy can be found at this fight. It's all on the flyer. Look, I gotta catch my flight back. I'm leaving México City now. You got a a fax? Call me at my office. I'll be back in L.A. in a couple of hours. I'll check my messages."

Don't make no sense. What's this flyer? Ultimate Wrestling. It's a joke. Go ahead. Put it in the fax.

Bobby's looking at the paper slipping out the machine. *Mi casa es su casa!* Bobby's screaming. The bastard! Is this a joke? Where is that hijo de puta reporter? He calls him, but it's the office phone. Reporter's in the air over México. Damn. What's this? A pinche poem? You sending me a poem? What the hell! He's supposed to find Sol in a poem? It's no use. He's talking to a machine. He's talking to Audex.

Little cuz looking at Bobby. Still hugging the Barbie in the box. Still asking the same questions. What's social security? They said you had to have it. Bobby can't think. He dials up a number and hands the cuz the phone. Keep the cuz busy.

"You have reached the offices of the Immigration and Naturalization Service. If you wish to hear this message in English, press one. If you wish to hear this message in Spanish, press two. If you wish to hear this message in Vietnamese, press three. If you wish to hear this message in Mandarin, press four. If you wish to hear this message . . . "

The cuz goes for the TV, fools with the remote. Remote turns on the VCR. Snaps on the tube. She don't know. She's just curious. It's all new to her. America's a surprise. Channels changing like crazy.

Bobby's not paying no attention. He's gotta find Sol. He's staring at the tube trying to think. Tube's got Korean channel speaking something. Maybe it's Russian. Some's Swahili. Spanish channel's speaking English with an accent. Everybody in the Mexican soap's speaking the Queen's English. Other hand, network's speaking fluent Castilian. Some's even in Mandarin. He understands it. He's thinking too it's not a mistake; it all makes sense. But! Does Connie Chung even speak Mandarin? Does that Trek character Chekov speak Russian? Or George Takei, does he speak Japanese? Does Anthony Quinn speak Greek, Turkish, or Spanish? Does David Carradine speak anything but slow English? Who's gonna understand all this all the time? This some joke?

Meantime cuz's channel surfing just like she's been doing it all her life. Youth catches on fast. Maybe it's the surfing. Faster she checks out, faster the lenguas check in. TV's gone crazy.

Suddenly he makes her stop. It's in Spanish this time. Lucha Libre. Gonna be The Ultimate Wrestling Championship. Some dude named El Gran Mojado. Unbeatable. To the death. Hey. Pacific Rim Auditorium. Noon. Sunday. June 28th. Tomorrow! Call Ticketmaster. Or check out the closest Blockbuster, Robinson-May, Music Plus. But hurry, tickets going fast. Gonna be sold out. Who's the sponsor? Drink called *Passion*. Drink Passion. That's it.

Bobby sets the cuz up with some frozen microwave, Famous Amos, and a glass of milk. Tells the cuz to sit tight. He's got some business to take care of. She's got the Barbie doll, her village dirt, and the remote. By the time he gets back, she's gonna be glued good. Now hit the road. Find the boy.

Pacific Rim Auditorium's not far. Something tells him he better go on foot. And he better leave now to make it by tomorrow. Not gonna move no machine, no Camaro, through these streets. Used to go everywhere on foot. Knows the alleys and the little streets. Been a while since he maneuvered the barrio. Been a while since any vato called him the Chino Loco. True, some things'd changed big-time, but he knew that. And some things never gonna change. Órale, it's still about moving the body with the flow. Still about keeping tuned to a sixth sense. Everything in control. Just pushing the air aside to pass. Don't disturb too much. Keep the memory of everything he passes. Like 360-degree vision. Surround sound. Don't miss a thing.

So pretty soon, Bobby's on a roll. Something taking him through some curves. If the cuz is back home channel surfing, this must be barrio surfing.

Next minute he's in the woods: Holly, Brent, Ingle, and West woods. Then it's the beaches: Manhattan, Redondo, Huntington, Hermosa, Topanga, Seal, and Long. Then it's the parks: Echo, Leimert, Griffith, Elysian, Monterey, and MacArthur. Then the hills: Beverly and Rolling. The saints: Monica, Bernardino, Ana, Gabriel, Pedro, Marino and Fernando. The Las: Crescenta, Canada, Habra, Mirada, and Puente. And the Els: Segundo and Monte. And finally, the big Los.

It's getting dark. Big Los twinkling like a shimmering sequined dress at a quinceañera. Clouds of smoke and haze getting those orange and purple stripes of sunset. Looking like a gigantic mural. Órale.

CHAPTER 41:

Prime Time *Last Stop*

Buzzworm climbed up the back ladder of the *NewsNow* van and peered over the top at Emi in a bikini and Ray-Bans stretched out on a beach towel. "Someone said this was the last stop before the sun goes down, but they forgot about Hawaii," she muttered to her intruder.

"It's not Hawaii neither," Buzzworm noted.

"Same person said you could rot here without feeling it. So-called paradise, see. Smoking, drugging, and sex are absolutely necessary to make you feel anything in paradise."

"If this is paradise, we're in trouble." He looked out from his perch, currently a tanning pad, and surveyed day five of the Harbor Freeway crisis in which every homeless person had for the moment found shelter. Funny how it looked like home. He looked over at a book squashed open on its belly. "What's to read?"

"Book I grabbed off Gabe."

"Easy Rawlins?"

"He likes this private dick stuff. Dark and dirty. Goes with wearing shades whilst taking in the rays." Emi rolled over on her stomach and propped her chin up on the triangle made between her forearms and the van's roof. "It's moving toward midsummer, and I do have a California look to maintain. You know, glowing health, tight muscles, New Age tan."

"I wouldn't know about no New Age tan. Got me an Old Age one myself."

"A New Age tan's like this: You arrive from some midwestern armpit, see. You've been raised on steak and potatoes. To you, veggie is like canned beans. Vegan is, well, it's a Trekkie term for aliens from Star Vega. Somebody on Venice Beach reads your astrological forecast. Someone else reads your aura. You find out you're a star-crossed Aquarian with a future as a bisexual. You get a tattoo on your right ankle and pierce your navel. You join a gym, start up on the Nautilus, and get regular bodywork. You take up yoga, do a thorough detox, and go macrobiotic: miso, tofu, and brown rice. You become religiously organic. You join an animal rights support group to heal your inner animal. You try to write a screenplay and get an agent. You go to bed under a pyramid with your therapist/healer. Your folks come out to see you, Disneyland, Universal Studios, and Marilyn Monroe's grave. They say, 'California seems to be doing you some good. Got some color in your face for a change.' Voilà! A New Age tan!"

Buzzworm looked blankly at Emi and shook his dreads. "Well, I'll be. And I thought having skin color was just so as to define what's white."

"It's total bullshit. I just needed to get away."

"I read you."

The hum of propellers was a constant, but the sound suddenly lunged in with the copter's shadow. "Damn. I told them to stay away!" She propped herself up and made a rude gesture at the flying machine.

"How did Balboa ever get involved with you?"

"Go figure. Behind that noir pose, Gabe's basically a romantic sort of guy. I'm the opposite. You want cuddly romance, you're better off with a Siamese cat. So maybe that's what it is. I keep the romance at bay."

Emi rolled over on her back again, pillowing her head on her arms. She looked over her toes at Manzanar on the overpass. She still had not had the courage to march up there to meet the man.

"That's why you won't go up there, isn't it?" Buzzworm nodded at the conductor. "That man's the ultimate romantic. You can hear his music can't you? Admit it, baby sister. Everyone can. It's painful stuff. Gets you right here. Times there's people down there rocking in the cars, weeping."

"I wouldn't know."

"He's calling you, baby sister. He's got your melody."

"I'm thirsty. I could use a drink." She leaned over the side of van and yelled, "Kerry, what's left in the cooler? Got a Coke? Or better yet, got *Passion*?" She took the dark glasses off and looked at Buzzworm. "Wanna hear a secret?"

Buzzworm's lips curled up in a wry smile.

"This is for real," she looked hurt and turned away.

"Baby sister," he nudged her with a soft voice. "Secrets are my business."

Emi nodded. "He was my grandfather."

"He is your grandfather," Buzzworm corrected.

She drew a sigh. "I can't believe it's him. I remember we were always singing songs together. It's the only thing that makes sense. I mean about that conducting or whatever it is. He liked to sing. I remember that. And then, he just disappeared. I knew he didn't die . . . no one said anything as if he did. I was nine or ten. I don't know why I should have even recognized him."

"But you did."

"And if I go up there, he couldn't possibly recognize me."

"No problem. I'll introduce you."

"What is he to me anyway?"

"Yeah, baby sister, the connection begs to be understood. I can't say I knew my grandma too well either, but when she died, she left me everything she had. It was just her house, but it was everything. You'd be surprised what comes with a house. Old letters, memories, ghosts, the meaning of ever having it in the first place. Maybe *you,*" he pointed at her, "get lucky. Get the baton and the overpass to boot."

Buzzworm looked at his watches. "I give you an hour to get ready."

"What's the point?"

"Between these TV microwaves and the ultraviolet, you gonna catch you some cancer out here. Time to put some clothes on and meet another human being. I'm gonna save your life yet."

"Is that so?"

Buzzworm stepped down the ladder and met Kerry at the bottom with a cold can of Coke. "Her Majesty will see you now," he smirked. As he turned away, the dull crack of a small but sharp thunder rumbled above his head. This sound was all too familiar, and it was not the pop of a flip-top jerked off an aluminum soda can. The rumble came again. Buzzworm jerked Kerry off the ladder and to the ground. "Get down!" he commanded and scrambled to the top of the van. He reached over, clawing at the beach towel, and dragged Emi toward him.

As he pulled her closer, she gasped, "I actually saw them out there aiming for the dish. It's such a dick in the air, you . . . wouldn't . . . think . . . they'd . . . miss."

CHAPTER 42:

Drive-By *Virtually Everywhere*

There was a time when the v-6 and the double-overhead cam did not reign. In those days, there were the railroads and the harbors and the aqueduct. These were the first infrastructures built by migrant and immigrant labor that created the initial grid on which everything else began to fill in. Steam locomotives cut a cloud of black smoke through the heart of the West. Yankee pirates arrived with cotton linens, left with smuggled cowhides and tallow. And the water was eventually carved away from the north, trickled, then flooded, into this desert valley. And after that nothing could stop the growing congregation of humanity in this corner of the world, and a new grid spread itself with particular domination. As someone said, now the freeways crashed into each other with flower beds.

Spread across these infrastructures was yet another of Manzanar's grids: his map of labor. It was those delicate vulnerable creatures within those machines that made this happen: a thing called work. Every day, he saw them scatter across the city this way and that, divvying themselves up into the garment district, the entertainment industry, the tourist business, the military machine, the service sector, the automotive industry, the education industry, federal, county, and city employees, union workers, domestics, and day labor. It was work that defined each person in the city, despite the fact that almost everyone wanted to be defined by their leisure. Every day Manzanar had watched the daily hires hugging their knees on the backs of pickup trucks, looking backwards into traffic, eyes fixed, challenging the pretensions of other workers inside cars that they imagined defined their existence. Now, for a scant moment in history, the poor looked out those same cars.

Little by little, Manzanar began to sense a new kind of grid, this one defined not by inanimate structures or other living things but by himself and others like him. He found himself at the heart of an expanding symphony of which he was not the only conductor. On a distant overpass, he could make out the odd mirror of his figure, waving a baton. And beyond that, another homeless person had also taken up the baton. And across the city, on overpasses and street corners, from balconies and park benches, people held branches and pencils, toothbrushes and carrot sticks, and conducted. Strange and wonderful elements had been added as well. Among them: lutes and lyres, harmonicas, accordions, sitars, hand organs, nose flutes, gamelons, congas, berimbaus, and cuícas. Manzanar nodded to himself. Not bad.

And of course the movement of traffic had almost altogether stopped, not only in the freeway valley below but virtually everywhere. The tenor of this music was a very different sort, at times a kind of choral babel. In its initial movements, a soft angelic quality with the repetitive chorus of the homeless encampment wafted gently above the smoking cinders of quenched fires. As the members of this choir grew exponentially, the thing began to have grandiose proportions only Manzanar could appreciate. The entire City of Angels seemed to have opened its singular voice to herald a naked old man and little boy with an orange followed by a motley parade approaching from the south. Once again, the grid was changing.

Manzanar charged into his music, frantically looking for help. The valley was no longer only ten lanes across or one mile long; it was becoming the entire city and bigger than a tiny island or a puny country the size of San Bernardino. And the approaching parade was dragging in the entire midriff (and maybe even the swaying hips, burning thighs, and sultry genitals) of the hemisphere. The rational forces of the North looked south at the naughty old man who waved his penis around and shook their big collective head. This was a gesture of war, was it not?

Despite the celebratory nature of Manzanar's great laboring choir, the terror of gunfire ripped across that valley of cars. Manzanar knew it had started with a single shot—the one that had penetrated the soft body of a young woman sunning herself on that news van. That was all it took. The sound of the shot penetrated Manzanar's very being with a vengeance he did not understand. The moment repeated itself again and again; he clothed it in desperation each time with pain and more pain. Great shuddering sobs welled from within.

The assemblage of military might pointed at one's own people was horrific, as was the amassing of weapons and munitions by the people themselves. If half of the homeless were veterans of war, then half of the current occupants of the valley suddenly returned to familiar scenes of fear and bloodshed, jumping into the foliage, cowering behind jeeps, lugging knives and rifles, carefully surveying the fray from that big ditch. A single shot heralded the ugly possibility of war. On cue, the thunder of a hundred helicopters announced their appearance on the downtown horizon, strafing the freeway along its dotted lines, bombing the valley with tear gas and smoke. The coordinated might of the Army, Navy, Air Force, Marines, the Coast and National Guards, federal, state, and local police forces of the most militaristic of nations looked down as it had in the past on tiny islands and puny countries the size of San Bernardino and descended in a single storm.

Manzanar recomposed with difficulty what the generals surveyed on their infrared monitors; a rainbow of putrid green gas and red, white, and blue smoke hid the fray from discerning eyes, muffled the shrieking and wailing. Lines of cars along the slow lanes south and north exploded into flames, golden clouds of boiling petroleum rising in two great walls, further obscuring the deed.

The motley community of homeless and helpless and well intentioned ran in terror, surrendered, vomited, cradled the dying. Manzanar recorded every scream and cry and shudder with dumb incomprehension. And the rising tide of that migration from the South—not foreign to the ravages of war—never stopped, clamored forward, joined the war with both wooden and real weapons, capital, and plunder.

And so the percussion of war cracked and thundered. Horns trumpeted attack. Strings bled a foul massacre. Oh say can you see by the dawn's early light the rockets' red glare, the bombs bursting in air?

SUNDAY:

Pacific Rim

CHAPTER 43:

Deadline *Over the Net*

First thing, I shot a bunch of faxes out: the feature story on the El Zócalo demonstration, insider interview with a revolutionary, plus the flyer to Bobby—hoping he'd know what the hell to do with it. Hoping he was going to find his kid. If I could get the rest of my stories pieced together, maybe I'd make it myself to the Ultimate Wrestling event.

Next off, I got back to LAX in time to meet Mexicana flight 900 for a second time to look for the woman with the baby and yellow bag. She turned out to be a no-show. I should have known. Rafaela had diverted the merchandise. I called the travel agency in México City. "I was expecting my cousin. Her last name is Juárez, traveling with her baby boy. She never arrived. I'm very worried," I lied.

"Why don't you just call her at home?"

"I don't have her number. Just this copy of her itinerary. It's very confusing. Perhaps you could provide a number for her?"

"Juárez? What is her first name?"

I fumbled for some common name with C. "Carmen," I tried. "No Carmen. Only a Corazón."

"Yes! How stupid of me. She goes by Corazón now."

"The ticket was picked up and paid for in cash. There's really no record. I wouldn't worry. She'll contact you, I'm sure."

Another dead end. As for contacts, I needed to renew speaking contact with Emi and Buzz, but Emi's cellphone still drew a blank, and I'd paged Buzz three times already. No answer. I needed Emi to help me fill in the blanks on my homeless conductor angle on the freeway crisis, and I never did get an answer about my package. If I could get the word, pin down the contents: kidney, heart, liver, whatever. As it was, it was somewhere out there playing limbo. If I got lucky, it might just limbo under my next deadline.

It was still daylight, and I still had to check out a lead on the poison oranges. The customs slips I'd taken from Doña Maria's indicated an address in El Segundo. I took a couple of freeway offs over to a legitimate brokerage, but no records could be produced to track the product. "Oranges from Brazil via Honduras. Is that the normal route?" I queried.

"Well, say Brazil's quota for oranges is exhausted, then Brazil exports to Honduras. Honduras to Guatemala, Guatemala to México, and México to the United States. Then it's cool even though everyone knows the orange harvest is dead in México in June. Keeps everyone in business."

So even the legal papers would have been bogus. As it was, I had a bunch of bureaucratic papers to make transactions look legal, to make the connections fuzzy. Anyone could fill them out. And no one had ever heard of the broker who signed the documents. The invisibility of those who fingered the threads mocked my every move. I said I'd be back with more information. It was going to take more time. I wasn't going to get this story right away, but I'd get it eventually. After all, it was *my* story.

I called Doña Maria's number and got Lupe on the phone. "How is Rafaela?" I asked.

"Sleeping. Always sleeping."

I heaved a sigh of relief, then asked, "Where's the X now?"

"Grapevine?" she asked. "El Tejón," she said with more confidence. "Where is that?"

"Good job," I encouraged her.

"What about the other channels?" Lupe queried.

"Other channels?"

"Two hundred channels. Coming to the dish invisibly from the sky. I have been thinking about this. The sky is wide and endless."

"Yes, yes. Keep watching."

"But," she insisted, "I've been looking. There are more maps than just one. More than just one X. Maybe another nine or ten. What does this mean?"

I groaned. More maps? Lupe was looping through channel after channel. She had trouble with the coordinates. She could be describing any of a hundred urban centers. I had to see it myself. International crime cartels with access to satellite tracking devices. Tracking illegal merchandise in dozens of cities. How do crime cartels get their own satellites? If a dish on the Tropic of Cancer could pick it up like Direct TV or GPS, why not any other? Lupe was right; the sky was wide and endless.

But where were the villains and what were they up to? Selling body parts from third world children for transplants? Smuggling drugs in oranges? Conceivably, there was a villain at the beginning and end of every signal. Multiple uplinks and downlinks to a constellation of satellites. But who was tracking all this? The commerce was on the ground; the threads pulling them around were in the air. Which conspiracy theory was this one? The cartel, if that was what it was, was a big invisible net. If I had a strategy, it would be to get in there and snarl the net without entangling myself.

As for entanglements, I was getting used to carrying on my relationship with Emi over the net. Maybe she was right. It was a lifestyle I had to accept. If things continued the way they were going, what with the jetsetting and newstime on a kind of dedicated speed, I was never going to be home. I was never going to be in one place for very long. My life had become frantic but constantly satisfying. Maybe that was because I had no time to think about it, but considering my mistake with Rafaela, it was probably just as well. Maybe I had finally lost my romantic notions; I'd become truly noir, a neuromancer in dark space.

Talking to Emi over the net was oddly satisfying. There was no voice inflection to imply anything, yet everything could be inferred from everything. Maybe some irony was indicated by ;-), but when talking to Emi, ironic notation was redundant. And it was quite a bit more private, if you considered the ears hanging on your phone conversations. It was a new dimension in communicating. Let your fingers do the talking. Digital connections. Digital manipulations. And she was right. It was incredible how sexy text could be. Well, I had always been a text man. As Emi liked to complain, I got my cheap thrills from black and white. But I could also deliver. Emi was always moaning it over the net; my descriptive powers really made her ache. And then there was the rest of the net; it was a big borderless soup and I was cooking. There were miles and miles of text stacking up at my address; I couldn't be alone ever again. Maybe the net was the ultimate noir.

I found a hookup for my notebook computer and zipped out a few lines to her mailbox: *Angel, you're gonna be proud of me. I'm finally getting the hang of hypertext.*

Bunches of her old messages popped up. I hadn't had the time to read them. I took a moment to scan a few: *So, Gabe, you've finally decided to write your own book. You certainly have read (or seen) enough of them. Is it going to be an L.A. Chicano private dick thing? Of course,* I'm *in it. I mean, I'm the private dick's thing, am I not? (kiss)* If she only knew.

I typed in my budgets, storylines that spun a net of loose threads: coked oranges traced to Brazil/Amazon via a Colombia shipment through Honduras, and since poison can be carried by the seemingly innocuous fruit fly, consequences could prove grave; international infant organs conspiracy—tip of the iceberg; voices in the valley of the homeless raised in choral symphony: *What's LAPD gonna do? Don't shoot! Don't shoot!*

Maybe it was a net of loose threads, but I was onto it. For every budget,

I set up a newsgroup over the net. For example: alt.soc.med.transplants .farming.infants was one; another hot topic was alt.soc.drugs.oranges (oranges continued to be scarce, worth their weight in gold, and floated invisibly through some parallel world). Almost instantaneously these groups were cluttered with commentary, hearsay, and even legitimate info. I waded through everything, ferreting out the good stuff and double-checking the sources. It was amazing what people out there knew or thought they knew and what they'd offer up for public scrutiny. On the spiked orange issue, I got a tip on an actual location for a lab somewhere outside Manaus, Brazil, doing the chemistry mix with medicinal rare plants and venoms provided by local aborigines. A coroner's list of the dead turned up. Another source even broke down the components; scary thing was it was not only scholarly, it looked like a damned recipe. Someone commented that if this was what it took to save the rain forest, so be it.

My infant organ farming newsgroup quickly self-divided into subtopics: Procedures. Ethics. Updates. Out of the blue, a chat group of people claiming to have received illegally farmed organs got scheduled. The chat here seemed driven by a combination of guilt-ridden angst and vicious survival types. The chat typically went like this:

—*If I thought for one moment that I was a recipient of an illegal organ, I would rip my heart out right now.*

—*So I say all transplanted organs are illegal. Rip it out now!*

—*We are all living on borrowed time. God bless the man on death row who willed me his kidney.*

—*This chat is about "farmed" organs, not "willed" organs.*

—*Death row's not close enough?*

—*I was a baby when this occurred. My folks were trying to save my life. How do I go on living, knowing what I know?*

This was all very well, but as a reporter I needed some facts. *What do you know?* I queried back. *Do you know the source of your organ? Who was the doctor who performed the transplant?*

Much of it was vague or not forthcoming. I waded through massive amounts of drivel to no avail, but I wasn't giving up. I was going to close in on the culprits. I wanted my link to the creeps who battered Rafaela. As soon as I had the goods on them, the entire story would be on every major mailing list on the net and e-mailed and faxed to the desk of every politician, every publication, and every public and private organization with an axe to grind.

Emi's old e-mail slipped back in. She never left me alone, even in the past tense. *I been thinking, Gabe. This L.A. net of crime theme you want to pursue: Isn't it a little dated? Gambling and racketeering condoned by the police: really now. Even the CIA/Contra arms-for-crack scheme is passé. I mean, have you seen some of the new chat menus online? For example, I accidentally discovered this newsgroup which is basically about human organ farming. El bizarro! It's crude I know, but check out the subtopic on "sales." It's buying and selling time. Baby hearts are going for a mere $30 thou. Sounds like a down payment on a Mercedes.*

Damn. I couldn't sleep on this. Look away, and I'd lose my lead. I rushed back into *my* newsgroup, but not before scanning a few more of Emi's Es. *Of course I'm assuming you're going to turn this newsprint of yours into a screenplay. If I were to direct it (smile), I'd be faithful to the black-and-white vision of course. Do something visually exciting: sunlight so blazing hot, it's casting those dark & dirty shadows. Remember, sweetheart, if L.A. hates it, N.Y.'s gonna love it!* Emi was rambling again. *By the way, I'm thinking of getting you a dog for company. Not a real dog. A fuzzy software dog. It's so cute! It lives in your computer in the corner of your monitor. Of course you have to feed it and clean up after it just like any other dog . . .* There was stuff here for days. It could wait.

I started to check out for the moment, but typed in: *I'm gonna be tied up, stuck to the desk here for the next few days. No time to chat. Keep me posted. Luvya Angel.*

I looked at the time, a digital reminder in the corner of my notebook. It was no longer daylight, but it didn't matter. I heightened the contrast on the screen, the harsh LCD light exposing a web of evil. In previous days, I would have even gone for a cold cup of pewter-colored coffee, but news itself had become my constant high. With the chaos of events, anything I put into the system got snorted up. Editors were going through the stuff with sieves, and what was sifted out went like toner, directly to print or the net. As soon as you had a lead, you had a deadline. It was now or never. I was tapping the very veins of news and shooting the stuff back into the system. I felt strangely powerful. Buzz and I were gonna share that Pulitzer yet.

I no longer looked for a resolution to the loose threads hanging off my storylines. If I had begun to understand anything, I now knew they were simply the warp and woof of a fraying net of conspiracies in an expanding universe where the holes only seemed to get larger and larger. It was like Emi with her multiple monitors, channel surfing, or reading a slew of books simultaneously. The picture got larger and larger. I could follow a story or I could abandon it, but I could not stop.

CHAPTER 44:

Commercial Break *The Big Sleep*

"Pull that goddamn dick down outta the air!" Buzzworm yelled at the *NewsNow* engineer, shoving him into the van with Emi slumped in the front seat. Kerry lowered the telescoping antenna, and Buzzworm gunned the van into action, jammed it between the spreading lanes. He could see the chasing helicopters in the rearview mirror approaching in a cloud of rainbow smoke. It could have been an air show, even with the strafing machine guns and multiple explosions. Emi, bleeding through her New Age tan and towel, appreciated the precision timing as if it were special FX.

"Can't you drive any faster?" she taunted as if this E-ticket wasn't E-nough.

Buzzworm wove the van through the droves of screaming and panic-stricken people like so many walk-ons, avoiding the sudden car explosions and shattering glass, careening around the digitally constructed dismembering of cats and dogs and even a horse. A cast of thousands—military and civilian—ran this way and that in an epic disaster. Emi looked on with dull approval; it was B fare. The explosions could be extended, the ride sped up, the sensation of violence and speed intensified. Strange, but she could actually smell the gasoline and smoke. Her eyes teared uncontrollably.

The van's rear tire blew, and Buzzworm forced the thumping vehicle up the side of the freeway valley, heading instinctively for some palm trees swaying against the wind of helicopter wings in a camouflage of smog. Stray bullets hailed from above as he crouched through the ivy, cradling Emi, and slipped with her between that tight constellation of palms. It was strangely and suddenly peaceful there.

Emi pulled a bloody hand up to her face and stared. "I give you permission *not* to touch my blood," she said. "I tested negative, but you never know."

Buzzworm held her close. He knew a dead cooky when he saw one.

In the corner of Buzzworm's eye, she could see the monitors in the van flickering beyond the palms. There she was, the *NewsNow* producer sunning on the *NewsNow* van. There was the shot and Buzzworm heroically scrambling up to pull her off the roof. The camera swung wildly looking for the direction of the shot. Easy does it. But what the camera caught was how the first shot was the push-button that set off all the others. It panned the barrage with a horrible urgency that made the viewer remember momentarily that a human eye directed its vision. Captioning ran across the bottom of the monitor: *Breaking News! LIVE footage from the downtown freeway interchange . . .*

Buzzworm wondered what could be *live* in this sense. Emi, on the other hand, lived for this. And it would repeat itself again and again to remind the world what the beginning of the end looked like. In this sense, she would never die.

Even so, Emi's mind wandered from current events. "I had a dream that I got buried in the La Brea Tar Pits, and years later I became the La Brea Woman. You know, my bones and a holographic image of me."

Buzzworm smiled his smile.

Emi winced, "Here I am in the healing capitol of the nation. You'd think some spiritual force would make its appearance at a time like this. Where are all the Jesuses and Mohammeds when you need them?"

"Making a living, I suppose." Buzzworm shook his head.

"Wonder where my private dick is?" Emi murmured.

"I know Balboa'd be here if he could." Buzzworm was unconvincing in the sympathetic mode.

"Are you going to sweet-talk me now that I'm dying?"

"Was hoping you'd leave a year's supply of batteries for me in your will."

"Only if you promise me the complete package: Forest Lawn, naked Davids, daily rosebuds, and eternal music. What's that you're listening to?" She nodded at his earplug.

"'S not eternal." He shook his head.

Emi smiled. "Who'd a thought you and I'd get this close?" She might have embraced him, but her limbs had ceased to feel. About all she could do was to look deeply into his eyes and flutter her lashes. "If *we* can jus' get along, maybe all our problems will go away."

"Gonna take more than holdin' hands to start that revolution."

"Oh well," Emi blew it off. "For Gabe. Did you try the net?"

"Baby sister, you know I don't know nothing about that."

"Gabe's into the net. Ever since he saved that village, he's been devoted to online."

Buzzworm looked around, wondering if the net could save anyone from the current situation. In the smoke, he could see the military, in jungle camouflage, making its move down the freeway canyon. The *live* monitor didn't show this. It was too busy repeating the beginning of the end, ad nauseam. Being the hero of this footage, he looked to her as the heroine. Finally, her death would be unforgivable. Emi's enraged media would see to that. A thousand homeless could die, but no one would forget her ultimate sacrifice.

She continued, "Last I looked, Hollywood wants to buy the rights to the guerrilla war in Chiapas."

"Why even go that far?"

"Tell Gabe, I got lucky and went to *The Big Sleep*." She pouted for effect. "Did you see it?"

"What?"

"*The Big Sleep*. There's a chauffeur who dies, see. His car gets pushed off the Santa Monica pier. Suddenly they stop the action. Someone asks the question: Who killed him? Script continuity, see. Nobody knows. They call up Raymond Chandler. He doesn't know either. Gabe told me this, so it's all hearsay anyway, but it's like that."

"Like what?"

"*The Big Sleep*. Just cuz you get to the end doesn't mean you know what happened."

"Oh." Buzzworm wasn't going to push it.

Didn't matter. She just rambled on anyway. "Hey, I read there's some guy digitizing L.A. Gonna put this treacherous desert outpost online. Maybe the big sleep is a big digital wet dream. And life is just a commercial break. Maybe Gabe can call me up in cyber, and we can do it in my sleep." She grinned and gasped, "Interactive-like."

"I'm not gonna remember to tell Balboa something I don't even understand. Can't you keep your message simple?"

"How about this? I just want to know one thing: What color is blood in . . . black and . . . white?" It dribbled down in a thick vein over her lips.

Buzzworm noted it would most likely be black, but he said, "It's all shades of gray, baby sister. Shades of gray."

Emi's voice sank to a whisper. "Abort. Retry. Ignore. Fail . . ."

CHAPTER 45:

Midnight *The Line*

Rafaela opened her eyes. "What time is it?" she whispered.

"What does it matter, my child?" Doña Maria rose from her seat of vigilance.

"The match. It will be starting soon." Rafaela grabbed the swaddled pocketknife from under her pillow, pushed aside the sheets, and slipped from the bed.

"You aren't well enough. You've been sleeping so fitfully. Where are you going?"

Rafaela stepped across the room, grabbed a small hand mirror from atop a chest of drawers, and stared at herself in horror, but the old woman snatched the thing away with a sudden fierceness. "Whatever are you doing?"

Rafaela bit her lip, adjusted the white lace straps of her cotton shift over her bruised shoulders and limped barefoot into the garden toward the orange tree. Doña Maria had applied a slather of poultices over her wounds; now dried, her skin had a chalky appearance. New red blood and old black blood spotted the white trim of her sheer gown. "You're still bleeding, my dear," Doña Maria called after

Indeed it was a long walk, the well-worn path the same path but a path disappearing forever northward through a thicket of sunflowers and cactus, and the orange tree a small green speck in the distance. Doña Maria's protesting voice was soon swallowed by folding space as was a blinking X on a map on a television screen. Rafaela kept sight of the tree and stepped lightly through the sand and dust. She only stopped momentarily to fold the pocketknife into the skirts of her gown, tying it in a secure knot in the bloodied trim. After several hours, she strained through the good vision in one eye to see the thin figure of a man leaning against the tree. "Bobby?" She hurried forward, pressing her hand to her side, cracked ribs shifting under her skin.

Bobby seemed to have seen her and was now walking toward her. They both walked and ran forever. The purple places on her face and limbs throbbed with every step. She stretched her arms across an infinite and yet invisible chasm.

But then she saw it: the fine silken thread she knew so well, the one that would lead to the orange and hopefully to Sol. It lay in the dust, occasionally whipping about like a delicate piece of tinsel. One more step and she could grab it. Take it in her hands and twist it about her body, pull herself toward Bobby. She held herself against it and, like a sweeping wave, rode forward.

Bobby held her bruised face in his hands and wept like a child. He stroked her dark hair and tenderly felt the crusting patches in her scalp where the hair had been ripped away. He lifted her lace shift away and kissed the welts on her bare shoulders and the scars along her back. He cradled her in his arms, heaving and groaning. He wrapped himself about her wanting to protect all the parts of her yet untouched, wanting to heal all the parts of her so tortured.

Rafaela pulled the silken thread around them until they were both covered in a soft blanket of space and midnight, their proximity to everything both immediate and infinitely distant. She kissed his palms and pulled his clothing and possessions and his work away. She tugged at everything and cast them all aside, folding and warming herself in his naked frame. They came together in a fleshy ball, wrapped and clinging one to the other, genitals pressed in a lingering fire, heart to heart, mind to mind.

But imperceptibly the silken thread unfolded and tugged itself away, caught finally between their ephemeral embrace. They straddled the line—a slender endless serpent of a line—one peering into a private world of dreams and metaphysics, the other into a public place of politics and power. One peering into a magical world, the other peering into a virtual one. "Will you wait for me on the other side?" she whispered as the line in the dust became again as wide as an entire culture and as deep as the social and economic construct that nobody knew how to change.

CHAPTER 46: **SigAlert** *The Rim*

Manzanar let his arms drop. There was no need to conduct the music any longer. The entire city had sprouted grassroots conductors of every sort. He peered through the din and smoke of the battle and saw a tall man coming toward him carrying the body of a woman wrapped in a beach towel. It was the man whose calling card read *Angel of Mercy.* It was the woman who had been sunning herself on the TV van. Buzzworm stood beneath the overpass and raised Emi's body like a gift.

Manzanar nodded. A well of silly tunes filled his old throat. Folk songs. Jazz bits. Rock tunes. Lullabies. *Are you sad today? I have a new song for you. How about that?* The words and the songs wandered around his head. He hadn't *meant* to leave her, or anyone else.

It was a curious thing. Manzanar had followed an ancient tortoise out into a deep place in his brain and stayed there year after year. Now it seemed he had surfaced. The infant heart had triggered the full range of memories. Slowly his head rose above the foam and floating kelp. He walked from the rim and looked back at the waves of natural and human garbage thrown back again and again. Everything would churn itself into tiny bits of sand, crumble there at the rim—the descending sun one gigantic blazing orange dipping behind, boiling the sea into steamy shades of blood. He had seen enough. And he had heard everything.

The deafening thudder of helicopter rotors dipped above him. Buzzworm was there struggling to place the woman's body on the hanging gurney. "Go with her!" Buzzworm's voice could not be heard, but Manzanar saw the words formed clearly on his lips and obeyed, climbing onto the gurney with his granddaughter.

"Hang on!" The words formed on Buzzworm's lips again.

Manzanar held on. He took her hand in his like old times.

The thing lifted, spun away from the freeway melee and around the Panasonic/Chrysler Coliseum sign. It was 78 degrees, but the time had long been dysfunctional. Manzanar looked up; it was the *NewsNow* copter requisitioned to save its own. Now, it dipped along the concrete sections of the L.A. River, skirting the Hollywood sign, flitting over the hills.

And Manzanar, peering cautiously from his higher perch, saw bird's-eye the inflation of thousands upon thousands of automotive airbags, bursting simultaneously everywhere from their pouches in steering wheels and glove compartments like white poppies in sudden bloom. All the airbags in L.A. ruptured forth, unfurled their white powdered wings against the barrage of bullets, and stunned the war to a dead stop.

But Manzanar heard nothing.

CHAPTER 47:

To Die *Pacific Rim Auditorium*

One of Arcangel's many voices boomed from the speakers, "Ladies and gentlemen! Welcome to the Pacific Rim Auditorium here at the very Borders. (And you thought it was a giant bookstore. Ha!) It's the Ultimate Wrestling Chammmpppionnnnshhhipppp! El Contrato Con América. Sponsored by a generous grant from the Ministry of Multicultures. Brought to you by the CIA, the PRI, the DEA, and the INS . . .

(a murmur ran through the audience)

"Of course the fight's not fixed. Why should anyone want to do a thing like that?

(sighs of relief, and snickers)

"Today, ladies and gentlemen, witness the battle of two of the world's greatest fighters: SUUUPERRRRRNAFFFFFTAAAAA . . .

(a great boo flooded the auditorium)

"and ELLLLLLL GGRRRRRRAAAAAAAAANNN MOOOJAAADOOOO!

(cheers)

"But first, let's meet and talk to the challenger and the champion before the battle begins."

Automatically, all eyes focused on any one of four giant screens. The flipping photographic image of a masked man in a titanium suit with a head of raging fire somersaulted and spread itself neatly over each screen. He stood, arms crossed and legs spread like the Terminator or Johnny Mnemonic or the Five Million Dollar Man. National heroes like SUPERNAFTA were usually replicants of some sort. The accompanying intro of majestic horns and a mean electric bass drowned out any disapproval from the crowd. A moment of awe and sincere speculation about the flames tripping off the top of his head dissipated into the embarrassment of being fooled by effects.

SUPERNAFTA never smiled. Humorless, he pointed his finger at the camera and intoned his cold bluster. "Today, my fight represents a challenge, not only to that Big *Wetback*," he spit, "in the other corner, but to all the children of the world. To that multicultural rainbow of kids out there." Upon saying *children* his eyes became slightly droopy like a puppy dog's. "Kids, this is your challenge, too. And the challenge is this: It's the future. And what's the future? Well, isn't it what everyone really wants? It's a piece of the action! And that's what progress is all about. A piece of the action.

How about 12 percent? You don't think 12 percent is enough? Look at it this way. What's 12 percent of a billion dollars? One hundred twenty million! That's multimillions. And it's not a lottery. It's your cut. And you don't have to do nothing to get it except to say no to drugs and sex. There's an entire machine of banking computers and technological research and development that's working day and night to put together this billion-dollar package so you can have your cut. That's progress working for you. Some people don't want progress. My opponent doesn't want progress. He doesn't care about the future of all you wonderful kids. He thinks you ought to run across the border and pick grapes. Think about it. Before any one of you can be truly free, you need to have enough money to do what you want. The only way that's gonna happen is to free the technology and the commerce that make the money go round. You're not asking for much. Just 12 percent. That's your ticket to freedom. Kids, it's about freedom and the future. Together and with the blessing of God, we're gonna meet this challenge today. We're gonna hasta la vista this baby's face!"

Fifty percent of the boos in the crowd turned to cheers. It was amazing what a 12 percent cut plus toys for all the children of the world could do for one's popularity. A lot of people started to think the fire FX from NAFTA's head was pretty cool.

But before too much thought could be devoted to any of this, the flipping photographic image of a personage in a ski mask of camouflage nylon, blue cape with the magic image of Guadalupe in an aura of gold feathers and blood roses, leopard bicycle tights, and blue boots, somersaulted and spread itself neatly over each screen. He stood, arms crossed and legs spread like a Power Ranger or a Ninja Turtle or Zorro. International heroes like El Gran Mojado were usually freaks of nature.

El Gran Mojado looked into the eyes of the people and smiled. "Hey," he asked predictably, "Have I finally lost my accent?"

"No!" Everyone yelled back in unison. With straggling voices also yelling, "You still sound like a Chihuahua dog!"

"You sound like Ricardo Montalbán!"

"Nah, he sounds like Marcello Mastroianni."

"That guy was Italian!"

"What's the diff?"

"He speaks English like an Argentine!"

"You only say that because you hate Argentines!"

"Only the Argentines love themselves!"

"Your mother is an Argentine!" Predictably, a fight broke out in the stands. In the meantime, the video continued. El Gran Mojado spoke plainly,

Noble people, I speak to you from the heart.
There is no future or past.
You all know that I am a witness to this.
There is no aging. There is only changing.
What can this progress my challenger speaks of
really be?
You who live in the declining and abandoned places
of great cities, called barrios, ghettos, and favelas:
What is archaic? What is modern? We are both.
The myth of the first world is that
development is wealth and technology progress.
It is all rubbish.
It means that you are no longer human beings
but only labor.
It means that the land you live on is not earth
but only property.
It means that what you produce with your own hands
is not yours to eat or wear or shelter you
if you cannot buy it.
I do not defend my title for the
rainbow of children of the world.
This is not a benefit for UNESCO.
We are not the world.
This is not a rock concert.
This is not about getting a piece of the action,
about dividing into tiny pieces what is always less and less.
How will 95 percent of us
divide 12 percent?

The fight in the stands was spreading. El Gran Mojado continued,

What will you each receive but a tattered piece
that will give you a pleasure as ephemeral
as a single night of torrid lustful juicy
prohibited sex?

He swayed and pumped his hips lasciviously with every adjective.

A titter floated through the crowds, and the commotion in the stands abated. "Sex? What did he say about sex?" People shifted in their seats and crossed their legs. The criers of Argentina felt all their erogenous zones swell and suddenly made excuses, running off to wait impatiently in lines for the restrooms.

"No!" El Gran Mojado looked squarely from his video.

I do not defend my title for the future of
starving children or the past of suffering ancestors.
I defend my title for life and death.
The life of our people or the death of our people.

Cheers and tears rose in the throats of young and old, the great anguish of life spilling into death filled their hearts. The heroics of this superclown would tell the tale. Laughter and tears. Tears and laughter.

The video image swallowed itself up into a pinhole, and all eyes rested on the square ring. The fanfare of horns, its theme song from *Rocky,* and dimming lights announced the entrance of the wrestler with flaming hair. It was the consummate effort of a Hollywood art director. Those who cheered, cheered for the twelve fabulous babe escorts whose bosoms preceded their buttocks in coordinated swimwear which, when pieced together (a gymnastic event), represented a big can of Bud. All that was worked into the soundtrack like one more digital element. Maybe no one offered a peep, but the sound of applause was explosive.

As for El Gran Mojado, he appeared by magic in the center ring, as if he had dropped in from the rafters above. He was accompanied by a choral symphony that came from outside the auditorium and slowly swelled to fill it by the people themselves. Everyone knew the music and the words in their own language, knew the alto, bass, and soprano parts, knew it as if from some uncanny place in their inner ears, as if they had sung it all their lives. Some people jumped up to conduct entire sections of the auditorium. It was very weird.

In the meantime, El Gran Mojado held Sol up on his shoulders and paraded around the ring. He juggled the orange and the ears of corn while Sol held on to his head. SUPERNAFTA, too, strutted the stage with his flaming head. People wondered if he was actually on fire. Occasionally the fire sputtered upward like a geyser or torch for heightened effect. No one had to remark that all he had to do was lower his head and El Gran Mojado would be a pile of cinders. Parents in the audience reached out for the little boy on El Gran Mojado's shoulders. Was that any place for a child? Even if that orange were not poisonous but undoubtedly a plastic representation. Even if he were a child actor. Indeed!

El Gran Mojado spotted a man sitting ringside with a big condom balloon, and announced with some irritation, "Where have you been? What do you think I am? A baby-sitter?" The wrestler slung the child over the ring and into his father's arms. There was one more thing, and Sol turned to get it back. El Gran Mojado tossed him the orange. Sol's hands were too little to catch it. There was the slightest moment of indecision, Bobby wondering how to keep the balloon and catch the orange. But the symphony of the moment spoke for itself as he released the balloon, letting it float into the spotlights, and caught the precious fruit in midair.

El Gran Mojado nodded, and the fight commenced. They faced each other like two toreadors, circling furtively. The choreography of the fight dictated the usual sparring and posturing. El Gran Mojado catapulted from the ropes and picked up SUPERNAFTA, twirled him around like a baton, and threw him to the mat. SUPERNAFTA lowered his head and singed Mojado's behind. Mojado, in turn, ran after NAFTA with a bucket of water, followed by a frantic referee. The crowd roared appreciation. Round after round they went—flying and leaping, dancing and taunting, scissoring necks, crunching legs, pummeling stomachs, pulverizing faces, butting heads. As everyone speculated and feared, SUPERNAFTA holographed himself into three, but Mojado instinctively knew the real villain, entered the visual range of the hologram, and gave the audience the pleasure of seeing the fight simultaneously from three different angles.

Finally the bloodletting and breaking of bones commenced.

Charred pieces of Mojado's cape
fluttered from the ring.
NAFTA's titanium body suit shredded,
bled in shiny tickertape to the floor.
Mojado's eyes were nearly shut in two purple lumps.
NAFTA's jaw hung to one side and his teeth
dropped like microchips,
one by one.
They flailed at each other,
the sound of human hysteria rising all around.
And when they could flail no more,
they wrapped each other in a grapple so tight
no one could distinguish one fighter from the other.
Inevitably the flames from NAFTA's head spread.
Mojado gripped his opponent like a splash of gasoline,

clawing the titanium suit and pressing the fire
into the flammable parts of NAFTA*'s body.*
It seemed that Mojado would be engulfed
and would also engulf his opponent,
taking them both in a vengeful double death.
But when the fire finally penetrated
NAFTA*'s superficial protection,*
Mojado released him and staggered back.
NAFTA *screamed within his titanium confines,*
for he had become a red cinder within,
a burning furnace.
Miraculously,
Mojado sprouted giant wings that
fluttered like white parachutes from his very back.
As NAFTA *thrashed about the ring,*
Mojado's great wings flapped back and forth
and back and forth,
fanning a great storm,
fanning the flames to cold smoke and
stoking NAFTA *to a live nuke.*
Everyone gasped as the great SUPERNAFTA *imploded.*

But only Bobby saw SUPERNAFTA's final weapon, his pointing finger a missile launcher that sent its tiny patriot into Arcangel's human heart.

And perhaps it was only the catastrophic finale to another fifty-two-year cycle.

The clash of a flat world
with a round world. The clash
of the same world
with itself, its hands
meeting in a prayer of blood.

The performance was over. The audience, like life, would go on. Perhaps they would abandon their labor for a short vacation—a contractual two weeks to celebrate, or perhaps, heaven forbid, they would never work again. Somewhere the profits from the ticket sales were being divided. A new champion was being groomed.

CHAPTER 48:

Hour 25 *Into the Boxes*

Somethin' about all those airbags burstin' on some kinda cue freaked out the population. The event had a spiritual quality, like a near-death experience, or Garbo herself slappin' some sense into your face. Some thought it was the talcum powder. TV stations showed it over and over in slow motion like thousands of white flags unfurlin' on the general humanity, with Pachelbel doing the honors in tinklin' golden baroque. Living huggin' the dead. Homeless huggin' the propertied. Motherless huggin' mommas. Childless huggin' kids. Armed and unarmed. Others their dogs. Everybody in a pure state of shock. Those that had them hugged their SUVs and actually drove them up or down the freeway ivy. Fellow with the Diego Rivera low-rider kissed the mother with her baby. Two of 'em drove away together. Grown men got teary-eyed. The killing stopped for a while.

Buzzworm sauntered through the wreckage with the Red Cross. Watched the safari of body bags creep up Limousine Way. End of the ramp, trio of homeless doing barbecue. Buzzworm knew this trio; they were hardcore. Lived their minds inside a crystal palace. Anything crossed their palms was traded for heaven. It was the only place provided respite, some kinda peace. Anybody else had their lives woulda killed themselves long ago. Skin wrapped around their bones almost without flesh between. No amount of rags or lice or grime or disease could cover it. Victims of hunger. But hunger got to them nonetheless. They were squatting around the fire, sticks poked with some kinda meat. Buzzworm noticed the scatter of blue-and-white baby Igloo coolers. Maybe five or six of them. He knew the coolers. And he knew the shape of the things getting toasted like marshmallows. One of the trio was working his mouth, picked something metal from between his teeth, flicked it out. Looked like a big filling, but he'd a lost all his long ago. Buzzworm skirted the trio. National Guard looking on. He walked away.

Made his trek outta the freeway valley, taking a detour by Margarita's old corner. For a moment, Indian momma there took him by surprise; coulda been his Margarita. This one had her wares out: big glass bottles of cold fruit juice. It was all passion. Not an orange in sight, neither domestic or imported. Paradigm had definitely shifted. Even so, Indian momma coulda been his Margarita.

Buzzworm finally went home. Grandma's house down Fifth and Jefferson was still intact. Took a bath. Took a nap. Swept the porch out. Watered the palms: the California and the Mexican fan palms, not forgetting the Washingtonia Robustas. Tossed some seeds out there. Seeds from one of the brothers doing urban gardening on the freeway. Grow there; grow here too.

Been some time since the radio frequencies were screwed. Power was doin' religion. AM stations were pledgin'. Jazz doin' hard rock. Hard rock doin' Warren Alney–like in-depth news coverage. In-depth news doin' Persian. Persian doin' Radio Free Cuba. Someone said radio'd become eclectic. Eclectic used to be Tom Schnabel, but he was doin' gardening. FCC guys must have been jumpin' off cliffs.

Buzzworm couldn't get no satisfaction from radio like this. Only thing he noticed with the jumble was that radio was like one big love song. I love you. You love me. I love myself. We love us. We love the world. We love God. We love ourselves but hate some of you. I hate myself but would love you if. You screwed me and I'm learning to love me or that other one. I loved you so I killed you. Radio was more tripped up than his own mind. He pulled the plug.

Same thing with the time. Couldn't get the coordinates on anything no more. It was like they said. No radio, no watch, nobody would give him the time of day. Once he made his decision, it was easy. Threw his entire collection of watches into a couple of large paper bags and distributed every one. Went up and down everywhere and handed 'em all out like candy. Antique, historic value, oddity, anachronism. They all just went.

Last radio frequency he'd tuned to was *Hour 25*. Talked about mythic realities, like everyone gets plugged into a myth and builds a reality around it. Or was it the other way around? Everybody gets plugged into a reality and builds a myth around it. He didn't know which. Things would be what he and everybody else chose to do and make of it. It wasn't gonna be something imagined.

He had some serious itineratin' to do. Homeboys fixin' to do good like a bunch of fool boy scouts, invokin' the name of Bobby Seale and the Black Panthers. Leftover homeless with their eyes on Worthington Ford's used-car deals. Congress woman Waters saying we gotta get to the bottom of this orange conspiracy. Contingent of New Age Santa Monicans talkin' 'bout plantin' a palm tree for every casualty in the freeway massacre. Vigilante groups disbandin' to Bel Air. Attorney General arrestin' and investigatin'. Heal L.A. or heel L.A.

And everybody was wanting to know how to get those airbags back into their boxes.

Unplugged and timeless, thinking like this was scary, Buzzworm gritted his teeth. Took a breath. Manzanar's symphony swelled against his diaphragm, reverberated through his veteran bones. Solar-powered, he could not run out of time.

CHAPTER 49:

American Express *Mi Casa/Su Casa*

Pacific Rim Auditorium's bigger than he thought. He's late. People already packed in like pay-per-view. Ticket windows all closed. Sold out. Scalpers hanging round with offers like it's the World Cup. People panting with wads of cash, putting out like it's life or death. Gonna go broke and not eat for one month. Gonna die to see this one. Bobby's a cash man, but this is more than he carries. Line in front of the Versateller's a mile long. So many fans pumping that baby, it's busted.

Bobby jives a scalper, "You take American Express?"

"Sure. Why not?"

That's it. He's in.

Inside it's a circus. Check for guns and hand grenades at the door. Giving away free condoms. Someone's got them blown up like giant balloons. Got ski masks on the ends. Safe sex. Liberation sex. What the heck. He buys a balloon.

American Express gets him the best. Ringside seats.

Sure enough. Sol's in the ring with the heavyweight. Looks like he's part of the act. What's Rafaela thinking? Putting the boy in the circus? Two enmascarados. One's got his hair on fire. Other's a juggling act. "Sol!" he's yelling. "Sol!" Enmascarado gives him the boy. Throws him an orange too. Sol wants the orange bad. Don't he want the balloon? No way. Had to lose the balloon to get the orange. What does Bobby know? He hasn't been around to know it's the last orange this side of the border. Don't know everybody else thinks it's a toy.

Fight gets started. Bobby's there with his son like it's a bonding thing. Kid's only two. You gotta be nuts. Thing gets going. It's entertainment. Stuff you see regularly on TV. Can't be too bad. Pretty soon, ringside, it's looking real. Bobby's like the crowd. He's into it.

Suddenly, Rafaela's there. She's back again. She's pointing at Sol's orange. Got that line that's tripping into town. That's why she's here in the first place. Can't Bobby see it? Can't he see the line? It's why everything is changed. He's looking hard, but what's this line she's talking about? Is it a dream? Mirage caused by lack of cigarettes? Go figure. She's saying this is no place for Sol. Sol shouldn't see this violence. Get Sol outta here.

It's too late. Everything happens too fast. The rudo with the head of fire is a goner. People cheering like crazy, but Bobby knows: winged warrior's a goner too. Rafaela knows it too. She knows this enmascarado. She tells Sol to give her the orange. Boy doesn't want to, but she gives him the look. He hands it over. Then she's yelling at Bobby to cut it.

"Cut what?"

"The orange." She's got a fancy pocketknife knotted in her dress. Hands it to Bobby. "Cut it now!"

"Okay. Okay." He cuts it. But then he sees it too. He sees the line where it gets cut through the orange. So he grabs the two ends. Is he some kind of fool? Maybe so. But he's hanging on.

Meanwhile, Rafaela's in the ring. She's peeling the orange and feeding the pieces to the enmascarado. Like it's gonna help. Like she's a soccer mom at half-time. Like it's the last rites. Enmascarado chews and smiles. It's all over. Crowds rushing in. Picking him up. Taking him away with orange peels scattered on his chest, stink of orange on his lips, like he's floating on a human wave. Gonna take him home. Home where mi casa es su casa. Bury him under an orange tree. Plant him at the very edge of the sun's shadow. Maybe grow another line right there. Mark the place. Tag it good.

Little by little the slack on the line's gone. Thing's stretching tight. Just Bobby grabbing the two sides. Making the connection. Pretty soon he's sweating it. Lines ripping through the palms. How long can he hold on? Dude's skinny, but he's an Atlas. Hold on 'til his body gets split in two. Hold on 'til he dies, famous-like.

Rafaela picks up Sol. Boy's straddling her hip and hanging on her neck. She's beat up bad, but she's some kind of angel. Never looked so beautiful. Tears running down her face, kissing Sol. Spent so much time worrying about her and the boy. Trying to lock 'em up. Lock out the bad elements. Then it happens anyway. Wasn't there to protect his family after all. Waves of people running past them. Look like a puny twosome. Fragile. His little family. What's he gonna do? Tied fast to these lines. Family out there. Still stuck on the other side. He's gritting his teeth and crying like a fool. What are these goddamn lines anyway? What do they connect? What do they divide? What's he holding on to? What's he holding on to?

He gropes forward, inching nearer. Anybody looking sees his arms open wide like he's flying. Like he's flying forward to embrace. Don't nobody know he's hanging on to these invisible bungy cords. That's when he lets go. Lets the lines slither around his wrists, past his palms, through his fingers. Lets go. Go figure. Embrace.

That's it.

Coffee House Press began as a small letterpress operation in 1972 and has grown into an internationally renowned nonprofit publisher of literary fiction, essay, poetry, and other work that doesn't fit neatly into genre categories.

Coffee House is both a publisher and an arts organization. Through our *Books in Action* program and publications, we've become interdisciplinary collaborators and incubators for new work and audience experiences. Our vision for the future is one where a publisher is a catalyst and connector.

LITERATURE
is not the same thing as
PUBLISHING

Funder Acknowledgments

Coffee House Press is an internationally renowned independent book publisher and arts nonprofit based in Minneapolis, MN; through its literary publications and *Books in Action* program, Coffee House acts as a catalyst and connector—between authors and readers, ideas and resources, creativity and community, inspiration and action.

Coffee House Press books are made possible through the generous support of grants and donations from corporations, state and federal grant programs, family foundations, and the many individuals who believe in the transformational power of literature. This activity is made possible by the voters of Minnesota through a Minnesota State Arts Board Operating Support grant, thanks to the legislative appropriation from the arts and cultural heritage fund. Coffee House also receives major operating support from the Amazon Literary Partnership, the Jerome Foundation, The McKnight Foundation, Target Foundation, and the National Endowment for the Arts (NEA). To find out more about how NEA grants impact individuals and communities, visit www.arts.gov.

Coffee House Press receives additional support from the Elmer L. & Eleanor J. Andersen Foundation; the David & Mary Anderson Family Foundation; the Buuck Family Foundation; the Dorsey & Whitney Foundation; Dorsey & Whitney LLP; Fredrikson & Byron, P.A.; the Fringe Foundation; Kenneth Koch Literary Estate; the Knight Foundation; the Rehael Fund of the Minneapolis Foundation; the Matching Grant Program Fund of the Minneapolis Foundation; Mr. Pancks' Fund in memory of Graham Kimpton; the Schwab Charitable Fund; Schwegman, Lundberg & Woessner, P.A.; the US Bank Foundation; VSA Minnesota for the Metropolitan Regional Arts Council; and the Woessner Freeman Family Foundation in honor of Allan Kornblum.

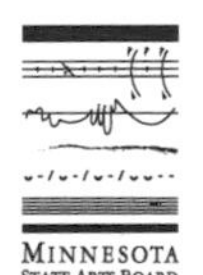

The Publisher's Circle of Coffee House Press

Publisher's Circle members make significant contributions to Coffee House Press's annual giving campaign. Understanding that a strong financial base is necessary for the press to meet the challenges and opportunities that arise each year, this group plays a crucial part in the success of Coffee House's mission.

Recent Publisher's Circle members include many anonymous donors, Suzanne Allen, Patricia A. Beithon, Bill Berkson & Connie Lewallen, E. Thomas Binger & Rebecca Rand Fund of the Minneapolis Foundation, Robert & Gail Buuck, Claire Casey, Louise Copeland, Jane Dalrymple-Hollo, Ruth Stricker Dayton, Jennifer Kwon Dobbs & Stefan Liess, Mary Ebert & Paul Stembler, Sally French, Chris Fischbach & Katie Dublinski, Kaywin Feldman & Jim Lutz, Sally French, Jocelyn Hale & Glenn Miller, the Rehael Fund-Roger Hale/Nor Hall of the Minneapolis Foundation, Randy Hartten & Ron Lotz, Dylan Hicks & Nina Hale, Jeffrey Hom, Carl & Heidi Horsch, Amy L. Hubbard & Geoffrey J. Kehoe Fund, Kenneth Kahn & Susan Dicker, Stephen & Isabel Keating, Kenneth Koch Literary Estate, Allan & Cinda Kornblum, Leslie Larson Maheras, Lenfestey Family Foundation, Sarah Lutman & Rob Rudolph, the Carol & Aaron Mack Charitable Fund of the Minneapolis Foundation, George & Olga Mack, Joshua Mack & Ron Warren, Gillian McCain, Mary & Malcolm McDermid, Sjur Midness & Briar Andresen, Maureen Millea Smith & Daniel Smith, Peter Nelson & Jennifer Swenson, Marc Porter & James Hennessy, Enrique Olivarez, Jr. & Jennifer Komar, Alan Polsky, Robin Preble, Jeffrey Scherer, Jeffrey Sugerman & Sarah Schultz, Alexis Scott, Nan G. & Stephen C. Swid, Patricia Tilton, Stu Wilson & Melissa Barker, Warren D. Woessner & Iris C. Freeman, Margaret Wurtele, Joanne Von Blon, and Wayne P. Zink & Christopher Schout.

For more information about the Publisher's Circle and other ways to support Coffee House Press books, authors, and activities, please visit www.coffeehousepress.org /support or contact us at info@coffeehousepress.org.

New and Reissued Works by Karen Tei Yamashita

Letters to Memory

Brazil-Maru

Through the Arc of the Rain Forest

Tropic of Orange was typeset by
Bookmobile Design & Digital Publisher Services.
Text is set in Arno Pro.